A JOHN STONE MYSTERY

MURDER WITH DECEIT

WINNFRED SMITH

Copyright © 2019 by Winnfred Smith.

All rights reserved. No part of this publication may be reproduced, distributed, or transmitted in any form or by any means, including photocopying, recording, or other electronic or mechanical methods, without the prior written permission of the author, except in the case of brief quotations embodied in critical reviews and certain other noncommercial uses permitted by copyright law.

This is a work of fiction. Names, characters, businesses, places, and events are either the products of the author's imagination or are used in a fictitious manner. Any resemblance to actual persons, living or dead, or actual events is purely coincidental.

Printed in the United States of America.

Library of Congress Control Number: 2019918780

ISBN		
	Paperback	978-1-64361-969-9
	Hardback	978-1-64361-986-6
	eBook	978-1-64361-970-5

Westwood Books Publishing LLC
11416 SW Aventino Drive
Port Saint Lucie, FL 34987

www.westwoodbookspublishing.com

Other Books by Winnfred Smith

Southern Shorts
Everybody Wants Madison
Best Tall Tales in Short Stories

More John Stone Mysteries

Murder Finds a Home
Murder Before Dawn

Contents

Chapter 1: The Long Cool Woman..........................1
Chapter 2: Knocking on Mama's Door....................9
Chapter 3: The Tower................................22
Chapter 4: Paris and Sudden Guests...................29
Chapter 5: Times Remembered..........................38
Chapter 6: Towering Events...........................49
Chapter 7: Skinny Visits.............................57
Chapter 8: Louvre Expectancies....................... 66
Chapter 9: Sofa News and Logs........................73
Chapter 10: Uncle John Arrives.......................80
Chapter 11: A French Connection..................... 90
Chapter 12: A French Deception.......................96
Chapter 13: Mothers, Meetings, and Magicians........112
Chapter 14: A Meaningful Discussion.................118
Chapter 15: An Unforgettable Short Talk.............131
Chapter 16: When Past Lives Meet....................135
Chapter 17: Speaking of Women.......................147
Chapter 18: A Visit to Larry's......................164
Chapter 19: Factory Factors.........................173
Chapter 20: Charade Assembly........................182
Chapter 21: Old Flames Arise........................199
Chapter 22: Picture Surprises.......................209
Chapter 23: Mainz, No; Créteil, Yes . . . Oops......217
Chapter 24: A New Kid in Town.......................224
Chapter 25: Newspaper News..........................232
Chapter 26: Dead Friends in Question................239

Chapter 27:	Radiating Questions	253
Chapter 28:	Old Contacts Emerge	263
Chapter 29:	Liars and Lies	275
Chapter 30:	Cell Mystery	282
Chapter 31:	Germany on the Horizon	289
Chapter 32:	A Derrière Exposed	293
Chapter 33:	A Surprise Homecoming	298
Chapter 34:	Buddha Conflict	310
Chapter 35:	The Mirage	322
Chapter 36:	The Smelly Announcement	328
Chapter 37:	Mainz on the Horizon	333
Chapter 38:	Secrets Outed	339
Chapter 39:	Mainz… ing Again	345
Chapter 40:	Paris and Mainz Collide	359
Chapter 41:	Ends Wrapping Up	367
Chapter 42:	Memorable Departure	372

Preface

There's a movie from 1944 titled *Laura*. In that movie, a body was found in Laura's apartment and declared hers. The police detective investigating the case falls in love with her. The shocking truth of her death and the murderer becomes clear in the final scenes. Such as it is with romantic mysteries.

For those who have not read my first novel, *Murder Finds a Home*, Nanna Bolton is not totally fiction. When I was five, I lived in the country. Maybe a couple hundred feet up the road was the home of my first childhood friend, JC. His was a black family.

His mother is my inspiration for Nanna Bolton. I never knew her nor JC's last name. I never knew her first name. Guess I was too young to think of that. I never saw an adult man there. What I do know is this: She had several children and lived in something close to a boxcar, just made of wood. Two rooms. Wood burning stove. There was no well or outhouse that I recall.

Her home was between Highway 16 and a barbed-wire fence. No ditch, just the edge of the road flat to the fence. I recall driving by there maybe thirty years ago. All flat. You'd never know a house was ever there.

When I think how she lived, she was an amazing mother. Her words you find in the story contain some fact and some fiction. All I really know is she treated me kindly.

Acknowledgments

Gail Williams has assisted by reading this book and providing spelling, grammar, and critical story corrections. She has visited France and on some subjects pointed me in better directions. **Nicole Stuart** has been reviewing and providing feedback on this novel and many of my short stories. Her feedback has given me a valuable perspective for the female point of view. **Becky Smith** gave me a varying perspective in the story. Points that needed more flare and some that needed less, all making the story more readable. **Main Street Writers Association, Cartersville, Georgia,** taught me about the many little things that make a story worth reading.

CHAPTER 1

THE LONG COOL WOMAN

Ever had a day start out normal, and then you meet a woman? Okay, there's more to it than that. You ask her to dinner and then find out her father was killed. Maybe murdered! Well, I did, but it didn't stop there. All I wanted was a friendly meal. Maybe a pizza. It slowly became a puzzle. You know, one piece at a time, only I had no picture to guide me. But . . .

Yeah, there's always a but. Clues were slapping me in the face, and I didn't have a clue what they were. Hey, I'm an IT guy. I deal with computers, and they don't lie. Here's the story. Oh, and thanks for listening.

I'd just finished dinner at a local bistro in Marietta Square. I crossed North Street to the sidewalk that surrounds the square, walking back to my car. It was a late Friday afternoon, close to six thirty, with the bright sun beaming down. I turned the corner and saw her.

I couldn't take my eyes off the woman. I remembered an actress from the fifties. This woman was a slightly younger Grace Kelly.

My eyes were so focused on her I could've tripped on a toothpick. Maybe it's something only a guy can understand. You think you have it all under control, and then *she* appears.

My *she* was walking and talking with another girl, both paying me no attention. She was wearing a long, black dress. It had one of those cuts up one side, way above the knee. You've seen 'em, and the only word is *wow*. The top was V-cut, circling her slender neck and bare shoulders, with never-ending, long, blond hair. Grace Kelly had blond hair. They both had all the right proportions, I might add.

She was walking straight at me. Do I keep walking? Maybe stop and force her to stop? I chickened out and stepped to the side. There was a fence around the park. I grabbed it. They walked past me. Never even took a look or anything. I couldn't let her get away.

Back on the sidewalk and a notch above my normal voice, I said, "They wrote a song about you." I'd like to say that came out bold and fearless. It didn't.

The two girls stopped and turned. With hands on her hips, the older one said boldly, "You talking to me?"

I took four steps. "Yes. The Hollies sang a song that had to be about you. It's called 'Long Cool Woman in a Black Dress.'" My confidence was building.

She was headed straight toward me, but stopped a foot or so from my face and informed me, "I'm five six."

I'd guessed she was five seven. The high heels must've thrown me off.

Without hesitating, and with a look that could not be denied, she said, "Sing it."

I didn't expect that. My dad liked the song and we listened to it on the radio. I hardly remembered any of the lyrics. The title just blurted out. But she had challenged me, and I had to take it. Singing best I could, mostly off key, I gave it a try.

I sang the only three lines I could remember telling how cool the woman in the black dress was. Having attempted to meet her demand, I confessed, "That's all I know, but I hope it gives the message."

As she leaned a little toward me, her arms slipped behind her back. Holding hands, I suspected. She smiled. "That was cute. What's your name?"

"I like your perfume."

"Huh?"

"You're wearing a Victoria's Secret perfume. It's called Crush. Aren't you?"

She delivered a smile with her green eyes twitching a little. "Yes. But. But, how did you know?"

"It fits you. My name's Stone. John Stone." Almost pleading, I asked, "Can I have your name?"

Her eyes were dancing all over my face. Maybe I had a pimple. No. The moment I thought she was mapping my face, her eyes stopped.

She flat out stated, "That can wait. I don't give it away that easy. You're trying to pick me up, aren't you?"

"Maybe." This was not me. I've argued with heads of state and dictators who had the power to execute me. I've stood in front of men pointing guns at me, and some who'd even pulled the trigger. You've had times like that, right?

Trying to get control, I said, "Look. I was just wondering if you'd have dinner with me tomorrow. I'll take you anywhere you'd like to eat."

She didn't answer immediately. If she was trying to add pressure, she was successful. Suddenly, she casually asked, "Anywhere?"

This woman was now inches from my face. Her eyes glistened as they feasted upon mine. It was a peaceful or, even better, a sexy intimidation.

I mumbled, "Yes. Anywhere. Can I have your name now? And your friend there?"

"Not yet. Stay!" She ordered. I did.

She was a cautious one, and I couldn't blame her. A total stranger starts singing to her on a sidewalk. I was pleased she didn't have a gun. I knew that because there was absolutely no place to hide it.

Her slender, smooth hand entered her purse and pulled out her cell phone. She stepped a few feet away, turned her back, and called someone. I couldn't make out her words. I hoped she wasn't calling her boyfriend.

She turned and, without hesitation, said, "I want to go to the Le Beaujolais restaurant."

Taking a chance, I asked, "Who's your girlfriend there?" Her friend was a few years younger but just as slender and pretty. She kept her distance. Her dress was red and quite short, leaving her slender legs fully exposed.

"My sister, Patty. Quit changing the subject. You going to take me to dinner, or have you chickened out?"

"Sure. I'll take you there." I managed to get that out with little surprise.

She smiled. It was obvious she doubted my words. Her hands rested confidently on her hips, again. "You've never heard of it, have you? You don't even know where it is?"

"It's in *Paris*. Paris, France."

The smile faded. The whole square went silent. Traffic must have stopped.

Her head tilted just a little as she tightened her eyes. There was a puzzled look, but for only a moment. Her doubt vanished and her hands regained control of her hips. "You just guessed that! It sounded French, and you . . . you don't really know, do you?"

I kept it simple. "I know the owner, Pappy, very well. I either see or talk to him every month or so."

Her steady eyes with scrunched eyebrows told me she questioned my words. Saying nothing, she turned, walked a few steps, and made another call.

Within seconds, she walked back to me. With a less confident voice, she asked, "What's his given name?"

I leaned a little toward her, and asked, "Who's giving you all the answers?" I quickly straightened up. Didn't want to be too close.

She stood erect, sounding very adamant. "My mother, if you really must know."

"You getting permission to go to dinner?" I really wished I hadn't said that.

"I do not need my mother's permission. I make my own decisions. Now," with a tilt of her head, "answer my question . . . Mr. Stone."

Her words came with a confident tone when she said my name. I suspect she didn't intend for me to like it, but I did.

I'd already said his name, but, I replied, "You've got to listen better. Pappy, or Pappy Armand." I paused. She said nothing as her hands dropped from her hips. I kept going. "You don't believe me. Hold a second."

I pulled out my own cell and held it where she could see the screen. I clicked a favorite with the name Pappy. After a couple of rings, Pappy answered.

With the phone between us, he and I exchanged hellos. I mentioned that the intoxicating woman standing beside me knew him. I told him to hold a second.

"Okay, beautiful, what's your name?" I added a little extra emphasis with a crooked smile.

Her mouth opened as if to speak, but paused a second, then the words came. "Nicole. Nicole Powell." As resolute as she had been earlier, she had become unsure of herself.

To Pappy I said, "You heard. Her name is Nicole Powell and she wants to talk to you." I handed her the phone. It was now in her hands, and I wasn't just talking about the phone.

Nicole stared at the phone about an hour—okay, maybe five seconds—when she sent a friendly "Hi."

They talked. She told him who she was and about her family eating at his place. I couldn't hear him, but I knew Pappy. He was asking the questions and she was giving him answers. After a couple of minutes, she returned my phone.

I listened as Pappy gave me the story. Nicole, her sister Patty, her mother, and her father, William Powell, had made a trip to Paris seven years ago. They ate at Pappy's restaurant several times. He remembered Nicole's mother's name was Betty. I knew he had a good memory, but seven years? Then he told me to be sure no one could hear us.

To Nicole and her sister, "It's my time. Stay put. He wants to tell me something." I walked away a few steps. "What's up, Pappy?"

"John, I want you to bring her mother with you." With an okay, he continued, "You will soon find that Nicole's father was killed in an automobile accident. I heard about it, but they left me no way to locate them. Your meeting her is fortunate."

"From what you told me, their visit was memorable. But why are you so interested now?"

"His body was burned and they couldn't identify him, so they used other items found nearby to resolve the problem. My sources told me it may not have been an accident."

"I see. So, why you telling me?"

"If it wasn't an accident, Betty and her family need to know. I want to know. The government has made its decision. I want you to see what you can find."

"Other than what you just told me, I don't even know where to start."

"Carefully and quietly, get as much detail as Betty and Nicole know. No. No, on second thought, just try Nicole first. Patty was very young. Nicole was eighteen, I believe, and I remember she was very close to her father."

"Okay, I'll give it a try, but I know I'll need some guidance from you."

"Thank you, John. I'll have more when you get here."

I told Pappy we'd be around to see him the next day and said our goodbyes.

That was an unexpected challenge, but not the first time with Pappy. And I'd had practice. I helped a girlfriend once, when I was much younger. She told me I had a knack. Knack. Stack. I just wanted a kiss. I got one and decided I should use that knack thing often.

I walked back to the girls to make the trip officially personal.

"Nicole. I said anywhere, and you said you wanted to go to his restaurant. May I take you to Pappy's place tomorrow for dinner?"

With arms behind her, again, with straight posture, she said, as if giving an order, "Yes. You may." She nodded her head gently and briefly.

Seeing her response, I then worried how she would handle my next bit of information.

"There's something you need to know. Pappy wants your mother to come along." Then glancing at her sister, I added, "You too, Patty." Patty gave me a positive nod.

Nicole's hands were no longer behind her in that feminine posture. Those arms were straight down by her sides. "Why does he want Mama to come?"

"Don't know. Maybe she made a good impression on him. You'll have to ask her. Guess we should bring your father, get the whole family involved." I wondered how that request would be answered.

It changed Nicole's demeanor. Her eyes focused on me. Her hands covered her mouth as she spoke, "Daddy's dead." Her low, calm voice cracked. She focused on the ground.

It had been many years, but her reaction was expected. I put my hand under her chin, lifting her head just a little. "Nicole, I'm sorry to hear that. I don't know why Pappy wants your mother there. Maybe your family meant something special back then and he wants to see all of you again."

I tried to keep my response as close to the truth as possible. At some point, I would eventually have to admit I knew about her father's death. I dreaded that moment.

Nicole's hands dropped from her chin. "Yeah. Maybe that's it. I was eighteen, and being in Paris with him was more than a special time. It's a time I'll never forget."

"That I can understand. I know you don't need permission, but let's see what your mother has to say about her going back."

Speaking soft and slowly, she said, "Yes. We should," along with a gentle nod.

Patty had been listening to all of this. She moved much closer and gave us her thoughts, "This is all really strange. And you better believe we need to talk to Mama." She brushed back her long, dark-brown hair and looked at me with sparkling blue eyes.

We had our decision. I added, "Sounds unanimous. I'll give you my phone number. You girls go talk with your mother and call me with the decision."

Nicole's eyes got wide open. Her head was shaking side to side. "I'm not talking to Mama about this alone. No way."

There was no question she meant that.

"Neither am I," Patty informed us.

Nicole gave me a hard stare. "John, you're going with us. If Mama needs a target, you're it. That's assuming you still want to take me to dinner."

That woman knew what she wanted. "I'm not sure if that was a command or a question. But, yes, I do. I'll tag along."

I may have sounded brave, but felt like Superman about to meet Lex Luthor holding a bag of kryptonite.

CHAPTER 2

KNOCKING ON MAMA'S DOOR

I pulled into the driveway behind Nicole and Patty. They had a moderately sized home. Two-story vinyl siding, two-car garage, no porch, and no steps.

We got out of our cars heading for the front door. They opened the door for me to go in first. I paused and said, "Ladies first." I wanted protection.

When their mother saw me, she did not look especially pleased. She paused, pointed a lethal finger at me, and said, "Nicole, who's this?"

"Mama, this is John Stone. He's the one I called you about. He's going to take me to dinner tomorrow," and with a slight pause, "in Paris." She cut right to the chase. Did not pause for formal introductions.

That sentence started a serious mother-daughter discussion that ended when she told her mother about Pappy. That Pappy remembered her. That he remembered her name. Whether she liked it or not, her mother gave only a tiny smile of recognition.

Seeing her expression, I figured it was my time. "Mrs. Powell, Pappy specifically asked for you to come with us. He would like to see all of you. I'd like to visit with him, too. Why don't we all go to Paris and spend the week? Pappy will keep us fed, and I can show Nicole around Paris."

Nicole's mother was not so easily convinced. She dug deeper. "How old are you, Mister?"

That was an easy one, and I accepted why she wanted to know. "Thirty-one, with a birthday coming up soon."

"I guess that's all right. But I can't let you spend all that money on plane tickets and hotel bills. I just can't. I don't even know you."

Nicole added her point with strength and determination, "Mama, I talked to Pappy and he knows John, and John is okay. And I'm going. I want to go back there where Daddy was with us."

I held my response a second or two. Her mother looked concerned. I think every word in the dictionary was going through her head looking for the right one, the right decision.

Assuming she was searching for the word to indicate a no, I decided to intervene in that choice and attempt to close her dictionary. "Before we go further, passports can be a problem. Do you still have passports?"

Nicole answered, "Yes. We have them. We kept them renewed. They're all current. It was probably crazy, but I often thought about Daddy and how he got us our passports back then." She wiped tiny tears from her eyes. "Guess it keeps the memory alive having them."

"I'm glad you did. So, we'll take my plane. I have things to talk to Pappy about. And I can easily cover the hotel bill. Besides, I need to see my team in Paris."

Nicole came back real quick, "You have a *plane*?" Her excitement enhanced her delightful smile.

I responded, "Yes."

Patty kept quiet. She was leaning against a doorway, smiling. I didn't know her age. A teenager, for sure, and she was certainly enjoying the exchanges.

Nicole's smile was captivating. "And you have a team? In Paris? What are you, a soccer coach or something?"

Mother Betty was catching all this. Her head was shifting back and forth.

"Sometimes that might be a good idea, but no. I own an IT company called Stanton and Stone Consulting, S & S for short. I have development teams in US locations. I also have an IT development group in England and am close to starting one in France."

She took a moment to think how to respond. "You do? You did?" The engaging look on her face caught my attention. Make that grabbed it. Her voice sounded as if she was trying to be sure she understood what I said.

"Yes, I do."

Nicole asked, "Is that how you know Pappy?"

"No. He had a problem and I helped him solve it."

Her head tilted. "Are you a spy or something?"

"No, Nicole, nothing like that. I sometimes help my friends solve a problem. Find something that was missing or keep someone from being hurt."

Their mother continued listening, but remained silent. I wondered if she was about to throw something at me. At that moment, she was only tossing questionable, unsure expressions.

Nicole's eyebrows went up and she tilted her head. "I see. You're a detective?"

"I've been called that. It's an old word, but it sometimes fits."

"Dad liked detective shows." Nicole sent a positive nod to her mother. "We always watched them, didn't we, Mama?"

"Yes, we did, dear." It was her moment to throw something. Fortunately, it was only a harsh expression. "Mr. Stone, just who are you? What's this all about?"

"I'm a guy who saw this beautiful woman and wants to buy her dinner."

That was my original plan until Pappy dropped his two cents in the pot.

Nicole presented her side. "Mama, that's what I want." After saying that, she gave me a pleasant, almost forgiving look. "John, I don't have to go to France. I was just trying to be difficult to this guy who stopped me on the sidewalk. And all you did was get sweeter." She never took her eyes off me. She sent one of those little female smiles.

She had me. "Nicole, I more than ever want to buy you dinner in Paris." Then speaking to everyone, I said, "Look. I can take all of you, and Patty, feel free to bring a friend along."

That got Patty's attention. "A Paris trip? Don't even think you're leaving me here. I'll even buy my own dinner." That young girl had a serious amount of confidence.

"Patty, this trip is on me. Listen, everyone. If we leave the Atlanta airport at, say, nine a.m. tomorrow, and with flying time and the time change, that will put us in Paris about four p.m. By the time we drive, check in, and unpack, it'll be close to six. I suggest we check in to the hotel, get rested, and see Pappy Sunday. Susan, my secretary, can make all the arrangements. How about it?"

Nicole's head shook. "I want to go, but I can't stay a week. I have a job."

"Where do you work?"

"Local paper. The *Marietta Gazette*. Why you ask?"

"Ah, Barry Goldsmith. Do you work for him?"

"Not directly. I'm in the publication department. Mostly just edit the stories they write. Why?"

"I know Barry. Hold on a sec."

When I pulled out my cell and started dialing, I saw heads moving in the no, no, no direction. I told them to pause and that I would take care of it.

Barry answered, and we shared a little business talk. I clicked the speaker button so all could hear. I told him why I called, and he liked the idea. He gave his okay with some stipulations. I told Barry goodbye and gave him my thanks.

"Nicole, as you just heard, you have two weeks off—with pay. Of course, you'll have to bring him a written report of your excursions, along with pictures."

"But, but, I only edit what they write. I just check spelling, grammar, and punctuation. I don't write anything."

"Nicole, that kind of editing and correction makes their work readable. Writing what you see and feel will be perfect. I'll critique it for you. It'll be fine. So how about you, Patty?"

Patty gave me a thumbs-up. If I'd guessed, she was smart enough to stay low and let the other two women come to an understanding.

Nicole came around. She clapped her hands then wrapped her arms around her chest. Her smile was endearing. "Daddy made me stay close to him pretty much all the time." She then dropped her arms with clasped hands. "Except twice, as I remember. This trip will be wonderful and so very memorable."

As she finished her excited words, she saw her mother. She went mute. Her mother was quiet. The two exchanged looks, and then aimed their composed look directly at me.

Nicole took on her smile again, walking slowly to me. She gave me a hug and a kiss on the cheek.

In some magical female way, they had reached a decision, I hoped. I gently guided Nicole to my side and asked her mother, "Is that a yes?"

Her mother said, "Yes."

"Oh, what about your cell phones? Are they set for foreign travel?" That got me three nos.

I took their phones, called their carrier, and had international added. With that done, I told them I'd cover the cost. I got complaints over that, but I told them it was the only way to keep good contact over there. Nicole agreed. Issue closed.

It was clear she was going to be handy to have around.

Her mother's face changed. "John, you said Pappy remembered my name. What did he say?" Her words were wishful. I saw refreshed memories blossoming.

"He just told me he wanted to see you again. When he remembered your name, I said something about how he'd remembered for so many years. He said, and I quote, 'She was too lovely to forget.'"

Nicole put her arm around mine and snuggled a little.

Mother Betty stood there silent for a moment, comprehending Pappy's words, I suspected. "Yes. I'd like to see Pappy again. It was a good time back then."

Still close beside me, Nicole added, "You're wonderful, Mama."

With that confirmed, I had my getting ready to do. "Good. Okay. I need to get some sleep and do some packing. I'll head to my apartment. I'll call later with what time I'll pick all of you up in the morning."

Nicole stepped in front of me, flat against me, again facing her mother. "I don't like that. He can sleep here, can't he, Mama?"

There was a pondering delay, then she said, "Sure. If he wants to. But he'll have to be on the sofa." Mother Betty gave me a studying glance when she said that.

"Wouldn't be the first time my bed was a sofa. Sure. But I still need to pack some things. That won't take long."

Nicole turned around, looking direct at me, inches between us. "I'll go help you." Then she quickly turned, facing her mother.

Her mother started to say something. I couldn't see Nicole's face, but those two were again sharing some mother-daughter, silent, secret-code discussion. In what was no more than three seconds, Nicole turned and told me, "Let's go," which brought that wordless conversation to an end.

We were in my car headed out when she asked, "So, where're we going?"

"I live in Riverside apartments. Nothing fancy."

"Don't try to snow me. I know better. I've heard of those apartments, and you have a great view of the Chattahoochee, don't you?'

"Well, from the balcony, if you hang off the rail and lean way over, you can see the river." Not true, but I didn't want to brag.

"I don't believe you. If you have a great view, I'll—I'll—well, I'm not sure what I'll do, but you won't like it. You understand?"

"Okay, I give. I have a great view of the river."

She gave me one of those girl hits. Never hurts. Now, if they're really mad you, it will hurt. We guys try to avoid that scenario.

"You live alone?"

That question was out of the proverbial blue. "Yep."

"Where does your family live?" She was digging as much as I've had to on occasion.

"You checking up on me?"

It was about time. I'd known her only a few hours and she was already deciding where I was going to sleep.

"Yes. Now answer the question."

Giving her a smile, I said, "My mother died when I was seven. My father died a few years ago."

Nicole understood how that would touch my childhood. "No mother. Your father had to do all the parent things. You're nice. He did a good job."

"He had some help." Unsure why I said that. She somehow had control of my mouth.

"Whadaya mean, help?"

"I had a nanny. We called her Nanna Bolton."

She tilted her head, and asked, "Please tell me about her."

"Sure. Well, Nanna was an old woman by the time I came along. When I was younger, she helped my dad's mother take care of him. So, when Mama died, my dad asked her to help, and we had a nanny."

"Was she nice?"

"Nice don't come close. Amazing is a much closer fit. When school was in, Dad would drop us off at her house. We'd catch the school bus and get off there after school. Dad would pick us up after he got off work. During the summer, we had lots of fun there. I loved her biscuits and sweet-potato pie."

"You said 'we' and 'us.' Who's *us*?"

"I have a younger brother, Jake Stone. Nanna took care of us both."

"Sounds like she was a very special person. Think you had more fun growing up than I did."

"It was more than the fun. Nanna was smart. Life smart. Her life was hard—had no money, lived from day to day. I learned more about life from her than anyone else. When I had a problem and let her know, she told me how to fix it. If it wouldn't go away, she told me how to live with it."

We were still chatting when I pulled into the parking lot. We got out and headed up to the twelfth floor and my apartment.

First thing Nicole did after I opened the door was head for the balcony. She was checking out the river.

She validated the view. "The river view is wonderful. This is a great place to live."

I sat down on my sofa and called Susan, my executive secretary, as she likes to be known. Nicole joined me on the sofa. She sat close. I know because, for a second, I thought she was wearing my shirt.

"Hi, Susan." I clicked the speaker button and held it so Nicole could hear.

"John, why on earth are you calling me on a Friday evening? It's after eight o'clock. Did some woman lock you out of your apartment? Or maybe she threw you out of your car and locked the door."

Knowing her, she had a big smile on her pretty face. I knew Nicole did.

"No, to all those possibilities. Here's the deal. I met a woman, and—"

Susan stopped me dead in my voice tracks. "Is she there now? Sitting beside you?"

"Uh, yes."

"What's your name, sweetie?" She wasn't speaking to me.

Nicole's head flew up from watching the phone and stared at me. I silently said, *Speak*, and she answered, "Nicole." Her name came out with uncertainty. Sounded like she was confessing.

Susan replied in a female to female fashion. The kind us guys probably should never hear. "Nicole, you watch out with this guy. Before you know it, you'll be falling for him and doing whatever he wants. So be careful."

Her confidence grew. "Yes, ma'am. I'll be careful. But if a girl falls for him, wouldn't he be a nice catch?"

"That's the problem. He's a nice guy. A loveable guy. If you don't believe me, ask half of the women in Atlanta." She let out a giggle with that one.

Nicole appeared to be inspecting me, then gave a softer laugh. She was enjoying this one-sided chat. I knew I'd be paying for it, and it wouldn't be the phone bill.

I tossed in my penny. "All right, you two. No fair ganging up on a guy."

Nicole ignored me. "Yes, he's a loveable guy. Oh, Susan, he's taking me to Paris for dinner tomorrow evening."

"Now that's one he hasn't done before. The big question. Whose idea was it?"

"Well, he met me in Marietta Square and asked. I told him I wanted to have dinner at a Paris restaurant. He said yes."

"And you want to go, right?"

"Yes. Very much."

"Nicole, he's got you."

"I like him, but he hasn't *got* me. Takes more than dinner." She kept a smile during that whole exchange. I kept a nervous itch.

"Okay, you two. I ain't got nobody, and I'm hanging up this phone." I shouldn't have said that. I said it and I knew it.

Susan ignored me. "Nicole, keep a close eye on him. John, why'd you call me?"

"Thought you'd never ask. I need you to contact Paul or Jane and get the jet ready. The small one. Probably need to leave Hartsfield about nine a.m., if they can have it ready. And tell 'em they get to hang out around Paris, too, at my expense."

"John, I'm sure they can have the plane ready. I'll call them now. That's a nice thing for you to do for them. Nicole, maybe we can meet and talk after you get back."

"I'd like that. Thank you."

Susan jumped in. "John, don't hang up."

"I'm here. What's up?"

"Mr. Kilpatrick, with Kilpatrick Pharmaceutical in Raleigh. Remember you saw him when you did the swing by Myrtle Beach?"

"Yeah, he wanted to go international but needed some IT work done, but he was very undecided about us."

17

"Not anymore. He called me. I talked to him almost forever. I was going to call you tomorrow. He's in. He bought your spiel—well, after I gave him my spiel. I'll send him the contracts, and he wants you back there to have detailed discussions."

"Maybe you should have Larry or Jamie do that and I can finish up later."

"Nope. I already chatted with Jamie, and he and I decided it was your turn."

"But I'm sorta stuck here for a while."

"John, sweetie, you've got a couple of months. He's got to get the hardware in, the servers and storage devices you recommended. You just get your cute butt back for that face-to-face with him."

I promised I would. And she would inform Kilpatrick of my schedule. We hung up.

"Wow. I was wondering who was working for who," said Nicole with wide eyes.

"It's been like that since she came on board. Half the time, I just do what she says."

"I hope you pay her a lot."

"I pay her well. You can ask her. She'll tell you. She's worth more than she'll let me pay her."

"If you're the boss, why can't you pay her what she's worth?"

"Can't afford it. She has more money than I do."

"Whadaya mean?"

"She's the daughter of one of the richest families in the South, last I heard."

With fingers spread, she asked, "So why is she working? And why working for you?" Her finger bent a little as it impressed my chest.

"She likes me. We'll talk more on that. Let's check the bedroom and I'll get my stuff." Nicole followed me.

After a brief look around the room, for at least five seconds, she picked up a picture. "Who's this?"

I'd forgotten about the picture. "That's Megan," I said. "We were engaged. She died in a car accident eight years ago." All that just came out. Something I never do.

Nicole put the picture down and told me how sorry she was and how pretty Megan was. I told her the picture didn't do Megan justice.

I didn't mean for her to see the picture. I usually put it away when women come over. It always seems to cause a happy time to vanish.

"You still have her picture here where you can see her. You loved her a lot, didn't you?"

Yes was the only word that could come out.

Didn't take long and I had packed enough items for a week. The picture had its usual effect. Nicole was quiet till we got in the car.

As I pulled out of the driveway, Nicole asked if I'd had any love relationships during those eight years.

"A few, but none went very far."

"Did you, you know, get real close to any of them?"

"All of them, but never in love—and they knew that. I never misled them." The chat had the feeling of an interrogation.

"Did they cry when you left them?"

"Some did. Most did, but I always let them know up front that I wasn't ready to get married. I didn't want to hurt them, but I—"

"You still had Megan."

"Yeah, that's how it was."

"Tonight you picked me up, and you've made me care for you in just a few hours. When will you dump me?"

That was one of those times a guy can really mess things up. I started this. What do I say? I decided to just be truthful.

"Nicole, when I saw you, I saw someone special. That's why I did that dumb song thing. I'm not sure we even have a relationship yet. After a week or so, we'll know if we really like each other."

"I guess so. I liked the song thing. And I know I like you."

I realized I was talking into the windshield, so I pulled off into a parking lot, stopped, and turned to her.

"You know, I'm thirty-one, and you look about twenty-five. That's a lot of difference. I can understand how you wouldn't want to get involved with me. And you're probably the one who'll have to do the dumping."

"Do you know what Pappy said about you?"

"I think I'm in trouble." That got a cute smile.

"He said you were the kindest, most truthful man he knows."

"I'll have to pay for that, I'm sure."

"He also told me to not let you get away. That you needed someone to finish the rest of your life with. He said I must be truthful. That you don't like liars. John, I've known you for maybe three hours and I like you a lot. And I'll be twenty-five in three months."

I pulled back on to the road, submitted a smile, took her hand, and held it the rest of the drive home.

When we got to her house, her mother had some cheese sticks, crackers, and iced tea waiting for us. She wanted to be sure we wouldn't get hungry before morning. That gave us time to talk, mostly them asking me questions. I told them about my brother, Jake, Susan, and my friends Mac and Elliot. I left my past girlfriends off the list.

We finished our evening snack and her mother made my bed. It was late, so we all said goodnight and I made myself comfortable on the sofa.

Guess I'd been asleep three or so hours. I woke up and maneuvered to better position myself on the sofa when I discovered Nicole sitting, legs crossed, on the floor right there, inches away almost touching the sofa. She may have woke me. Don't know. If I'd gotten up, I'd have stepped on her. This was unexpected, but pleasing. She had some frilly top on and some short, silky bottoms—what there was of them.

She said nothing, so I figured it was my time. "Hi. Can't sleep? Did I forget something?"

"You didn't forget anything. I couldn't sleep. Kept thinking about you and wondered why we met."

"We met 'cause I got lucky." I tried to be funny. She didn't laugh, and she didn't respond. "We both had someone close to us die. What happened to your father? Tell me about him."

She tilted her head down, seeming to focus on the floor then back at me. "Seven years ago, he was killed in an auto accident. I never expected that to happen. It was a tough time then. Still is. We didn't have much money. I'd planned to go to college, but when I graduated high school, I started working full time to support the family. I was the oldest."

"Your father would be proud of you. That took a lot of courage."

"That's nice of you to say, but I had no choice."

I held out my hand. She put hers in mine. "I didn't expect to see you when I opened my eyes, but you were a pleasant sight. Now, I like talking to you, but you need to get some sleep. The day will be a long one."

She gave me a smile and went to her room.

CHAPTER 3

THE TOWER

Saturday morning came early and sudden. It was about six thirty and someone nudged me on the shoulder. I was lying stomach down, head sideways. When my eyes opened, Nicole was a few inches from them. She was on her knees, fully dressed. Her chin was almost on the sofa pillow, eyes focused on me.

She gave a soft, "Good morning." I mumbled something unidentifiable. "You might want to get up, Mr. Lazy. Remember, we're having dinner in Paris."

I had an urge to kiss her right then and there, but it was not to be. She stood up, pointed a finger at me then at the bathroom, and said, "Move it!" The command worked.

Her mother prepared us all a great breakfast. No poison. Maybe I was winning her over.

Nicole was wearing a white blouse, long black pants, and sandals, no socks. I mention that because I, like most guys, would have been hoping for short shorts. But the pants fit well.

I called my rental agency and the minivan picked us up along with Lizzy, Patty's friend. Lizzy had a passport showing her brown eyes and long, brown hair, now with blond stripes. I made sure all the others had retrieved theirs. At least that was out of the way.

Hartsfield, be prepared.

Paul and Jane, my pilot and copilot, also man and wife, had my Learjet ready. This was my smaller but faster jet. It seated ten comfortably in normal, seat belts included, living room type chairs and sofas. The sofas could lie flat to accommodate passengers who would not fit in the small bed in the back. It wasn't long before we reached cruising altitude.

I took Nicole, Patty, and Lizzy to the cockpit and introduced them to Paul and Jane. They were fascinated that a married pair were both pilots. I often thought the same thing. The plane was a gift from Elliot, one of my two closest friends. I helped him find the guy who killed one of his managers. Paul sorta came with the plane.

That was less than a year ago. All was going well, till on a trip to Australia I needed a backup pilot when my primary one got sick. I pulled in Jane, and the long trip was all it took. She's now two months preggers. I've been trying to figure how I can adjust the copilot seat to fit an expectant mother.

I know what you're thinking. What if she starts having the baby over Dallas or Indiana or the Pacific? Not to worry. I'll find a midwife.

We didn't get off as early as I wanted. Still, all were sitting calmly chatting and staring out the windows. Nicole's mother had prepared sandwiches, several varieties thereof. When I mentioned those varieties, everyone suddenly got hungry. With Nicole's help, we got the vittles ready for eating along with chips, iced tea (sweet, of course), and Cokes. Of course, we didn't forget the pickles.

I broke out a deck of cards and asked if rummy was okay. Most knew how to play. Poker would have been more fun, but figured I needed to stay on Mother Betty's good side.

The games lasted couple of hours, extended with questions about some of my exploits. It was midafternoon and Mother Betty and the young girls decided to take a nap in the bed, leaving me and Nicole in the cabin, alone.

I put the cards away and did my tooth-brushing thing and sat down watching Nicole clean the food counter.

She reminded me of my passenger days. "I must admit. I miss the stewardesses on planes. Make that flight attendants. They brought me food and drink and would even chat a little."

"Then why don't you hire one?"

"And miss all the fun watching you do the serves?"

She finished her chores and stood in front of me, with arms crossed. "Careful, or I may spill a drink on you."

With a little bye-bye wave, she went and did her teeth thing. She came back and sat down on one of the sofas and did a hand pat meaning I was to sit beside her. Who was I to argue? Besides, the bed was packed.

Nicole curled up on the seat, legs neatly folded under facing me. "You ever been shot?" That was a sudden question but easily answered.

"Yep. Once. Nothing serious."

"Where?" she quickly asked.

"Hong Kong."

"No, you ninny. Where on your body?"

"Oh. Once in my left upper arm. Bullet just grazed me. Needed some stitches. That's all."

"I don't like that."

I responded with, "I didn't either," and a smile. "Well, such situations do happen, but most of the time nothing serious occurs."

It got quiet. I was curious about Patty and her father. "How old is Patty? She looks nineteen or twenty."

"She's eighteen. I'm six years older. And you're going to ask why so many years, so be quiet." I obeyed her wish. "I was supposed to be an only child. But something happened, and Mama got pregnant and Patty popped out."

I must admit, I was enjoying the situation. "When love is in the air, that can happen. So, tell me about your dad. Was he good to you?"

"Oh, yes. He was more than good to us. So sweet. He never forgot a birthday. And boys. Daddy told me a lot of things to watch out for." Her words were accompanied by waggling eyebrows and a grin. "When I told him I wanted to play basketball, he put up a goal in the backyard. I tried and I tried, but I was no good at it. He saw that and when we played, he'd miss almost all his shots. I know he did that, on purpose, for me."

"That's understandable. Dads will do that."

"And when he could, he would take us to school and pick us up. Mama didn't like it, but he taught me how to shoot a pistol. I was good at it. Still am." That was accompanied with a wink. "We went swimming a lot of weekends. We went on lots of trips. Florida, Tennessee, once to Arizona. Saw the Grand Canyon."

Her description fit my father. "Sounds like a great guy."

"He was. His job caused him to travel a lot. He could be gone for a month. I didn't like that. I missed him."

"I bet you would. Where did he go on those trips?"

"Daddy never said. I must admit, that was always a puzzle. But when he returned, he always brought us a present. He always gave Mama a big, long-lasting hug and a kiss. I can remember her standing there snuggled against him. Her head would lay on his chest. That was so sweet."

"I remember Mama and Daddy hugging, but guess I was too young to see it like that. Daddy never remarried. Why hasn't your mother remarried? She's an attractive woman."

I'd often wondered why my father never did.

Nicole was speaking calmly and looked to be enjoying the conversation. "I think so, too. She's dated some guys but just didn't let them get close. Like you, I think. Mama told me once that when a woman truly loves a man, she always wants him to be loved, even if not by her."

"A man can always hope. Does your mother know you came to see me last night?"

She dropped her head just a bit, with eyes peeping at me, with a soft, "No."

"Don't think she would trust me being alone with you."

"You know, I thought about joining you not long after that. I was going to sleep on the floor by the sofa."

"I'm glad you didn't. Your mother would've put handcuffs on me."

"So, what if I had slept on the floor there during the night? What would you have done?"

"I would've picked you up and put you in your bed. Okay, I probably would have kissed you."

"You would have?" That brought a little smile to her lips.

"Put you in bed or kiss you?" I couldn't resist asking.

"Kissed me, you ninny."

"I probably would have."

"That would've been a sweet thing to do."

"Yeah, but I didn't. Actually, if you'd done that and your mother wasn't watching, I would've ripped that flimsy nighty off you and . . . covered you with a blanket and went back to the sofa."

Along with a smile, she hit me in the chest with one of those girl love taps. That let me know she cared.

"Well, I do like you, but I think I'm glad you didn't rip anything off," she whispered.

"That was just my wishful thinking. I'd prefer to stay on your mother's good side."

"Don't worry. I'll take care of Mama's good side. I suggest you consider mine, or you won't be on any side."

"I'll remember that. Nicole, with all these deep thoughts, I'm getting a little sleepy. How about you?"

She gave me an eye-to-eye stare for a moment, then said, "Yes."

I thought she was going to kiss me. Instead, she leaned her head on my shoulder.

Off came her sandals and she snuggled in. I let the seat back a little to make us more comfortable.

In an untimely moment, Jane came into the cabin, but she saw the, shall we say, situation. With some sign language, she told me it was another five hours to touchdown. I replied asking her to dim the cabin lights. She would be back at least an hour before landing.

Susan had made hotel reservations at the Hotel La Boulogne. I didn't ask anyone, but I got my customary room with a great view of the Eiffel Tower. To keep appearances, I got the others a room below mine one floor down. Also a great view.

When we landed, I'd planned to call the hotel and clue 'em we were on our way. Check-in would take very little time.

Nicole had gone to sleep holding my arm, and I enjoyed her being near, remembering I'd started all this.

Jane returned with the one-hour notice. I let the seat back in upright position, kissed Nicole's cheek, and whispered it was time to get up.

She stretched a little, pulled herself up, and kissed me back. Smiling, she said, "Okay, sweetheart, I'll get up. What's for breakfast?"

"A glass of wine. Go wake your mother."

Those words gently reminded her where we were. "Oh, okay."

With that, she stood upright and headed to the bedroom. I headed to talk to Jane and Paul to see if we could land quick, or if we'd need to circle the country.

I liked the answer, but Jane had a request. "John, would you mind if we went to Mainz? It's near Frankfurt. I have a close friend who lives there now and would much like to see her. She got married last year and moved there."

"Sure. That sounds like a cool thing to do. So, you knew her back in Australia?"

"Her family moved next door to mine when I was ten. She was ten. We grew up together."

"Well, the plane will be ready to go. Enjoy yourself."

"Oh, no, John. That's kind of you, but I want to drive. It's only about five hours, and I'd like to see it by country."

"Well, okay, if that's what you want. Hmm, you know, the drive would be more pleasant. Don't recall why, but I remember Mainz. Old, but popular town. I'll have to put some thought in remembering why. Anyway, enjoy yourselves. Call me if you need anything. Oh, and the car rental is on me."

Paul jumped in. "No you're not, John. You do too much already. We can cover the cost. Just being over here and going there is special. From our past trips here, I know the guys at the hangar, and they'll take good care of the plane."

"Okay, I give. But you two call me if you need something."

Jane gave the last word. "We will. Now go sit down so we can land this thing." She ended that with a hand waving bye-bye.

I took her command and headed back to the cabin. We were heading straight in, but that caused problems. The girls. Four females and one not so roomy bathroom. I took a leak and relinquished the bathroom to the ladies.

With all that done, the women sat and buckled up. Nicole stood and took a couple of pictures. Her story reporting had got underway.

Seating arrangement was important. I made sure they were by a starboard window. I provided the direction to look and what they might see. I like, and prefer, Orly Airport. If you must do the circle, you come quite close to the Tower. Even landing straight into Orly, the Eiffel Tower is visible—small, but visible.

I should mention, landing in Paris at night is a captivating sight. The city lights up. A pilot who knows the landmarks will let you see streets lined with lights. In the winter, the trees along the main streets are draped in lights. That would have to wait till winter.

It was unplanned, but I knew the timing would give the ladies a spectacle to enjoy.

In the daytime, the Eiffel Tower is massively tall, but it lacks flavor. They saw it at a distance, at night, at its best. They witnessed a small, colorful, flashing gold tower, causing a fixed stare.

A block or so behind the tower is the Seine River. It circles a good chunk of the city. If you saw the movie *Charade* with Cary Grant and Audrey Hepburn, you saw the river. Audrey Hepburn played the character Regina Lampert. I always thought that was a cool name.

CHAPTER 4

PARIS AND SUDDEN GUESTS

The landing was smooth. The Hotel La Boulogne check-in also went smooth. It's one of the few hotels in Paris high enough and positioned such that other buildings do not obstruct the view of the Tower. You just have to know which rooms to ask for.

By the time we landed and got to the hotel, it was a late Saturday evening. Having reservations made and being a familiar guest, all I had to do was sign the papers and head for the room.

I left my other companions standing at the lobby as our luggage was being brought from the car. I told them check-in wouldn't take long.

As I approached the desk, the charming Adrienne was there. She was always on the day shift. I'd taken her to dinner and a movie or a club several times.

"Adrienne, did you get transferred to the night shift?"

"Bonsoir, John. Am pleased to see you. It has been much long." She shook her pretty head. "No transféré. When moi know you to come moi, non, I get evening time. I hope that bon certain? I mean okay. Here you reservation paper to sign."

The papers were simple enough. After a couple of signatures and checks, they were done. I handed them to Adrienne and answered her question. "It is okay, ah, bon. I understand," I shook my head and tried again, "comprends." She gave me a smile, so I assumed I got the word right, as I know so very few French words. *L'amour* being one I'd practiced a lot.

While talking to Adrienne, I saw Nicole heading for the desk. Within a nanosecond, she was standing right beside me. Based on the expressions of the two women being in close proximity, I was sure the coroner would soon be cutting away some body parts. Mine.

I placed my arm on Nicole's back, adding, "Adrienne, this is Nicole Powell. I brought her mother and family to Paris to have dinner tomorrow at Pappy's place. We've eaten there, remember?" Where this was going was unknown and spine-chilling.

Adrienne glanced at Nicole as if inspecting her, but said in very good English, "Hello, Nicole. Is good to have you and your family here. I hope you find hotel abasourdissant—non, non, amazing—as John has. Some we believe John that make it amazing."

Nicole had her own comeback. "Hi, Adrienne. John says the view sparkles, and I can say for certain that he makes any place amazing. Good to meet you, Adrienne." She ended the sentence with a manufactured smile and turned to me. "John, we better get to our room. We need to try and get a little sleep." She took my arm and led me away.

While being escorted, I managed to turn my head to give Adrienne a smile with a bye-bye wave.

After a safe distance, I whispered in Nicole's ear, "Nicole, you said *our* room. You left the *s* off rooms."

Without looking at me, she said, "I know," and led me onto the lift. Her family followed.

On the way up, Nicole told me to come back to her room in case they forgot something. I told her to be sure to open the window curtains. The Eiffel Tower would await their oohs and aahs.

Leaving the women at their floor, the porters and I continued up to my floor. Having left my bags in the room, the porters departed. I only had a carry-on bag, my laptop, and a suit bag. With my unpacked luggage awaiting my return, I headed down to the tenth floor.

I knocked on the door, which opened about an inch and left me standing there with a "Come in," which I did. I'm not sure who opened it. I could believe the door opened itself, afraid to do anything else.

There were four women inside deciding which bed to use, who gets the bathroom first, and in what order. I'm not being critical, just amazed. There was an amount of order in their play.

Taking a scenic seat, I sat and watched. I asked myself why was I there? Then Nicole appeared in a short *negligée*. There was truly not much material. I wondered if it had been planned due to my impending presence.

It was getting very picturesque, so I decided to face the other way and did a U-ey in my chair. Then asked, "Anyone need anything? I can go get whatever."

As I waited, Nicole suddenly materialized in front of me. My eyes instinctively closed.

"What's the matter?" she asked while leaning forward, with her hands behind her back.

"Huh?" came out sorta sudden. I didn't open my eyes.

"Why are you staring at the door? And why are your eyes closed?"

"I saw you and was getting evil thoughts. Retreat seemed the best solution."

I imagined a smile on her face. "You sweet thing. You can open your eyes. I won't bite."

"You're not the one I'm worried about doing the biting." I opened one eye. I smiled. She smiled back. I immediately closed it. "Can I go now?"

"You may go, you sweet man. I promise to miss you."

I stood up, opened my eyes, took her hand, and walked us to the window, where the curtains were closed. I stood her at the center of the window, facing the curtain. The other women standing around behind her stopped and started wondering what I was doing. I walked to the window side and pulled the cord. The lights of the Tower caressed Nicole and flooded the room, followed by aahs.

My work was done. I gave Nicole a light kiss on the cheek and left. Okay, I could have stood around and got hugs and kisses. I figured points were made. Why gloat?

It was well past eleven when I got to my room. Late, yes, but I needed to talk to Pappy.

I clicked the buttons and he answered. "I take it you got in? Is everything okay?"

"Yes. Everyone's checked in and are probably asleep."

"You only call this late when you have something on your mind."

"Just had more questions. I did find that Betty's husband was dead. Now, tell me how you knew."

"After they left, I checked the internet on occasion hunting for their names."

"You have some sort of crush on Betty?"

"Crush? What does that mean?"

"Like her very much. She made a deep impression when she was here."

"Yes. I had and still do have a crush, as you said. When you called, it brought back many good memories."

"Thought so. Thanks for the info. We should be by for lunch tomorrow and dinner. I'll be showing Nicole the sights, so we may not see you a lot. She's considerably more beautiful than your restaurant."

That got a laugh out of Pappy. "If you spent all your time at my restaurant, I'd have a physician check you out."

I told him I'd let him know when we got to the restaurant. It was late and being wore out, I added, "Let's get to bed, my friend. See you in a few hours."

We said our goodbyes.

I did minimum unpacking, including my laptop, of course, brushed my teeth, and turned in. I left my curtains closed.

The Tower is great, but it's like sleeping with a spotlight over your bed.

There was a hard tap on the door, which woke me. It was 1:00 a.m. I got up, walked to the door, and peeped through the peephole. Nicole was peeking back at me. I didn't expect that. At first, I worried that something was wrong, but that worry didn't last long.

I opened the door. She was wearing her PJs, accompanied by her purse.

"Can I come in? I couldn't sleep and wanted to talk to you about Daddy."

"We could talk in the morning."

"No, I want to talk now. Please?"

I held the door fully open, and she walked over to the sofa.

It didn't seem the time to sit before saying what I was thinking. "You know, if your mother finds you here, she'll have me strung up by my thumbs."

"Yes, she would. But my daddy would just want me to do what's right."

She patted the sofa and I joined her.

Her visit opened the door for more knowledge. "Tell me more about your dad. You told me he was a great guy who travelled a lot. What else do you remember?"

Nicole thought a bit. "He taught me how to play tennis, checkers, and cards. Poker. He always let me win. He hid Easter eggs for us and the neighbors' kids. He enjoyed watching all the kids scrambling for eggs. He always got us a fresh Christmas tree and helped us decorate it. But things changed."

"What changed?" She had captured my interest.

"His time at home. In those last years, he was gone for two or three weeks. Once for a month, and another time for nearly two. Next thing I knew, he had the accident."

"Tell me what you know about the accident. I mean, if you can. If remembering causes you too much sadness, don't say anything."

"John, it's been so long and I've thought about it so much, I no longer cry when I remember it. Let's see. Well, he'd got home from a long trip. That night he got a phone call and needed to go meet some of his company guys."

"What kind of business? What kind of work did he do?"

"He worked for the Federal State Department at the Atlanta office. But he got laid off and went to work for a company that did security for other companies. I asked him once what all he did, but he said best not say. Said it would get him in trouble."

"So he went to meet some of his business contacts with the new job? Do you know the name of that company?"

"Yes, it was Signature Security Consultants. On the way, his car hit," she paused, "a tree."

"Maybe you don't need to talk about it." I had to ask. It was a gruesome topic.

"Actually, I do. I need to. When he hit the tree, the car blew up and the fire burned him, everything, very bad. He was so badly burned they couldn't even identify him. But it was his car. They found his wallet in the dirt."

"So they never identified the body as his, they just assumed it was him due to what little evidence they had."

"Yeah. Oh, they did find his ring. It had a diamond in it, a real diamond. The ring melted, but the diamond was there. He always had that ring. It meant something, but I don't remember. Mama would know." She paused for a moment. Her eyes closed briefly. "John, I shouldn't have talked about it. I'm tired. I woke you up. I'm so sorry."

"Don't even consider that. You have nothing to be sorry about. I'm glad you did."

"You're so understanding, but it's late. I should go back to my room."

I wanted to know more about that ring, but it didn't seem the right time. "Yes. You should go."

Nicole walked to the door, then turned. "It's not just late. It's very late. John, I may wake them up and maybe scare them. Can I sleep here on the sofa or the chair?"

This didn't seem real. "Please don't get angry, but you see how this looks. Did you plan to sleep here?"

"No. I promise you I didn't. You're easy to talk to, and I couldn't sleep, and—"

Her emotions took over, and it was my time.

"You can sleep here, but you'll sleep in the bed. I'll do the chair."

She walked to me and kissed me on the cheek. "Daddy would've liked you."

With that, I found a blanket and pillow and took over the chair. Sleep was needed.

About an hour later, a knock on my door woke me. As I was getting up, the door opened and closed, leaving a creature wearing a pink robe. I took a few steps and the robe dropped to the floor, exposing Adrienne, along with her long, brown hair.

"Hello, John. I come myself for welcome you. I miss you."

She started walking toward me. Watching her close in on me, I said, "This is not a good time."

"I on break. I not be missed. It you and me."

We both heard a grunt coming from the bed. Nicole quickly flipped off the covers and stood by the bed for a second. The next thing I knew, she was standing beside me with her arm resting on my shoulder. She was shorter, but her presence got her point across.

Adrienne stood still, with her light-blue eyes wide open staring at Nicole.

I stood still waiting for the fight to start.

Nicole broke the silent standoff. "He belongs to me. Now get out." She minced no words.

Adrienne picked up her robe, threw it around her, and was out the door. Before what, I had no idea. I was more worried what the woman hanging on my shoulder was going to do.

Nicole stepped in front of me, with eyes on me. "You'll make sure she understands you're off limits, won't you?"

"I took her to dinner three times and once to a movie that was in French. I never understood a word."

Then I realized I'd done nothing wrong. I leaned close and shook a pointed finger at her. "And you understand that I didn't invite you to my room, either. Now, go back over there, get in bed, and go to sleep."

I stood back just in case.

Without a word, she walked to the bed and sat on the edge. Her head was down, but her warm eyes were on me. "I'm sorry, John. I shouldn't have done that. You didn't do anything wrong."

Her mood was about as enjoyable as a woman can be. I went and knelt down. "I'm glad you were here. You did what I'm not sure I could've done. In case you don't know it, I'm thanking you."

"You're just trying to make sure I don't cry."

"Every man wants to prevent that. I meant what I said about you being here. Now, you get back in bed, and I'm heading back for the chair." Having said that, I stood, tilted her head a little, and kissed her.

I had a wake-up call for 8:00 a.m. I hoped it wouldn't show up suddenly.

There was another knock at the door, at 5:00 a.m. It woke me up. I checked the peephole again. This time it was real trouble. Mama. Any sleep left in me became extinct.

When I opened the door, she didn't move, just asked, "Is she here?" That was an easy question because I knew the *she* she was referring to.

There was only one answer, "Yes," as I pointed to the bed. Before I could explain, her mother let me have it.

"I thought you cared about her. You don't. All you want to do is please yourself."

Keep in mind I wanted to defend myself, but my words were stuck in cement.

Finally, there was a slight crack and I jumped in. "She slept on the bed. I slept over there." I pointed at the chair with the blanket and pillow.

"John, you didn't ask her up here, did you?"

"No. She showed up unannounced about one o'clock. She couldn't sleep and wanted to talk with me about her father. We sat on the sofa, talked a while, and then I headed for the chair. Word of honor." Think I crossed my heart.

Mother Betty was cooling down a bit, at least with me. Nicole was still asleep. I started to go wake her when her mother stopped me.

"Let her sleep. When she wakes up, send her to our room."

Now, you must get a feeling of what just transpired. Possibly you just survived a fall off Mount Everest, or maybe you were vacuuming out the space shuttle and it took off. Okay, you get my drift. I had just survived a mother's wrath.

Her mother had known me less than a day and she was going to leave her daughter sleeping in my bed. You better believe I knew what I needed to say about that.

"Sure, that's a good idea. She needs her sleep. I'll make sure she's safe, and when she wakes up, I'll walk her to your room. Ah, her room."

Her mother turned to Nicole briefly, then back at me. "This trip, the plane, all of this. Are you trying to get her away and alone? Please don't hurt her."

"As I told you yesterday, all I wanted to do was take a lovely woman to dinner. Nicole picked the location. If it had been some island in the middle of nowhere, I would've never agreed to anything like this. She knew Pappy. I thought it was okay. Nicole was happy with it. Please know I would never hurt her."

She listened to me. I know she did. Her eyes were boring holes in my head, but she didn't respond. She turned and opened the door. Holding the door open, she took one last stare at me and quietly left.

I sat down in my chair bed and got to thinking. Her dad had traveled all the time, never saying where he was going or why. He died in a burning car and they couldn't identify him. Instead, they made an assumption.

My suspicious nature kicked in. Teeth don't burn easy.

CHAPTER 5

TIMES REMEMBERED

The wake-up call I was expecting, which over there was a knock on the door, came at 8:00 a.m. Paris time. That's 2:00 a.m., Sunday morning, Georgia time. My eyes opened with my mind wondering why and hoping no one was waiting at the door.

Nicole hadn't moved. That *tap-tap* didn't discourage her sleep and left that chore for me.

I walked over and stood by the bed. She was sleeping on her side, facing me. I didn't want to startle her.

Dropping to my knees, I leaned close to her ear and whispered, "Time to get up, sleepyhead."

I'd always wanted to tell someone that. She didn't move. I whispered again with no response. More drastic measures were needed.

Bending over, I planted a kiss on her left cheek, then on her right. A tiny smile emerged, so I went for best effect and kissed her, on the lips. She kissed back.

As her eyes opened, "You make a great alarm clock. I like your method."

"It was sorta spur of the moment."

Her arms went around my neck. "Feel free to spur that moment anytime."

Letting her arms slowly leave my neck, I straightened up, saying, "You should get up."

She threw off the covers, giving me a stunning view. "Still want me to get up?"

Her PJ bottoms were shorts. I was happy she was wearing something, anything.

I stepped back in awe. "Yes." At least that's what the verbal side of my mind said. Suspect you know what the nonverbal side had to say.

"Well, you're no fun," was her reply as she threw her legs off the side of the bed. With a minor movement she was on her feet, stretching and yawning.

"You need to go back to your room. Your mother gave that order."

Her response was, "Are we still okay with what happened last night? When she, that, that woman came in?"

"Are you kidding? I had two women about to fight over me. It was a bit tense, but I liked it."

"Typical man. I'm going to my room." She started walking to the door.

"You're not going alone. I'm taking you down to your room."

"Okay," was her reply. Her face showed no expression. It was as if she was being submissive, which was, in effect, in control, of me.

With me holding her hand, we left my room and stood by the lift. "Now, we'll take the lift to your floor, and—"

"Lift? What's that?"

"It's the elevator. The British word for an elevator is lift. The French word is tricky to say and spell, so when I say lift, think elevator."

"I see. You're trying to be European."

It wasn't a question. It was a statement. How did she know that? She continued to puzzle me. It was a pleasant puzzle, but a bit worrisome.

In a few minutes, we were standing in front of her door.

As I knocked on the door, she said, "You didn't want anyone to hurt me, did you?"

"True."

She was right. Tying that to her mother's wrath, I made it my stay-alive plan.

When the door opened, I said hi to Nicole's mother just as she let go of the door and disappeared into the room.

I grabbed and held the swiftly closing door open as Nicole went inside.

She turned and said, "You be back here in an hour, or I'll be back to your room without PJs. Understand?"

I refused to let her have the last word. "The Eiffel Tower tour starts in an hour. Be casual and be ready for some fun."

The door closed with no other words spoken. I took the lift. I needed my own safe space.

I returned within that hour. It was close to nine o'clock. The girls were not ready. Nicole grabbed me at the door and sat me down in that same see-all chair as yesterday. Fortunately, they all had clothes on; they just had some last-minute female touchups to do.

With all dressed, I gave them some offers. "There's lots to see. The Tower, the river, Pappy's place, and the old Paris landmarks. If we do the Tower and maybe a couple of landmarks, we would be ready for Pappy's place for lunch. What do you want to do?"

Nicole spoke first. "John, I want to see the Eiffel Tower and the river with you, then do lunch." She was wearing snug blue pants, medium-heel black shoes, and a pink blouse with several of the upper buttons untouched.

Patty and Lizzy were wearing white blouses and shorts, with sandals. Patty spoke, "We just want to walk around Paris and see the stores and places."

Mother Betty was quiet, but I could see something different on her face. "I saw so much last time. I'd really like to go see Pappy and maybe talk and remember some of the old times."

It felt like my time to join in. "That's a perfect thing for you to do. Pappy would like that. Okay, everyone, here's the plan. We'll drop your mother off at Pappy's place, then we'll head for the Tower. At that point, Patty, you and Lizzy can go as you please. I would say you should keep to this side of the river. There are some areas of Paris that are best only to go with an adult, preferably a man."

That got lots of stares. My first thought was I'd gotten my point across, until the stares quickly turned into grins.

First thing I did was call Pappy to give him a heads-up then called a taxi to get us to the Le Beaujolais. I made a mental note to get a rental. I normally get one at the airport, but I had four distractions that prevented the norm.

Avenue de Suffren is a busy thoroughfare, as it should be, being within walking distance to the Eiffel Tower. Standing on tiptoes, you can see most of it. The trees are taller than the few small businesses near the Tower.

I was going to be a gentleman and open the doors for the ladies, but they nearly ran me down leaping out of the taxi.

Nicole saw my distress. Having been one of the causes, she helped me out of the taxi. "Sorry, John. We were sorta excited."

"I noticed. Next time I'll bring along my football pads."

"You played football?"

"No. Just making a joke." But I got a smile out of it.

The taxi left with my tip in his hand.

Holding Nicole's hand, I followed the gang into the restaurant. There was no sign of Pappy. He must have been in the back room, or most likely the kitchen. I told everyone we'd just let the hostess seat us so we could surprise him. Then I saw the hostess. The surprise skedaddled.

"Good morning, Mr. Stone," she said. "Mr. Armand said you would be coming. It is good to see you again."

"It's good to see you again, Celeste." Her long, light-brown hair, dark-brown eyes, and supermodel figure added to the viewing.

"Come. I will seat you." She directed us with a hand.

As we followed her command, I noticed the ladies kept quiet. I was holding Nicole's hand and she began to squeeze it firmly. I whispered to her, "Why are you so quiet? And why are you holding my hand so tight?"

Nicole whispered, "How well do you know her?" ending with a twisted lip smile.

Continuing to whisper, I responded to the hidden accusation. "Whoa. I don't know her *well*. I eat here a lot, and she's always here. She knows the names of all the regulars."

I felt I was about to have handcuffs attached.

Whispering back, she said, "I believe you, maybe." With a moment's pause, she squeezed my hand again. "John. This is . . . is . . . so surreal. I remember walking in here the very first time holding Daddy's hand."

"I wish you could be holding his hand now." And it wasn't because of the hand squeeze. I remembered holding my mother's hand.

She loosened her grip on my hand and grabbed my arm. "I like holding yours." She leaned her head briefly against my shoulder.

Celeste guided us to a table with a window and had us sit down, thoughtfully leaving menus in English. "I will tell Mr. Armand you are here, Mr. Stone."

"Celeste, you're his daughter. Why not just say Daddy? Or guess it would be Papa." It was only a suggestion. I added a smile just in case.

She leaned forward a little as her hands went behind her. "Papa likes me to be formal." She added a brief body wiggle for emphasis. The moves gained the attention of several pairs of male eyes, but I don't think it was intentional.

"Well, you do it perfectly and cutely."

Her hands swung around in front holding each other, "Cutely. What that word?"

"Better ask your papa."

With a delightful smile covered by her fingers, she accepted my thank-you and departed.

Whispering to me, Nicole asked, "You could've told me she was Pappy's daughter. I don't remember seeing her."

Returning the whisper, I added, "Seven years ago, she would've been in diapers." I was kidding and she knew it. The look caused me to add, "Just kidding. Maybe a teenager."

If a female snicker can tap your face, hers did.

Through our murmuring, no one else was speaking. I waited a few seconds. It remained quiet. You'd think we were attending a funeral. Everyone was looking at everyone else.

I figured they were afraid to speak, so I injected a bit of misguided humor. "Okay, someone can say something. Has the typical cat got your tongue?"

I ended that with a grin. I found I was the solo act.

Nicole's mother spoke first. "It's just as I remembered it. We sat at this table almost every time. I think Pappy always kept it ready for us."

Patty added, "I don't remember much. I'm not even sure I liked the food."

Lizzy had a different opinion. Her brown eyes were wandering all over the restaurant. "I wasn't here, but I'll never forget it. It's delightful and romantic."

"Lizzy," said Patty, "we've only seen a few blocks of this place and I like it too."

Nicole turned to her mother. "I remember it too, Mama. I sat next to Daddy every time."

I saw Pappy heading for the table, then Nicole and her mother saw him. I also saw Nicole pull out her phone. Photos would be taken. These would be memorable. Didn't suspect anyone would mind, and they didn't.

Giving him a wave, I stood. "Hey, Pappy, good to see you again."

Pappy grabbed my hand, shaking it, and we shared a hug. He signaled for Patty to get up. "Patty, you've grown. Now a beautiful young woman."

Those words brought a smile to her face and her eyes opened wide. They hugged, and she was the one hanging on a little extra longer.

When they parted, Patty's smile did not leave her face. "Pappy, this is my best friend, Lizzy."

Lizzy stood and Pappy gave her a gentle hug, "Lizzy, I welcome you to my little eating place. I hope you enjoy it." Then added, "Paris now has two beautiful young women to explore its wonders."

Lizzy was in heaven. "Oh, Mr. Pappy, it's all so wonderful. I know I'll enjoy every minute here."

Pappy put his arm around her. "Paris will help you do that. Now, Lizzy, if you don't see anything on the menu you like, you tell me what you want and I'll have it cooked for you."

"Oh. That is so kind," said Lizzy, with wide, bubbling brown eyes.

Pappy waved his hands. "The same goes for all of you."

Lizzy sat down. Her expression told me she was having an unbelievable experience.

With that out of the way, he pulled a serveur over and we ordered. When the serveur left, Pappy remained standing and gave us some history of his restaurant.

After a couple of minutes, he said, "Forgive me, everyone, but there's some business I must do. John, I need you, too."

He signaled me to follow him. I saw we were heading to his office.

I turned to the table and gave a ta-ta wave, saying, "Gotta go." I spread my arms, palms up, hoping to show them I wasn't sure why Pappy was pulling me aside. Patty, Lizzy, and Nicole all took my picture. I could only hope I was a blur.

Pappy sat down behind his desk. I took my seat waiting for him to let me in on why I was sitting there. His office, except for a laptop, printer, and other internet devices, was a step back in time. I think Napoleon once owned the chair I was sitting in. Yet, it was in pristine condition. Same for the sofa. I'd never thought of Pappy as an art collector, but he had three paintings that looked original. He told me they were copies.

The oddest thing about his office was the heavy bolted door, which is not so unusual, but there were no windows. First time I was there I asked him why. He said he'd seen everything outside his office too many times with too many reminders. I didn't take that further. One day I may get braver.

"John, when you called, it brought back many memories of that time including Betty. But more importantly, her husband. Tell me again what you've learned."

"Nicole told me the night he died, he had gotten a call to meet someone. She didn't know who. Next thing she knew, his car had hit a tree and he was burned bad. They found his wallet, a diamond, and a melted ring. They declared the body as William Powell based on those two items. That's pretty much it."

Pappy had a puzzled look and added. "That doesn't seem like much to declare it was Powell's body. What about dental records? Don't you think it's a coincidence he was burned beyond recognition?"

He had the same doubts. "How'd you know that detail, my sly friend?" I asked.

"I have my sources. Just because you're thousands of kilometers away, news does get here. So, was it a coincidence?"

He saw the same ambiguity I did. "With the methods of identification today and the possibility of burns that bad, no. You're on target. Why no mention of dental records?"

Pappy had no identifiable expression to my words. As for me, maybe somebody just forgot. Hah, not gonna happen.

From just watching him and knowing the way he can be ahead of the game, I hadda ask, "Okay, partner, you know something more. Let's hear it."

"When they were first here, Powell always ate with the family. When they did some touring around Paris, they would stop by here. He was with them. Then there was the time they were here seven days. I don't recall when, but after three or four days, that changed. Once as they were eating lunch, he got a call and left. I had to get the family a taxi to their hotel. That happened more than once. Sometimes they came and he wasn't with them."

His words caused questions needing answers. "Were his absences mostly daytime or nighttime?"

"Both. When I asked why he was not with them, all I got was he had something to do. Never much more than that. It was really none of my business, at least at the time."

"Pappy, when a man with a family is not with all of them or even with one of them, he's seeing a woman, or something more secretive is in the works."

"You're thinking as I am, John. I never mentioned this to you, but my father was with the French underground back in the war. I was young, but I remember he would disappear for days at a time. After he died, my mother told me of things he was doing that got him killed by the Germans."

"Ah. Nicole said her father worked for the Federal State Department and got laid off. Then he got a job with Signature Security Consultants, where he would do a trip ever so often. The trips started lasting longer. He started being gone for weeks and then a month. She never knew why."

Pappy picked up on that. "So, he did similar things, absences, when at home?"

"Yes. And he got a call the night he was killed. He told them he had to meet with some of his company's business associates. Are you thinking he was working with the French government on some problem?"

Pappy replied, "I do not know, but there were and are always things brewing that regular people have no knowledge of. If his trips were security related and somehow connected to French government actions, maybe against a company, he was in a very mixed, dangerous company."

"Yeah. I can see that."

"John, if he was murdered because of something he was working on, I want to know who killed him. If he's not dead, where is he? In either case, the search alone will be dangerous for you and for me."

Since I'd known Pappy, it had been a habit of his to expose the unknown even when he should not.

I gave him and myself a warning. "You know by digging up the past, it could also hurt Betty and the family."

That was no surprise to Pappy. "Yes. I know. But if he's still alive, they should know."

With a questionable nod, I said, "I agree. At least I think I do."

"You're one of my closest friends. And I understand the issues as I ask you to consider this matter. Now, I do have some names and places to start."

I pulled out my cell phone. "Okay, give 'em to me."

"Here's the names: Jules P-e-l-l-e-t-i-e-r. Ludovic R-o-u-s-s-e-a-u and Alivia Béringer. I believe you can spell that one."

"Yep. You wouldn't happen to have phone numbers or addresses?"

He opened his middle desk drawer, pulled out a small note, and handed it to me. "I suggest you not call but visit them. Tell them you got their names from me because you wanted to know more about William Powell. Do not tell them I have you checking up on them. You are just trying to give some closure to his wife and daughter."

"Any side thoughts on the three?" His knowing those three existed had to come from some source or personal experience.

"There may be some unlawful actions and government connections. I do not believe there's any spying or government secrets involved. They are not that intelligent."

"I'll keep that in mind when I approach them. I'm thinking of paying a visit to Signature Security and the US Embassy tomorrow. Do you know their hours?"

"Signature is open twenty-four hours, seven days a week. I believe only a select few Signature locations are open on weekends. You should check that. The American Consulate is not open today. Maybe for visas and passports, but that's it. But you might go by there just in case."

"Good info, Pappy. I believe I have enough to begin. We better get back. Food may already be on the table."

"They will bring it when they see me walk to the table."

"Pappy, you *do* have it under control."

He gave me a smile.

When I sat down at the table and as Pappy stood there, the food came out, as he predicted. When everyone had their plates in front of them, along with a red wine, Pappy put some scenic brochures on the table. Where he had those hidden, I do not know.

"These are some of the most entertaining and memorable places to visit. For those who have a partner with you or want to find a partner, use the walkway alongside the Seine. For you two young ladies, be on guard, for you will be noticed."

Patty and Lizzy sent us twisted, pursed-lip smiles. They knew very well he was referring to them, and I suspected they were planning to be noticed. Nicole gave me a light punch in the side, getting my attention.

"Betty, what are you planning to do this afternoon?" asked Pappy.

"I really have no plans. I was hoping we might have time to talk about the past and now."

Couldn't speak for the others, but she had her own plans. Those plans only included one other person—of the French persuasion.

Nicole turned and winked at me. I returned the wink.

"Betty, my afternoon is yours," Pappy said, then, speaking to us all, he added, "Enjoy your food and the afternoon. I must bid you adieu to address a shipment of food waiting in a truck out back."

He left us to devour the French dishes. I personally enjoyed his chicken cordon bleu. Just as we finished our meals and were rising to leave, Pappy magically made another appearance.

"My serveurs all said you enjoyed your meals. Is that true?" he asked.

Everyone gave their yeses and thanks.

We left Pappy and Betty standing by the table. As we had just exited the front door, I turned back to see them sit at a table for two, near a window. Alone.

CHAPTER 6

TOWERING EVENTS

As we walked up the Avenue de Suffern, I made sure they saw the Tower because the closer we got to the base, the more our heads would experience an unpleasant view straight up.

When we were about to get on the lift, I informed Patty and Lizzy it was everyone for themselves. Nicole took my hand, indicating we were a pair. The young girls took off for one of the lifts, helping the doors close before we could join them.

I didn't mind. It was obvious we would be distractions to their hopes.

Nicole and I reached the top and rested on the handrail, side by side, both looking at Paris.

With Paris in her eyes, she asked, "What did you and Pappy talk about? You were there a long time."

The woman didn't waste any time. "Just some business stuff he wanted my advice on." I was unsure how much to share and probably was already in trouble.

She kept her eyes on Paris. "I do not understand how you can be successful in business," she started, "if you don't know how to lie better." She turned to face me, with a devious grin.

My goose was cooked. I don't lie much, and certainly not to customers, but sometimes you have to fib a little to keep the peace.

Like when a woman asks if the dress fits her well. If the guy says no, she may not speak to him for the rest of the day or night or whenever.

I turned so we were facing each other. "Forgive me, but we just talked about your father. He knew your father was dead."

"How did he know that? How could he know?"

"He has his ways." I threw my hands out. "They do get news over here, you know."

"Don't gimme no bullshit, Mr. Stone." She was on the verge of anger.

"Nicole, I truly don't know. From what I do know, he has sources to get many things, news included."

Her head tilted just a tiny bit, and a small smile emerged. My hand was on the rail. She put her hand on mine. "I can understand that. Did you tell him how my father died?"

"Yes. Gave him all I knew based on what you told me. I hope you know he cares about you, your mother, and Patty. He just wants to make sure you're okay. He cares about all of you."

"John, thank you for telling me." She added, "You do know why Mama stayed with him when we left?"

She saw it too. I added my thoughts. "She has some feelings for him. When Pappy and I were talking back there, it was really obvious he feels the same."

Nicole's voice became almost solemn. "Since Daddy died, Mama hasn't been involved with anyone. I think I told you that. Maybe Pappy's the reason? I know Daddy was away several times and Pappy spent a lot of time at our table every time we ate there. But I don't remember any romantic connection. I mean, they didn't hug or kiss."

"I have to believe your mother loved your father back then. If she had any feelings connected with Pappy, I have to believe your mother would have suppressed them."

"And then because Daddy traveled so much and was gone so many times, then died, maybe his death let those feelings loose."

"Then I showed up." I said that, even though it didn't fit. But the words were out.

"Yes, you entered my life. You, a strange man who swept me off my feet, as Mama would say."

"And all I had was a song."

She looked at me for a moment, then put her arms around me. I added mine around her. I accepted a kiss that lingered for an extended time.

Pulling back a few inches, but still within kissing distance, she asked, "Have you ever kissed a girl up here?"

"First time. And that's the truth." Unsure why, but figured I should add that.

She grinned at my admission. "I believe you, sweet. Now, I want you to tell me the rest of what you and Pappy are planning to do."

Okay, now that was a good play on her part. It's a female thing. She closes in on you, plants a super kiss, and next thing, the topic changes and the guy is hooked. But we like it. At least I do.

My next steps could be dangerous—make that *would* be. Me, a stranger, finding and talking to those names Pappy gave me straight out of the blue. If her father was dead, and he probably was, that would offer some challenges. If he was still alive, my asking could be a reason for someone to end *my* existence.

Offering her a curled lip, I said, "You're a sneaky woman. You bury my lips with a never-ending kiss, your warm, slender arms still around me, and you ask me a question I'll have to answer."

"It's a girl thing. Now, you tell me or you'll have to find another girl to sing to."

With no choice, I started, "All I ask is that you keep your arms around me."

"So long as you tell me the full truth, you have my arms." I could only hope she wasn't Super girl.

"Okay. Pappy gave me some names to talk to that may tell me why your father spent so much time away from home. What he may have been doing and why. Maybe even with whom."

"You know he was working for that security company. That's already a lead."

"Exactly. And he may have been contacted by the State Department because they just might want to dig deeper if his company had a record. We just don't know yet. Pappy wants to know, as do I. Maybe more. We believe you and your mother need an answer."

Nicole's eyes teared up a little. She gave me a pat on the cheek. "That would mean so much to me and Mama. When do we start?"

"It'll take some time away from you and the family, but I was planning to start the probing tomorrow. You'd have to do any sightseeing alone." I had ignored her words, hoping she wouldn't catch me.

Before I could respond, she'd won the race. With her arms still around me, she said, "Oh, you won't miss me. I'm going to help. You can be Sherlock Holmes and I'll be Watson."

When we met, I had seen—make that felt—her strengths. She was the type to be involved. It was time to get out of her grip, her arms, and her will.

I pushed her back, holding her firmly. She looked startled.

"No. I'll do the searching alone. It will be dangerous, most likely very dangerous. You are not helping."

She stood straight up, eyes wide and fisted hands on her hips. "You sure know how to screw up a nice feeling. I'm going to help. He's my father. If you try to stop me, I'll tell Pappy and everyone I see what a mean person you are. That's the end of the discussion. Oh, but I'll let you be in charge."

My hands went into the air. I let out a large breath of air, shaking my head. "You tell whomever you want. I'm going to tell your mother."

Nicole's lips pursed. Her eyes tightened. She took a wide swing, landing her open hand on my upper arm. It was not a love tap, even though it didn't hurt. It was her frustration showing.

I grabbed both her arms and held them tight. My words were firm. "Neither of us can win this. You've given me no option. I will let you help, but please let me keep you out of danger when I see it coming. Please? I do not want you to get hurt."

That released a smile from her lips. Her hands went to my shoulders. "We both won. And I do want you to protect me. What do we do first?"

She had me on the spot. I hadn't planned to have a plan so quick. "You do realize all this came to reality an hour ago?"

"Sweetie, if you don't have a plan now, that's okay, because I know you'll have one soon. That's what you're good at. I can tell you're thinking of one now."

That came with a grin. How she knew that, I didn't know. Must have been that woman's intuition thing.

"Okay, ya got me. Two things. I want to pay a visit to Signature Security Consultants' office. And I want to see these addresses. See what part of town they live in. I'll have my friend look up the names."

I pulled out my cell phone and showed her the names.

Nicole had a bit of sudden wonder on her face. "Your friend?"

"I'll have Mac get me info on Signature and these names. If those three have any arrests or any type of record, I want to know before meeting them."

"Mac?"

"Mac. MacKenzie Stanton. He's one of my two very close friends. If there's anything to be found out about a person, he can find it."

"Oh, that's the one you told us about back home. Maybe I can meet him sometime?"

"That could be difficult. I never know where he is or who he's with. With girls that is. But, if the chance happens, I'd like for you two to meet."

"Is he with the police or something? How would he find out anything?" Her words didn't seem as firm as they had been. I wondered if she felt she'd won or lost.

I took both of her hands and held them gently. "He's not with any organization now, but he was in the past. The CIA. And I don't question how he finds things out, I just ask. He delivers."

Speaking softly, Nicole shared, "I don't expect this to be fun, but helping you find answers about my dad will mean so much. You give me hope."

With her relaxed words, we headed back to the hotel. The Eiffel Tower didn't seem the place to start an investigation.

We got back to the hotel about two o'clock and went straight to my room. We needed some certainty of privacy. I stood by the window while Nicole took her shoes off, turned down the covers, and sat down on the bed, watching me.

I sent those three names to Mac with what little info I had on them. What I didn't know was when he'd get back to me. Also, I asked for whatever he may have on Signature Consulting.

When I hung up, she asked, "When will you hear from him?"

"Hard to say. I told him it was a rush and I needed the info bad. More often than not, he gets tangled up with a woman, and often it's two—at a time, that is—and his availability becomes limited."

Nicole got a suspicious look on her pretty face. "Give me your phone?" When I didn't immediately offer it to her, she got up and joined me at the window.

She took my phone out of my hand, turned, and sat back down on the bed. She patted the edge, indicating I was to join her. I did. Beside her.

"What *are* you doing?" I asked with fear, wondering what I'd gotten myself into. I wasn't thinking of the phone call.

"Be patient." I watched her click the redial button. I remember thinking, *Oh shit*, but it was too late.

"Mac, this is Nicole Powell. I'm John's girlfriend. He's lying here in the bed beside me. I want you to get him that information he just asked for, real soon. If you do, when I meet you, I'll give you a nice present. Goodbye, sweetie."

She ended the call and put the phone in my lap.

A thought came out verbally. "That actually might work."

Nicole turned to lie on her side, resting her head in her hand and looking up at me. "If you took off your shoes and lay down beside me, it would be more fun."

Sometimes you must obey the greater power.

With shoes on the floor and me on my side very close to her, she said, "I'm a little warm."

With a wink, Nicole sat up on her knees and took off her blouse and bra. Without warning, she leaned forward, putting her hands down on either side of me. She planted a short kiss, and with a few enchanted moves, she was lying beside me, head resting on her hand, as before, wearing only bikini panties.

"I must admit, I have never had a woman do what you just did in my presence. You're not only beautiful, but you have beautiful moves." I wasn't kidding.

"Take off your clothes," she asked with a demanding tone.

Again, I obeyed and lay back down beside her.

"So, what do we do next?" She smiled as her finger tapped my nose.

I leaned toward her, put my arm around her, and was about to kiss her, when she said, "Not that. Not now. I mean about those people we need to find."

Disillusioned, I moved back to my previous position, obeying her wish.

"You're a very tempting and disappointing woman. But a pleasure to look at. Are you sure you want to do this? I mean this. Now."

I began to wonder where my manly confidence was hiding.

"Yes. You really must pay attention to what's happening. Now, any woman can be tempting when she wants to be. I'm glad you like what you see." Then with brief shakes of her head, she added, "I'm waiting for an answer."

The choice was made. "Before we can do too much, we have to wait for Mac's reply. He'll probably send it to my laptop. As for now, when we get our clothes back on, we'll take a look-see at where they live. And look for getaway methods in case such is needed. We'll pay a visit to Signature Consulting. Just gotta find it."

"I've never been on an investigation. What should I wear when we interrogate them? Something sexy or businesslike? Maybe provocative?"

"We're not interrogating them, my dear. Just asking questions. Provocative might be a good idea."

With a shameful smile, she teased, "How about short shorts, a tight blouse, and sandals that wrap up my legs?"

I liked her suggestion. "You can wear that for me anytime. Annnd it would also be okay for our discussions. The men would be highly distracted."

"Enough about clothes," she said. "I think it's time you got on the subject."

"Huh? Now, what's the subject?"

"Me."

CHAPTER 7

SKINNY VISITS

With our early-afternoon festivities completed with delight, I had a rental delivered to the hotel. With transportation in hand, so to speak, Nicole and I headed for Alivia Béringer's residence. It was an apartment building over in Montrouge on Brossolette.

It was the typical four-story building in the area from what I'd seen. Nothing fancy, at least on the outside. Inside was a bit above average with a lobby, a small one, furnished with a sofa and a couple of chairs.

I was about to press the lift button for the fourth floor when the door opened. Out stepped an eye-stopping, delightful long-haired brunette in her mid to late thirties, who smelled very feminine. She never gave us even a glance as she headed for the door. I pondered if we were invisible. Most, even strangers, at least give ya a nod. I do. I turned to look at her.

Nicole noticed. With a squinted-up nose and a tilted head, she asked, "See something you like?"

"Huh? No. I was trying to decide if she was French or German."

"Sure you were. She was looking at the door. You were looking at her ass."

"I was not. Okay, maybe I did glance at it." I motioned for Nicole to get on the lift.

She declined and motioned for me to enter, which I did.

I pressed four. Before my finger left the button, she added, "You're a man. It's what you men do. We women know just why you men came up with that 'ladies first' thing. We know why, and you just tried to get me to do it. To go first."

"Huh? Hey. I was just trying to be polite." Believe me, I was.

"Bull! It's so you men can watch our butts move."

"I didn't start that, ya know." Must admit, I blurted that out.

"Do you look at my ass when I'm walking?" If a look can feel hot, hers did. "You *do*, don't you?" Her accusation shot by my ear like a bullet, listening for the truth.

Unfortunately for me, there was truth in what she asked. "Okay, Nicole, I confess. Yes, I do. Sometimes. Not all the time. Understand, you're an enchanting woman and, and, it adds to your mystery."

Physically I was standing. Mentally I was on my knees.

The doors opened. I went out first.

Nicole stepped near me as the doors closed behind her. Softly she asked, "Do you like my ass better than hers?"

How I got myself into this I do not know, but I needed to get us moving. "Yours is much shapelier. So is everything else about you." I took her hands. "When I first saw you on the square, I thought of a movie actress, Grace Kelly. Gorgeous is the word that comes to mind. You have the same hair, eyes, and all the other feminine attributes that exceed even hers."

"I don't know her, but that's sweet of you to say." As she gazed at me, she added, "John, I give you a lot of trouble. I'll try to stop. I promise." She was near tears for being right.

"Don't you dare. You keep doing what you're doing. I like what you do, okay? Now can we start our searching?"

Her hands tightened on mine. "You're a kind man, and yes, we should. So, who we looking for here?"

I pulled out Pappy's notes. "Alivia Béringer."

Nicole noted, "I don't see a picture there. You don't know what she looks like, do you?" She was getting in the mood.

"Nope, but we will. For now, we need to examine this floor. She's in D1 over there, but I want you to look around and tell me what you see."

She glanced at me, then began, "Well, I see a door to the stairs, I think." I used my hands to direct her to the door and investigate. "No keyholes, so it can't be locked. What else do I look for?"

I added, "Can the door be opened? What's behind the door?"

"Oh, I see." She turned the knob and opened the door. "It's just stairs. Goes up, goes down. Nothing else there."

"Good point. In this case, nothing. We've learned if we need to make a fast exit and can't use the lift, we hit the stairs. We know we can escape either way."

"But we don't know what's upstairs, except the roof."

"Another good point. Funny, but in movies the good or the bad guys always seem to go up the stairs to escape. Let's see what's up there."

We walked up the stairs and approached the door to what should give access to the roof. "Give me your analysis of the door."

"Analysis? It's obvious." She turned the knob. "No key needed."

"Come on. We're checking out the roof."

As I stepped out, I held the door. Nicole followed me and turned when she saw me stop.

"I want you to turn the door knob on the roof side."

She grabbed it. "It won't turn. There's no keyhole. That's dumb."

"You don't see it often, but that's done so that if the police are chasing a criminal who heads for the roof, he gets stuck up here."

"I can see that, but what if a regular person gets stuck up here?"

"When repairs are needed, the carpenters will place a plastic attachment to the knob that makes the latch stay in. What all that means is the apartment owners do not want their tenants wandering around the roof."

"But if they open the door just like we did, and get locked up here, what do they do? Jump?"

"Some might, but there's an easier way. Hand me that brick over there."

She got it for me, and I placed it in the doorway so the door could not close. "Follow me."

We stepped to the side of the entrance wall. It protruded about a foot.

"See that button?" I pointed at it. "That's the way out for a person who's not supposed to be up here. Press it and the building security rescues you."

"I don't think I'd want to do that. They'd be angry."

"You get the point. There's no fire escape, but if you had a rope, you might could swing down to one of the balconies and break into a room. That is also not a good thing, but it may be the only way down."

"If I were a bad person, I'd bring a rope or have a helicopter pick me up."

"Now you're thinking. Let's go."

Once inside the door, I moved the brick to one side and gently let the door close. I had wondered if opening the door would cause an alarm. No one had showed up, so figured we were safe.

When we were back in the lift, I asked her, "Do you now understand why I asked you to examine the floor?"

"I think so. If you're dealing with bad guys, know your surroundings."

"Now, that was beautifully put."

We headed for our next stop.

Jules Pelletier also lived reasonably close in Malakoff. The Grand Marque du Sud apartments. Five stories and kinda nice was about all I could say for his place, which would be an exaggeration. Similar lobby as the last place, but the building looked old. Cheap would be a good description.

Once on the fifth floor, I told Nicole to look around and examine the possibilities.

She looked down both aisles near Jules's door, and then opened and went up the stairs. In under five minutes she returned to the fifth floor and me.

"Okay. The roof's accessible and there was no fancy door lock like the prior building. There was a fire escape down one side allowing the possibility of escape. Oh, it went down the side of the building into an alley."

Nicole was learning. I complimented her on her good eye. She used one to wink at me.

The last was Ludovic Rousseau. He, too, was in Montrouge, southwest corner. Amargo de Paris apartments. Six floors. This was not a cheap place to live. High class, if the entrance was an indicator. It had two tall, white columns supporting a narrow but long blue canopy. As for my opinion, it was all mostly for show.

The lobby looked more like a hotel, without the concierges. After checking the third floor and roof, there were no obvious oddities noted. The next visit here would be for more details. We vacated the premise.

No sooner than we were sitting in my rental, Nicole gave her opinion. "John, what have we found about these three that made our time useful and beneficial?" It was a good question.

"We know the layout of their dwellings, but there is one other thing that's interesting. What do you think that is?"

"I have no idea. You tell me?"

"They all live less than three miles from each other."

"Maybe they're friends or relatives. So what? Oh, but they could be spies or something."

"I doubt they're friends and really doubt they're relatives. If not spies, crooks, thieves, or killers, we know they have something in common because Pappy wants us to question them. It would appear they live close so that, if needed, they might have safe refuge nearby."

"Still seems a waste of time."

"Probably was. But I got to spend time driving around Paris with a charming woman."

"No fair. You changed the subject."

"If I recall, you liked being the subject."

"Okay, stop the playing with words trying to get me to like you more. What's next?"

"We're paying a visit to the American Embassy I'm not sure what I'll tell the Consul but he may have heard of your father."

She gave me a questioning glance. "You sound like you know where it is. Do you?"

"Yep. It's up on Gabriel Avenue, or Avenue Gabriel as the French say it."

"It's Sunday. Surely they're not open today?"

She called it. After a thirty-minute drive, I found that both Pappy and Nicole were right. Closed. Note to self. Check the website.

It was late in the day, almost six thirty, and we were at our last stop of the day, Signature Consulting. Having learned my lesson, I checked their website. As Pappy suggested, they were open but with skeleton staff for emergency purposes. I was going to be an emergency.

Their office was in the northwestern suburbs of Paris on Rue de Clichy, off Route 5, near the town of Clichy. It's colorful French that translates "of Clichy" to "de Clichy," attempting to mean "in Paris on street of Clichy." Yeah, I'm not sure how it works either.

Signature was a single story among a variety of single- and multistory buildings. It and the others were less than picturesque. There was a small flower shop nearly buried between two buildings. It furnished some needed color to the street.

We entered the front door, one of the double-door types. It was open, so I assumed they were available for business. Or I just notified the police to stop by.

A young, pretty woman greeted us, in French. I gave my hello in English and she responded in English. I told her why we were there and gave her Powell's name. She told us to wait as she made a call, speaking French for obvious reasons.

She finished her call and pointed to a door. "Monsieur Naude will see you."

Following her point, we entered and a man greeted us. "Good afternoon. My name is Duane Naude. And you are?"

We introduced ourselves and I attempted to make sure he knew the relationship between Nicole and William Powell, her father.

He continued, "Thank you. Have a seat. How can I help you?" He sat down as well, at his desk.

There was also a circular table with a chair. He chose the desk, I suspect, to appear more formal. Another man was sitting over in a corner to our right. No introductions were made. He said nothing. Just stared as us.

To get things moving, I said, "You've probably checked your records, so you know Nicole's father was killed in an automobile accident in the States. We know you're a security company, but we're hoping you could share with us the kind of work her father was doing. And maybe what he was working on back then. Anything that could give Nicole some closure would be appreciated."

"Actually," he began, "I'll have to look that up. Give me a minute. I'll bring it up now."

His fingers were typing, but the screen never changed. He was lying. The dimwit had put a large picture with glass frame to his right, giving me a reflective view of his computer screen.

"Oh, forgive me." He pointed to the silent man in the corner. "This is Bastien Vadinoye. He is with our security team and we were discussing another subject. I wish him to remain. He may assist with your question."

Vadinoye saw us but made no recognition of our existence.

Naude continued, "Yes. I see." He paused a moment, pretending to read, I guess. "He was working on a security project at the time but had taken a few days off. He wasn't working on the case when the accident happened."

Possibly he was reading words from some document he could share. "That's odd. He told his family he was meeting some of his company contacts when he left the house."

Naude typed some more. "It wasn't business. It may have been a personal meeting." The screen didn't change.

Nicole wasn't happy with those words. "No, it wasn't personal. I heard what Daddy said. I was there. It wasn't a friendly meeting and it was after dark. It was business."

"Miss Powell, I wish I could help you more, but it's not in my records. He was an excellent investigator. It's possible he was working with one of our US branches, but I have no record of that."

I saw a movement out of the corner of my eye. Naude's attention suddenly shifted to the corner.

Vadinoye stood and walked to the edge of Naude's desk. "I am familiar with Monsieur Hoywell. He was working on security issue with one of our clients. With his death, we cleared the details from Hoywell's account. There is nothing more we are able to share."

His English was surprisingly good. He just didn't know how to say Powell.

Naude never took his eyes off Vadinoye till he finished. Then his eyebrows tightened, and he glared at everyone in the room. My impression was he didn't know what had just happened.

That was enough. I took Nicole's hand and stood up. She rose reluctantly. "We appreciate your time, Mr. Naude, and you, Mr. Vadinoye. We'll do some digging of our own elsewhere."

Naude stood looking at me. Nicole was also looking at me. Neither look was pleasant. Vadinoye never even flinched.

Giving Naude a brief bow, I turned my back to him and whispered to Nicole, "Need to go. Tell you why later." As I got to his door, I turned. "You should fire whoever hung that picture behind you. Gives visitors an informative view."

With a salute, we left.

When we exited the building and got to the car, I started to open the door but Nicole stopped me. She grabbed my arm, stepped in front of me, and let me have it.

"What in the hell did you do back there? And what did the picture have to do with anything?"

"It was a show. He was either lying to us or had no intention of giving us anything, or it was nothing but a show."

"You're making no sense. Have you suddenly gone crazy?"

"I could see his computer screen reflected in that picture. When he typed, we heard the clicks, but the screen didn't change. His screen had four lines on it. I couldn't read it, but it never moved."

Her anger switched from me to Naude. "What? He can't do that!"

"But he did. I don't know the purpose behind that whole scene, but he had no intention of giving us anything, and neither did creepy Vadinoye. When that happens, there *is* something to be told."

Nicole turned to the car and leaned against it. Her arms were crossed, and she was crying softly.

I took her arms and pulled her to me. Speaking gently, I said, "That dirtbag was just one source. Here's the point. When you know there's something hidden, it must be something you need to know. And I promise you, we'll find out."

She lifted her head. Eyes wet, she said, "You can't promise that, John. But I keep hoping."

We headed back to the hotel. Nicole's outlook lifted, and she sounded more positive as she talked. That's always a good sign, not that I'd done anything to help. I remembered her comment about hope. I wasn't sure I had hope. I was in a foreign country with different laws, fewer freedoms, and people who may decide they want to turn me into dog food.

CHAPTER 8

LOUVRE EXPECTANCIES

Sitting with Nicole on the sofa in my room, I got to thinking of Patty and Lizzy. It was close to seven o'clock, not dark, but they had been out of our sight for a long time.

"Maybe we should've ridden around the Tower area a little. The girls aren't here, and I'm worried."

Nicole didn't seem concerned. "If they need us, they'll call."

"Maybe you should call them, just to be sure."

Her nose crinkled like she smelled a dead rat—me. "Okay, Mr. Worrywart." She stuck out her tongue. It was a cute tongue.

She made the call. They answered, said they didn't need any help, and said bye quickly.

"See? All I did was bug them." She did the tongue sticking out thing again.

"Your tongue is cute and sexy." The words came out of my mouth with little thought.

"If you keep being—being whatever you are, you'll see it more."

We were inches apart. I took her hand. "Okay, I apologize. I just don't want anyone to get hurt while we're over here. And that includes you."

"I know you don't. Pappy was right about you."

"Well, maybe a little. Oh, when we do our talking tomorrow, it will send a smoke signal to people we have no knowledge of. People whom I suspect do their deeds under the radar."

Her face had a soft look about it. "I like the way you talk."

That caught me off guard. "You have a graceful way of muddling my thoughts. Now, where was I? Oh. We most likely will then be in the line of fire. I'd like for you to stay here when I talk to them."

I knew that suggestion would be of no value, but I had to give it a chance.

She pulled the hand I was holding, along with mine, and held it against her chest. "You make perfect sense, but I'm still going with you. If nothing else, I can be a backup. Now, is there more we can do today?"

With that reaction, I gave up on keeping her away. "I've been trying to think of something. I need Mac's information. When we talk to those three, I want to have some details I can allude to and maybe cause them to act. Do something to provide us a clue to all this."

Still holding my hand, she leaned back and rested her head on the sofa, looking at me. "And I'm no help. I guess I'm dragging you down."

"Actually, you're a big help. You give me a reason to do this." I was about to add more when she cut me off.

"You hungry?"

"Yes."

"Me too. Let's head for Pappy's. Might as well see how Mama's doing."

It was after seven and certainly food time. If we hadn't gone, I suspect we'd have been delayed again, subject wise.

When we entered Le Beaujolais, Patty, Lizzy, and Mother Betty were all sitting at that same table, with Pappy, I might add. We got seated after Pappy gave hugs to Nicole and me. No clue why he hugged me. I would've stopped with Nicole.

Before I got a word in, Patty asked, "How'd it go at that signing place today?"

Lizzy corrected her. "Signature something. That's the place, right?" She glanced at me.

Why they cared, I didn't know. *How* they knew, I wondered, but I replied, "Boring would be a good word. We learned nothing. Got the runaround. If it weren't for the flower shop across the street, there'd be no color on the whole block. Okay? Now, you two don't care about my day. That makes me even more interested in yours."

The girls inspected each other as if they were deciding what to say, or possibly what to omit.

Patty started. "It was great. We must have walked a mile down the Seine. It was beautiful. Lizzy, should we tell them who we met?" Lizzy nodded. "Well, we met these two French boys. They were walking alone, too. We saw them behind us, so we stopped and sat on a bench. They stopped. We talked, and when they offered to give us a tour, we said yes."

Her mother's face shifted to not happy. It was totally absent a smile, and she let them know. "You mean those two boys picked you up, and you let them?"

"Mama, they were very nice, and there were lots of other people walking. We were never alone."

"I don't like it," said Mother Betty, continuing with the displeased frown.

Patty ignored what her mother said. Speaking to me, she added, "Mr. Stone, they want to take us on a tour of the Lower museum."

"Not Lower. It's the Louvre, pronounced like 'loova.' That museum is probably the best in the world."

Lizzy joined in. "Yes. And we want to see it." She shot me a questioning gaze, then added, "We'd like you to go with us. Not all the time, but to help get us going. The boys are sweet, but we don't know French and they know very little English. Please?"

Bad news was coming, but they needed to know. I was going to be the untimely bearer of that news. "Lizzy, Patty, the Louvre closes at six on Sunday. Sorry, girls, but the tour will have to wait." My gut told me those boys should've known that.

Lizzy wasn't pleased. With a hint of displeasure, she asked, "How do you know that? Maybe you're wrong." Then it turned to a gentle begging. "Please be wrong. Please." Her voice and face had a youthful sweetness about it.

Patty jumped at that possibility. "Yes. Maybe you're wrong. It's a famous place."

I wish I could have granted their wish. "I'm sorry, girls, but last time I was here, a friend told me. If you don't believe me, ask Pappy."

Nicole gave me the look. Trouble was brewing. I saw it. The look women get telling us to say the right thing, to take a different path, or else.

My brain provided a solution out of desperation. "I have an idea. Ask the boys to come here? We can meet them. Their dinners are on me."

That got me a smile and a tiny nod of approval.

Nicole withdrew the look.

I heard a pair of yeses, indicating I was again on their good side.

Mother Betty added, "I'd like that better." She turned to the girls. "Do you know where they live?"

Patty pulled her phone from her back pocket. "I have his number. I'll call him."

My finger went up. "Now, you know when you call him, he has your number. Being a man, I always like to have the woman's number. Do you want him to have your number?"

Lizzy gave her an option. "If you don't, Patty, they can have mine. I'd love to have the number of a Frenchman if nothing more than a souvenir." She finished that with a young wicked grin.

"I like that, too, Lizzy. We'll share."

Patty held her phone so Lizzy could add it to hers.

Nicole was getting impatient. "Will you call 'em? Let's get this show on the road."

Without delay, Patty said, "Here goes." She dialed the number and the boy answered.

She asked, "Nathan, is that you? This is Patty." I couldn't hear his reply, but she gave us a big smile along with a wink and nod. Then she asked, "Nathan, the Louvre is closed, but we'd love for you to have dinner with us. Can you join us?"

Nicole got impatient with one word. "Well?"

Patty gave us another nod, then kept speaking. "At the Le Beaujolais restaurant. Yes. My friend will pay for our meals. Do you know where that is?" She listened to him, then added, "Oui. He will pay for the taxi." There was another pause, and we all heard her reply, "Super. Oui. See you here soon." She hung up, smiling.

Nicole looked inquisitive. "Did you know anything he was saying? Did he understand what you wanted?"

She had a quick response. "Not really. But he was happy and said oui lots of times. Believe me, he knew what I was asking."

I had to ask, "Do either of you know where they live?"

Patty continued with the unknowns. "No. No exactly. It's not far."

"How do you know that?"

Lizzy joined in. "That's what they told us. Not far."

"But they don't know English. How could you know?" Why I continued this I do not know.

Lizzy didn't give up. "After a while, we understood. I know we did."

Patty did her corroboration, "That's right. We kept exchanging words, and we know they live close."

They weren't gonna give in. I gave an "Ah. Gotcha," and ended that side of the conversation. We began to chat about nothing while waiting for the boys.

Nathan and Andre arrived within minutes. Either they were next door or they took a jet. It was neither, just a simple taxi, which I paid for. The driver said they were about twenty miles out and the town was Créteil, wherever that was. I quit digging. My brain hurt.

The dinner went well, after which I saw there were some couples who wanted to be alone.

With dinner done, we went back to the hotel, including the boys. We chaperones, meaning me, Nicole, and her mother, left the boys and the girls in the lobby to have some alone time. I realized I was referring to them as boys. They were maybe twenty at best. I made a reminder to ask.

However, before we left, I pulled the boys aside and made sure they knew to do their talking there, never leaving the lobby, and that they were to go home alone. I gave them cab fare and added a few "or else" words.

I pulled the girls aside. "I know you'll do what you want, but try to keep it at a couple of kisses, okay? Until I know them better, I just don't think it wise to be out alone with them at night. Because I'm the one talking to you, your actions can get me in a lot of trouble. I could lose my head."

After getting a hug from both, I added that I had spies behind the hotel desks.

Patty let me know their position. "Thank you for caring."

Lizzy said, "Me too. We understand what you're saying. We promise to stay here in the lobby. Course, we might have a drink with them in the restaurant."

I figured that was the best I could do. They both kissed me on the cheek, spun me around, and with one on each side, gave me a gentle goodbye push.

With that, Nicole, her mother, and I went to their room, where I figured I'd be run through the notorious wringer if I was forced to tell them what I'd said to the girls.

No sooner than the door had shut, Nicole's mother was standing in the doorway, as if guarding the room.

"What did you say to the girls?" She minced no words.

Owning up, I said, "First, I told the boys to not leave the lobby and to leave the hotel alone, or I'd make them disappear. I privately told the girls to keep it friendly, stay in the lobby, and not to leave the hotel with them. And that I had desk-clerk spies."

Nicole gave me a foxy smile bordering on the edge of Machiavellian.

Nicole's mother saw it and came back at me firmly. "I do not like that. They are not your children. You cannot give such permissions."

Before I could start begging forgiveness, Nicole stepped in. "Mama, he did what I would have. They're not children. You and I both know, at least I hope you do, that the girls will kiss those boys anyway. John told them what any father would. I believe they will obey what John told them. They pay him more attention than you or me. Maybe it's because he's a man, but he certainly got their attention."

Nicole's words ended that sticky parenting session. Mother Betty was not happy, but she went to her bedroom, leaving Nicole with a coquettish gaze at me.

I replied with a goodnight kiss on the cheek. I figured it may help, and then left for my room.

When Nicole followed me, I knew rest was unlikely.

CHAPTER 9

SOFA NEWS AND LOGS

I headed for the sofa. It was getting a lot of use. The bed did too, but when talking is needed, sitting is better than laying down.

Nicole joined me. "I really like what you did for the girls. I was surprised Mama even let the boys have dinner with us. I believe what you said and did gave her a little belief that the boys are trustworthy."

"I'm not so sure about that, with the look she gave me before we left. For me, those boys seemed okay. I just wanted to put a bit of fear in their minds."

"You did," she agreed. "The girls whispered to me they still wanted to go to the Louvre. I'm wondering if the boys will pick them up tomorrow."

"If they have no ill intent, they'll show up."

"How often do you show up with ill intent?" she asked.

The subject needed new direction. "Never. Better check my laptop." She grinned and gave me a positive nod.

With her approval, we moved to the desk and powered up my laptop. Nicole was hanging over my shoulder. No time for surfing, I needed e-mail. And there it was.

Hi Little John. This was too much for a voice call, and ditto for texting on my cell phone.

You should send me a picture of Nicole. She gave me encouragement to get back soon.

As to Alivia Béringer, born in Germany. Has a record for collecting money from the unsuspecting elderly. Started young after twenty, maybe twenty-five, so I was told.

Jules Pelletier will take some time. Will get back to you. Now, Ludovic Rousseau was also connected to Signature. May still be. Didn't check that far. My unofficial sources tell me he removes troublesome personnel or individuals. Watch out for him.

Because you asked about those characters, you also need to be aware of Yanis Allard. I classify him as a Frenchman who should never know your name, unless you're a priest. He has been known to help people disappear permanently. Avoid him.

As to Signature Consulting, they have offices in the US, France, Germany, and Sweden. Their first foreign location was London, but they were kicked out when it was proved they allowed certain types to get though their security on purpose.

Oh, William Powell. When he was with the State Department, he had no trouble till he was assigned to investigate Signature Consulting. He found they were stealing US high-security documents. Our government had him appear to be guilty of espionage and laid him off, quietly. His undercover assignment was Signature. That could easily have gotten him killed. I'll dig a little deeper on that.

That's about all for now, old buddy. Give Nicole a kiss for me.

Be in touch. Mac.

Nicole was reading over my shoulder, and before I could even log out, Nicole reacted without tears and not so much anger, but surprise. "My father was a spy? Oh, dear God, spies get killed all the time. He probably is dead. John, I don't think I wanted to know all that."

"Most spies don't get killed. Very few do, and your dad must have been good at it or they would never have put him on such an assignment."

She looked at me; still no tears. Maybe she realized it was more satisfying by knowing. "I'm going to believe what you said. It gives me hope. And I really need hope."

"My plan is to keep building on that desire. Keep remembering that."

"I will. But how does Mac know all that? You said he was retired. He must have contacts all over the world."

After closing the laptop, I headed for the sofa, talking on the way. "He's retired, and he does have contacts. Ask and he will find."

Nicole sat beside me. "I wonder what he would find out about me?" Her face looked worried.

"Knowing Mac, he could find out why you came with me and what you've been doing since you got here."

Nicole had been leaning close to my shoulder. She shifted her position a few inches, with a querying look at me. "He can't do that. Can he? That's, that's not possible. He hasn't been to my home, to this hotel. He's not even in France."

I gave her something to think about. "How do you know where he is? He could be in the room across from mine."

Her eyes widened. She sat up straight and frozen. Then the thought must have grabbed her. She jumped, or close to it, into my lap, with arms around my neck.

Speaking near strangulation, I said, "All right, now look, Nicole. He's not that kind of guy. Now, get off me and let's put some thought on how we want to approach those three creepy, foreboding people."

She shifted her head, softly saying, "Do you really want me to?"

"Yes."

"Jeepers, you're no fun," she uttered as she backed away, but she stopped and fell back on me. "Little John? He started the e-mail with it. Why'd he call you that?"

"You sure do switch. Never mind. I hoped you wouldn't notice. He's one of my two closest friends. Mac, Elliot, and me. Both are taller than me, so I got the Little John moniker."

The grin was all over her face. "That's so cute. Little John."

"Now don't you start."

"They must really like you to be that sweet. I like the nickname. It's as cute as you."

Attempting to change the subject without using that word, I said, "Let's visit Alivia Béringer first. She may be the least dangerous."

"How do you know that?" She was back in the game.

"Just a hunch. Alivia deals with the elderly, meaning she probably doesn't carry a gun. And with you there, that makes two women. She'll be outnumbered." I hoped she'd accept the compliment.

"I appreciate the thought, but my being there won't matter."

"Ah, but it will. As a woman, you'll see things a man won't. If you do, warn me or pull me aside and tip me off."

"Thanks for the confidence, but we'll see. What time is it, John?"

"Little after ten. Why?"

"The boys? The girls? We need to check on them."

She grabbed my hand and headed for the lobby.

In the lift she paced forward, back, side to the side, her hands in full random movement. "John. What if they aren't there? Oh, God. What've I done."

"Nicole. It's ten o'clock. If I know girls, they still have the boys corralled."

And they did. As the lift doors opened, there were the four of them, smiling and laughing. When the girls saw us, their hands went up, waving for us to come over. Now that I didn't expect.

Next thing I noticed was they had paired up. The girls had picked their guy. So, what's new?

Patty was first. "Nicole, this has been so much fun. John, thank you for all you did to let them stay."

"Hey, I didn't give permission. I'll accept the thanks, but your mother gave the okay."

Lizzy chimed in, "Mr. Stone, we know if you hadn't done all you did, they'd be gone."

Nicole was still a little antsy. "That's true, girls. John made it happen. But it's getting late."

The girls' joy dropped a step. They needed a fresh boost, so I took a shot. "What about the Louvre? Do you still want to go?"

That got an excited yes from the girls.

To the boys, I said, "Visit Louvre." They got the message with a multitude of ouis.

Lizzy asked, "When can we go?"

That was again my cue. I signaled for one of the women behind the hotel desk to come over.

While on her way, I said, "It opens at nine, so we do breakfast at, say, eight thirty and leave after you do your teeth and girl things." I got okays.

"Monsieur Stone, may I assist you?" I jumped a little. The desk clerk had crept up on me.

"We're going to the Louvre tomorrow morning, and I need you to help me communicate the times with the boys, here." I pointed to them.

That got another "Oui, Monsieur."

It took a while, but the boys agreed to show up at the hotel at eight thirty to eat breakfast with us, then do the tour and return here. With that done and the clerk back at her desk, Nicole and I were standing there when all were quiet.

I noticed the girls were staring at me. Then it dawned on me—Nicole and I were in the way. I gave some taxi money to the boys. That got me a wink from the girls, along with a stare indicating Nicole and I needed to exit, which we did.

Must admit, I wondered why they didn't have a car. They looked old enough, or maybe they weren't.

When the boys had departed, the girls joined us. We both got hugs.

Nicole said, "It's obvious you enjoyed your time with them. But how could you know what they were saying?"

Lizzy said, "We learned a few French words, and they knew some English. If we had trouble, we went to the desk clerk to help. The one Mr. Stone got to help him."

"It was so romantic. It was wonderful." Patty was oozing romance.

I was tired with all this girl stuff happening. "Girls, and I mean all three of you, I'm bushed. I'm heading for my room."

Both girls' heads tilted, eyes tight with uncertainty.

Nicole helped. "He's tired. He doesn't have the stamina he once had."

Yeah, she said that. I chalked it up as no way to get even.

All three knew what that meant and got a good laugh—at my expense.

I uttered, "Good night," and headed for the lift, followed immediately by all three. Two got off at ten. Nicole held the doors open till the girls had disappeared into their room, meaning no one was to hear or see whatever was about to happen.

"I'll be joining you in a few minutes," she said, smiling, as she let the doors close.

With nothing else to do, I continued to the eleventh floor. I managed to do a quick shave and brush my teeth, when there was a knock on my door. As I opened it, I was asked to step aside as Nicole came in with her night things in hand.

"I've brushed my teeth. Are you through with the bathroom?" she asked.

"Yes, I just—"

She didn't let me finish. "Then it's my turn. Oh, put your pajamas on," she commanded as she shimmied into the bathroom. I didn't mind.

There was nothing for me to do but the PJ thing, then climb in bed and wait.

Nicole came out of the bathroom wearing very little, and if I didn't know better, she glided across the floor into bed, beside me.

With her lying on her side, inches away, I asked, "Is your mother going to knock on my door at five in the morning?"

"She knows where I am, and you have nothing to worry about."

"Maybe I do." Those words came out suddenly. Explaining them was not going to be pleasant.

Her head tilted and her eyes tightened. "I know you worry about me, about keeping me safe, but you're doing that perfectly. Most of all, you're helping me—no, you're *wanting* to help me—know what happened to my father." Her voice got softer. "And you're sweet."

"That's nice of you to say, but I worry about us. Us together. Our feelings about each other. I like you a lot, but I don't, I mean—"

With a quick move, her chin was resting on her folded arms as she lay on my chest looking into my eyes, inches away. "You're not in love with me. I know that. You're worried about that, and you don't need to be. I woke up and saw you cuddled up on the sofa. You were so sweet there. That told me the kind of man you are. John, I'm not an innocent woman. I've been with three men, but they didn't last long because they wanted to please themselves. They didn't truly care about me. You do, and I love you for that. Just like all the others."

"What others?" Suddenly this got scarier than some guy with a gun pointed at me.

"The women you've dated and who loved you."

"There haven't been that many. Beside, how would you know?" She was grinning. Then it hit me. "Susan?" Her tiny grin turned into a wicked one. "Do you women keep some sort of a log about men and pass it around?"

She inspected the ceiling with a hmm, then me, without a hmm. "There was Elizabeth."

"I don't know an Elizabeth." I said it, then remembered.

"You were going to take her to see *Cats*, but you got called away. When you came back from somewhere, you flew her to San Francisco and made up for it. She was happy, and she made you happy."

"There *is* a log! Ouch. We men don't have a chance." She only smiled. What else could she do? It was the truth. "Okay. Look. I must be a dumb dummy because we've done it twice today. I do want to make love with you again, and yet I'm tempted to say no now that I know of that log."

She softly and confidently said, "Consider that temptation melted. I'll put a double star by your name in the log."

CHAPTER 10

UNCLE JOHN ARRIVES

Monday arrived at 7:00 a.m. I know because that's when I had set my alarm. The intent was to give us time to do baths, teeth, dress, and get to breakfast by 8:30. That was the plan, until the woman I was sleeping with crawled over me and turned off the alarm. I mentioned it was time to get up. She said, "Not yet."

"Yet" came about twenty minutes later after we spent some up-close time together, again. Preparing for breakfast and our interviews, I donned a T-shirt, sports shirt, blue jeans, and shoes with socks.

Nicole was wearing the items she planned to wear for our interviews. Items included a tight pink sleeveless blouse along with short shorts and sandals. She was gorgeous. I asked if her bra was uncomfortable.

She said, "What bra?"

We joined other guests on the lift and arrived for breakfast at 8:20. Nathan and Andre were already there. I got us a table for seven, where we sat and waited for the remaining three.

I asked the boys if they had been to the Louvre. I remembered and used the word visited, which was close to the French word, and got a pair of ouis.

With the little French I knew, I may have asked them if they'd ever pissed in the Louvre.

I won't bore you with the breakfast orders and conversations except to say Patty and Lizzy sat close to their new boyfriends. As girls usually do, they sampled what their boyfriends were eating. Nicole fed me several bites of her French waffle as she ate several bites of my eggs. The only times the smiles left the boys' faces were when they had to chew food.

We finished eating and everyone was ready to go, but there were some instructions needed for the younger crowd, specifically the two French ones. I asked the concierge to join us. Her name was Adele. I told her I needed her to translate my words. I had my reasons.

With Adele beside me, looking at the boys, I said, "You have permission to join us at the Louvre, and if the girls wish it, to show the girls around Paris." I stopped as Adele translated. The boys were very happy.

I added, "Now, these two are very precious to me. You will treat them with respect, kindness, and allow no harm to come to them." Adele did the translation.

The boys agreed to that request, although their expressions were more of concern and fear, which I liked.

It was time for the pièce de résistance. "Now, boys, if you do anything beyond holding their hands and a kiss or two, and you know what I mean, I will find you and remove a body part that will prevent you from ever fathering children. Oh, and it would not be my first time doing such. Do I make myself clear?"

Patty's blue eyes went wide and her mouth opened. Lizzy smiled and put her arms behind her back. She was enjoying it. So was Nicole.

With my words and the girls' reactions, dread filled the boys' faces.

Adele had a different expression. Shock would come close to what I saw. I nodded back and she translated.

Nathan and Andre instantly went from a happy posture to one with their legs suddenly close together and each with their hands clasped below their waist area, as if protecting something.

As I watched their movements, I saw they were speechless and probably needed some encouragement. "I want you to have a good time, and I want the girls to enjoy themselves. Do I make myself clear?"

Adele translated.

Andre nodded.

Nathan nodded.

"Nods won't do. I want to hear your voices." She translated.

Each of the boys said the French version of "We will treat them as you said." And got real quiet.

Nicole's mother didn't say a word.

Nicole's hands were glued to her own mouth to keep from screaming with laughter.

I gave a thank-you to Adele. I couldn't hear, but when she got back to the desk, I believe I saw her sharing something with the other women there. My suspicions were confirmed when the women kept darting a look at me as Adele spoke. After which, they all blew me a kiss with a little sexy finger wave.

Nicole didn't see it. Luck was with me.

Patty and Lizzy pulled me aside and gave me their thanks, along with a hug and a kiss. I took that opportunity to give them some secret instructions. When we rejoined the others, they told all they just wanted to tell me how much they appreciated what I did. I was relieved they left my additional instructions confidential.

With that done, the girls each grabbed their guy and gave him a cheek kiss, which struck me as encouragement.

Mission accomplished. Next stop, the Louvre.

The museum's entrance is its own piece of art. Before we went in, I said, "Now, you can walk through the museum on your own or use a tour guide. But keep in mind, you could spend the whole day in there."

Nicole got interested. "John, we don't have a whole day."

With a nod to her, I continued to speak to everyone. "I understand. I really don't have time to do that either. Nicole and I need to do some research."

That got a confirming nod from Nicole.

The girls glanced at each other with corresponding shakes of their heads.

Patty gave their answer. "We didn't know it could take that long. There's too much else to do. We only want to do just a couple of hours. Can we?"

That was what I needed. I pulled a small guide book I had hidden and handed it to Lizzy as her hand leaped at me.

"Yes, you can. There's a lot to see and that guide will help. I've been told there's so much, it's best to do multiple visits. Suspect if you're the type to stand and gaze at something, that would be best. If you want to make multiple trips while we're here, I'll fund each visit. My gift to you."

On their tiptoes, the girls gave me a hug. Nicole, who was already standing beside me, gave me a body bump. I counted that as a thank-you.

She then checked her mother. "Mama, what about you? Do you want to see a lot or a little?"

Mother Betty pondered her reply a moment or two. "A little is all I need, for now." I heard what I thought she was thinking. She wanted to be elsewhere.

Nicole pulled me aside, whispering near my ear, "I'd very much like to see this, but I'd rather spend the time with you looking for my father. We can see more later. I know Mama would rather see it with Pappy, and the girls do not want us adults hanging around."

I whispered back, "I agree." Then to all, I said, "Seems due to the size of this place, we each want to see bits and pieces at different times, which is cool. All agree?"

That got a lot of yeses. I was going to add something, but Nicole beat me to it.

"Mama, why don't you join John and I and let the young ones do their own tour?"

"Yes, I'd like that. Maybe you can drop me off at the restaurant when we're done looking." Then she added, "Patty, you and Lizzy, you call me if you need anything, okay?"

"We will, Mama," replied Patty.

Taking my turn, I waved a pointed finger at the boys. "You two comporte!" Think I told them to behave. I got a pair of nods. I would've added "or else," but didn't have those words. "Girls, you call Nicole when you leave here and tell her where you're going. Is that understood?"

Lizzy replied, "Yes, Uncle John." I smiled and gave her a finger point. She returned the gesture. That was a new one. Never been an uncle. My father had one brother, but he's dead, too. I wasn't that close to him. I made a mental note to ask why she called me uncle.

They were about to turn and leave, when I added, "I want you two back at Pappy's restaurant by four today!" I held up four fingers, wiggling them, and pointed to my watch. I made sure the boys also understood.

Patty did her own "Oooookay, Uncle John." She sounded like she was teasing. Lizzy hadn't. I appreciated both.

For me it was just more confusion dealing with the younger crowd. I had a feeling I needed an advance course, immediately.

They waved goodbye and headed off. Nicole's mother watched as they gave her a last wave. She stood there even when she could no longer see them. I had no intention of interrupting her unmistakable concern.

Seeing they were out of sight, Nicole stood beside her mother, holding her arm. "They'll be okay, Mama. I think Uncle John got his point across."

I couldn't let the uncle opportunity pass. "And Nicole will call them every hour."

Still beside her mother and watching the place where the four left our view, Nicole said, "Mama, he may not be related, but he makes a charming Uncle John."

She gave me a wink over her mother's shoulder. I had a feeling the uncle label would return to haunt me.

With the kids' departure, we ventured into the Louvre for about an hour when her mother let us know she was ready to go. We were, too.

We managed to see da Vinci's *Mona Lisa* and the *Venus de Milo*. If you recall, Miss Milo is said to represent Aphrodite, the goddess of beauty. Most likely the woman posing was comely. Personally, I like women with arms.

We dropped Mother Betty at Pappy's restaurant. It was late morning, and I knew she would get in. I figured there was an open-door policy where she was concerned.

Before we left for the embassy, Nicole called Patty and all was well. It was a short call, which I expected. "Didn't have much to say, huh?"

"I was bugging her. She was enjoying her time with Nathan, and I took her away from him."

"Sounds like a girl thing. Give me your phone."

"Why?" Nicole was suspiciously not pleased by my asking.

"I'll tell you later. Now, give it to me." I added a delayed "Please."

Nicole didn't like my avoiding her question. I knew because she didn't exactly give me the phone. It was more of a slap—into my palm. I was happy it wasn't to my face.

But I had it. I clicked the redial button and turned on the speaker so Nicole could hear. Patty answered and I said, "You remember those two movies I told you about? And wanted to know which one you wanted to see?"

"Yes, I do, Uncle John. I may change my mind, but I like *The Moon Is Blue*."

"I'll remember that. Now, I may need to call you back later, but no worries for now." We said our goodbyes and pressed our associated buttons.

"And *just* what was that all about?" Nicole's question didn't have a happy vibe. I decided to keep the phone for a bit.

"Simple. I set up a code with the girls to be sure they were okay." She started to speak and I shushed her. Must admit, that felt good. Normally she's shushing me. "'The moon is blue' means all is well."

"And when were you going to tell me about this?"

I continued to hold the phone. "About now." Her arms gripped her chest. I felt a little frustration seeping in. "Look. I wanted to see if it worked, before explaining. It did."

"So, Mr. Secret-Keeper, what if all is not well?" Her arms were still in place.

"There are two other possibilities. If she's unsure, she will say *Casablanca*. If someone had joined them, she might add, 'And all those people came into his café.' And I may ask something."

"How does she know all that?" Her arms relaxed a little.

"Hold on. Now, if things are bad and we need to come quick, she will say *Strangers on a Train* with something like 'I loved how they could see the river and the big church' or some such to give me a clue where they are."

"You didn't answer my question!" Her frustration renewed. "And just how does she know all that? She doesn't watch old movies. I like them but she—"

I jumped in. "True, but Lizzy had seen all those and many more old ones. She was coaching Patty."

"And just when did you get all this done?"

"Remember when the girls pulled me aside this morning? That gave me a chance to privately make a plan. Look. I wanted to know all was well or if the boys were holding them hostage or something. It had to be confidential, so I used that time."

"Damn you!" She hit me with her fist. Didn't hurt, but her point was made.

"What'd I do! I thought it was a brilliant idea."

Tears started again. I was getting good at causing them. I started to say more when she put her fingers to my lips.

"When I told Mama you were like a father, I didn't really know just how much you were. Mama or I should have done something. But, but, what—I mean, how—oh, I don't know. Just explain. Please?" She turned in her seat to face me.

I turned best I could and gave her the phone. Bucket seats ain't for face-to-face talking. I needed a '57 Chevy. "When the girls pulled me aside and were thanking me, I recalled something Nanna Bolton told me."

Her hands clasped the phone. "Oh, yeah. Your nanny. I like her."

"You remembered. Yeah, she was a special woman. Her youngest daughter, sixteen, if I recall, was going on a date with this eighteen-year-old boy. They'd known him awhile, but Nanna was always looking out for her brood. She told her daughter if the boy started to go somewhere to get her real alone, soon as she knew it, to tell him it looks like fun. Then to tell him she needed a phone to call one of her girlfriends, who might want to come, too."

"I see. She had to make the boy think he'd have two girls to have fun with. Why didn't she just use her cell phone?"

"Well, you get the idea, but there were no cell phones back then."

"Oh. Yeah, right. Dummy me." That came with blinking eyes and a shaking head.

Her expression was not what I wanted to see or have her believe. "You're no dummy. You caught on quick. Her date didn't and took her to a gas station. Nanna's older son arrived and took care of the boy. Nanna's daughter found out early who to date and who not to."

"I'd loved to have known her."

"She would've loved you without a doubt. Okay, let's head for the embassy. It's almost noon. Maybe we can cause someone to delay their lunch."

After parking the car, Nicole and I entered the facility by showing our passports. I hadn't asked her to bring it with her. Her father must have taught her the necessity in a foreign country.

We gave our names to the receptionist and sat as we were told. It took close to thirty minutes before we were invited into her office. Funny, but her office door never opened while we were waiting, meaning no one entered nor left. I figured she wanted to appear busy, or maybe just needed to finish her lunch.

"Good morning, I'm Carol Phillips." She presented her hand and we both shook it.

"Ms. Phillips, we—"

She interrupted me. "Mr. Stone, it's good to meet you. I must apologize for not being here when you came, last year, I believe. You saw my assistant, Harold Graham."

That really was a year ago. Why would she remember me?

"Oh, yes, I did." He had been close to useless, but I kept that to myself, for now. "He took care of my needs. This is Nicole Powell." I placed my hand on her waist.

They did hellos and she directed us to be seated.

"So, what may I help you with, Mr. Stone?"

"Nicole's father died in an auto accident about seven years ago, back in Georgia, but he spent a good bit of time here. She would just like to know more about him, so she asked me to help. His name was William Powell, and we know he once worked for the FBI or US State Department, but had been working for Signature Security Consultants, a US-based firm. I believe they have offices and customers in many countries." I was only guessing.

"Miss Powell, do you know when, what years, he was in France?"

The two of them did some calculations and came up with an approximate window.

I provided a little clarification. "Now, we are certain he was in France several times during those years. We also believe, not totally certain, that he may have been in other European countries as well, just not as frequently."

Nicole gave me a scary stare. I knew she was wondering where I got that information. I planned to tell her later that I made it up. We didn't know, but we did know he was gone from home weeks at a time. And considering Pappy's contacts, I felt her father spent most of that time in France, but maybe not all. Yeah, I know, total guesswork.

Ms. Phillips gave me a thoughtful gaze. "I don't personally recall him, but being with the US government, they usually check in here, often upon arrival." She turned to Nicole. "But not always. Still, our government does keep me informed of who may be coming."

Nicole leaned toward her and responded in a kind, thoughtful voice. "Whatever you can share will be very much appreciated."

Phillips responded with a similar tone but with a government slant. "Some things have security tags, but I will gladly share what I can. You might speak with Duane Naude, with Signature Consulting Services. He may can offer some assistance."

Nicole gave her a sincere thank-you.

I replied, "We understand for government security reasons, all may not be shared, but anything encouraging would be appreciated." I don't use such words often, but it couldn't hurt to toss 'em out.

Ms. Phillips stood, giving us the universal indication to leave. Her parting words were that she would give us what she could.

I had a feeling she wouldn't need much ink.

CHAPTER 11

A FRENCH CONNECTION

Without thinking, we got in the car and I headed to Alivia Béringer's apartment. Then I realized we'd missed something. "You hungry?"

"Yes, but I want to meet this Alivia person. I'll feel like we got something accomplished."

That was good to hear. I needed all the positive words I could muster. I added, "I'm wit' you kid."

That brought a smile with her opinion, "Now you're trying to be cute, quoting Bogart."

"Man has to try for all the points he can get."

She returned with a command. "Yeah, you got a point. Now, hit the peddle."

Alivia was really a blank. All I knew was what little I got from Pappy. All I could do was ask about Nicole's father and hear the replies.

It was about two thirty when we got there. I stopped just inside the building entrance. We were facing the lift. I took Nicole's hand. "You ready for this?"

"I guess so. I just wish I had some idea of her relationship with my father. I would feel more comfortable. I mean, she could lie and we may never know."

"Ya got that right. We'll listen and ask questions and see where the answers lead us."

Entering the lift, I pressed four. We were alone, yet no words were spoken. I expected Nicole to say something, anything, but she was quiet.

When the doors opened at the fourth floor, I took Nicole's hand and led us to Suite D1.

I knocked on the door. Within a few seconds, it opened with a woman standing there saying something in French. I asked if she spoke English, and she replied, "May I help you?"

"You may. My name is John Stone, and this is Nicole Powell. We'd like to speak with Alivia Béringer regarding Nicole's father, William Powell. Are you Alivia?"

"I am not. Why you present?"

Nicole spoke, "My father, William Powell, was in an automobile accident a few years ago. We were told Miss Béringer might have known him, and . . ." Nicole pulled a tissue from her purse and attempted to speak through the tears. "I'm so sorry. I thought I was beyond crying."

The woman replied, "My name is Nicolette. You may come in and sit."

As we entered, she led us to a couch and she sat facing us in a chair.

Nicole continued, "You are so kind for letting us in. I hope you will forgive us."

Nicolette replied, "There is nothing for to forgive." With a smile, she added, "When I heard your name, I needed to meet you. Nicole is a short version for mine, Nicolette, but no people call me Nicole. It is French thing." She displayed a smile with that bit of info. "So, tell me of your father."

"You are so kind to let me speak to you. It is really appreciated."

Nicole handled the contact so well, I kept quiet.

"Please tell more. Your father was killed in automobile accident. Was here in Paris?"

Her interest came across positive. I had no background on her, so I didn't know if she was just asking questions or had an ulterior reason to know more.

"No, it was in Georgia, where we live, but he worked for a company here in Paris."

"I wish I could give more, but I not know him."

Nicole kept at it. "We were hoping Miss Béringer knew him and we could speak with her. Maybe we could come back when she's here?"

"You can return, but Alivia not be back for at least a month. She's visiting parents in Germany."

There was something fishy there, and I smelled it. "I wish we could have come here sooner. When did she leave?"

"It was week ago."

"Ah, you know, I may have seen her. I was here with a business associate on the fifth floor, and a woman got on the lift as we were going down. She had very long, brown hair with blond tints on each side, right? Oh, and her fingernails were a shade of blue, if I recall."

"Yes, but why you remember her?"

From the corner of my eye, I saw Nicole glaring at me. She knew I was lying.

"Actually, it was my associate. He'd been an agent for some French actresses and he's always looking for new talent. She was a lovely woman, such as you. Oh, please forgive me. I don't normally say such things."

"That was sweet for you to say, and is easy to forgive."

This was playing out well. "Nicolette, do you have a picture of Miss Béringer? I'd really like to know if it was her."

"Sure. One moment," said Nicolette as she went into a back room.

Her cell phone was right there on the table, three feet from me. It was an iPhone and I couldn't resist.

Nicole's whisper was near silent. "What the hell are you doing?"

I put a finger to my lips as I took two steps in two seconds.

It was right there inches away. I pressed the power button, and the main screen appeared. No password, or she'd used it and the lockout hadn't happened. I pressed the phone button and took a quick look at the recent contacts. It was an endless list. Some with names, others just the number. I saw Rousseau. Two of the numbers looked familiar. I memorized the last four of each, clicked the home button, turned it off, and spun around as if talking to Nicole.

Nicole's eyes were wide open and her head was doing short, quick shakes.

At that second, while I was sweating, Nicolette returned with a framed picture. "Here she with brother. It taken few weeks at his birthday party."

It was her. The one with the cute ass. Catching my breath and trying to be calm, I said, "Yeah, that's her. May I ask where the picture was taken?"

"It taken at her parents' home in Mainz, small town south of Frankfurt."

"Thank you for letting me know. If you don't think she would mind, I'll tell Mr. Kaplan, George Kaplan, I know who she is and that I met you."

"Thank you, Mr. Stone. She won't mind. If that all you have, I must go visit a friend. She expecting me."

As we were leaving, Nicole gave Nicolette a thank-you. I added mine as well.

No sooner than the door shut and we were in the hall, Nicole asked me who Kaplan was.

I whispered, "I'll tell you later."

Nicole's expression gave me worry.

We managed to get into the lift, and when I pressed one, Nicole let me have it and it wasn't a kiss.

Without the help of her hands, her mouth throw harsh words at me. She dug in, "What the hell were you doing there? She was a nice woman being helpful. You did nothing but lie to her."

"She was the first liar" was my short reply. I held back on the phone thing.

Her fingers spread as if grabbing at my own words. "How do you know that?" She paused a second. I saw doubt appear on her face. Her hands dropped to her side. Less harshly she asked, "How did you know about her hair and fingernails?"

"Alivia is the woman with the ass."

Her excitement shot up again. "What? John, you're making no sense."

"Remember yesterday, when we were here first?"

After a moment, she said, "Yes."

That may have been all she said, but I saw a question emerging.

"Remember the woman who got off the lift as we were standing there? She walked right past us. She in no way recognized we were there. Like we were invisible. She had very long, brown hair with gold tints and blue fingernails."

Her head tilted a bit. "You saw all that looking at her ass?"

"It was you who accused me of looking at her ass. Falsely, I might add. I was looking at her hair and hands and shoes and her ass. She didn't just walk past us. She ignored us. I think she recognized you or me and didn't want to talk."

That got an "Oh," then a more pronounced, "Oh, shit. It was her. Nicolette was lying."

Quite calmly, I added, "Think I mentioned that." I couldn't help but offer a toothy smile.

I expected a physical slap, but she did it with words. "Don't be a smartass."

Her brief reply gave me the opportunity for one last fact.

"You said your father was in an accident. You didn't tell her your father was dead. She told you."

"I think she just assumed he was. I mean, we were looking for information. If he was alive, we'd ask him."

Ouch, she had me. "Miss Nicole, you made a good point."

The lift deposited us on the first floor. I put a finger to my lips till we could get outside. Our conversation was to be a two-person discussion.

Sitting in the car, Nicole had time to go over all of this in her mind and let some slip out.

"John, so now what do we know? She's a liar. Course, you were better at it than she was."

"I think you just gave me a compliment." She gave me a gentle tap, I think meaning she agreed that I was. Course, I'd had practice.

Her eyes lit up. "We saw her yesterday. She's still in Paris. She could be watching us now." An excellent conclusion.

With a nod, I said, "Correct on all three points. And, she had recently been in the apartment."

Her hands flew up and out, fingers spread, "Now, how do you know that? No. You can't know that."

"It was the perfume."

"Nicolette's perfume? What's that got to do with anything?"

"Not Nicolette's. There was another perfume smell in the apartment. And, that smell was the same as the woman who brushed by us out of the elevator. I mean the lift."

She got it, and it filled her pretty, nodding, smiling face. "The woman with the ass?"

"Yes. She flew by us so close it flooded my nose. Don't know the name. Must have been a French version."

"Who is this George Kaplan? You never mentioned him. Do you really know him? And why do we care?"

"You do know how to switch gears. Okay. Sorta. He doesn't exist. It's a name used in several Hitchcock movies and some TV shows. Enough of that. It's a little before three. Let's get some lunch."

"Yes, I'm starving. Must have been all the smelly lies."

She leaned over and kissed my cheek. At least she was on board. Maybe George helped. Hey, coulda made another point.

A puzzler was why Nicole hadn't brought up my checking Nicolette's phone.

I left that one unanswered, hoping it would go down as a wrong number.

CHAPTER 12

A FRENCH DECEPTION

Pulling up to Pappy's place made my stomach growl and my mind wander.

Alivia must have known us. She knew us that first time stepping out of the lift. How she knew was a mystery. I didn't yet know, but she certainly did not want to meet us. Just another question I could run by Pappy. Might ring a welcome bell.

I parked, then remembered. "Give me your phone."

"You're gonna bug her again!"

"Yes. Give me your phone, very please."

She reluctantly gave it to me, and I pressed the redial button. As last time, I turned on the speaker.

Patty answered with "Hi, Sis." When I returned a male hi, Patty recognized my voice. "Oh. Hi, Uncle John. I thought it would be you. I know it's close to four. We're on our way to Pappy's place. Be there in a few minutes."

"Good to hear, Patty. Any change of heart on the movie?"

"Nope. *The Moon Is Blue* is perfect. Thank you for caring, Uncle John."

We said our goodbyes and did the buttons.

After giving her the phone, Nicole gave me her opinion. "You planning to adopt those two? They're already your nieces."

"Now, I didn't start that. Lizzy did. And you know it. I'm not trying to be a relative. I just want to be sure they're okay. They're bright, young, and pretty, and that can draw not-so-nice people."

Without a word, Nicole unbuckled her seat belt, sat up on her knees, grabbed me, and planted a serious kiss. She backed off a few inches, and said, "When the right woman corners you, you'll make a wonderful father," then sat back down.

When I recovered from the stunning lip attack, I said, "Wow. That was a first. A really nice first. I wasn't trying to get you to do that. I just want 'em to be safe."

She gave me a head nod. "I know that. We best go inside before I try a new attack."

I took that as a warning, got out, went to her door, and opened it for her. Her hand touched my face and went down to my hand as she led me into the restaurant.

Once inside, I noticed there was no Pappy and no Mother Betty. I was about to bring that to Nicole's attention, but she'd noticed it, too.

Celeste was at her hostess stand.

I waved at her. "Hi, Celeste. I don't see Mrs. Powell. Is she here somewhere?"

Celeste flipped her long, brown hair with an air of confidence. "Mr. Armand took Ms. Powell to see the Tower. Not think they be back soon. I can seat you." Thought she might have said Papa.

Her expression caught my interest, but the hook hadn't yet set in. "Better give us a table for seven, so we're ready when they get here."

I got another formal, "Yes, Mr. Stone" as she led us to the table we had last evening and left menus. Fortunately, they were once again in English.

As she was about to leave, I got her attention. The hook had caught me. "Celeste, since my first time here, you're speaking with more English words. I was Monsieur Stone, and now I'm Mr. Stone."

"Thank you, Mr. Stone. I met this American man. I try learn speak English."

Nicole had been quietly listening, her lips shifting from a smile to a pout.

I tried to give her encouragement. "You are learning well. He will be impressed." I attempted to go easy on the contractions.

"That kind for you to say," she added and left with an over-the-shoulder wave.

Nicole's expression turned into words. "Now you've got another girl liking you." She opened her menu staring at it.

I began to wonder if I was on the menu, about to be roasted, along with the menu.

"All I did was compliment her. She's trying to impress her beau, not me."

Before she could do a comeback, Patty and Lizzy walked in with their boys. I threw my hand up and they came to the table, followed by Celeste with more menus.

The boys shook my hand and sat down beside their girl. Nicole asked them if they had fun, but instead of answering, Patty and Lizzy shared glances.

Lizzy took the lead with her brown eyes darting back and forth between Nicole and me. "Now, please don't get angry till you know the whole story."

Her starting words sounded like times past. Times when I should have left town instead of listen.

"Lizzy, I can abide by that, but whatever this is we don't know about, when did you find out?"

The girls stared at each other with puzzled faces. Lizzy continued, "How did you . . .? I mean, you can't know."

She was stumbling, so I gave her a push. "Look. I've heard those words before, and the end result was rarely pleasant. And no, I don't know. But I'm willing to take another chance. Just tell me your whatever."

Lizzy's mouth opened and closed at least three times before she found the words. "Ah, well, first, you should know that Nathan and Andre speak English pretty well. We didn't know till this afternoon after we left the Louvre."

She saw me tilt my head. I included a small smile.

"Please, Uncle John. I promise you we didn't know till today. They found a place by the river with people around, so we wouldn't be afraid, and told us. They were afraid to let us know because of a family thing that's happening."

Nicole wasn't happy. Looking at the two boys, with arms resting on the table and fingers spread, she shared, "You lied to us. You made us look like fools trying to talk to you."

Patty tried to help. She took Nathan's hand. "Nicole, they're not mean. They made sure we were not hurt or lost. They did whatever we asked. But they had to know us and if you were friends or enemies. There's a reason for it. We want to tell you."

Nicole wasn't fully convinced, but gave in, a little. "Then tell us. Tell us before Mama and Pappy get back."

Nathan was about to start when he got encouragement from Patty. She had his hand clutched in both of hers.

I kept quiet. It was getting interesting.

His eyes leaped from mine to Nicole's and back as he spoke. "We," he pointed to Andre, "are brothers. Name is Gagnon, and Mother is Noémi. Our father was killed seven years ago. The police enquêté, non, non, investigate. Found nothing, but we believe they know and not tell us."

Nicole was shaking her head. "John, I know what you're thinking. They will ask you to help. But you can't. We need to know about my father. Please, John?"

"Your father will not be forgotten. We'll find the truth." I put my hand on hers. It relaxed as I gave it a gentle squeeze. She turned her hand to hold mine. "And it's something I want to do almost as much as you. And, we will, but we can at least hear what they have to say."

"Okay" was all she said. I gave her a confident nod with a wink. I turned to the boys. "Okay, tell me what the problem is."

The boys eyeballed each other. Nathan took the lead. "You must know, when we first met Lizzy and Patty, we saw two beautiful girls and wanted to meet them. We promettre, non, non, promise, that is, was, all. But we heard last name Powell. Please, understand. Our father worked with American named William Powell."

Nicole almost jumped when he said that. She squeezed my hand, hard.

That was sudden, significant news. I asked the obvious question. "What was your father's full name?"

Andre took the lead. "Gustav Gagnon."

His focus was on me. But as he spoke, Lizzy's eyes never left his as she seized and smothered his hand.

I asked, "Nicole, you ever heard that name?"

In the search for her father, we had just found another fork in the road. The question was and is always the same, which do you take?

"No. Never. But Daddy never told us much. He just said it was government business and he couldn't tell anyone about it. He had a job he couldn't talk about. I got scared. Not for me, but for him. Now, it's even more frightening."

I didn't know if the girls knew all this, but that didn't seem to matter. Heads and eyes were riffling each other, as if a sniper's bullet was visibly waiting to hit someone.

Directing my attention to the boys, I said, "That information is unexpected but welcome. Do you have any idea what they were doing? Or where they were doing whatever?"

Andre's eyes stopped and rested on mine. "He spoke to Mother. They were working on project with Signature Consulting. Something that touché, non, inclus, non, non . . ."

He was having difficulties, so I quickly added, "I understand. Touched or included. There was a connection."

"Oui, yes, French American connection, but never he went into it more."

"Do you think he was afraid?"

There had to be fear. That can ensure secrets remain secret or you vanish or the worst result, your family can be harmed at your expense.

Andre kept at it. "Afraid, oui, yes. For us." Even when he stopped speaking, he kept glancing at me and Nicole.

The girls were quiet. I gave them a nod, eyebrows raised, hoping a signal might cause them to join in. They saw me, but did nothing.

I felt they wanted me to help, and I wanted to, but if I did, I'd have that forked road to travel, and both might lead to the door of a French police station. I already had a couple of US police districts that were pleased I was out of the country. And I had three women staring at me, and Mother Betty would probably join them.

As the saying goes, we were getting nowhere fast. "Boys, I understand your concern and need, but you've given so little." I paused, hoping for help. Didn't happen.

Then I thought. I never throw anything away. I have a birthday card from Janet Shaw. Eleventh grade and so long ago.

"Boys, do you still have any of your father's personal things? Letters, cards, keys, papers, notepad? Anything?"

That got more eyes bouncing between each other. I threw my hands out, spread open as if asking.

Nicole grabbed one, squeezed it, and planted it on the table. My face gave a silent *ouch* as she spoke. "I do. I have lots of Daddy's things. I just couldn't throw them away. It's like keeping him there." She stopped, then added softly, "But they're not here."

Nathan had an answer. "We have. I have things. Andre has, and Mother has many of Father's things."

He ended that with a smile. The boys did the high-five thing with their spare hands. The girls did not let go of the hand they held in their clutches.

Things were looking up. Their father's personal things could lead us closer to Nicole's father. "I want to see everything, but not now. Nicole and I have to eat and talk to people helping us with her father."

I was finishing up my sentence when Pappy and Mother Betty walked to our table. My mind was so cluttered with our talking I hadn't seen them come in. And I could see the door!

Attempting to shift the attention, I asked, "Pappy, where've you two been all day? We've been waiting here close to an hour."

Mother Betty didn't wait. "What is the everything you want to see?" She'd heard me.

They were standing to the side of Nicole and me. I looked up at Mother Betty. I was the fish at the end of the line with hook in mouth.

I glanced at Nicole, hoping she would remove the hook. She glanced back with a delightful face, tilted and happy and quiet.

I was hooked by two women.

Shifting my attention to Mother Betty, with her dark-green eyes roving between her and Pappy, I said, "We've had an amazing find. Nathan and Andre's father worked with your husband. Please sit down. We have a lot to tell you." As they were sitting I told Nicole, "Why don't you get it started. I have to go pee."

Without hesitation or further words, I got up and headed for the restroom.

I took a quick glance back seeing Nicole's mouth open and eyes firing darts at me. The girls had covered their grinning mouths with their hands.

After sufficient time to empty my bladder, clean the sink, dust off the counter, and wash my hands, I returned to the table. After careful inspection of my chair for pointed objects, I sat down.

Nicole took my hand—gently, I might add. "John, I gave Mama and Pappy a shortened version of what we discussed. Mama is pleased with what you found, and Pappy wants to talk to you about it. When he does," she looked at Pappy, "I'll be there, too." After another pause, she asked, "Any objections, gentlemen?"

She directed that question to me and Pappy and got rid of the hook. No way was I going to object, so I joined.

"I had the same idea. We need your viewpoint." I got the boys' attention. "Andre, Nathan, are you okay with the plan?"

They nodded and were about to speak when Nicole stood up and wiggled her fingers for me to follow. Before I could offer a yes, she turned and headed for the door.

I wondered why but had no choice but to follow. From their expressions, the rest of the table had the same wonder.

She stopped just outside the door, turned, and gave me the scoop, "It's after five and we haven't eaten. And, if you remember, there's one guy Mac didn't give you anything on."

"Jules Pelletier. I know."

"And the other guy. All I remember about him is he makes people disappear."

"Ludovic Rousseau."

"Yes. And it'll be well after six before we get to either place. How do you remember these names so easy?"

When I finally separated the statement and the question she slipped in, I pulled a small note from my pocket and waved it at her.

"Okay. So you keep notes. Let's wait till tomorrow midmorning before we talk to those guys. I'd feel more comfortable, safer then. Please?"

"I agree. If they know each other, they may already know who we are, and maybe where we are."

She gently put her arms around me. Her face rested on my shoulder, her lips touching my chin. "I'm scared."

"Me too."

Without moving, she said, "No you're not."

"Nicole, maybe I don't show it, but things do scare me, too. If we were in the States, I might not feel it so much. But in a foreign country, surrounded by unscrupulous characters, it's a different story. The one thing that helps is an enchanting woman with her arms around me. That alone can cause a guy to forget everything."

Still in position, she murmured, "You make a girl feel safe in spite of it all. I'll do what I can to help you forget. Oh, you need to know what was said when you left."

"Maybe I should go pee again?"

She shifted to facing me. Her eyes were so close to mine, I was afraid to blink. "Not now, Mr. Stone. After I finished, Mama started to put you down. You know what Pappy said?"

"Think I prefer a kiss."

She pulled away several inches and did a light tap on my cheek. "Later. He said sometimes your mind doesn't know what your instincts know. That you take off not certain where you're heading, but end up at the right place. He said to just remember to let him, you, go. He'll get there."

Reality threw its arms around me. Only one thought leaped into my mind. "I can imagine what your mother said."

"I'm with you, kid," she said with a smile and a wink. "Mama said that was crazy. Pappy said it sounds that way, but to just give you time and space. Then he told me to trust you. That you'll keep me safe. John, I believe that."

"I've only known him a couple of years, but I think he knows me better than I know me. So, you think we should go back inside?" I wanted the subject changed. It was getting scary.

"Sweetie, I know exactly what to do. Let's eat quick and get back to our room."

With a sheepish grin, I said, "You mean your room, with your mother."

She retuned my grin with a smile and a couple of pats on my cheek. "You know very well I mean your room. Now's not the time to be cute."

"I like the thought."

And I wasn't thinking of being cute.

As we got to the table, Mother Betty said hi and thanked me for watching over her daughter. Yeah, I was surprised, too. We ordered food and all started eating. Pappy had shifted to doing restaurant-owner things in the kitchen.

We were taking our last bites when I asked, "Mrs. Powell, how'd you like the visit to the Tower?"

That caught her off guard. She started to speak but stopped for a moment. I suspect she was carefully gathering her thoughts.

"It was good to visit it again. It's been so long, it had a new, fresh feeling about it." She paused a moment, and added, "I must admit, Pappy made it special."

Nicole was sitting between me and her mother. She put her hand on her mother's shoulder. "I'm glad you did, Mama. It's good to see you with someone."

Betty looked at the table with a small smile, then back at Nicole. "Well, I'm not sure I'm with him yet."

"Mama, I can see the happiness in your face when Pappy's near. And I like it very much. Patty, what about you? Don't you think Pappy is a sweet man?"

Patty let her feelings fly out. "Oh, yes. Seven years ago, I had no idea how I felt, but now, I see, as you said, Nicole, just how sweet he is."

Lizzy wasn't about to be left out. "He's a kind man, but I think there's a little piece of him that causes me to want to know more, you know?"

Patty's eyes went wide and her hand waved a yes. "Lizzy, that's so right. Maybe it's Paris, but he sometimes seems mysterious. It's like he's telling you something and is leaving out a little to pull you in closer."

Lizzy replied, "Patty, that's what I said," with a distinct nodding of her head. Lizzy's reply wasn't in anger, more of a wakeup call.

Patty hands quickly covered her mouth. "Oh, you did. I'm so sorry. But, well, it must be true. We both noticed it."

They looked at each other with a wide-eyed stare. Patty was hooked. They were both hooked. Pappy was pulling them all to his corner of the ring.

Nathan and Andre were sitting quietly, with eyes jumping between speakers.

I needed to get them in play. With hands in the air, I said, "Girls, it's getting late and I need to make tomorrow's plans for Nicole and me, and for Andre and Nathan as well."

Suddenly all four women were talking to each other all at once. I had elected myself as the subject, and the responses were not compliments.

Without thinking, I stood and clapped my hands, then motioned palms down trying to say be quiet. The women ceased as they stared at me. However, my clap inadvertently alerted the other customers.

I spun around, saying, "Excuse moi," and sat down real fast. Giggles and laughs spread through the place.

Celeste rushed over to our table and said something in French. Looking up at her, I asked, "Ah, what did you say?"

"Told femmes, non, women, to forgive as you are but a man."

I thanked her and told her to go seat someone. The women at my table were laughing, and it wasn't at Celeste.

Attempting to ignore the whole place, I said, "Nicole is tired and so am I. We're headed to the hotel. Tomorrow morning I'll be checking on leads related to Nicole's father." I shifted attention to the boys. "As for you two, please set a time tomorrow afternoon for Nicole and me to visit your mother and look over your father's personal things. We may find clues related to both fathers."

Andre thanked me and added, "We will speak with Mother, and she recueillir. No. Put together Father's things. Will tell you time when know."

"That's good, Andre." With that done, someone had to figure what the girls were going to do. I picked up the opportunity. "Lizzy and Patty, did you have any plans for this evening?"

As always, the girls were silent, deciding who should speak. Lizzy must have gotten the nod. "Uncle John," she gave me a wink, "Andre says there's a movie with English subtitles that we might like."

"Mrs. Powell, guess I should back off and let you handle this?"

Nicole singled out her mother with a suggestive gaze. "Let John handle it, okay, Mama? Please?"

They continued to focus on each other. It was brief, but Mother Betty must have reached some silent agreement with Nicole. This time my eyes were doing the flipping.

Mother Betty turned to me. "John, please continue. I haven't been to a movie in decades."

Felt like I got a reprieve from the warden.

"Thanks for your encouragement." To the boys, I asked, "What kind of movie is it?"

Nathan was ready. "It is a romantic movie. It is your Americans call 'G' movie."

"No naked women, right?" Hey, I hadda ask.

That got a serious smile from Nicole and the girls. Mother Betty was not impressed.

Nathan returned, "Non. Nothing like that. It's about a writer who meets a little girl then fall in love with her mother. Is Christmas time."

That got my attention. "Think I know that movie. It's called *Love Always, Santa*. Right?"

"Yes," replied Nathan. "That's the one. You know of it?"

"Good movie. It was made a couple of years ago. So, boys, why did you pick that movie to watch?"

Both went stone silent. Guess they figured one of them had to speak. Andre took the honors, or maybe the blame. "Patty told us you were writing a book, or will write a book."

"I see. So, you two guys chose that movie?" The stream smelled fishy.

Andre and Nathan did that stare at each other. I thought they were going to speak, but Patty took the floor.

"Uncle John, we picked the movie. Nathan and Andre showed us the movies we could choose from and translated the titles. When they told us about that one, we wanted to see it. That's when I told them about hearing you talking to Nicole about writing."

"Why didn't you just tell me you wanted to see it?" I knew the answer.

"Please don't be angry, but I wasn't supposed to know. I overheard you tell Nicole and not to mention it to anyone. Please understand. Lizzy and me both wanted to see it because you want to write."

That's when Nicole's leg slammed against mine. Meaning she got my attention. She gave me a tiny nod and a tiny smile. My choice had been made.

With my focus on the girls, I said, "You girls will like it. I understand why you were hesitant to tell, but it's okay. And you have my approval."

That got a clap from the girls. But there was a restriction to be disclosed.

"Boys, you will have the girls back to the hotel no later than eleven. Is that understood?"

Andre took that one. "Yes, Uncle John. Before eleven." Nathan gave repetitive exaggerated nods. I swear I thought his head would fly off.

Mother Betty jumped in line. "No. Ten o'clock!"

The girls' smiles went north. I know the term is went south, but if going south is so bad, why do so many northerners retire to the south? Not too many southerners retire to the north. Anyway, you get my drift. Now, where was I?

Patty's head was shaking. "Mama! That's too early. The movie won't be over."

Nicole added, "I agree with Uncle John. Mama, you're outvoted. Boys, you will have them in the hotel by eleven or Uncle John will make you vanish."

I could see the boys' mouths silently saying the word vanish. Guess they figured out what it meant, because their eyes were wide open.

"They be in hotel by eleven," announced Nathan.

Funding was in question, and I knew that was in my corner. "That's good to hear, boys. Now, do you have money for drinks and popcorn or whatever you will do?"

"We could use a little," said Lizzy with the kind of girlish expression a man can only obey.

Young now, but one can only imagine what she'll accomplish in the next few years. Bonnie and Clyde came to mind, but I abandoned that unpleasant thought.

She won. I gave the girls about fifty euro. That's about sixty dollars.

"Now, are there any other comments or orders they need from the adults here?" I waited for about ten seconds. "Okay, you boys and girls get out of here and enjoy yourselves."

That got handshakes from the boys. Both girls gave me hugs, as they said, almost overlapping, "Thank you, Uncle John." That alone felt good. But they topped the words off with cheek kisses.

It was nearing seven, not so late, but I was tired. Pappy came to the table. Nicole told everyone we were going to the hotel. She was tired, too. Her mother turned to Pappy and he said if she wanted to stay, he would take her there when she was ready. She took him up on the offer, which I expected. Nicole and I were hotel bound.

It was a long, busy day, and I knew Tuesday would be no different.

Once in the room, I dropped on the sofa as Nicole dropped beside me. She snuggled up to me and I put my arm around her. We were without movement for at least five minutes.

I was about to doze off, but it was not to be.

Nicole helped keep my eyes open. "I hope you know those girls love you." She touched a tiny finger to my nose.

My arm was in place, so I gave her a little hug. "Oh, they don't love me. They're just happy I got it okayed to stay out till eleven."

That caused a reaction. Her legs stationed themselves across my lap and her eyes focused on mine. "Either you can't see it or don't want to see it, but they do."

I started to speak, but her fingers sealed my lips.

"You don't know this, but Lizzy's father died last year. Cancer. It was an awful time, and then you showed up. They'd call you Father, but they know not to. So it's Uncle because they see you watching out for them, like their fathers did."

Those words were unexpected. "I didn't mean to cause that. But Patty asked her mother when her mother said ten. I mean, I just gave an opinion."

She grabbed my shirt. "I know that, and so do they. When Patty complained to our mother, she didn't look at her. She was looking at you. You! Did you see that?"

"Looking at me? No. I missed it. They don't need to look at me that way. When this is over, I'll go my way. They may never see me again."

"John, if they told you they loved you and wanted to see you sometime, would you totally abandon them?"

"Of course not. I could never do that. But I can't go live with them."

She took hold of my hands. "You'd visit them on birthdays, anniversaries, graduations, maybe some trips together, now, wouldn't you? And you'd bring them back to France if they asked, right?"

"Of course I would. I could never say no."

"I know you wouldn't. John, I don't think they'd expect anything more."

I heard what she said, but her earlier words did more than shake my memory. She dropped a brick on it.

"Whoa. Whoa. Whoa. Who's at home with Lizzy's mother?"

Nicole raised her head. "No one. Lizzy is an only child. Lizzy has an uncle, but he lives in some other state. John, I know what you're thinking. You invited Patty's friend. Lizzy's mother was happy, even overjoyed for her daughter to go to Paris. She would never say no."

"But her mother could've come with us. She's there alone. Does she work?"

"No. She doesn't work."

I started with "Then she—" I was stopped by Nicole's hand landing square on my mouth. Guess she saw my eyes jump wide open.

Then she grabbed my face, giving it a gentle shake. "Now you listen. When Patty called Lizzy to invite her, I talked to Rebecca, Rebecca Patrick, her mother. I asked her if she'd like to come. I knew I'd have to ask you, but I wanted to know."

She let go of my face as her hands dropped to her lap.

"Well, I—" She stopped me again.

Her hand went firm against my chest. "Be quiet. I'm not through yet." I kept quiet, and her hand relaxed. "Rebecca wanted her daughter to have fun without her mother around. And she didn't want to impose on you. Okay, you can talk now."

I wasn't giving up, even if my chest took another hit. "But she's there alone. I can get her a plane ticket and have her here tomorrow. Don't you think Lizzy would like her here?"

Her fingers were lightly stroking my chest as she spoke. "Of course she would. Lizzy told her mother she'd like her to come. But Rebecca didn't want to intrude. Now, just relax about it. There's nothing you can do. I know you want to, but it's her decision. Okay?"

"Okay. I guess." I said it, but I didn't like it.

My plan was to keep thinking of a reason to get her over here. But that thought would stay hidden, for a bit, mostly to protect my hide.

Nicole's hand grabbed my chin and gave it a shake. "You're a sweet man for wanting her here." She went up on her knees, with arms around me. "I'm tired and ready for bed. You take a bath, and I'll go get my night things and take my bath when you're done. Okay?"

She put her fingers to my lips. A reply wasn't needed.

It was a bit after eight and I'd just finished my shower and night stuff when Nicole opened the room door.

"Get in bed," she ordered. "I'll be there in five minutes. I have no intention of letting you get lonely."

"Whatever you say, lady." I scratched my head. "Do I know you, ma'am?"

"Yes. I'm the woman who follows Uncle John around. Remind me to tell Susan about Uncle John?"

Uncle John decided to worry about that later.

CHAPTER 13

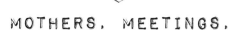

MOTHERS, MEETINGS, AND MAGICIANS

My alarm was set for 6:00 a.m. for some unknown reason. Fortunately, my alarm is always low and always on a music station. That is, with the exception of Paris. There I get static, but it's low static.

Nicole was still asleep, lying on her side facing me. I carefully flipped the alarm off, put my hands under my head, and focused on the ceiling.

It was Tuesday, and I wasn't totally looking forward to the day. Not because it was Tuesday, but because the first half could prove dangerous. The latter half could be enlightening or disheartening.

Nicole needed to be diverted to a safe place, but she didn't divert easily. Actually, she didn't divert at all. Probably any man would like her. That's why I liked her. There was no holding back. You always knew what she wanted and when to run.

The new information from the boys was filled with questions. Why did they suddenly appear to have a father who worked with Nicole's? Why were both fathers killed? And by whom? What could be so devastating or dangerous that needed two dead? My thoughts caused me to question their deaths. Powell's was a question. Gagnon's shouldn't be, but did they see his dead body?

"What are you doing? Why are you staring at the ceiling?"

She startled me more than my alarm. I should have felt her eyes boring holes in my brain.

With a short head turn, "I was counting the plaster circles in the ceiling. Did you know that—"

"Bull. You were thinking about something. Come clean?"

My arms and hands slid from under my head to my chest. "Okay. You got me. I was thinking about you lying there and—"

She cut me off again with, "Bullshit!" Within seconds of those words spoken, her elbows were resting uncomfortably on my chest. My hands ducked. "You tell me now or you'll need 911."

I was captured. "Is there nothing I can get away with?" Why I even said that was a waste of words.

"No."

"If you must know, I was thinking about the boys and their father."

That changed her attitude and position. She shifted her elbows flatter to, I think, ease my pain, yet we were still eye to eye. "So, what were you thinking?"

"What was so disguised or secretive that would need two men dead?"

"John, sometimes I'm not sure I want to know. Daddy was a sweet man. Spending time with him was always so special. I just don't want anything to harm the memories." She put her hand on my cheek. "Please don't let that happen."

"Beautiful, there's no way to promise that, but this I believe. From all you've told me, your father was a good man. I can't believe anything he may have done will change that."

"There's no way you can know that, but I believe you're right because you have no clue." She gave me a grin.

It was one of those grins women show when we men have lost all control of our future.

Clueless replied, "You win. I'm hungry. All this thinking has boosted my appetite."

I suggested we invite Mother Betty and meet her and the girls for breakfast. Nicole cancelled that thought. We dressed and headed down only to find her mother and the girls in the hotel restaurant already at a table.

Nicole stopped suddenly. I know because I was doing the lady-first thing and was clasped against her still body.

Progressing to their table, Nicole announced, "Mama. It's seven thirty. What are you, all of you, doing here this early?"

The girls' heads were downturned, but their eyes were gazing up expressing mischievous grins . . . saying nothing.

The mother-in-charge had the answer. "I had no choice. These two," Mother Betty firmly pointed at the girls, "practically dragged me out of bed. They wanted to see the boys."

What's new? I was trying to decide who had control of the relationship, the boys or the girls. If you don't know the answer, I'd like to know what universe you're from.

I dove in and asked, "Sure. Ah, where *are* they?"

Lizzy took her time at bat. "Morning, Uncle John. We thought you could pay their taxi and they could come here. And they could show us more of Paris."

She said that with one of those cute, tilted-head smiles, along with raised eyebrows.

Truth is sometimes obvious, but it can offer some humor. "So I'm to pay to get them here, and then pay for the day's sightseeing?"

Patty added, "Oh, no, Uncle John. We'll just walk around. There's so much to see."

Lizzy was almost bouncing as she nodded, agreeing. Then she added, "And we can be with them when you meet their mother."

Patty gave an attending nod to that.

"And, how did you know when I was coming to breakfast and give you the funding?"

Patty came clean, "We were going to call you but, well, Lizzy and I thought it best to give you more time to do things."

Their eyes were flashing between me and Nicole.

Mother Betty must have seen their actions, because, as I was about to speak, she said, "Let's leave it at that."

I held off for a moment or two to let their reactions decline. Their only reactions were tiny smiles. Mother Betty had no smile.

A subject change was needed. I spoke to the girls, "There's something I've been wondering about. It's summer break for you girls. I know nothing about French schools. Is there a summer break for the boys?"

Patty said, "They don't have as big a break, but they don't start school till next month."

"Good to know. I thought they were playing hooky."

Lizzy came back cutely, "No, Uncle John. They go to school and they get good grades."

"Hmm, that's good to hear."

The topic ended when the serveur came over to take our orders. I asked the girls if the boys were going to eat breakfast with us. When they said no, I had the serveur take our orders.

When she left, I had one of the girls call the boys and get 'em over here. With all that done, it was then time to be Uncle John.

"Girls, I want to talk to you about when I speak with Mrs. Gagnon. Now, I don't mind you being there, but please understand. It's not a date, and it may not be a fun visit. With Nicole's help, I'm trying to find why Mr. Powell was killed. And why the boys' father was killed, and if there's a connection. Last, if you do attend, I must ask you to stay till it's over, till I'm done. You okay with that?"

The girls did their usual stare at each other as they always do. Maybe they were trying to appoint who would reply to my words.

After a few seconds, Patty spoke. "We understand the importance of meeting her. For me, being here and listening to you and Nicole, I finally feel the same way. He was my dad, too. If there's anything you want me to do, I will." That got a nod from Lizzy. "Lizzy will, too. We want to help."

I needed a second opinion. "Nicole, anything you want to say about them attending and maybe helping?"

"No, John. I trust you to tell us all what to do. Mama, are you okay with the girls being there?"

"I think it will be a good thing." She turned to me. "John, I appreciate you doing all this. You met us a few days ago and look what you've gotten into."

Her words were appreciated. "I'm glad you approve. I'm hoping for a positive outcome for us all. As to this special situation, I've been in worse things."

Our food arrived, we ate, and within a few minutes of finishing, the boys arrived. I paid the taxi and gave Lizzy funds to cover the morning and get them to the boys' mother's house. Lizzy shared their expense money with Patty.

It was then time for some orders. The boys had asked their mother, but she had said any time. That being the case, I told the boys I wanted to meet their mother at 2:00 p.m. that day. They were to ask her and have Patty confirm to Nicole the time. Both boys said yes and both girls nodded their heads, but I wanted a bit more.

I waved my finger at them all. "Do not forget. I want to know before noon. Do you understand?" That got verbal replies from all four. Then I asked, "Is there anything else you boys have to say?"

Andre answered, "That is all. We will be there."

I had been waiting for that. "Andre, I will need the address."

"Oh. Yes. It is twenty-nine Rue du Buisson. The city is Créteil. Not so far there."

"Thanks, Andre. I'll find it." Nicole was already writing it on a napkin.

Nathan added, "It is eight US miles." He liked giving the info. His French grin spoke for itself. He added, "Is one level with up storage," maintaining the grin. Guess he meant attic.

The boys were working with me more than I expected. That cooperation should get us lots of new information.

"And thanks to you, Nathan. I compliment you both for speaking English so well."

That got good glances, nods, and tiny claps from the group. I didn't get any hugs, but they weren't needed. My joy was the happiness I saw in the girls.

The girls and boys left. Mother Betty went back to her room. I later found that Pappy was to pick her up and they'd spend time together. It was obvious those two were becoming fond of one another. Nicole didn't mind, which I thought was a good thing.

The breakfast gathering had accomplished some good things, the best of which was meeting Mrs. Gagnon and where that may lead.

My concern was Jules Pelletier, next on Pappy's list. The one who makes people vanish. I wasn't especially excited about knocking on his door.

I kept telling myself he was a magician.

CHAPTER 14

A MEANINGFUL DISCUSSION

It was a few minutes past nine, and we were, hopefully, heading for a friendly visit with Jules Pelletier. We knew nothing about him. I had to believe—make that sorta believe—that he knew something about Nicole's father.

It took about twenty minutes until we arrived at the Grand Marque du Sud apartments. Still cheap looking. Only part of the name I knew was the Sud, meaning South. I clicked the five button on the lift.

As the lift opened, I pulled out my note. Room 503. When we got to the door, I knocked and told Nicole, "If he opens the door and has a gun in hand, tell him you're looking for donations to add fifty feet to the height of the Eiffel Tower."

She pressed her elbow into my side as the door opened, then held my arm.

He didn't have a gun, but he was tall, about my height and maybe thirty pounds heavier. He completed the look with boots, a beard, and a white, heavily stained T-shirt. He said something in French. I made a note to start bringing an interpreter.

As before, I asked if he spoke English. He gave me a "Oui."

I added, "My name is John Stone, and this is Nicole Powell. We'd like to speak with Jules Pelletier regarding Nicole's father, William Powell. Are you Monsieur Pelletier?"

He came to a sharper attention, with a firm "Yes. I ne pas non Powell." From his attitude, I believed he said no.

Nicole jumped as he spoke, grabbing my arm a bit tighter.

It was time for a variation. "My apologies. That was someone else. I meant to ask if you ever worked for Signature Consulting?"

His head, with gritted teeth visible, moved so close to mine he could have bit my nose. "Non Signature!" My nose survived, but I thought he parted my hair. Okay, maybe not, but his attitude could have left a crack in the atmosphere.

Nicole gripped my arm even tighter. If I were holding her arm, I would've done the same.

At least I was still vertical.

Attempting to keep some control, I went after his attitude firmly. "That's odd. I spoke with Duane Naude, who said you did." I lied, but I needed more reaction.

His head shifted a couple of inches forward. "Non Journée." He pulled back and slammed the door.

I turned my head to Nicole and put my hand over hers, which was at that moment cutting off circulation in my arm. "I don't think he wanted to talk much. Maybe he don't like Tuesdays."

Nicole didn't hold back. "Tuesday, Muesday. He was pissed. Let's get out of here!"

She turned, heading for the lift, dragging me with her. She pressed the one button. After about ten seconds, she kicked the door, growling, "Where the hell are you?"

I was thankful she was pissed at the door. I buttoned my own lip on the way down.

Once we were outside and walking to the car, I said, "I gotta ask Pappy why he gave me that man's name."

"No, you won't, Mr. Stone. He's your friend. I WILL ask Pappy why he gave you that man's name. That man looked like he was ready to kill someone."

I didn't question that determination, but I added, "It's nine forty-five. We've got time this morning to check out the last name."

It must have been frustration that folded her arms tight against her breasts. "Is it a man or woman?"

It wasn't an amiable question.

"A man. Name's Ludovic Rousseau," I answered.

Her displeasure continued. "Another man. Huh. Nicolette lied, but she didn't look like she was ready to kill us. What did Pappy say about this one?"

I pulled out my tiny notepad. "Pappy said he helps people disappear. Mac said he works, or worked, for Signature and . . . and I do not like the sound of this one."

Her arms freed themselves from her chest and flew out. "Why? Tell me why."

"He removes personnel." Just saying those three words locked my mouth shut.

"Dear God. He could be the one who killed the boys' father and my father. And what happens to us if we go asking him questions?"

With only her arms to hold, I pulled her close. "Don't worry. We'll figure this out."

She looked at me, offering a nod, and said nothing, even as I held the car door open for her. Even then, she settled back into her seat and stared at the window.

Nicole's question needed an answer, which I didn't have. The word *yet* came to mind, but so did the cost when the yet was known. I could only think of one man who might know, and that's where we were heading.

I burned rubber to Pappy's restaurant.

The drive wasn't boring. The topic shifted to one more pleasant. Pretty much each mile—no, make that each inch—I answered Nicole's questions about Mac. Things like, where did you meet him? Was he ever married? How'd you meet him? How does he know so much? To name a few.

Most everything I gave her was not real specific. Among other things, I told her he was never married. "All I can say is he was a very good, make that an excellent, agent and a very close friend. He protects me, and I protect him." That seemed like a good end to the interrogation.

Keep in mind, I was driving and attempting to keep my eyes on the road, with a glance at Nicole ever so often.

Still looking ahead, she replied, "From everything you said, it all means you either don't know anything or you're not going to tell me anything. I think it's the latter." She turned toward me and let me have it. "You don't trust me!"

The last sentence came with the force of a tornado.

"Now, wait a minute," I started, looking at her, then at the road and, well, you get the gist. "I do trust you. That's not the problem. Knowing too much about Mac can cause the knower harm."

Gently shaking her head, she said, "I would never say anything about him."

She said what I knew, in just the short time I'd known her, was the truth. I quickly submitted my opinion. "Well, not on purpose, but you could be forced to. Now that you know he exists, it has to be your secret—forever."

"I can keep a secret, John. I promise. And I think I understand about not knowing."

My eyes kept darting between her and the road. "Believe me, I know you do. I'm sure you'll talk to him before this is over. You'll like him, and he'll like you."

That I knew. Mac is a woman magnet.

Nicole was calming some because her eyes were watching the road and sights out the side window. "Well, I do know women like him. You told me that."

The, shall we say, discussion continued till I parked the car. Mac has rescued me in the past. I was hoping that wouldn't be necessary here, 'cause it only happens when I step into some serious doo-doo.

It was close to ten thirty as we stepped in the front door. I walked up to Celeste and was about to open my mouth when she said, "Mr. Armand and Mrs. Powell are in his office."

Wasn't sure if that was just informational or a warning to stay away. No choice but to ask, "Celeste, is it okay to join them?"

She nodded. "Yes, Mr. Stone. He said he was expecting you."

That was odd. We were to see the names he had given me, but I hadn't told him any more than that. And I hadn't said I was coming to see him. I hadn't called him. Certainly I'd see him at some point, but with this delightful woman by my side, I could easily be detained.

I felt an arm grab mine. It was Nicole.

She waved her hand in front of my eyes. "Hello in there. You're thinking again."

"Huh? Oh. Yeah. Ah, thank you, Celeste." With that said, the arm-grabbing female led me to Pappy's office.

Next thing I knew, Nicole opened the door, allowing me to follow her. Once there, I was just my usual self, wondering why I was needed.

But Nicole had a bright-eyed, happy feeling about her as she got things going. "Hi, Mama. Hi, Pappy. Whatcha doing?"

Ah, the light came on. The one in my brain. You're thinking the same thing as me. She thought they'd be hugging or kissing—but they weren't. They were sitting side by side, sorta close, looking at a book.

Her mother took the lead. "Hi, Nicole. What've you two been doing? Been out there having fun?"

I took control of the arm dragging me around and dragged it and us to the sofa. On the way, I asked Nicole, "You want to tell them, or me?"

When she said, "Sure. I'd be glad to," I got nervous.

Nicole's expression turned from friendly mother talk to determined daughter talk.

She jumped right to the point. Her words and feelings were illustrated with stiff, spread fingers.

"Pappy, where on earth did you get these names you gave John?" Not waiting for a reply, with those fingers waving, Nicole said, "Yesterday we found Nicolette looking for, what's her name, Alicia, or something like that."

I leaned a little close and whispered, "Alivia."

"Yeah, her." Her hands grabbed her knees as she leaned toward Pappy, "She was a big liar. This morning we met—no, we didn't meet, we ran into—that Petler guy." Her words were filled with frustration.

Leaning in again, I whispered, "Pelletier."

"Yeah, him, and he could barely talk. Think he only knew three words, and if he hadn't slammed the door, I think he was about to beat us up."

I whispered, again, "Beat *me* up."

The back of her hand landed on my chest. "Yeah, John. He was a creep. Not John. Petler." I let that one slide. "A useless, wormlike, creepy, creepy worm. And now we've got one more to see. I don't know his name."

I whispered, "Ludovic." Frankly I was afraid to join in.

With a half nod toward me, she said, "Thanks, John," then turned back to Pappy with a sharper nod and snappy words. "So, Pappy. What can we expect from creepy Luddywick?" Without looking at me, "Be quiet, John. I know I missaid it. Will we finally have someone shoot us, or actually give us some decent words?"

She ended that tirade with arms folded across her breasts, looking direct at Pappy.

Her mother was sitting up straight, eyes wide. Her mouth was open as if she wanted to say something but wasn't sure what.

Me? I didn't move.

Pappy was the only one enjoying her words. He had a smile. "Nicole, I should hire you as an interpreter. You described those three perfectly. Here's the situation. Nicolette and Alivia share the apartment. They must lie, or de police would have them in prison. Alivia is here, in Paris."

Nicole's hands went up and down in opposite directions, and then rested on her knees. "But Pappy. Nicolette knew my father was dead, at least she may have."

My worry now and since I got into this was how much Nicole would learn about her father that could change her feelings for him.

Pappy leaned forward, arms lying on the table. "Yes, she might know, but I wouldn't think so. First, let me tell you of the others.

Pelletier is a follower, and a poor one at that. I not think he could look at a calendar and decide what day it is without help. He hasn't worked at Signature, but his leader, Ludovic, has and is still with Signature. He's the bad one. He's been known to make people disparaître. That's the French word, and I suspect you did the translation."

By that point, Mother Betty, sitting next to Pappy, was sizzling. "Pappy, I can't believe you let my daughter get anywhere near those type people! I never thought you were like that. If anything happens to her, I'll, I'll—oh, I don't know."

She stopped and rested her face in her hands.

Nicole rushed to her mother and dropped to her knees, holding her mother's head on her shoulders. That same angry expression her mother had grew on Nicole's face as she gave Pappy her own stare.

I was ready to throw in my two cents, but Pappy had a nickel. "Nicole, Betty, this I can assure you. Both of you, and John, and the girls have protection you will never see. But it's there. I promise you. I would never put your family in harm's way."

That surprised me. From my past experience helping him, I felt or maybe even believed he had underworld connections. If I'm allowed to think out a few light years, there was the French underground, if it still existed. He just told us he had people, agents, I guess, at his disposal.

I had to dig into that arena, but only when we were alone.

Pappy was always truthful with me, best I knew. "Pappy, I believe you. Not sure why. Maybe it's because I've known you for a couple of years, but I do."

I turned my attention to the two women. "Mrs. Powell, from what I know, this man is one of the good guys. I believe he has given us leads, if not clues, that even he may be unsure of. We can dig in so we can know what happened to your husband."

Nicole peeked up at me, offering a smile. I needed that. Maybe she knew using that woman's gift of intuition. I returned a wink.

Pappy lightly tapped the table to get my attention. My eyes jumped in his direction. "John, when you meet with Noémi Gagnon this afternoon, be sure you dig into what happened to her husband,

Gustav Louis. I know you will, but she may not trust you. Those two boys will be the only way into her confidence."

Our attention moved to Mother Betty as she stood. "John, if you have time, would you take me to the hotel? I need some time alone."

Nicole also stood, but said nothing.

"Of course I will. I think we're done here. We can go now. Shall we go, Nicole?"

"Yes, John." Her reply came with an agreeing smile and a gentle nod.

Her arms were hanging down by her side. I reached out my hand and she embraced mine.

We left Pappy's office with him standing silently watching us leave. Once we had reached the eating area, I made an excuse to tell Pappy something. I asked them to wait and promised to be no more than a minute.

Back in Pappy's office, alone, I told him, "That was a difficult time for both, but I know you're sincere in your feelings for Betty. I'll do my part to bring her around to your side again."

He put his hand on my shoulder and made the other available to be shaken, which I accepted. "I know you will, John. You know I care for that woman more than I ever have. Possibly as much as I did for my wife, even long after she died."

That had come to my thoughts also. "Not to worry. Betty will come around. Just be patient, my friend."

Our hands departed friendly. I was about to turn, when it hit me he knew of the Gagnons. My suspicious nature kicked in. "Hmm, so just how did you know of Noémi and Gustav Gagnon? I haven't mentioned them to you."

"Wondered when you'd notice," he said with a smile. I returned it with a grin and a squinty eye. "I had the boys checked out. They led to their mother, and from my knowledge, they are a good family. You can trust them."

With a twisted grin, I asked, "Is there anything you can't find out?"

I was joking. He got serious. "Unfortunately, there's too much unknown. I haven't found much on those names I gave you. My people are checking, but whatever they've done is still unknown. It is only their reputations that I have knowledge of. And that is limited."

With that done, we hugged and I headed back to the restaurant.

No sooner than I was standing beside the women, Nicole asked. No, gave me a verbal order. "What was that all about? And if you lie, you know your life will perish."

Her finger pressed against my chest strengthened her words.

I knew I'd have to explain. I clasped the finger for emphasis, then let go.

"Now, don't interrupt me. I told him I knew that was a difficult time for both of you back there. I also told him I knew he wouldn't let anything happen to any of us. Don't ask me how I know that, I just do. He cares for you two and is trying to find answers that will bring closure about your father, Nicole, and your husband, Mrs. Powell. That's his goal."

Yes, there was more, but for that time, I wanted their confidence in Pappy to be unquestioned.

Nicole stepped close to me and put her hand on my cheek. "I believe every word you spoke. You told the truth, and I trust you more than you know. Mama, you need to trust John and Pappy, too."

Mother Betty gazed at us both. "Okay. I will, but I need to be alone to think through all this."

I hoped there was some emotional mending in the air. I then attempted to reply with what needed to be done, "I follow that. Now, let's get you to the hotel. Nicole and I need to do some planning for the day."

That got okays, and we were hotel bound.

Nicole and I parted with her mother at the tenth floor. Actually, Nicole did the parting and took me with her to my room. Once inside, she flopped on the sofa and pulled me down with her. Very close. I had one arm over her shoulder; her hands rested on my leg.

It was close to eleven thirty and Tuesday was half over. And it would be if it was a nine-to-five day. Course, that was wishful thinking. She'd turned a little to better face me. "All right, John, how do you—" Her phone rang. She grabbed her purse and pulled out her phone.

"It's Patty," said Nicole as she answered. After about three sentences, she ended with "That's perfect. Thanks, Patty. Uncle John says thanks, too. What? Of course, he will." Patty hung up.

"Patty said we'll meet Mrs. Gagnon at two and texted me the address. Guess she didn't remember I had it." She shook her head briefly, then put the phone down. Her hands were back on my leg.

What I heard was a relief. I put my free hand on hers. "I must admit, I'm glad that's happening. It can mean a lot to our search." I paused a second. "And, what did that 'of course he will' mean?"

That got both her hands holding mine. "Everything's okay. Patty just wanted you to be kind when you meet Mrs. Gagnon. I told her you would be." She gave my hand a gentle squeeze.

Her hands needed company. I shifted my arm from her shoulder and added it to her pair. "I appreciate the thought. Hey, it's lunchtime. Let's get something to eat."

"Not yet. You haven't answered my question."

"What question?" I really had forgotten.

"This one. How do you know Pappy has people looking after us that we can't see? How do we know they're there if we can't see 'em? I want to know."

I still had her hands captured. I lifted them a little with, "Oh, that question." I tried to be cute. Didn't work. I got the look. Our hands dropped. "Okay, ya got me, again. I don't know. What I do know is he does what he says."

She shook her head and freed one of her hands, jabbing a finger in my chest. "John, the man owns a restaurant! He's not an FBI agent. He knows how to cook."

"And he makes a great crème brûlée." I displayed a full-toothed smile with that one.

Did no good. The free hand tapped my cheek. Three times. Wasn't hard. Think she was trying to make a point. "Stop attempting to be cute. It's not the time. I'm serious."

One of her hands was now on my shoulder, with her cheek lying on it. I still had the other one in custody.

Figured I had to come clean. "Now, listen and don't interrupt." I lost both hands. She crossed her arms. "You're very sexy with your arms crossed."

Her arms flew to her legs. I tried to take hold of her hands, but they were welded to those legs. However, I succeeded. I'd captured them again.

"Now, cut that out. For now. When I went back to talk to him, he told me he had the boys checked out. They're okay and so is their mother. That's all he knows."

Her eyebrows tightened. Maybe disappointed. "Why didn't he tell us? We were there." Her hands were calmly holding mine.

"If you recall, you—we—had walked out. Left him standing there. But he would have eventually. There's so much going on, I believe he just forgot with what happened between him and your mother. He cares for her so much; I know it hurt him."

"How does he do all this? And how did you meet him? You said you'd been over here for your IT business. But—but how's that got anything to do with Pappy?"

Those were good questions. I knew because our hands, which she had control over, gently rose and fell emphasizing her emotions as she spoke.

It was time to pull in the history. "About three years ago, Mac asked me to help a friend. Pappy was that friend. They knew each other from, let's say, past lives."

"Oh, dear God, they were both spies!" The calm vanished. She said that as she came close to crushing my hands.

"Well, not exactly spies. And please let up on my hands. I wasn't planning on doing any wrist wrestling."

She loosened her grip. I shook one of my hands, only for fun, then collected her hand again. "I'm so sorry, John, and I'm interrupting you. I promise to be quiet."

"Hmm, now where was I, when Godzilla tried to rip off my hand." That brought a pleasing smile back to her face. She did a quick lean against me.

After recovery, I gave it another try.

"Feel free to rip off a hand anytime." I quickly added, "I don't expect a kiss. Just trying to be funny."

She kissed me. Success.

"Now, finish the story, Mister."

"If you insist," I replied with a sheepish grin. "Pappy's son had invested some money—"

She jumped to full attention. Felt like she'd grabbed both my eyes in her hands and was staring at them. Then it came.

"Pappy has a son? You never mentioned that."

She poked my chest. I grabbed the finger, then her hand, quickly.

"I've about decided I shouldn't have." Her hand attempted to remove itself, but I held it. "Now, cut that out. And listen, please." Her hand relaxed a little. "I would never have gotten involved, but I was already over here working on an IT location."

"Sure. You just happened to be in France and were prepared to help?"

I started speaking, slow but emphatic. "Will you let me finish?" Switching back to normal, I said, "I was in Paris and had never met Pappy. Now, where was I? Oh, yes. A pair of would-be crooks had scammed his son out of a million dollars. Pappy couldn't get involved or they would kill his son."

She added, "John, I'm so sorry I interrupted you. I do it all the time."

I lifted her hand and gave it a kiss, "No apology is needed. You care. Besides, you were kinda cute when you apologized."

She smooshed my hand and gave me a smile and a nod, which I took as an okay to continue.

"Now, the French police were doing nothing, so Pappy called Mac and they got me. It really wasn't that difficult to handle. That's how I found Pappy."

Nicole was quiet after I finished. She let go of my hands and slowly straddled my legs, allowing those green, sparkling eyes to stare down into mine. The straddle was cool. The staring was spooky.

"You're a very nice, sweet man to have around. And all you wanted to do was take a girl to dinner, and here we are."

"Well, she was a fairly pretty girl."

My word was just a tease, but it was a stupid, dumb thing to say. It's like when your woman asks if a dress makes her look fat. Best not lie, and in most such cases, go easy on the truth, which can be how your heart sees her.

"Fairly pretty?" She added pouting lips to her reply. But they were cute pouting lips.

Attempting to recover, I added, "At a minimum, you must be the most captivating woman in Georgia. Could we please change the subject?"

"Not to that subject. We need to talk about meeting the boys' mother in less than two hours. And . . . we haven't eaten."

"If you recall, Miss Powell, I brought that subject up half an hour ago. Now, if you'll get off my lap so I can get up, we can go."

Without a word and only a smile, she flipped of my lap and rested on the sofa.

I stood up and held out my arm. She stood and accepted it.

Lunch was finally on the agenda.

CHAPTER 15

AN UNFORGETTABLE SHORT TALK

Nicole called her mother and we three met at the hotel restaurant, where I'd planned to make it a long lunch. Long because we had to plan the time with Mrs. Gagnon and her boys.

We ordered. I did a sandwich; the ladies did salads and hot tea. No iced tea available, so I ordered hot black tea and a glass of ice. And sugar. Not the first time. That's how I get iced tea over there. The serveurs always give me an odd look, possibly shock. The girls watched closely with grins as I was preparing it.

I recall saying, "One must improvise when in Europe."

The grins got a little grinnier but I held my cool glass of sweet iced tea with pride.

Lunch got underway and after a few bites, Nicole broke the ice. No, not my ice. "John, how do you think we should approach Mrs. Gagnon?"

"Well, her husband has been dead about as long as your father. In that length of time, things change. Feelings change, don't you think so, Mrs. Powell?"

Her expression told me she'd been there. It was somewhere between happy and sad. "John, I missed him so much, but after a point the missing became less because life goes on. I had two children to worry about, to support. Before I knew it, one of them began to support me. The memories were different."

"I understand what you're saying. Over time, when we lose someone close, the memories remain, but they are just—memories. Not reality. We face life's challenges and know the past is just that—a time that can't be brought back."

"That sounds like a man who has lost someone. Did you lose someone, John?"

Nicole decided to answer. "Yes, he has, Mama. I saw her picture in his apartment the night before we left. It was a beautiful young woman." Nicole put her hand on mine. "Oh, John, I'm sorry. I shouldn't have said anything. It wasn't my place."

"Not to worry, Nicole. You spoke the truth. She was my life. Now, she's a pretty memory. And memories are just that, times past, and they can't stop your life. Knowing how women feel about such, Megan would not want me to go off in some corner and hide."

Mother Betty placed her hand on Nicole's. "I see why you like this man."

Nicole beat me to a reply. "You see it, too? When we get into a situation where my mind gets scared, he tells my heart to trust him."

It was my time. "I'm ignoring all that, girls, mostly 'cause I got no idea how to reply. Except to say that's why you need to give Pappy a chance. He would never cause any harm to you or your family. He has his ways, and we should give him our trust."

"So, what're we doing next?" asked Nicole. Unsure why, but she ignored my plea to trust Pappy.

"We need to plan our meeting with Mrs. Gagnon."

Mother Betty cut in. "While you two do that, I'd like to go back to Pappy's place. I owe him an apology." She began looking in her purse.

I suspected she was looking for cab fare. "I can take you back to the restaurant."

"Oh, I don't want to bother you two. I can take a taxi."

Nicole had her own firm opinion. "You will not take a taxi. John and I will take you to see Pappy. And that's final."

That exchange settled the issue. We were delivering a sweetheart to Pappy.

We dropped her mother off at Pappy's place but didn't go in. Instead, we went and parked near the river, searching for a place to sit, watch, and talk.

We walked a short distance holding hands and found a bench facing the river. I motioned for her to sit, and I joined her.

She decided there was too much space between us and inched closer. As she had often done, she pulled her legs under her, resting them on my legs, with an arm on my shoulder. She took my hand.

The sun was bright and warm. Holding a woman's hand or not, this was not the place to think of leaving.

I had a concern. "Nicole, I hope the relationship with the boys will let their mother open up and share with us. There's a lot I want to know." That was an understatement.

She nodded. "I've heard some things. I guess we all have, but tell me what you want to know."

There was one thing that continued to bug me. "The most important thing I want to know is if she saw her husband during the funeral. In the casket."

Nicole's face saddened as I said those words. Her head shook gently. "Please don't ask her that. Not first. It's much too personal."

"No, I won't. We'll lead up to it. I want to know if she knew of your father and what she thought of him. And if he ever came to her house. The personal side of things can help reveal many secrets. I hope she'll share them. Just that sort of stuff."

"That all?" I wondered if she was getting impatient.

Then a thought dripped out of my leaky brain. "I just remembered something. Did you mention the boys' father, Gustav Gagnon, to Pappy?"

"No, I didn't. Why do you ask?"

"Maybe your mother did. I know I haven't, yet Pappy knows. He used the name just before your mother stood up asking to leave."

"Ah, yes, I remember. Sure, I'll find a time to ask her when we're alone. I'd like to know, too."

There was something I needed to share. I should've mentioned it earlier. "When I went back to see Pappy, I was about to leave and thought to ask him how he knew."

Holding her knees in position, the rest of her sat up. She was forming grooves on my legs. "And you're just *now* finding time to tell me?"

"Believe me, I sorta forgot."

"You *sorta* forgot? Bull hockey. What did he tell you?" I knew she wouldn't believe me. I didn't believe me, but I had forgotten to tell her.

I attempted to give my reply some importance. "Hey. I did remember, ya know. Now, please listen. I was going to tell you and things got jumbled. I just remembered."

"Well? Go ahead. I'm listening. At least for now."

"He had the boys checked out and then their mother. He told me they were okay and trustworthy. Would you mind sitting back down? My legs are getting indentions."

"Your head may get indentions. That's good information. Not complicated. What was so difficult to remember about that? One sentence."

"Actually, it was two sentences. And my legs really hurt."

She suddenly realized what I was saying and sat back down, lightening the load on my legs. "Oh, John, I'm so sorry. I didn't realize what I was doing." Then came an attitude shift in a somewhat irritated direction. "You do know if you'd told me when you first knew, those legs wouldn't be hurting."

"If I promise not to be forgetful, can we go? I think my legs need movement."

"Yeah. Guess so." Then she surprised me. "I thought you'd have much more to ask her. But that's okay. I suspect you'll dig into each answer till all is known."

"That's the plan."

She stood up, still holding my hand. "Let's go make it happen, Mr. Forgetful."

CHAPTER 16

WHEN PAST LIVES MEET

It took about thirty minutes to get to Noémi's home. It was a small house south and a bit west of Paris. With GPS we found her street. A street I can type but fear attempting to pronounce.

On the way, there were the usual businesses and apartment buildings. There was a pharmacie—yeah, with a *cie*—which sounded more accurate. Bet our spelling was Benjamin Franklin's doing. Why do you think we have realize and the Brits have realise? I saw that in one of Dad's ancient history books. Must have been accurate. It was handwritten.

As we ventured into more single-family residential streets, some houses had small grass yards. Others were behind concrete walls or a thick grass covered fence, meaning real grass and the houses were somewhat hidden. Before we reached her house, the homes were large, two-story structures, still with tiny yards. As we moved farther out, houses got smaller.

One oddity. Even with driveways, cars were often parked on the sidewalks, leaving just enough room for pedestrians.

Noémi's house was also hidden behind a protective, light-colored concrete wall and a double-wide gate of solid wood, accompanied by a smaller gate for humans. The house itself was made of the same material and color as the wall.

We arrived right at 2:00 p.m. and I did the sidewalk park. We used the human gate and walked to her door. No steps. No porch. Just a square slab of concrete. I was about to knock, when the door opened with Andre standing there.

"Hi, Mr. Stone. Miss Nicole. Please come in." He was very cordial. His mother had taught him well on how to engage guests. Course, I hoped we were more than that.

Just through the front door, we were in a small wide foyer. Andre stopped and told us his mother only spoke a little English. We were to keep words simple.

He added, "Mother knows a lot that happened back then. She told us some, but with you being here improved her interest. Say nothing till I introduce you. Nathan or I will translate for you."

Lizzy walked up just as he finished. "Hi, Nicole. Uncle John. She's a special woman. And kind. You'll like her."

"I think I will, Lizzy." Then to Andre, "Does she know of Nicole's father being dead?"

"Yes, she does, and that he and Father were partners. She met him many times. She not know that deaths may be connected." I asked Andre how old she was. He told me forty-two. That would've made her twenty-three or twenty-four when Andre was born. Younger that I thought. Unsure why I thought that.

By then we were entering her living room, where Noémi was standing, hands clasped in front of her. She was a light-haired brunette, with eyes to match. Her hair was long, but put up in curls. Not tall, maybe five foot three, and slender. I wouldn't say she was beautiful and not a centerfold type. Still, I felt she was on the better side of attractive.

It had been seven years since her husband died, and I wondered why she hadn't remarried.

The living room was not too small, yet it had little furniture. Only four chairs. Could've made room for a small sofa, but funds may have been the reason there wasn't one. The only table had a lamp on it. There was a three-shelf bookcase about two feet wide. There was only one book. Looked like a Bible.

There was a fireplace with the traditional shelf across the top. On that shelf was a small, empty vase on one end and in the center a picture of a man, a woman, and two boys. The usual family photo. The boys were young, so the man in the picture was probably the father.

The kitchen was visible, but from my viewpoint, not large. I could see a gas stove and a refrigerator. From my limited view, it looked new. It had the water dispenser in the door. Course, that's been around a decade or two. I saw button selections for cracked or cubed ice. That's fairly new.

All total, it appeared life had not left her much. My hope was to add something positive and memorable.

She offered us chairs. As I approached her, I did a short bow and remained silent. Nathan asked if he could get us a glass of water. No one accepted. There was nowhere to set it. We'd be holding it for the whole visit.

Us guys motioned for our women to sit down. They accepted our request, and we each stood behind our girl. I wasn't sure of the custom in France as to who sits and who stands. The old photos of my parents had the woman standing. Keep in mind, that was prehistoric times.

Andre stepped close to his mother and started the meeting. He spoke in French to his mother, pointing at us. Then to us in English, he said, "This is Nathan and my mother, Noémi. She prefers you to call her Noémi. Uncle John, you can be first to give her a hello. You may remain there or step out closer. Whichever you want. She would like you to speak in English."

He moved back behind Lizzy.

I was still behind Nicole. "Noémi, I am happy to meet you. Nicole, here," my hands were on her arms. I moved my hands to her shoulders to draw attention, "knows that your husband and her father worked together. She wishes to tell you more and learn from you."

Noémi had been looking at me. When I finished, she turned to Nicole. "Nicole, is pleasure you here. Tell moi about you father?"

It was good to hear Noémi asking. That would make it easier to ask about her husband.

Nicole told Noémi about her father as a dad and that he worked for the US government then with Signature. She talked about his travels and him being away from home so much. Noémi never took her eyes off Nicole.

Noémi spoke, "If my boys not told of their father, moi will. The kindness you spoke of you father was as they father. Gustav and you father was much time together. They are friends. When you father die?"

"He died seven years ago in Georgia, in August. It was an automobile accident."

Noémi interjected, "I sorry you remember sad thing."

Nicole had been there. "Time has helped. And John," she put her hand on my hand, still on her shoulder, "has given me hope to know more."

Noémi gave me a tiny head bow, then said to Nicole, "He must are special."

"He is." Sometimes only a few words can make you feel good.

Noémi asked, "You there when he die?" I liked her digging. It would help my use of a shovel, when it was my time.

"No. The accident was a few miles away. His car burned."

"When you saw him, what look like?"

Her digging intrigued me. Why would she ask that?

That was something I felt Nicole did not want to remember. She glanced down for a moment, then briefly leaned her head to my hand, then to Noémi. "He was burned so bad there was nothing to identify." Her hands went to her lap.

Having understood, Nathan clarified, "Identité." He turned to Patty. Think he wanted to be certain of what he said. Patty gave him a gentle touch.

I stepped beside Nicole and raised my hand. Noémi gave me a nod to speak. "Nicole's father was working for Signature Consulting, but before them, he worked for the United States FBI. Did your husband work for a French government agency?"

"Oui," said Noémi. "He laid down work for Signature Consulting."

More pieces began to gather. Two men working for similar government agencies are laid off and start working for the same private company. That was mysterious. If one was to consider that a coincidence, it would fail coincidentally.

My hand went back to Nicole's shoulder. Her hand joined mine as she looked up at me. She gave me an almost unnoticeable shake of her head. She had the same thought. I returned her shake with a nod of agreement.

It was time for my next questions. Our focus was now on Noémi. "Could you tell us how your husband died? If it is something you wish not to remember, it is okay not to speak of."

My words must not have been clear. Andre repeated them in French.

Noémi said, "Oui. I can speak. He was on an assignment in Saint-Denis and was killed."

"Noémi, you asked Nicole what her father looked like when she saw him. May I ask what your husband, Gustav, looked like when you saw him after the accident?"

Andre translated my words.

"Oui. I understand. He had fall in tank of *acide*. His body was not known."

Nathan added, "The word was acid, and he was not identifiable."

Nicole clenched my hand tight then lifted it and held it with both hands. There were tears running down her cheeks. His words had brought her past to the present.

Every now and then the boys would say a word that would not normally be in a conversation, like identifiable. These boys learned well. My guess, they were maybe ten or eleven when their father died. At that age, they would've been sponges.

I put one of my arms around Nicole. Next thing I knew, her arms flew around me, pulling me firm against her.

Noémi saw the reaction. "We are so sorry to say those words."

I answered for Nicole. "Noémi, the past is always with us. We can hide it with the present. But sometimes that present opens and memories flood us."

Noémi turned to Andre. He translated.

"You have kind words, John."

"That's kind of you to say. If I may ask, did the boys see their father after the accident?"

"No. I kept the cercueil closed."

Turning to Nathan, he said, "Casket."

She continued with, "Was not much maison funéraire could do."

Nathan quickly said, "Funeral home."

"Thank you, Nathan. I not wish to see him either. His mother and father did not wish so, as I did not."

With tears on her cheeks, Nicole said, "I can understand. I wanted to remember my father as he was. Not like that."

"Oui. Is a woman thing. He was good man then. He is good man." Noémi's brown eyes were isolated on Nicole.

Suddenly, Nicole left me and was down on her knees in front of Noémi. They hugged. In a flash, Patty and Lizzy were there as well, bringing their own tears to share.

The boys went somewhere and found handkerchiefs, sharing them with the women. Not something we in the States see so often anymore, but it was perfect for the time.

When the tears lessened, the girls remained seated around and at the feet of Noémi. It was as if they were at the feet of their mother. Her short arms were around them all, if not physically, in spirit.

The boys looked at me and I motioned for them to join their respective girls. They leaped at the offer. I pulled out my phone and took a couple of pics, as unnoticed as possible. That had to be remembered. I joined them.

I had no idea this would occur. I was just trying to learn what had happened to Nicole's father. Someone had to say something. Whatever any man says at a time like that could easily be frowned upon. It had been a minute, but the meaning was unforgettable.

I took the plunge. "I must admit, I've never seen anything like this before. I'm just a man, but I will remember it."

Nicole reached over her shoulder offering her hand. I took it. Still looking at Noémi, she said, "I know this man. He didn't say it, but he wants to ask something. John, it's okay to talk." She never took her eyes off Noémi.

Noémi gave me a pleasant gaze. I took it as a permission to speak. "May I ask you a question?"

"Oui. Please."

"Your boys speak very good English. How did that happen? Did they have lessons?"

She smiled. "They learn from William. I did, me. The boys," she again asked Andre, then she said, "fast learners, and William told we much stories, much about America. They listen to him." She spoke a French word to Andre. He answered and she replied, "For hours."

"I can tell, Andre and Nathan are good sons."

"Kind for you so speak. They are life of my life."

That was a cool thing to say. "Boys, your mother has her own way with words, and those words are precious."

Her stare told me she didn't understand. Andre gave her the French version, and she gave me her first broad smile. Believe me, that can make your day. I rose and found my way to an available side and gave her a hug. She returned my action with a kiss on my cheek.

I moved back behind Nicole, trying to decide what to do. I was standing beside two boys with sad faces, but no tears, and four women with water dripping from their cheeks. Being a grownup and a man, was I supposed to bring this thing, this emotional thing, to an end? No way. I'd rather have been facing a firing squad.

Noémi saw me in my time of peril and gave me a reprieve. She said something in French to the boys. Nathan gave her an answer. "We women show amour for our men. Rise and *rester*, sit. This spécial time. Nous. Non. Non. We remember."

That gave the girls permission to take their seats, along with wet hankies, and us guys to stand behind them.

I leaned down to Nicole. "Is there anything else you need to ask about?"

After a final wipe of her eyes, she replied, "I've heard all I need, John. Thank you."

Looking over at Patty, "Patty, how about you?"

"I'm okay, Uncle John."

Turning to Lizzy, "Lizzy, I believe this could have brought sweet thoughts of your father."

"It did, Uncle John. Father died differently, but he's still gone. I love those memories. I will always remember this time you made happen. I love you, Uncle John Stone." She stood and, in a flash, grabbed me with a super hug. Patty did the same.

There were more questions to be asked, but they would have to wait. It was a time for remembering. And I was not gonna be the guy breaking up the hugs.

Nicole stood. "Noémi. You have been so kind to let us share this time. I would like to come back and see you again before we leave France."

Noémi said, "Oui. I wish you *à tout moment.*"

Andre added, "Anytime," with a smile.

With that ended, everybody hugged everybody and us guys got kisses on lips from our girlfriends and kisses on cheeks from the other girls. I asked Noémi if I could have a copy of the picture on the mantel. The boys said they would have one made and get it to me tomorrow. I gave them funds to cover the cost.

There was more to know, and I felt it was a good time to ask. "Boys, almost forgot. Ask your mother if we can look through any of your father's personal things. There may be clues that could help us find Nicole's father."

Nathan said something to his mother and she replied. "Uncle John, you may, but we need to pull them from above . . . ahhh, attic. Can you return tomorrow afternoon?"

I said yes with a glance at Nicole. She returned an approving nod, which was all I needed. With that done and goodbyes said, Nicole and I left. The girls wanted to stay. They may have been a bit intrigued with France, but mostly it was the boys. I gave the girls cab fare back to the hotel, including enough if the boys were to come with them. I got a couple of hugs.

Nicole and I left heading somewhere. With all we'd just experienced, anywhere would give comfort if not relief.

We were heading toward Paris and Nicole hadn't said anything for the first couple of miles, when she said, "I know we went to find out about my father, but even with that, I learned more than I knew about him. Those boys must have loved him, too."

"Yeah. Think you're right. He had to be close to a second father, or maybe an uncle."

I certainly learned of her father's personal nature, and it was good to know. It was at least a side puzzle piece.

She turned toward me for a moment as best she could with a seat belt. "You may not know it, but you've become a real uncle to Lizzy and Patty."

That was a nice thing to hear, but the end result could be hurtful to the girls. "We talked about that. I never wanted that to happen."

"Of course you didn't. You're just the kind of man who can't help it. And, it was more than just protecting them from the boys. Sweetheart, you showed them what it's like to have a man helping them know about life."

Her conclusions were appreciated. I glanced back at her. "What do I do now?"

She put her hand on my leg. "Just keep doing what you're doing. Be yourself. When all this is over and you leave, they'll cry again, but they'll understand. Our youth lets us be foolish sometimes, but you, John, are real. They will never forget you. Neither will I."

Now, keep in mind, she brought up the uncle thing again. But she took it to a whole new level with, "Neither will I." I'd known that woman less than three days, and she knew more about me than I did in my thirty-plus years. This was one of those times I'd like to sit in Nanna Bolton's lap. She always had an answer.

There was no answer and no certain solution. Glancing back between her and the road, "You really know how to slow a guy down. I can't say for sure how all this will turn out, but in the end, I'll try to lessen the effect on the girls and you. Course, you already know me, don't you?"

"Yep."

Watching the road. "I really got no way out, right?"

"Right." She grabbed my ear to emphasize her word.

I pulled off into a parking lot. Listening and driving and trying to see her reactions wasn't gonna happen. I flipped off the seat belt and turned as best I could in the driver's seat. "Now, don't start the one-word replies, please!"

She removed her seat belt and sat up in her seat, on her knees, facing right at me. "Okay, I won't. Sweetie, all I want you to do is get the answers we need and take us home."

That was a decent request. I needed the diversion. "Let's go over what we heard. Both men worked for a government, got laid off, and then both worked for the same private company, Signature. Then the same two died in different countries, same year, I think, in ways that would hide their identity. How chancy is that?"

"You're saying it was planned?"

"Sounds like a cover-up. They found something or knew something or both, and someone within the government had to make them stay quiet forever. From what I've learned, it's not that difficult for any government."

"Why couldn't it be Signature that killed them?"

Her thoughts were taking the same path mine had.

"The cover-up was too well done. The federal medical examiner and the French equivalent had to be in on it. Including their bosses, and who knows how high up it went. Can't say how bad the acid was to Mr. Gagnon, but they could've identified your father with his teeth, but they didn't. At least that's what you were told. Signature could not have made all that happen." At least, I didn't think they could.

"Dear God. John, we don't have a chance." She paused and came to another conclusion. "Oh, no. If you dig too deep, they'll come after you." Her head was shaking. "I don't like this."

"Don't think it's that bad. It's been seven years and Noémi is still alive, and so is your mother—and you. Granted, there probably haven't been any probes."

My words got her finger pointing at me. "That's exactly what you're doing. And I got you started." The finger wasn't pointing anymore. Her hand rested gently on my shoulder.

I put my hand on hers. She needed to know I liked it. "Actually, Pappy got me started. As soon as he knew you were coming and asked about your mother, he got interested. And when he saw me in the restaurant, we went into his office."

Her hand on my shoulder did a little grab. "John, he still cared for Mama. That's what got his interest roused up all over again." Her hands began to fly all around, accentuating her words and emotions. "His feelings resurfaced. Came to life. And I'm beginning to favor it, at least I think I do. She's had no one for so long."

Her hands settled back into her lap.

She had a point, but if that was all there was, why'd he give me those names? And why hadn't I asked more questions?

We weren't talking of the past. It was now. "You make a good point, but it's not cared for. It's cares for."

Her right hand punched my arm and she bared her teeth at me. "Yes, you ninny. The man loves her."

"I know that! All she wants to do is be with him. For all I know, I'm gonna have to rent her a taxi."

Her arms crossed at breast level. She returned my absolute with, "Keep up that talk, and you'll have to rent *me* one!"

The only word I had to say was "Women," and I said it calmly.

With arms still crossed and staring out the windshield, which appeared to be heating up, "Men!"

I couldn't keep it in. I started laughing. Could not stop. With something close to the speed of light, her adorable head was suddenly facing me. A better word would be immersed. There was a distinct possibility I was about to melt.

Looking at her, the only word that came to my feeble mind was a soft "Cute."

It took about three seconds before her hands dropped to her lap. She turned her head down, eyes gazing up at me. With those cute, pouting lips, she gave me her feelings, "That's no fair. I'm angry at you." She paused a moment. "Maybe not." Then she started to cry.

"Hey, now, don't do that. I'm sorry. I didn't mean anything I said, except that you're cute. Okay?"

With the poetic grace and ease of a gazelle, less the thorns, she flipped up on her knees, totally facing me, wiped the lonely tear away, then smiled and let me have it. "Do you actually think some man, especially you, is gonna make me cry?" On the word cry, she grabbed my shirt right at the neck, pulling it and me near her. "Now, hear this. I'm hungry and we're going to Pappy's place to eat and get some info from him. You got that, Uncle John?"

Well, that will tell any man he's outnumbered and must be sure the woman knows who's in control.

I cranked the car and headed toward Pappy's place with a, "Yes, ma'am. Whatever you say."

As I said, the man must know who's in control, or he's in deep doo-doo.

CHAPTER 17

SPEAKING OF WOMEN

We had gone about a mile. A pleasant mile, when Nicole changed her mind. "I don't want to go to Pappy's yet."

There were other things we could do. "Well, it's only four o'clock, so we can chase a lead or something, then eat."

I took a quick look and saw her lip and nose squish up a bit, informing me I had a lousy idea.

She confirmed it. "I don't want to chase any leads. We can do that tomorrow."

"Hmm. We could go swimming, but there's no beach nearby and the Seine ain't a place to swim." Why I even brought that up I have no idea. Okay, okay. It was the vision of a bikini.

Out of the corner of my eye, I could see her looking at me. "If I had my bikini over here, I'd probably want to go there, but not now." See? I wasn't the only one. I did my own quick glance at her. She gave me a wink.

As it had crossed both our minds, I offered my position on that subject. "If I knew you had a bikini, we'd already be somewhere."

I'd stopped looking, but I heard her say, "Me too."

I couldn't help but check her expression. The look was not mean, no smile, no grin. It was more intriguing.

Even with all that, nothing was working. I was at a loss. I truly did not know where I was going. I had actually thought of visiting

Nicolette again. A surprise visit. Might find Alivia there. That got me to thinking. Their room was on the front of the hotel. It was possible she could see us coming. But, no. She'd have to look out a window every five minutes. I decided to scratch that dumb thought totally.

"John. You thinking again?"

She startled the heebie-jeebies out of me. "Huh? What? No. Yes? Geez, don't do that."

That same female tapped my shoulder with her fist. "Knock-knock. Then stop thinking to yourself. I might want to hear your thoughts."

Having no choice but to open up with shorter thoughts, "Ah, well, I was just thinking about Alivia and Nicolette."

I heard a "huh" from the lady, then, "I'd rather you be thinking about me." Her words had a frustrated sound.

"No, not that. Just trying to think of a way to find her. Even Pappy knew she was in town. That's another question. How'd he know? We didn't tell him."

"He's probably got a spy somewhere." She said that as if it was a . . . who cares.

"That's it. He has a spy. He said he had people looking after us. If he can do that, why not look after others? I think it's time we confronted him on that. We can go there now and do it."

Staring at the windshield, she said, "Sometimes you men just don't get it."

"Get what?" I was clueless.

She abandoned the windshield to look in my direction. "I've just heard things about my father I never knew. I love him even more, but I can't hug him or sit in his lap and hear him tell me sweet things. I never can. I just want to be close to someone I love. And that's you. I want to go to the hotel."

At least now I had a destination.

We were sitting on the foot of the bed next to each other, looking at the Eiffel Tower. The curtains were always open till bedtime.

Nicole had unlatched and removed her sandals and said something about how pretty it was. I said something about how pretty she was. I got a thank-you. As I mentioned, we men gotta always try to get points.

"Daddy liked me wearing sandals. He didn't like flip-flops. The sandals didn't have to lace up far. He just liked them. He told me I was pretty. He was my father, so I just thought he had to say that."

"He said it because you were and you are. He wasn't complimenting an image. He was complimenting reality."

"That's sweet of you to say." She paused a moment. "He didn't like me wearing bikinis, so I wore the old single-style swimsuit when he was around. I have several of them. As I grew older, I bought more. I also have several bikinis, which he never knew I had. I wish I'd told him."

"Did your mother know?"

"Yes. But Mama said she'd never tell him."

"Tell ya what I think—he knew. Don't believe your mother would keep that a secret. And because he loved you so, he would never have spoiled your fun."

"John, I never thought about it that way. He would do that. I wish I'd told him. I was lying to him." I saw tears emerging.

"Now you understand. He knew it and he still loved you. And protected you. And gave you or your mother the money to buy those bikinis. That's how much he loved you."

She kissed my cheek. "I'm glad I told you. Thank you."

I did a little brush of her cute nose.

We needed to get off that thought. "Thank you for sharing that. Okay, it's now about four thirty. What's next? Supper? Talk some more? Want to go hunt for Alivia?"

She quickly pulled one leg up on the bed as she rolled those green eyes, glaring straight at me. "You still don't get it. I'm sitting here next to you on the bed, and you bring up another woman."

Attempting to be understanding, and yet a little confident, I said, "I wasn't thinking of her *that* way. We need to find her only to *talk* to her. I mean, for all I know, she might shoot us."

She put her hand on my cheek tapping it gently, "I know what you meant. Most any man sitting here would have tried to get my clothes off. You didn't. I was just teasing you a little. I don't want to spoil the moment here with you."

"Sometimes I think I need an instruction booklet on how to deal with women."

Yeah. That book would have all the words not to say. Hmm, not a good idea. I'd lose most of my vocabulary.

"John, all you have to do is be sweet and think only of the woman you're with. That will make you a good man."

I couldn't see them, but I felt my eyes open wide. I had a revelation. "That's what Noémi said about her husband."

Nicole's hands flew up and back down. "You did it again," shaking her head. "Another woman. Must I put duct tape on your mouth to stop it from messing up?"

"Hey. That was a wild thought about *her* man. I didn't mean anything. Don't know why I even thought it. Believe me, no man can be where I am now and be thinking of another woman."

I closed one eye, waiting for the next assault.

"Okay, you're sweet again. Wanna get something to eat? I'm hungry."

I woulda went. Hungry or not.

We landed at Pappy's place, hungry for food and explanations. When we entered the restaurant, Celeste led us to a table, leaving menus. She only said, "Follow me." I didn't get a mister or a monsieur.

I sat beside Nicole, knowing we'd have company. Celeste also told us Mother Betty was in back with Pappy. After we submitted our orders, I caught Celeste's attention and told her to tell them we were there. Mother Betty and Pappy joined us, rather quickly, I thought.

We gave them the gist of our visit with Noémi. We didn't go into deep detail of the men's deaths, for I knew that would birth many questions. Pappy didn't appear surprised, but his eyebrows raised on more than one occasion. I got the feeling he was looking for more info.

Mother Betty started first, and it was venomous. "I didn't know just how much I hated Signature Consulting. They killed two men, and no one was held accountable. Someone there should be dead."

She picked up on some of the mystery, while offering a snake in a box to Signature.

I saw Nicole's anxious countenance and did the customary backstep. She took control. "Mama, we don't think Signature did it."

Her mother said one surprised word with wide open eyes, "Huh?"

Nicole turned to me. "Tell her, John."

I had the pointer, but it felt more like a hot poker. "Thanks, Nicole. I think." I gave Nicole a blink and addressed her mother, "First, you should know the girls are still there. They've taken a liking to Mrs. Gagnon, Noémi Gagnon."

Nicole decided to share the details herself, by sending the words about to leave my mouth down a dead-end street. "They like the boys and now their mother. You should have seen and heard John, he's truly become their Uncle John." She gave my arm a hug.

Mother Betty jumped at that remark and directed her words at me. "John, you shouldn't do that."

With my words still blocked at the end of that street, Nicole picked the reply. "Mama, he didn't do anything but keep them safe. They both had a man looking after them. And I like it, too. They needed it, him."

"But Nicole, he can't live with them. He has his own life."

"Of course not, Mama. Yes, he has his own life, but if they asked him to come to a birthday party or a graduation, he'd be there in a flash with gifts." She didn't ask, but gave my hand a couple of pats.

She'd dragged me into the thoroughfare. With a clear street in sight, I did my thing. "Yes. I would. I'm not some super father guy, but I wouldn't want to hurt them."

"See, Mama? He won't desert them, now or never." She ended that by patting my hands, again. The street was clear, so I smiled.

The question wasn't directed at me, but I was the subject so I grabbed the moment. "I won't. And could we change the subject?

This makes me nervous. And Pappy's sitting quietly enjoying my nervousness."

Nicole placed her hand on mine, leaving it there.

Pappy saw I needed help. "Betty, you need not worry about John. He will do as Nicole said. Changing the subject, John, is there anything else you leaned?"

I suddenly detected our subject could be overheard, so I took a looksee. The restaurant was about half full of customers, but none close to us. I provided Pappy my conjecture.

"Nicole covered what we heard. That was about it. But the unlikely event of both men dying accidently at virtually the same time," with a slight shaking of my head, "just don't fly." I leaned a little toward Pappy for emphasis.

Nodding his head, Pappy said, "I'm in agreement on that aspect."

Another puzzling sentence from Pappy. A short one. That man probably knew more of all this than the police. Now, that was a guess on my part.

There was something I needed to know, and I hoped this was the time. "Almost forgot to ask. Pappy, how'd you know Alivia is still in Paris? I didn't tell ya. I just found out myself."

"John, my friend, I told you I have someone looking after you and Nicole. That's all I can share, but my cohort has been watching her hotel. She comes and goes periodically."

"Any idea where she goes?" Couldn't hurt to ask.

"She does some shopping when she's in Paris, but she'll be visible then out of sight for a couple of weeks. Then show up. How she does it, I don't know, but she's very good at eluding my spies."

He got my attention. "You have spies?" From what I'd seen and heard, that was a total shock to my ears.

"No, John. Just a word. Just friends who help me look after loved ones." As he said that to me, he had a more fixed look at Nicole and Betty.

He triggered a thought. My hand with pointy finger went up wiggling. "Now, Noémi did mention a factory in Saint-Denis. Her husband was on an assignment there when he was killed."

I got his attention and silenced my finger.

Then his expression caught my interest. "Did she know the name of the place?" His question was asked very tranquil.

Pappy was curious. At least, he gave me the impression it was new to him. However, at that point, I wondered if anything was new to him. In any case, I wasn't gonna bring it up. Time usually tells all, and I could wait.

"No, she didn't." I left it short. I wanted to hear his reply and where it may go.

Pappy added, "That's a very large city with several manufacturing plants, and even more that have closed."

Specifically addressing Pappy, I said, "If you got even a syllable of which plant it might be, let me know. I want to see it. Actually, I want to visit it in detail."

"So, what's your next step?" he asked.

Before I could answer—actually, before I could think about it—Nicole provided the info. "Tomorrow morning, we're going to see that Loodvic guy."

I was about to correct her when she gave me a tight-eyed stare. I kept silent.

She asked Pappy, "What can you tell us about him?"

"I know he works for Signature and spends most of his time out of the office. He visits their clients, but I don't know his role with them. I do know he is well spoken in several languages, including English. And he's a cordial man. Friendly talker, but I don't know much more except my sources tell me not to trust him. Be careful what you tell him."

Nicole's expression jumped to not pleased. "Then why the hell should we see him?" That language got a stare from her mother, whom she ignored. "That's just another man who could shoot John. Seems like a stupid thing to do."

That woman was not happy, and several of the restaurant patrons knew it as well.

Pappy was not smiling, but his expression was more of concern. He put his hand on the table as if placing it on hers. "Nicole, I would never send John into such a place. If I were, he would not be alone. I don't believe this man would harm John, or you. By not trusting him, I only meant he might tell others to not talk to you."

I thought he was on track. "Pappy, I believe I understand. We should tell him just so much. Keep it simple. Point no fingers. We're just looking for a loved one and know very little."

"John, that's exactly right. Now, he will know if Nicole's father worked for Signature, so you can ask about that. If he says he knows nothing, he's lying. You can press him up to a point. Hey, maybe even have Nicole start crying."

That did not set well with Nicole, and she let him know, with stern words,. "I will not cry unless I need to. That's bull—" She stopped short of the word, glanced at her mother, and finished her sentence with, "Hockey." That's twice she used that word. Maybe she had a reason to favor it. I did not wish to know.

I leaned over next to her ear with a low whisper, with her mother only seeing the back of my head. "Nice recovery." Her elbow went into my side. I uttered a grunting noise, which she totally ignored.

When I regained my composure, I saw Pappy was grinning. Mother Betty was not.

Pappy then laid both hands flat on the table. Spreading them open, he said, "Nicole, I didn't mean to belittle you. Only to show the control you lovely women have over us meager men. And, this may be a time to use that talent." He clasped his hands together, still on the table.

I knew I would regret it, but I spoke anyway. I also slid my chair away from Nicole a couple of feet. "Pappy, you got a point there. That guy wouldn't have a chance. I mean she's already got—"

Nicole stopped my sentence with a long arm crash into my chest, two feet away. She wasn't even looking at me.

Pappy burst out laughing then gave those hands a slap and said, "Nicole, you like that man, don't you?" He was pointing at me, the guy in pain.

With a look, she gave me one of those female smiles, with eyes telling me to obey. "I'm sorry, John. I shouldn't have done that. Please move close to me. Please?"

She added to that plea with her finger doing the come-here wiggle.

I shifted my chair so it was touching hers. She put both arms around me and gave me a public kiss. Not long, but touching. Once our lips parted, she wrapped her arm around mine and grabbed my hand.

Mother Betty said nothing. But Pappy did. "John, she may elbow you every now and then, but she's still fond of you. I highly suggest you keep that in mind."

Nicole's eyes were focused on me. I felt she was giving me permission to speak. For my own safety, I kept it short. "I will, Pappy."

Nicole smiled. Pappy laughed, again. Mother Betty was still not happy.

I gave an eye to Nicole and a head tilt toward her mother. Nicole picked up the intent.

"Mama, you'll have to forgive me with all this. Sometimes our guys say dumb stuff and we have to remind them not to."

The next woman really surprised me.

Mother Betty looked to Pappy. "Nicole, you're so right. We women must keep these men in their place. They'd be lost without us, wouldn't they?"

You can guess who was the only person at the table with permission to answer that. "Very true, Mama," said Nicole.

It was time to get out of that frame of mind and keep my hide attached. I took the chance. "Anybody hungry? I am."

That got a pleasant response from all. I mentioned that Mother Betty didn't have a menu, but she said she didn't need one.

We ordered, ate, and the food was delicious as usual. Pappy managed to eat with us while heading for the kitchen a couple of times. Mother Betty asked about the girls. It was well after six and I was worried, too. Nicole called them. They wanted to eat with Noémi and the boys. I asked to speak with one of them.

Nicole handed me the phone.

"Hi, Uncle John. You worried about us?" It was Lizzy. I pictured her grinning.

"Well, maybe a little." I could hear their soft laughter.

"We're okay, Uncle John," said Patty. I could hear them both breathing. The phone must have been between them, inches apart.

"Whatcha got planned for tomorrow?" I asked. I also knew those at the table would not be part of it. I held the phone so Nicole could hear.

Lizzy answered, "We're doing some shopping. Nathan and Andre know some places to look."

Nicole and I exchanged looks and I asked, "I take it I'll need to fund that spree?"

Patty got in on the call. "It's okay, Uncle John, we'll probably just be looking."

"Girls," Nicole added, "you need to get back to the hotel soon."

Patty again. "Don't worry. We'll be back there by eleven."

Nicole was not pleased. "That's much too late."

Lizzy said, "No it's not. Uncle John, please let us stay till eleven?"

When Nicole heard that switch I saw tears in her eyes. She pulled away just a little and whispered, "You talk to them."

"Okay," came out quiet.

I left the phone where it was and gave them the order. "I agree with Nicole. Now, you leave there at nine. Exactly nine. The boys will watch you get in the cab. You'll get here about nine thirty. We'll all feel better knowing you're safe. Is that understood?"

My voice was firm but kind.

I heard two sad replies in unison. "Yes, Uncle John."

"And, if they want to kiss you, that's okay. A hug and a kiss is always a good thing. Not sure why I even brought that up. It's gonna happen anyway."

The two girls giggled. "That's so sweet of you, Uncle John. You understand, and it means so much." Patty had a happier sound. "The boys heard what you said. They liked it, too."

All four were pleased, and that wasn't a surprise. Been there a few times, myself, in the distant past.

Nicole leaned close to the phone with an, "I love you." I said the same. The girls returned the words and the call was over.

Pappy heard it all but said nothing, just watched. Mother Betty said, "John, I really didn't expect that from them. They do love you. Please don't hurt them."

Speaking directly to Mother Betty with a brief shake of my head. "I would never do that."

My last word had barely left my mouth when Nicole quickly added, "No, he wouldn't, Mama. And they know it. That's why they didn't listen to me. They had to know what John wanted." Nicole took my arm. "John, I'm tired. Let's go to your room."

Her command was taken and we said our goodnights. Pappy asked that I keep him in the loop of what we were going to do tomorrow. I told him I would.

Nicole and I headed for the eleventh floor.

When we entered my room, she flipped off her shoes and led me to the sofa. I was tired, too. We sat there leaning on each other, in silence. She dozed off before I did. When she was fully asleep, I eased up and put some money in an envelope and put it on the table. Then rejoined Nicole.

Acting like I'd woken up suddenly. "Boy, that was scary."

I startled Nicole. She did a little jump. "Why do you keep saying that? What's so scary?"

"What they said. I'm not used to that, at least not from teenage girls."

"You'll get used to it. Let's go over our plans for tomorrow. I need to be ready in case I have to cry." She added a soft giggle to keep it pleasing.

"We'll see Loodvic, as you've so named Ludovic."

That got her going. With hands moving all around, you would think she was swatting imaginary houseflies. "Now, cut that out. I can't remember his name. It's too weird."

"Just think of it as Lou-door-vic. On second thought, forget that. Call him Larry."

That got a pleasant response from her. "Then it's official. We'll see Larry tomorrow morning. But what can you ask him? About all we know is Larry works for Signature and is rarely in the office."

"I can ask him if he knew your father. If it's a no, I'll bring up Gagnon and see where that leads. If it's a yes, I'll lightly lead him into your father's accident and pursue any answers he gives, attempting to keep it friendly."

"Then what?"

"I feel like I'm the one being interrogated."

"You are. Answer my question." Nicole wasn't giving up.

"We'll go where that leads. Ah, and, I want to know more of that Saint-Denis place. Sounds interesting. And, maybe another visit to Signature, and then back to Noémi's place. I'm hoping to learn a lot more there."

"I don't expect much. Daddy told us so very little about his job, too secret, he always said. And if it was, Noémi can't have much either."

"Could be. Some people are keepers and some are tossers. My dad never threw anything away. I found old bank statements. Pictures from his childhood. Things about his first jobs, while he was in high school. Even found a handmade tablet where his mother wrote down the movies she saw when she was a teenager."

"Mama has that sort of thing. Daddy had some old pictures but not much more. Guess he was a tosser. But he did have pictures of me and Patty."

In the midst of our chatting there was a knock on the door. Nicole went to answer it. I heard the door open, as Nicole said, "John, put your clothes on. There's two young girls at the door."

I heard laughing, then Patty's voice. "Hope we're not disturbing you."

It was obvious who it was.

"Okay, you two. Get in here. I have clothes on."

Next thing I knew, they were standing in front of me with smiles.

With hands out and palms up, I said, "I do have clothes on, as you see. And, I had them on when you knocked, just so you know."

Why I felt the need to tell them all that still puzzles me.

In a flash, the girls were on the sofa, one on each side of me up on their knees. Nicole joined them, sitting on the floor. I was surrounded.

They were quiet and smiling. I was at a loss. "So, what's this all about? Think I've been captured by a tribe of women."

Next thing I knew, the one on the floor was planting a kiss on my lips and the two beside me did the cheeks. All were giggling, at me, best I could tell. I couldn't see through all the hair.

"Okay. Okay, girls, enough," I uttered firmly. They backed off. "On second thought, that wasn't enough." A man must go along with a trend, sometimes.

They did the kissy thing again and backed off on their own.

"I must admit, that was a first. Can you tell me why you did that?"

Lizzy started with, as best I can describe it, a pleasantly serious expression. "I lost my father two years ago. I have missed him so much. He would kiss me night-night every night. He'd sometimes sit on the edge of the bed and tell me things. He was wonderful. Since he died, I've cried most every night."

Her eyes teared up, but no water on her cheeks. She controlled her emotions well.

I knew of her story. I gave her a little flip of her nose with my finger. "Lizzy, I was young when my mother died, I don't think I was near that affected. When I lost my father, I shed my share of tears." Then I looked at Patty. "You were so young when your father died, it had to be the same."

"Yes, it was," said Patty. "I cried so much it hurt, but over the years it got easier. Then you came along. I know it's only been a few days and I don't expect you to replace him, but it's been so special having a man watch over us. I found how much I missed it."

Lizzy added, "Same for me. That's why I called you Uncle. And when you told us to leave at nine, I didn't want to, but I knew I had to.

Oh, when we told Mother Noémi, she said we should do as he, you, say. And, that's the words she used."

That was a special time, one I'll never forget, but I couldn't resist. "It's good to have her on my side. I'll have to make my commands less acceptable."

That got me three faces with twisted lips, and my hands trying to stop the three love taps, unsuccessfully.

"I'm kidding. I'm kidding. So, what are your plans for tomorrow?"

Patty chipped in on that one. "Uncle John, we already told you, remember?"

Nicole had to have her say. "Girls, he's sometimes the typical man. Never listens to what we girls say."

It was my time to have the last word at least once. "Ha, gotcha. Shopping. You're going shopping. I remembered. Just wanted to hear what you'd say." I got more love slaps. "Would one of you get that envelope on the table?" I pointed to it and Lizzy retrieved it. "That belongs to both of you. Go ahead. Open it up."

When Lizzy opened it up, she let out a light scream. "There's a lot of money in here. I don't know how much, but—but—"

I said, "It's the equivalent of five hundred US dollars for your shopping trip."

Nicole was first to respond. "John, it's sweet, but you can't do that."

Patty added her feelings, "No, we can't. It's sweet of you, but we shouldn't."

Lizzy started to speak, and I put a finger over her lips. "You girls have appointed me your uncle, and as an uncle, I can, at my discretion, provide shopping funds. Now, it's yours. Not much, but it might buy you a couple of something nice. It's your money to spend on you; don't give it away. Uncle John has spoken. Got that?"

Nicole replied, "This reminds me of something Uncle John told me." Speaking to me, she said, "Tell them about your nanny."

The girls looked at each other, smiled, and almost in unison asked, "You had a nanny?"

Lizzy picked up the hint. "Tell us about her."

That was not something I expected to do. "We called her Nanna Bolton. Her first name, Mattie Mae."

Nicole helped get it going. "From what you told me, she must have had a big house with all those children."

"You might think so, but it was nowhere near normal. She only had two rooms. I never knew, but later in life I wondered if it was a railroad boxcar."

Patty picked up on that. "Uncle John, no one can have a family and live in a boxcar."

"I was young, and I only know what I saw. It probably wasn't, but the front door was wide. And, you had to move it sideways like the one on a boxcar."

Lizzy asked, "Surely there was a living room?"

"There was no room. When I walked in the door, the back door was straight ahead about twelve feet. The kitchen was on the left. The immediate left. I remember a wood-burning stove and an old-style icebox and a sink with only one faucet. The bedroom was on the right. There were only two beds—one full, one twin. No sofa. One chair and one lamp sitting on the floor."

Nicole was hearing more than I'd told her earlier. "Dear God, John. No one could live there. How many children did you say she had?"

"Three girls and two boys. Her younger son was JC. We played together a lot."

"She had to have money. Where did she get it?" Nicole's question was on point.

Patty gave the opinion most would think of, "Her husband would've made money. That's where she got money. That's the way it works."

"Patty, in all my years there, I only saw a man one time. It was a cousin, I think. I have a vague memory her husband died years before."

Lizzy jumped on a possibility. "Insurance. They probably had insurance, and when the father died, she got that money to live on." She ended that with a smile and a nod of her head.

"Her husband may have been there when she looked after my father, but from what I remember, except for children being older, her home didn't change. I can't believe they could afford insurance."

"That can't be real," Lizzy said, almost confessing.

"I never knew where she got her money. Too young to think about it. In those days she probably got money from churches and the state. I know Daddy gave her more than she asked for. He would bring food to help with what she fed me and Jake."

Nicole added, "John, your father must have been as sweet as you. I can't begin to imagine what it was like living like that." She was shaking her head through all we were saying.

"Doubt anyone could, but she did. This I know. She never went to school, but when it came to living a life, she was smarter than anyone I've ever known. She knew what made you happy and what made you sad."

Nicole was still sitting on the floor, but by then was resting her arms on my legs. "I think she taught you more than you know. She would be proud of you. I bet she's watching you now."

That got nods and yeahs.

Lizzy closed her fingers together and put them on my shoulder. Speaking soft and slow, she said, "I guess there're very few people who will remember her or even know she existed. I'm glad I'm one of them." I wondered if she knew how true those words were.

Patty added, "Me too. Thank you, Uncle John, for telling us about her."

That sorta brought things to a close. The girls gave me hugs and cheek kisses, and I shooed them out. It was after ten, and they needed to be in their room. Besides, I was tired.

Nicole moved to the sofa. "That has to be the sweetest thing I've ever seen. Those girls will love you forever. Me too."

"You know as well as I, they'll find their man and fall in love with him and build a longtime relationship. Well, I hope they do. And, they'll slowly forget the old guy they met years ago. That's life, and that's okay. I'll remember them, and that's my treasure."

"Sometimes you make too much sense. Daddy had no brothers or sisters. Mama had one of each, but they've moved to different places out west and are getting old. We don't see them much."

"It's called life. And we have to make time for older relatives."

"John, sometimes you make too much sense. I'm tired and sleepy."

"You just said that."

"I know. What time is it?"

Checked my watch. "It's a few minutes after ten."

"Let's go to bed. You take your bath and I'll get my night things."

"Hope your mother isn't there."

"I'll leave her an absentee note. It's approved by Uncle John."

CHAPTER 18

A VISIT TO LARRY'S

Wednesday morning arrived calm and quiet. I didn't set the alarm, on purpose. It was close to nine. As to breakfast, the girls had money to get the boys to the hotel, or they could go to their home. I had added extra in the envelope for any needed transportation.

The woman lying beside me was still asleep. I found myself staring at the ceiling, again.

Now, if Larry makes people disappear and his partner is Jules, then Jules must be the one who does the doing. But they wouldn't do the autopsy, in either country. I'd thought it before, and my mind brought it up again. The two governments had to be in cahoots. And, maybe Signature, with Larry and Jules's help, could have successfully eliminated both men. But why?

In novels, I've read and the movies I've seen, William and Gustav could have discovered something embarrassing to high government officials. In a dictator run country, the government would just kill you. The worry would be gone. But not in France, nor the USA. Too many possible leaks. Like John Kennedy. One guy shoots him, but who was really behind it? The real truth we'll never know.

The big question in this case was, did I want to discover the why? I could end up wearing a pair of cement boots waving at salt water fish on the way down.

In the midst of my pondering, I felt a wiggle, turned my head and observed a pair of green eyes watching me, "I see you're awake." It was obvious, but I needed to say something.

She was still lying on her pillow with her hands tucked under it. "You're staring at the ceiling again." No particular expression accompanied those words.

With eyes still looking at her, "You noticed? Yeah. Trying to put pieces of this mystery together."

"Why weren't you staring at me?" Keep in mind, she was talking with her face half hidden in the pillow.

I shifted to an elbow and gave her nose a little finger swipe. "Seeing you lying there causes my brain cells to fog up."

One eye was partially visible but open, while the other opened wide. "Is that a good thing?"

I'd gotten her attention and enjoyed the view.

"It's a yes and a no." Think I uttered those words trying to cover all the emotional bases.

"Huh?" At least it got her a little more, shall we say, attentive.

I pondered a moment, searching my brain for an answer. "Yes, you're a pleasant thing to look at, which causes me to only think of you. No, because you're a pleasant thing to look at, which causes me to only think of you." I was confident all bases were covered.

Next thing I knew, she raised up on her elbow and wiggled her nose. "That is the strangest thing I've ever heard you say."

"See?"

She leaned close and kissed me. "I understand. So, look at the ceiling and tell me what you were really thinking about."

Per her command, I put the ceiling in focus. "I was just rolling the things I know over in my brain hoping to connect the pieces. Both governments had to be involved, but what would be so bad to kill them?"

"Well, I have no idea. Did the ceiling tell you anything?" She added a grin with that.

That caused me to chance a peek at her. "You're being cute and I like it." I shifted my gaze back at the ceiling. "Governments will get rid of people usually because they find out something the government does not want anyone to know. Dictators will just kill you, but that's not so easy with these two governments."

"I see what you mean. But with so many employees, it would be hard to cover up, wouldn't it?"

"Good thinking. And true. But, somehow, they did. I must confess, I want to know more about that factory where Gagnon died. It's too much of a mystery."

Nicole suggested rather firmly, "It must be nine thirty. I'm excited and hungry. Let's do breakfast."

"I'm for that. Ah. The ceiling went silent. Must have been looking at you."

Kiss received.

After dressing and eating, it was after eleven, and we headed for Larry Rousseau's place. Those early mornings kept happening.

Nicole was wearing a tight-fitting shirt, shorts, and sandals that laced almost up to her knees. A very sexy look.

There was nothing to slow us down. We discovered Mother Betty hanging around the hotel waiting for Pappy. The girls had left, and with a phone call, we knew they were at Noémi's place with the boys, and safe.

It was about a half-hour drive and we were back in Montrouge, pulling into the parking lot at the Amargo de Paris apartments, again.

Before we even stepped through the door, I remembered the six floors and the impressive entrance. With a touch, I discovered the silver poles were plastic. The other two hotels we visited were more common pain brick and stone. They had double doors but not fancy ones. This one had double glass doors, with gold trim and classy lettering. Okay, not real gold but a good imitation. The revolving door was a good addition. We stepped inside and took the lift.

In a couple of minutes, we were standing in front of apartment 302. I was deciding if we should knock. Why, I don't recall.

Nicole caught me deciding. "Well, you gonna knock or just examine the door?"

"Hey. I'm thinking. You just remember to cry when ready." She pulled back her hand that became a fist to let me have it, then backed off. I knocked.

In a few seconds, the door opened and a five-foot-eleven, slim but well-built man with dark brown hair and tanned skin stood there. He was about an inch shorter than me.

I started with my usual question. "Good morning. Do you speak English?"

"Yes. Who are you and what do you want?" He spoke English right out of the shoot, and, I might add, was well spoken. His tone wasn't angry, but only approaching friendly.

With language settled, figured I'd try for the who. "We'd like to speak with Mr. Rousseau."

His expression didn't change much. "Why?" was his noncommittal reply. He wasn't quite ready to be friendly.

Pointing to Nicole was my next-best chance to get more than one-word replies. "This is Nicole Powell. Her father worked for Signature Consulting several years ago and was in an accident."

Nicole raised her hand slowly accompanied with a gentle smile. "Yes. Hi." She took control and captured his attention. Good timing, I thought. "I'm trying to find more information about my father's accident. It was seven years ago. He was killed in America, in the state of Georgia." His head tilted almost unnoticeably. "I know so little, and John," she pointed at me, "brought me here to see if we can learn more about his death."

The man held off for a moment, then asked, "What was your father's name?" The tone of his words changed. Not so much friendly, but curious.

"William Powell. He worked for Signature Consulting at the time."

Larry put his hand to his chin as if thinking about what she said and what he would do. "I am Rousseau, and yes. I believe I do remember him." He paused and regrouped with a hand extended for us to enter. "Forgive me. Please come in."

His English wasn't just good; it was close to perfect.

We entered his nice—make that expensive—furnished apartment. There was a bar and several wine and liquor bottles displayed.

He led us to a leather couch as he took a chair in front of us, causally leaning back in it. He rested his outstretched arms on the chair arms. "May I get you something to drink? Hot tea, water, a beer?"

His position didn't seem like he really wanted to get us something. In my book, it was a polite gesture.

"Not for me. Nicole, anything for you?"

I only wanted info. Besides, I wasn't sure I wanted to consume anything he had to offer except information.

"No. I'm okay, just anxious. I know so little." Her hands were clasped together resting in her lap. A guiltless and submissive posture.

Larry picked up on her words. "I can understand your urgency, Miss Powell. Are there any specific questions you wish to ask? That may help me provide the information you need."

"Yes, I have questions. I do know he had left France and was back at home, I think, for a few months. Do you know what project he was working on? I wonder if it was some top-secret thing."

"That's something I wouldn't be privy to. Any projects he and his department would have been working on would be above my pay grade. It's been so long, I might could do a little digging and see what turns up. What would that give you?"

He had a good question. Possibly he was wondering if it was worth his time. His eyes shifted from her to something then back at her.

Nicole's face went sad with hands tightly gripping themselves. "I'm sorry. I just don't know what to ask." But, she wasn't done. As soon as she said that, I saw her hands loosen. She paused and tilted her head, which lasted at least a second. Then, with her body and hands at full attention, she took off. "Now. He was working with another guy." She turned to me. "John, what was his name?"

"Yes. It was, oh my, ah . . . yes, Gagnon. Gustav Gagnon."

Larry Rousseau's eyes lit up. "Yes. I remember him. And they worked together, often. If I recall, Monsieur Gagnon was killed. I must admit, I haven't thought of this in years."

If this guy wasn't for real, he was good at sounding like he was. Nicole smiled. "Yes, they did work together. I was told he had died. Could they have been working together on the same project when they were killed?"

Larry leaned forward in his chair, with hands clasped together and eyes darting between Nicole and me. "I think we can cease this useless probing. You probably know more than I do. You've been to the homes of my friends and to Madame Gagnon's home. You're in effect interrogating me. A useless effort at that. I suggest you zero in on what you truly want, or leave."

I gave Nicole a nod. Our game was up. "Monsieur Rousseau, I do apologize. We only got a little from Madame Gagnon and from two others, a Pelletier and Nicolette Martel, pretty much nothing. Nicole's father was burned to the point of identifying him only by his wallet and a ring. There's so much we don't know. And, we had no knowledge you would be any different than the others we've questioned."

"Monsieur Stone, I appreciate your honesty." And he knew who we'd questioned.

He'd just finished those words when Nicole intervened, and it wasn't a slow, polite intervention.

She let him have it with a full blast of emotion. "Those two men worked together a lot, and both died in the same year. I need to know what they were working on and if that's what got my father killed."

Her words caused the need for a tissue from her purse. She dabbed her eyes. Not a lot of tears, but it was certain her words had exposed hidden emotions.

"Miss Powell, your sincerity is appreciated. Here's what I know. Yes, they were working on the same project. I know they were because it was secretive. Being secretive, I was not privy to it. Most general projects, I knew of. This one, no."

I saw it. He looked away from her, then back again. There was a window over to his left, but I saw nothing distinctive, only a distant tall building and clouds.

But, he may have been opening up, so I added my question. "Do you know where Monsieur Gagnon was killed? I know it was in some city called Saint something."

"Yes. That's Saint-Denis. Northeast of Paris. A very old heavy manufacturing town. Let me think." He put his fingers to his lips and glanced around the room. "Karthos Manufacturing. It was somewhere near the canal. Dépôt Street, I think. It's been much too long."

That was good info. "Could that plant still be open?"

"From what I recall, it closed very soon after Gagnon was killed. Many of those plants have closed. Business moved to other places and countries. Ah, I recall. It's at Rue Dépôt Raspail. I don't recall much of the building, but knowing the manufacturing buildings around France, it will be at least two stories and long. And abandoned."

I was surprised he gave me so much detail. I wondered the reason. "That's appreciated. I'll give it a visit and remove another piece of mystery."

Larry did an agitated shake of his head sending me a firm reply, "I suggest you do not. If you break in, the police will know and arrest you. Unsure how they do it, but they keep track of such things." His eyes did not waver even for a moment.

I didn't expect that. "You're probably right, but I must at least try."

"Then please be careful."

His reply came across as somewhat sincere, which caused me to wonder why I doubted his sincerity. I felt he knew more about us than he let on. And, just as Pappy said, he was very polite.

He had good knowledge. I dug more. "As best you know, both men died? Were actually killed. Is that right?

"This I will share with you, but I ask you not to repeat it, as it could be dangerous for me. And for both of you, should the wrong people hear it."

He paused, eyeing us both. I replied, "Monsieur Rousseau, you can be sure it's our secret. There's too much unknown about all this."

Nicole gave a friendly "Me too."

He added more. "There was something both men saw or heard, and started tracking it. That's when someone decided they had to be silenced. I heard they knew something they should not have known."

"That's what I was thinking." And it was.

Larry continued, "I only know that because I overheard those few words in a chance conversation behind me. I was suddenly distracted and missed whatever else was said. I never heard nor read anything else."

His words connected to my thoughts. "Do you think only Signature had it done, or were the French and US governments involved?"

"I believe Signature would have done the deed, but there had to be someone else, someone high up to continue the cover-up. Unfortunately, that's all I know. Over time the issue was silenced."

He did it again. As he spoke to me, his eyes changed their focus to the left again, then back to me. What was so distracting out that window?

Nicole was crying. I took her in my arms. "Monsieur Rousseau, you have given us so much good information. If there's ever anything I can do to repay you, please let me know."

He smiled and yielded his hand. I shook it as he added, "There is nothing to repay. Go and take care."

We said our goodbyes and left his apartment.

In the car Nicole said, "Did you hear what I did? Daddy was killed. He's dead. There was always hope, but no more."

"That's what I heard. I want to go to Pappy's. We could spend some time there and tell what we heard in a roundabout way. I don't want to cause Pappy troubles."

"I want to go to the hotel, your room. I feel safe and loved there."

"Me too."

Driving to the hotel, Nicole was quiet. with her head laying against the seat in my direction.

I wasn't ready to give my true thoughts to Nicole, or anyone for now. I heard what Larry said, and he sounded truthful. But was he? His words were a carbon copy of my thoughts. Someone high up in either government, with help from Signature, could have had them killed in falsified accidents. Killing them because of their knowledge.

And, when Rousseau was talking about the project being secretive. It was the way he said it. I was watching him. Something wasn't right, but my senses were blurred.

That visit caused me to remember one time when Nanna Bolton and JC were out picking blackberries. I got there in time to help. There were some growing wild near the barbwire fence behind her house. A snake bit JC. She grabbed him, went inside, and did the cutting on his leg and sucked out blood.

After watching her do that, I asked how she knew. She told me that snakes put stuff in ya that ain't supposed to be there. She topped that off with "Sometime some man'll do dat. Dat ain't so easy to shoo way. Ya jist gotta know a bigger snake."

I'll always remember the grin she had.

It was hotel time. I hoped it would offer Nicole some peace. Next was to be a visit to Karthos Manufacturing. The plant could be useless, but I had to know.

This investigation was getting too calm. I wondered, no felt, it could become adventurous, or most likely dangerous.

I decided I may need the help of a bigger snake.

CHAPTER 19

FACTORY FACTORS

We got to the hotel about one o'clock without lunch. And, from some unknown hunch, I suspected lunch was not on the menu.

When I opened the room door, Nicole walked in, removed her sandals, and lay down on her side of the bed. She patted the bed for me to join her, and I did, also after removing my shoes. I turned to face her but didn't lie down.

She remained quiet for a couple of minutes. "I've wanted so much for him to be alive, but he's not."

"So was I, for your sake."

"I know. John, I'm so depressed, I can't think. Are we ready to go home?"

"I'd like to stay and do more digging. I can't believe those two men did something so bad they had to be killed. There has to be more to this."

"If the government is involved, you won't find anything. They could harm you for even trying. I can't bear to see you hurt."

She had a point, and I didn't want her to get hurt either.

The odds were against us, but I wasn't ready to give up. "This is just speculation, but I have a feeling Pappy and a group of activists or some such has ways to keep their government under control."

"John, you're a smart man, but that can't exist today. The French Revolution ended when it did. It can't still exist."

"You're right, but I've got a little more digging to do. Pappy's behind-the-scenes procedures may be fictional, but this is bugging me more and more."

"Yeah. And, they may swat you like a fly." She had no happy face when she said that.

"Good analogy. I'll watch for swatters." She didn't think that was funny. "Look. I want to know what was so bad a man had to be killed. I want your father's killer exposed and his name cleared."

Her expression was filled with both hope and distress. "So do I, but not with you being hurt. I want to know what happened, and I don't want you to be. I can't even say the word. Let's just go home."

"Sweetheart, if I don't go after this, I'll always wonder. I don't like to wonder. You stay here and rest. I'm heading for the factory."

I knew that would never happen. But she needed to get out of her somber mood.

As expected, it didn't set well.

She was up on her knees in a flash. I think the Big Bang took longer.

Her expression and words were not in anger. More like determined. "Like hell I am. I'll be there and learn what you learn. You got that?" Her finger was digging a hole in my chest.

My reply was going to hurt—me. "I knew you would." I felt the urge to run.

Her hands went to her hips. If eyes could burn, hers would be flaming. "You! You!"

"Now, be careful young woman. Words can hurt. Mostly me." I ended that with a grin.

She hit my upper arm with her fist. It hurt a little.

Her finger waving at me embellished her reason up a notch. "And don't tell me it didn't hurt, because I saw it on your face. Ha!"

I leaned a little closer to her. "Okay, it hurt a little, and you're coming with me. I have no choice, for there's no way out. Are you happy?"

With volume down a notch, she replied, "Yes, I'm happy, and I know what you did." Then her voice got softer. "You pulled me out of my depressed hole." She moved close and held my face in her hands. "I'm glad you don't give up. Daddy would've liked you."

"I guess you realize, the rope I pulled you out with just got wrapped around my neck."

"I know. It may be an imaginary rope, but I gotcha." Her face acquired a pleasant glow.

"Now that I've lost all control, can we leave?" If that sounded like I was pleading, I was.

It took us about forty minutes to get to Saint-Denis and locate a street leading to the Rue Raspail. Finally, I turned one last corner, and there it was, eating up the entire block. Scratch the eating thought. It was so old and abandoned, I'd believe it starved to death.

The building was three stories tall, some brick in front and concrete walls of what I could see. The windows were large, of the factory variety, encircling at least the sides I could see. Each window had a foot-tall metal fence at the base. Had no idea what that was for. But it was still there after seven years.

One odd thing. There was a blue plastic trash bin sitting by the curb at the end of the building. Looked new. Why would it be needed with the factory closed?

Getting inside would be the challenge. The front door was large and metal, both to prevent unauthorized entry assisted with a healthy dead bolt and a padlock. No visible rust, but the area was full of dirt and other trashy stuff. The cleaning crew hadn't shown up lately.

Nicole had been watching me check things out. She kept scanning the street with eyes like radar in all directions.

"You nervous?" I queried.

With her arms holding each other against her chest. "Yes. This whole place looks, looks old, and eerie."

"I agree with that. Let's see if the rear has an entrance."

"Do we have to?"

She could not keep still. If I didn't know better, her feet were dancing. She kept turning to watch in all directions, more than once.

"Well, it's a maybe, but I wanna see the inside. Go sit in the car. It shouldn't take me long."

That got her riled up. The dancing feet froze as she let me have it, with words just under a yell. "You're crazy. I'm not going to sit there alone. Go do something. I'll follow you. Go!" Her hands were flapping at me to move.

I had my orders, but as I headed for the trash bin, the hand flapping stopped. She was a half step behind, clutching my hand. Make that gripping. Felt like she wrapped our hands in duct tape.

It took a couple of minutes to reach the back of the building. Behind the main structure, there were some smaller ones. Wasn't a good view. The thing took up the full block, or whatever the French call it.

Approaching the bin, which was at the curb, I turned and saw a loading dock with several large, vertical entry doors with space to back up eighteen-wheelers. None were present, but there was a green door, a normal sized door, locked, which needed only a key.

She was watching. "You're going to pick that, aren't you?"

"I'm going to try. I want to know what's behind the green door."

"Hah. I heard that. Green door? It's not the time to be cute. Like Larry said. The police will get you."

I was down on my knees working the lock. I looked up at her. "Not if we're quiet."

That got me a "Hmph!"

The lock clicked. I stood up and turned the knob. The door wasn't stuck, but it did crack a little as I slowly opened it.

"Okay, you come behind me." I was inside just past the door frame when she grabbed my waist. "Not that close. If there's anything in here, I want you to be able to run." She let go. I stepped inside. Something hit me. I felt myself falling to the floor, and everything went blank.

I regained consciousness with my head spinning as I heard Nicole say, "Wake up, John. You okay? Please wake up. Oh, dear God, please wake up."

It was hard to move. Took a bit to find I was lying on the floor with my head in her lap. My vision was fuzzy, but I saw her looking down at me. I vaguely remember asking where I was and what happened.

"Oh, thank God, you're okay. That man hit your head with a bottle. He knocked you out."

The head she was referring to was hurting. My hand went to the top of my head, but not for long. It hurt. "What man?"

"That old guy. Him!" she declared as her arm flew out pointing at something.

I started to rise. Didn't work. With her help, I managed to sit up. There he was. An older man was also lying flat. "Him?" I tried to point, but my arm fell down.

Her eyes focused back on me. "Yes."

Still looking at him. "What happened to him?"

"I knocked him out!" Her words were happy ones. No fear at all.

My consciousness was returning, but all I had was "Huh?"

"You were just past the door inside. You turned to me to complain about making noise and he hit you. I didn't know what to do, so I kicked him you know where, and when he bent over I used my knee to hit him under his chin. Saw it in a movie. And, there he is. I must admit my knee hurts a little, but it was fun."

Admiring what she did, I added, "Remind me never to sneak up on you. Help me up."

Once on my feet, with Nicole holding on tight, I saw we were at a side entrance. The area was large and must have been the loading dock area for whatever they made. There was an office over to the left, or what was left of it. The real eye-opener was no trash or heavy dust far as I could see. The whole area had been swept clean.

My arms spread wide. "Do you see how clean this place is? The whole place?"

She saw it, too. "Yeah. It is. But why? Maybe that man lives here."

"Maybe. No idea."

With my head approaching normal, he then looked to be in his fifties or sixties.

I bent over him and tapped his face. He was breathing, and his heart was beating.

Facing him, I said, "He's alive. Possibly our friend here can tell us." I looked up at Nicole. "Stay close, but see if you can find some water."

With one arm fully extended and pointing, she said, "There's some over there in the office. There's a bottle sitting on the cabinet."

"Must be his. Get it. I'll stay here with him."

He wasn't moving, but I kept my knee resting lightly on his chest. He could've been faking it.

She took off quickly and was back in a flash. I took the bottle and splashed a little over his face. He didn't move. I gave him a heavier splash, which worked. His arms were moving all around then his hands hit the floor and sat him up. He was not happy.

He said something in French. No interpreter, just when I needed one.

Nicole's excited voice sounded off. "More French. I'll call the boys and get them over here."

She got the old man's attention. "I speak English. Why you here? No one is supposed to be here?"

Figured it was time for intros. "My name's John. This is Nicole. Be nice. She's the one who put you to the floor."

Still on the floor, he said, "Yes. No sooner than I saw her, everything went black. Now, old bones hurt."

Nicole asked him, "What's your name?"

"Marcel Moe Clair."

I presented our intentions. "Marcel, we're not here to hurt you. Only to look around. If I help you up, will you not run or try to hurt us? We mean you no harm."

"Help me up. I won't hurt anyone, and I got nowhere to run."

As I helped him to his feet, he began dusting himself off and calmly said, "If they find you here, they will arrest you and *feu* me." He shook his head. "I mean fire me. Please leave."

When I heard that, I shut the green door and flipped the lock.

Nicole answered, "We will leave. I promise. But, you see, a friend of my father died here, and my father died soon after in America, near my home there. I know so little, and this place may tell us more. Please let us look around, just a little?"

The old man dropped his head then brushed his finger across his nose as if he felt a tear. "But only for a while. If they come, they will be angry." She gave him a hug. He hugged back a little, then said, "Enough of that. Do your looking." He ended his command with a short smile, with his hands moving as if pushing her away.

She stepped away, then back, and gave him a brief kiss on the cheek. He flapped his hands again, but it was obvious he liked the attention.

I was curious. "Marcel, how is it you speak English so well?"

"My wife. Camille was born in your Virginia. We met when she came here with her parents over forty years ago. I taught her French. She taught me English."

Nicole liked that. "Marcel, that is so sweet. How old was she when you met?'

"A beautiful, unforgettable eighteen." His face grew sad but no tears.

He got another hug from Nicole. He didn't let go till she stepped back.

She wasn't done. With her hands snuggling his arm, she asked, "Marcel, how did Camille die?"

That girl got personal fast, which was good for us. But she wasn't thinking that. She was truly concerned for him.

"A cancer in her brain. She didn't suffer long. She's been gone five years now."

She had more to know. "I'm so sorry to hear that. Your English is so good. She must have been a good teacher."

"She was. We would speak and challenge each other with words. She would say something in French, and I had to come back in English. I did the same in French. After a while, in our daily conversations, she would speak French. I would reply in English. We did that for years. Every day was special. I loved that woman more than life."

Nicole asked, "You must miss her so much?" I too was captured by his story. And, proud of her.

"Every minute of every day. You remind me of her. Camille had blond hair. Wore it long like yours."

There was a tear in her eyes as she spoke. "I'll take that as a compliment, Mr. Moe Clair. Oh, did I say that right?"

"Yes, my last name is Moe Clair. It's a family thing." He smiled, and I don't think it was to be friendly. He was proud of his name.

"That's so sweet. But what are you doing here, now? This place is so old and abandoned. Please don't tell me you live here. Do you live here?"

Her true sentiment came through even with her question. A real concern for him had grown quickly.

"No. I watch over the place. No one has bought it, and vandals come and steal sometimes."

We got lucky. He was better than searching alone. I had a guide. "Marcel, do you remember a Gustav Gagnon? He died here seven years ago."

"No. Never a Gustav Gagnon work here."

"No, he didn't work here, but he was with Signature Consulting and was on a project here in the factory."

"I've heard of Signature Consulting, but not that name." He was shaking his somewhat gray-haired head.

That was a start. I waved my arm around. and asked, "Did this place have large acid tanks?"

"Yes. There were five tanks. Two with hydro acid. Three with sulfuric acid."

I was surprised by the confidence he had in his voice but it told me he knew what he was talking about.

"That's a lot of acid. I'd hate to fall in a batch of it." I used those words to lead into a possible answer.

"Wouldn't happen. Some acids are kept covered and chilled, others just covered to prevent you dropping in. I say that, but in my time here three accidents happened. No deaths, and all was because of a leakage, which was repaired each time."

He was giving good info. I wanted more. "Gruesome, if ya ask me. Guess you'd have to open up a tank and throw someone in it on purpose, which I'd hope would never happen."

"I worked the day shift. Never happened on my shift."

From his words and movements, he was proud of that. But my attempt to get information in roundabout ways wasn't fully working.

"Hmm, so you never heard of anyone accidentally falling into a vat of acid? I'm just curious. I mean, there was so much of the stuff, and running twenty-four hours a day?"

"To be truthful, if it did happen, they'd cover it up and would've been successful. This I know. I've heard it has happened in other factories, but it never got out through official channels. It would be disastrous to the company. Any company. The government would probably attempt to close it down."

Nicole's hands went to her face as tears began to flow.

Marcel stepped close to her and gently put his hand on her arm. "Forgive me for all I said. I didn't mean to discourage you."

She put her arms around him. Through her tears, she said, "I know you didn't do this on purpose. It's just the way it is. And, you've been so kind for telling us all this."

"I'm glad to have a time to do it, my dear." He separated them from their hug to see her face. "You added a pleasant memory of my Camille. I will remember it and you forever."

It was time to go, and I saw my chance. "Marcel, we've been here every bit of thirty minutes. We best be going. You've been a great resource, and I don't want to cause you any troubles."

He shook my hand, letting me know he was glad to help. I exchanged phone numbers in case we had more questions or he remembered anything else. Nicole gave him a hug and we left.

Once outside, I had us cross to the other side of the street. I quietly told Nicole to hold any talking till we got in the car. If anyone was watching or drove by, I hoped it would look like we were not associated with that factory, nor Marcel.

Nicole was thinking hotel. I had been thinking lunch but that factory just didn't play right.

I've seen abandoned factories and that's just what happens. No one hangs around. I kept thinking what was so unique that it was still being watched.

CHAPTER 20

CHARADE ASSEMBLY

We headed back to Paris and our hotel. It wasn't even three o'clock and we'd found another piece of the puzzle. Could be a corner.

On the way, Nicole and I replayed what we'd heard. We found that no one had died there with acid. But, we know someone did. Marcel's notion of a cover-up with no one knowing was possible. Well, possible if very few knew of it.

I wanted the opinion of the blond sitting in the passenger's seat. "Do we believe Noémi's husband died of acid in that factory?"

"Well, he died of acid somewhere. We don't know for certain if that's the factory where they found his body. Everybody has a different story. How do we know who's giving us the truth?"

She had a point.

I knew this was going to be another big discussion. I told her to hold a sec as I pulled over to a parking lot and got back in the groove. She turned sitting on her knees to face me.

Turning best I could. "That's the problem. We don't."

Her hands went up. "I believe Noémi. She would have to be telling the truth based on what she was told and saw. Course, she can't be certain what she was told is the truth. And, neither can we."

"That's our problem. Can't speak for France or any business, but I've worked third shift in the past, many times, and there were always fewer people on that shift."

"I see. With fewer people there, it might be possible to divert their attention long enough to toss someone in the acid and get them out and away."

"Yep. You got it. I'm ready to believe that Gustav Gagnon could have died there. All that's needed was a few of the right personnel to do the toss, get the acid off him, and cart what's left of him away."

"Even easier with my father. He was in a car by himself." She was strong and calm up to that point, but she changed. Her face became tight with anger. "John, if you find them, I want them dead! I'd like to kill them myself."

I started to answer when my phone rang. It was Patty. I held the phone between me and Nicole. "Hi, Patty. What's happening?"

"Me not Patty," came a man's gruff voice. "She tell me you Scone. That right?"

He didn't have my name right, but I knew it was me. "Yes, and why are you using her phone?"

Nicole silently asked what was going on. I held the phone so she could hear, but answered her silent question asking to say nothing.

"Shut up and listen, Scone. I got them two boys and two girls, and you going do what I ask."

Nicole grabbed my arm tight.

"You have her phone, but I don't know you have either of them. I need to talk to Lizzy. Then I'll know."

Nicole started shaking her head. I gave her a silent *Not to worry*, as best I could.

He came back with, "That not happen."

"Do you even know who you're talking to?" I had to be certain, and I wanted to hear his voice more.

He said my name, and added, "I know which you are."

"Good. Then know this is not going any further till I talk to Lizzy. I'll ask the person you have and know if it's them."

He blurted some words that I prefer not to repeat. He gave Lizzy the phone. His last words were "I be listen."

"Hello, Uncle John." It was Lizzy. I'd know her voice anywhere, but he didn't know that.

I had to know more of where they were, and I needed time. "I need you to name a movie, so I can understand if you are who I think you are."

I hoped she would understand what I was doing. Nicole didn't, but I kept whispering for her to not worry.

"Oh, yes. *Charade* is a good one. Do you remember when Cary Grant was at the hotel across from his future S&S office? He said there was a flower shop there and wished it was a pencil shop. And he'd have to use the back door."

She picked up on my game. Felt like the king was in check. Her description was nothing like the movie, but she did a brilliant job of creating needed dialogue, for me.

Before I could reply, he cut off our charade. "Enough. You're will stop looking for Gagnon and Hoywell, and take two girls and family from France. When know you gone, I free two boys."

"And what if I don't?" That's a question always asked. And, even knowing the answer would not be acceptable.

"I kill them all." His anger was certain and expected.

"Okay, okay. I understand. I need some time to get the trip arranged and get the girls from you." That was the truth, but I didn't need it for a plane trip. It was for a rescue operation.

"You got three hours. Call me when ready, and I release girls at location I decide."

"That's not enough. I need more time." I didn't expect him to give me more time, but it never hurts to try.

"That all you have." He went silent.

Nicole's eyes became moist and glistening. She leaned close slapping my chest. "He's going to kill them and all you did was talk about movies."

I grabbed her arms and spoke gently but firm, "I know where they are."

She was crying. Frantic. "No, you don't. No, you don't. You can't know that. Please don't let them get—" She couldn't finish the sentence.

I shook her arms. "Lizzy told me their location with the movie. That was that guy we met at Signature Consulting. Creepy Vadinoye, as you renamed him. Remember he couldn't pronounce your father's name? He couldn't say Powell. He said Hoywell."

She calmed a little. I ran my hands down her arms and held her hands. I kissed her hands, hoping to calm her enough to talk.

Through her fear, she said with shaking words, "You know that? Are you sure you know that?"

"Yes. That's him. He called me Scone. That's too much of a coincidence. It's the Signature guy."

Panic appeared on her face again. "Oh, dear God, what do we do? How do we call 911 over here?"

"Pappy."

It was a crucial time. I needed Nicole to believe I knew what I was doing. I whispered positive words more than once. It didn't take long, and Nicole nodded her head. She was on board.

Luck was with me. Pappy answered his phone. I told him what had happened, all the details and the address in Clichy. He was on his way, and so were we.

And yes, Nicole was with me. I had plans for her.

As planned, we met on a side street out of view. Pappy brought four of his personal compadres. I'd never seen them before, but they were associated with Pappy. Meaning I had a suspicion they had all seen me. They probably knew what I had for breakfast.

No one offered any intros, so I held back with mine and Nicole's.

There was no way to enter from the front without announcing our presence. One of Pappy's guys said something in French, and Pappy said to follow him. With us tailing him, he went back down the side street to an alley. That alley passed the back door of Signature. The back door, just as Lizzy said. She needed a present.

Then it dawned on me, again, that her mother wasn't with us. Under no circumstances could I let anything happen to her. That extended to all of them.

Speaking to the guys, I started, "First, I need to introduce Nicole. One of the girls they have is her sister. She's not going inside till we have the girls in our hands. Meaning this will turn out as I hope."

Nicole did the stare. "You're going inside, why can't I?"

"Could be some guns fired, and I don't want you dead. You're needed when we get the girls and boys out of there. They will be frantic and overwrought with fear, I suspect."

She was about to chew me up when Pappy intervened. "Nicole, he's right. My agents will protect John and anyone needing it. You need to remain outside the front entrance. Please?"

That please must have done it. Excited and speaking fast, she said, "Okay, Pappy. I understand. Tell me what to do."

I told them more details. "Okay, everyone. Lizzy said we would have to use the back door. He must have brought them back here." Then it dawned on me. "Do you guys understand my English?"

"Name's Franco. Glad to finally meet you and Nicole."

"Olivier, here." His hand went up with a nod to Nicole.

"Roger." His hand went up as well, including the nod.

"And I'm Jacques. We all speak English. Nicole, it's good to have you here." He got to the point. "John, you've not been in this back entrance, correct?"

"Correct. My only time here I only saw a door from the front entrance area."

Jacques gave us a risk. "If we open this door, we will most likely warn them."

Crazy thoughts were filling my brain. "How about I go in through the front door, with one of you, and ask to speak to Vadinoye? He may just wonder why I'm there and come out from wherever and confront me."

Pappy was quiet. From his actions, he was letting them take charge.

Franco jumped in. "I'll go with you. Once Vadinoye comes to meet us, I'll call Jacques."

Jacques added, "Pappy, Olivier, and I will go in this door. Roger and Franco, along with you and Nicole, will head for the front entrance."

"Sounds like a plan, but I have one addendum. As soon as I see Vadinoye, I'll have my phone ready and will call Patty's phone. If he doesn't have it, it will ring wherever they are."

Jacques gave us the last piece. "Agreed. Then we'll raid the back area. If the ring is back there, we'll find it. If not, we find the kids."

The plan was good, but there was an unknown. "Vadinoye may have a gun. I don't. Do you?" I queried them all.

They each pulled hidden 9 mms, held them up, and hid them back. Pappy pulled a spare and gave it to me.

Then Franco gave me my actions. "When all this starts, you hit the floor. Vadinoye will know what's happening and start shooting. I suggest you make like no gun." I gave him a nod.

With the plan in place, Franco, Roger, Nicole, and I headed for the front door.

We entered as I'd done before, but that time it had been for a peaceful purpose. Roger remained outside with Nicole. I didn't know why he was hanging outside and didn't ask, but he would keep Nicole safe. Well, for as long as she wanted to be safe. He gave me a thumbs-up as I passed him.

I gave Nicole a brief kiss, "Now, please stay out here." Knowing her, she would remember those words for the same three seconds it took me to say them.

The receptionist asked what we needed. I politely gave her my name and asked to see Monsieur Vadinoye. That it was urgent and we needed his help. She made a call, and in under two minutes, he was standing in front of us.

Vadinoye didn't show it, but he must have been at least a bit surprised. His smile was pleasant, but it had to be make-believe. "It good see you again, but what can I do for you? I not understand why you here." His calm was riddled with lies.

"When I was here last, Naude wasn't much help, but you seemed to be the man who would. Someone has kidnapped the two girls and their two French boyfriends. I'm very concerned he will hurt them. Could you possibly help me find them? It will be dangerous, but I don't know anyone else who could do it."

I did not intro Franco.

Vadinoye kept his composure amazingly well. Had to be due to a multitude of witnesses. "Your words of confidence appreciated, but I not believe I be of help. You should go to police."

He was playing the game well.

I played my part. "I can't do that, he'll kill them."

Just to my side, I could see Franco's finger positioned on his phone, ready to press a button that would alert his comrades out back. I had my cell phone in hand about to scare the piss out of Vadinoye. I displayed my phone and pressed the call button.

"No. No. Not do that." His hands went up waving in an attempt to stop me.

With the phone against my ear, I said, "It's okay. I'm calling him now. He has Patty's phone. I want you to hear him."

The phone in his pocket sang out. I heard Franco say, "Now!" as he stepped further to the side.

Vadinoye backed several steps as his hand swung around. It was obvious he was reaching for his gun. He didn't make it. Franco put three heartfelt rounds in his chest. It was quick. I didn't have time to move.

The receptionist screamed as she and the rest of the office watched him drop to the floor.

Roger came in the door, gun in hand. The lookout was suddenly in the game.

I yelled to the receptionist and others in the office. Even Naude was standing there. "That man was a kidnapper. Stay in your offices. Now! Naude, that goes double for you. Sit down and stay put."

They all took my order except the receptionist. She was frozen with fear. Pointing to her, I ordered, "You! Sit!" I pointed down. She sat quickly and refroze.

Leaving Roger to man the front, Franco grabbed me and we rushed through the door heading for wherever Vadinoye had been before biting the dust. Doing that without knowing what was on the other side was unwise, but we did it. I remember thinking it was my last unwise action.

We were fortunate. We were not dead, yet. The door led to a hallway. From my first glance, there were four doors. Other offices, I guessed.

I saw Jacques and Olivier at one end. In the opposite direction, two men had just launched themselves into the hall with guns drawn. Screams came from the room behind them. I went flat against the wall. Franco said to stay put as he flashed to the other side and did his own flat against the opposite wall.

Jacques and Olivier went down on their knees, firing rounds. Franco and I did the same from our flat surface. All causing more screams from rooms unknown.

Within seconds, there was an eerie silence.

Along with two dead men lying outside the door, where the first set of screams had been heard. All my team was unhurt. All were frozen, still waiting for what the next second would bring.

After a few moments of calm, I had to know. I yelled, "Lizzy, Patty. Stay in the room you're in. Are you okay? Are the boys okay? Are you alone? What's that favorite movie of yours?"

With her crying voice, Patty screamed, "Yes, Uncle John. We're all okay. We're alone."

Lizzy gave me the clue to their surroundings. "And because of you, it's *Blue Skies*."

Those were good words. My concern was any remaining guns in the room. Thanks to Lizzy, that concern faded. "Stay where you are. I will come and get you soon."

It was time to see what the five remaining rooms had to offer. I yelled again for more actions.

"My name is John Stone. The two dead men in the hall kidnapped my family. I want all of you in the hall. Leave any guns you have behind." With emphasis I added, "In the hall, NOW!"

Franco translated for me. He told me he added they should have their hands in the air. Wish I'd thought of that.

There was quiet along with crying as seven women and four men emerged from the other rooms, with hands in the air. They looked like office types based on their apparel.

The men were wearing slacks and white shirts and ties. The women wore pants and blouses and had tissues in their hands. Probably HR and finance personnel. I doubted the two dead ones were sales.

The tissue holders needed instructions. "You women may drop your hands and clear your tears." Franco did the translation.

Within seconds Pappy's team was checking for other unknowns and weapons with the men. I don't know at what point, but Pappy had already called the police.

My goal was the girls. I rushed into the room and was pleasantly attacked by the arms of two girls and two boys. The girls had no tissues. They accepted my shirt.

I heard my name. Nicole wanted my presence. I yelled, and within seconds she was in the room joining the hugs. Tears prevented any talking.

Franco stopped at the door. "John. All is under control. Stay in the room. Police will be inside maybe two minutes." I gave him my thanks.

The crying had slowed, and I asked all to sit and calm down as much as possible. With what they had been through, I didn't expect instant calm.

There was a small table with chairs. Each girl took one and joined her guy, mine included.

As we were sitting, Nicole asked them, "Are you okay? Did they hurt you?"

The boys nodded nos. The girls shook their heads, almost in unison.

Patty spoke first, with hands and arms darting around as if fighting the air. "They scared us. They were evil. They kept threatening us and grabbing our arms making us go or sit where they wanted."

Lizzy added with more descriptive words of what they experienced, "They kept poking us with their guns. Uncle John, it was an awful time." Her arms caressed her breasts. Andre pulled her closer. "Patty will tell you. We kept praying you'd find us. When you called, that was a blessing." Tears were running gently down her cheeks.

Patty was calmer but still wiping tears from her eyes. "Yes. Yes. When you called, I got hope. Uncle John, you gave me hope." More tears appeared on her cheeks as her hand rested in her lap.

They appeared to be calming when both girls leaped up and headed for me. Nicole did her own leap clearing room as the girls filled that space and put their arms all around me. I'd been in a lot of tough spaces, but nothing like this.

I gave them what I hoped were soft, comforting words. "Not to worry. You're safe now." Then a confession appeared in my mind. "I guess you know this is all my fault."

That got me two tearful looks and a not-so-pleasant gaze from the older female.

"My digging put you in harm's way, and I'm so sorry for that."

Unexpectedly, Patty spoke first. She leaned back a little, still holding on. "You, you're looking for my father. I wanted you to, and I still do. Those men wanted you to stop. Please don't." With harsh words, she added, "And…and I'm glad they're dead." That started her tears again.

I gave her a snug hug. "Don't you worry. I'm not going to stop."

Lizzy leaned back just a tiny bit. "Me too. Please don't stop. I know you can find the answer." She snuggled back close, but no tears were shed.

Nicole added her thoughts, "He won't stop, girls. If I know this guy, they just gave him more ammunition." She put her arms around my neck. It all felt good.

With that, I heard an attention-getting grunt from the doorway. Nicole pulled back as our heads turned in unison seeing, best I could tell, a French police officer quietly standing there.

Speaking gently to the girls, I said, "Okay, we need to sit down. There's a police officer needing to talk to us."

After wiping tears on my shirt, all three women took their places with their boyfriends.

The policeman had a suit and tie. Figured he was a detective type. "Good afternoon, Officer. I'm John Stone. I guess you want to talk with us."

He stepped into the room keeping a decent distance, possibly not to alarm anyone. "Good afternoon. I am Détective Thomas Bernard. At your service."

He gave a tiny, almost imperceptible bow. I half thought he was going to click his heels. Guess I've seen too many movies.

I asked the obvious. "I guess you need to ask us some questions. I was with the rescue party. These two girls and boys," I pointed at them, "were the ones who were kidnapped. Do you want us to leave the room as you interrogate each of us?"

With a formal sound, he answered, "That will not be needed. I just need to ask. You, sir, Monsieur Stone, were with the rescue party. I believe you entered from the front entrance. Is that correct?"

"Yes. I did."

"And you were in the outer lobby when Monsieur Vadinoye was shot?"

"Yes, sir. I was."

He nodded to me and turned to the girls. "You two girls and you two boys were taken by the two men dead outside the door here and the third one who left just a few minutes ago?"

The four gave him a yes.

He gave them the nod. I got a nod with words, "Thank you, Monsieur Stone, for assisting me with my questions." With a brief glance to all of us, he finished, "I will leave each of you to go as you wish. I appreciate your assistance."

Everyone's eyes were drifting between him and me. I surmised they were attempting to see what his next move would be. He actions so far were shy of reason. He didn't seem to care.

Before he got completely turned around, I asked, "Three men are dead and there was a lot of gunfire. Do you not wish to take our names?"

"That will not be necessary. I have already received that information from Monsieur Armand. My team has, as you have seen," he did a little head movement in the direction of the hall, "removed the bodies and collected the necessary forensics. I must go now. I have reports to complete. Bonne journée."

He gave another tiny bow and left the room. The whole thing would've been more exciting if he'd clicked his heels.

Everyone at the table looked bewildered, including me. "Okay. What did that guy do? I'll answer that. Nothing. I've felt more investigated when I got a parking ticket. If I didn't know better, I'd say he was taking our names for a raffle."

My poor excuse of past events brought unexpected smiles to my listeners' faces. Didn't mean for that to happen, but glad it did.

I wanted to know more. "Now, if you don't want to talk, just tell me. But I'd sure like to know how they managed to get all four of you."

Patty started, "It was all my fault. I'd bought a dress and was showing and talking about it. I was going on and on and didn't think about where I was."

And she shouldn't have. Nothing like what happened could have been expected. But it did and I knew I needed to be more careful of all of them.

"No, it wasn't your fault. It was mine," said Lizzy. "I was twisting around waving the pair of pants and paying no attention." Again, perfectly normal behavior.

Patty disagreed. "No. It was my fault."

"Oh, no, it was mine," added Lizzy.

Enough was enough. "Okay, girls, let's not fight over this. It was neither of your fault. You did nothing wrong. Now, someone tell me where you were when they took you hostage."

The girls looked at each other. Patty got voted to speak. "We had just come out of a dress shop and were about to get in Andre's car when the three men were just suddenly there with guns, ordering us to keep quiet."

"Yeah," added Lizzy, "we'd never seen them, but we knew we had to do as they said."

Andre saw an opening. "We might could have fought them off, but they were just there so quick."

Nathan had his say. "And, the beards and mustaches were false and came loose couple of times, but they kept them on. They had hats on till they got here."

Lizzy gave her head a brief shake, with lips parted and eyes narrowed. "But Uncle John, when we got here," her eyes swept around the room, hands in the air and palms open, "I knew, we knew, where we were because of how you spoke of it."

"Huh?" And I meant what I said.

Her hands went flat on the table. "Oh, come on, Uncle John. You were talking about the place and how boring it was. That it needed a flower shop across the street." Her hands flipped palms up. "Remember? Please remember?" Her head tilted a tiny bit. I thought she was going to cry.

Nicole gave me a quick glance then told Lizzy, with a finger pointed at me, "Believe me, he remembers. He doesn't talk much, but when he does, he sometimes makes a little sense."

I felt like banging my head on the table, but I refrained. Just had to regain some awareness of where I was. "All right, girls. No fair ganging up on a guy. And I do remember." I said that sticking my tongue out at Nicole.

Laughs filled the room. Even the boys took a chance and smiled.

Rescue was in sight. Pappy stepped into the room. His timing was good, mostly for me.

With a hand flying high, I attempted to switch the attraction. "Hi, Pappy. Been wondering when you'd join us." And wondered where he was.

Pappy threw up a hand and waved it at us to keep some serenity and move thoughts elsewhere. "Just had a few things to clear up. From the laughter, I suspect everyone is okay."

I wondered what those *things* were, but now wasn't the time to ask. I didn't want to lose the joy.

Lizzy's hands were closed together as she spoke, "Hi, Pappy. Uncle John took great care of us. He's wonderful."

"He sure did. He's better than wonderful," added Patty, taking a glance at me.

I wasn't going to take that credit. "Girls, you should know that Pappy and his team did the most, nearly all, the work taking out those guys. I was along mostly for the ride."

Pappy wouldn't let that stand alone. "Sure, I had my team do the cleaning, but if it hadn't been for John, we would not have known where to clean. He figured it out."

Patty reached over and laid her hand on Lizzy's. "And if Lizzy hadn't remembered the flower shop, Uncle John wouldn't have known."

Enough was enough. I was about to speak when Nicole added, "All of you should know that Uncle John knew it was Signature people who did the job. He knew from what the Vadi guy said. He recognized words the kidnapper used. I can't imagine anyone doing that from a onetime three-minute conversation." Her hand brushed gently on my cheek. She also gave me a wink, which I took as a command to speak.

"Ah, now, don't go saying all that. I just got it started. Not much use after that. Pappy took over. He kept everyone safe."

Pappy added, "Guess we all had some part in this. And the police have it under control. They don't need us here. It's close to five. Anybody hungry?"

That ended our gathering. Pappy's gang, which I planned to know more about, faded away. Pappy gave a ride to the boys and girls, leaving Nicole to ride with me.

When we got in the car, she immediately let me know her mind. "John, I can never repay you for what you did. You knew where to go. You knew to call Pappy. Patty could've died, if not for you. I know I keep saying things, but I can't get it out of my mind."

Things in my past have never gone away, but time and friends made it easy to ease through time while remembering.

I didn't want her to get discouraged. "I know it's difficult to get it out of your mind, but it will ease some. Slowly, maybe, but it will. And, you need to, because you and I have more work to do."

Nicole's wishes emerged. "Sometimes I want to quit. Don't let me. Going back to looking will help us both. What'da we do next?"

Those words were music to my ears. "Let's just say I'm working on it." I added a little wink for emphasis and got quiet.

I cranked the car and pulled away from the killing scene, knowing I'd be back there. This piece of the puzzle was done. Still, it was difficult to believe Vadinoye did this on his own. And, I couldn't believe the company would've authorized it. Problem was the participating parties were all dead. A wounded bad guy would've been helpful, but if we had one, who'd do the questioning?

"You thinking again?"

She caught me, again. "Yes. Food first. Then back to the hotel to do some planning."

"I like that thought. But first, I need to go to a pharmacie."

Her words came out calm, but how could they, especially when connected to a pharmacie?

My eyes tried to watch both the road and her. "You not feeling well? Are you sick? Are you hurt?"

"No, John. And this is a little embarrassing." She paused. "I'm starting my period." Her pretty face was a tiny bit red.

"Nicole, there's no need to be embarrassed. It's a natural thing."

I caught her looking at me, then at the window and me again. She didn't look unhappy, but something was maybe causing her a little shyness.

She put me in the know. "It's not being embarrassed. John, it'll be five days before we can . . . you know."

Searching for something I could say to perk her up, I tried, "Hey. I'm good with kissing and hugging. No kidding. Ah, there it is." I nodded at the pharmacie. She smiled. I gave her another wink.

I parked the car and started to get out, but she stopped me. "I'm going in by myself, okay?"

"Of course." I pulled out some money and handed it to her. "I'll be right here when you get back."

She gave me a cute little smile, took the money, and glided into the pharmacie, peeking back every few steps.

After about twenty minutes, she was back in the car and not happy. "Everything's in French and they had several types of pads. It took forever to even get anything close to what I use. I finally got a clerk to help, but she only knew a little English."

"But ya got 'em. That's good."

She let go. "Will you stop trying to be so positive? That was frustrating, embarrassing, and it took FOREVER!"

"I thought you girls used those . . . new, different kind of things?"

"Can't say tampons?" She grinned.

"Maybe."

"Just so you know, I like pads. You can say pads, can't you?"

"Yes." She had me.

It wasn't something I'd ever had to deal with, but I could understand she needed the pads and had to buy them here and in front of me. My past reminded me this wasn't new to me.

I held out my hands. She took them. "Nicole, I really do apologize. I can't even begin to imagine how frustrating it was trying to buy the pads over here. I don't know what I can do, but just ask."

There were no tears, but her eyes were glistening. "John, it's me who should apologize. Maybe it's all this going on. My father's dead and my little sister almost joined him."

She rested the side of her head to the seat, with eyes resting on me.

Still holding hands, I said, "It's about five thirty. Let's go the hotel, and you do whatever you need with the pads. Then we'll go to a restaurant where it's just us and do dinner. Would that help? Want to do that?"

A tiny grin emerged. "You're just too sweet and understanding. I'd like to do that. But after the pad thing, I want to see the girls. Then we can eat. That okay?"

I gave her hands a kiss and added, "Your wish is my command, my lady."

As we headed for the hotel, we kept talking with happy words. But the one thing no one brought up was lingering in my subconscious. What would have happened if I'd accepted his terms and gone to pick up the girls? Only one answer. Death. We'd all be dead. Me, the boys, the girls, and Nicole, too, because there'd be no way to hold her back from being there.

There were some unknown questions dawdling around. Why did Vadi do it? And, who had him do it? And, why were they so desperate to silence us? And why not just me? I was the one throwing probing rocks at 'em. I was lifting the covers to see what was there.

Then another thought tarried. Maybe they weren't done trying.

CHAPTER 21

OLD FLAMES ARISE

Nicole did her pad thing in my room. Then we dropped in, unexpectedly, on the tenth floor, where we found not only the two girls but the two boys. Although a surprise, it was a good thing to see. The atmosphere was a happy one. Stepping in the door, there were smiles and laughter, but not from everyone.

Mother Betty had a little less pleasant expression. But that didn't spoil the reception.

Nicole got hugs and I got hugs. It was good, so I added, "Wow. This is good to see what with all that happened today. Amazing."

The grinning girls each grabbed an arm, offering me a hi.

Lizzy said, "It was real scary, Uncle John, but when I saw you standing at the door, I knew we were going to be okay. That's all it took for me."

Patty added, "Yeah. You were wonderful. Wasn't he, Nathan?"

Nathan stepped close and shook my hand. "Yes. I felt the same way."

Andre joined him and did a handshake. "Me too. When you did the movie thing with Lizzy, that gave us all hope. It was a frightening time, and that helped so much."

I have to admit, I was getting much too much recognition and too often. I really didn't do that much. I found them, but did little to rescue them. I saw Nicole looking at me. I gave her a tiny upturned grin. She caught on.

After capturing my arm and pulling me aside, she said her thing. "Okay, everyone. That's enough. John appreciates your compliments, but you're wearing him down. Let's all give him some room to breathe. Meaning give him some rest. That experience was tiring for him, too."

That woman hit the time-honored nail on the head. The girls said okays and let me go. I gave Nicole a whispered thank you into her available ear.

I wanted to give them some positive words about their future. "It's been a tiring day, but I hope you've learned something from all this. This really was a team operation. Everyone played their part, shall we say, well." With a pause, "So. Does anyone want to throw out any thought of the future?"

Lizzy asked, "Not sure I understand, Uncle John."

"For instance, anytime you're out, always, always know your surroundings."

Before I could say another word, Lizzy was there. "Oh, yeah. Instead of totally focusing on, say, the clothes we buy, see who's around."

She got it. I added, "Exactly. People get robbed or car stolen often. Park and walk where there are other people. Never walk down a dark alley alone. Actually, never walk down one. Thieves are cowards. They want to catch you alone."

Patty added, "And if something seems odd or not right, get out of that place."

"You got it. Both of you." Then I turned to the boys. "To you boys, everything we just said goes double for you. This may not be true today, but the men are usually stronger than the women, so it is your duty to watch everything. Got that?"

Nathan put his arm around Patty. "That's true, and if I had been watching around us, we might not have been kidnapped."

Andre hugged Lizzy, repeating with his words.

Nicole asked, "So. Girls. What do you think of their ideas of protection?"

Both girls did their own boyfriend hug, saying they liked the idea of being protected.

Nicole said, "Me too. It's good to let our guys know what we want." She took a peek at me, just as she said, "Everyone. John is taking me to dinner, and we really need to leave. Please enjoy the rest of the evening. I know I will." She added emphasis with a little hip bounce on mine. "We'll see you in the morning."

As Nicole finished her say, the two girls smiled. That's when I saw them in absolute unison smiling and staring at each other. I knew something was cooking in those pretty little heads. I just knew it.

They'd flipped an imaginary coin, and Patty had won the toss because she asked, "Can we go, too? That would be fun."

Nicole's expression shifted a bit. It wasn't unpleasant. It was more of a *You gotta be kidding* look emphasized with one eye about half shut. "Nope. This one we're doing alone."

The girls grinned and clapped hands. Mother Betty was standing over to the side, watching but with little reaction. Like she was in another world, or maybe another time.

Holding Nicole's hand, we walked to her. I asked, "You haven't said a word. Is there anything I or we need to do?"

The girls and boys were watching. And, listening.

Mother Betty put her hand on my arm. "I think I'm just tired, John. I didn't see anything that happened, and that scares me more."

I did a tiny peek at Nicole. She took the hint. "What can we do, Mama? If you'd like to eat with us, you can." I expected her to make that offer. It was the thing to do.

Mother Betty came back with, "No. You two go alone. I suspect you aren't going to Pappy's place. Maybe something more romantic, and to be alone."

Good guess on her part.

"Yes, Mama. John is taking me someplace different. Special." Nicole kept it short.

We said our goodbyes.

Once in the car and having driven about a mile, out of the corner of my eye, I saw Nicole turn to me. "When are you going to let me know where we're eating? You've been known as a secret keeper, remember?" Fortunately, her words were accompanied by a smile.

The name was going to get comments. "It's really more of a café. It's a little place on some street that translates to 42 Barnyard. It's called Villa le 42. That's the English version."

She was surprised. I thought the name sounded kinda romantic in French, if you ignored the street name.

With a little head tilt, "You mean it has the street number as its name? That is so weird."

"I must get you out into the real world more." That alone got a stare, but I continued. "There's another one on rue 24 and there's one in Decatur, Georgia, that uses its street number in the store name."

"I should really get out more. What's it like? The restaurant?"

"It's more of a bistro. Not too big, but it has a very romantic setting. Always dimly lit."

"And, how do you know that?" She stopped smiling.

"Well, I—" She stopped me cold.

"Who was she?" Her words came out fast covered with ice and accompanied with tight eyes and curling lips.

"Will you cut that out? Her name was Gabrielle. She worked at Pappy's place. I met her on my first trip over. She changed jobs. I don't know where she is. Are you happy now?"

A smile appeared on her cute lips. "Very. I was just checking on the competition."

It was time to turn the tables. "So, now that you know someone of my past, who was the last man you dated, and where did he take you?"

"We had lunch, a dinner, and a movie. More than once. He was sweet and courteous. The rest you'll just have to wonder about. We girls have our secrets, too."

"Okay. I give. 42's about three miles ahead," which was a pleasant thought.

She knew she'd won. She had one of those sheepish smiles from then till I parked and opened the door, when she took my arm as we crossed the street to the door of Le 42.

I liked this café because it was small and cozy on the inside. There was an awning that covered small, colorful round tables and chairs for two on the sidewalk. The sidewalk must have been at least twelve feet, providing plenty of room to offer some privacy, if only for conversations.

The small tables told me they liked couples, most likely male and female. Just outside the awnings were two umbrella stands, with table and chairs, for those preferring more privacy.

The front had tall glass windows, one each side of a brick wall, which was about five feet wide, with the name attached. One of those glass walls provided the entrance, also of glass.

Approaching the café, my next problem occurred when I opened the door.

The hostess saw me and immediately said with excitement, "John. Pour toujours. Good see you. It été forever." I assumed she said we hadn't seen each other forever. I was pondering running forever.

The light skinned, long haired brunette speaking was Gabrielle. Her attributes were obvious. A bikini model figure with brown eyes that could mesmerize a man to the point of capturing his mind. She was, probably still is, a human magnet. Attracting men and repelling women. She was the essence of physics. Opposites attract. Likes repel.

Nicole was still holding my arm, just a bit tighter.

I had no choice. "Hi. It's been a while. How are you?" I wasn't really ready, make that prepared, to say her name.

A puzzled look appeared on her face as she asked," You no no moi name?"

My hesitation gave passage for Nicole, still holding my arm firmly, to turn her head and ask, "Well, do you, my dear? Do you remember her name?" Her female intuition told her I knew the girl's name.

I felt like the guy sitting in a strapped chair with a man asking if you had any last wishes.

With no choice but to reply, "Of course I do, Gabrielle. It must have been two years, and you're as beautiful as ever." I figured I had nothing to lose. I was already lying flat on the mat and the count was nearing ten.

Then the unexpected happened.

Gabrielle ignored the arm holding my arm and gave me a cheek kiss and a firm hug. After the lava stopped flowing, Gabrielle backed away from the hug and told Nicole, "Oh, pardonne-moi. Moi know sweet man pour forever."

Then, with only two feet between the two women, Nicole said, "That's what they all say."

I was cooked.

Gabrielle politely agreed, "Oui," as she paused and backed away more. "Oh, moi désolé, no, no pardon." Her hands went into her hair. She was frantic. "Moi, non, non. Me, me, no thinking. Forgive. English non good."

She had trouble with the "me," but frankly, I always thought "moi" sounded kinda sexy.

It was my time and I decided I needed to spread it on thick. I was already on the floor watching the referee count.

"Gabrielle, there is nothing to forgive. Your speech is as captivating as you. And, you are as fantastique as ever." I added a twitch of French to that word on purpose.

Her hands went behind her back as she wiggled her derrière. "John, sweet—you—speak."

That brought a smile to her lips. And a wide-eyed gleam to every man in the place.

The arm Nicole was holding was growing numb.

Attempting to gain some control over the situation, I finally asked the obvious question, "You work here now?"

It was pretty obvious she was, but any update she might give may extend my lifeline a few days.

"Oui. Moi, non, non, me at Villa de Coursou for time. It non good. It *classe*. Non, non, upscale for moi me. Non like." Yeah, me too. I needed an interpreter.

Best I could tell, she didn't like some upscale place she was working and ended up at Le 42. It brought a comment to mind where Bogart spoke of all the gin joints in all the world when an old flame walked into his place. This time I walked into hers.

Nicole decided to stop the lava flow. She had been impatiently watching and listening to all this. "John, these are good memories, but perhaps we should get a table." At least she got us back to the main agenda.

Gabrielle's eyes shifted between me and Nicole at lightning speed. She picked up on Nicole's command, gathered menus, and regained her attention with one word well spoken, "Come," which we did.

Even it sounded like something we use on our hair. A comb.

When she had us seated and menus on the table, she said several words in French, most likely on purpose as she left. The only two words I picked up were bientôt and reverrai.

At an opportune time, I wrote them in my notepad. I told Nicole I was making some notes. Later I looked up the words and found Gabrielle had told me we would meet again. I couldn't decide if it meant now or later. Neither time would be good.

I disposed of the note at an opportune time.

A serveur, a male serveur, came and took our orders. That provided some relief, and I'm not talking about the food. I attempted to let Nicole know Gabrielle and I only had three dates and that's all they were. Dates. Lunch twice and dinner once.

I was nearing the end of my confession when my phone gave a ping. It was my pilot Jane calling me. I showed Nicole the screen and signaled that I would need a minute. She returned a silent okay.

With a reprieve in hand, I said, "Hi, Jane."

"Hi, John. Got a minute?" She replied with a bit of excitement in her voice.

I wasn't sure I even had a second, but returned Jane's question with "Sure. What's up?"

Her voice came at a timely time. She sounded good. I know Paul and Jane had started a drive to Mainz, a town south of Frankfurt, the morning after we arrived. I was glad to hear her voice.

Jane was calm but a bit thrilled as she spoke. "John, we've been here just a couple of days. Oh. You should know we were enjoying the drive so well we spent Sunday night in a motel somewhere and got here Monday morning. It's wonderful. Thank you so much for letting us come here."

"That's good to hear, but I didn't give you permission. You ain't flying, so it's your time. I'm glad you're enjoying it." My usual flying all over the US couldn't be as pleasurable as this trip.

"Well, thank you for not giving your permission." I heard a short giggle. "John, it's been a fun time. My friend loves where they live and she's happy."

"Looks like I'll have to be here several more days myself, so keep yourself busy there."

"That I'll do. Oh, I'll be sending you some pictures soon. I took 'em this afternoon. There's a popular place here where people always take pictures."

"Hey, I'd like that. I'm already excited to see them."

Okay, so maybe I was super excited, but I've not been to Mainz. Haven't even been to Germany. Those two were getting around more than I was.

"You'll see me and Paul and a picture of my friend, Jessica, with her husband, Erwan. I also took one with Erwan's sister and her little girl. They're a great family. So friendly and hospitable. Guess that's an old word, but it fits the bill."

"Hey, send them my way." I was truly interested to see her friend and family.

"I will, but right now my phone's having trouble sending them. But, I'll get them to you soon." She didn't say it, but she sounded sorry she couldn't do the send.

"Might consider a letter." She couldn't see my grin.

Must admit, I still like sending and getting actual birthday cards in the mail. Hmm, guess I need to join the real world.

"Ha. Ha. It's getting that bad. Oh, and Jessica has an amazing house inside and out. I'll send you a picture of that. Well, guess I better let you go."

We said our goodbyes to an encouraging call. I was glad to know she was enjoying herself.

As I hung up, a smiling Nicole asked me about it. She'd heard most of it but needed the full scoop.

She said, "They must enjoy being pilots for you with all your travels. Getting to see new exciting places all over the world."

"They seem to. Now, a lot of my trips are in the States, but they enjoy seeing and visiting places."

Our food came and we began to eat. After a couple of minutes, she stopped, which got my attention. "John, I apologize for giving you so much trouble with Gabby. She's very pretty, and you have good taste."

"Now, her name is Gabrielle, not Gabby. And I accept your apology, but it wasn't needed. I was surprised to see her again. Must admit, it was sorta fun." When I said that, I knew I was in trouble and attempted to gain back some ground. "Wait. What I meant was seeing her again. It wasn't fun, but it's good to see she's still around."

Nicole gave me one of those stares that freezes a guy's will. I told her the dinner was just that, dinner. I had taken her home. Gabrielle lived with her mother.

When I said that, Nicole started a silent laughter. Her head went back, with her hands on her mouth attempting to contain her laughter. After an exaggerated time, she settled quietly and started eating.

After a few bites, I had to ask, "Will you say something?"

She placed her hand on mine. "I know she's just one of many women you've dated. It's okay. You're a kind man to let Gabrielle and I enjoy the fight over you. I'll let you decide who won."

I didn't bring up Gabrielle anymore and shared some of my past business experiences, as well as a little more about Nanna Bolton and my dad.

That brought to mind seeing an older man at Nanna's shack. They were outside talking. I saw him give her some money. After a while they hugged and he left. Wasn't any of my business, but I asked her who that was. She told me it was her cousin Jimbo and he wasn't doing well. When I asked her why he gave her the money, she said, "He dying and he know it. My daddy took care him, and now he taking care ah me."

My dad helped her, too. I suspect my dad gave her more money than needed to care for us. Course, he knew it went to a good cause. I've since wondered how she ever managed life at all.

Nicole and I did a lot of that personal sharing through the meal.

We were finishing up and trying to decide on dessert when Nicole switched gears on me. "John, are you sure you want to keep on this? My father is dead and Noémi's husband is dead and, and, I'm worried about you."

My hand was on the table. Her hand landed on mine as she said that.

"That's a super offer, and here's the but. I believe there's more to know, and I think Patty would like to keep going. And, for me, there just seems to be more fuzzy pieces that need clearing."

"Sweetie, do you have any idea what those fuzzy pieces are?"

"No. Well, maybe. But, if I keep looking, I hope the fuzzes will clear up. I'm just not yet ready to give up."

She signaled and I put my other hand on the table. She then had both hands under her control.

"John, I want you to clear them up, too. I promise to help as much as I can. You just tell me what to do and I'll do it." She gave me a wink, and added, "I'll even cry on your command."

It was after nine o'clock when she decided to have dessert at the hotel. We left.

CHAPTER 22

PICTURE SURPRISES

No sooner than we were settled in, Patty called asking permission to come to my room. I looked at Nicole nodding my head, she nodded back, adding a wink. I told Patty, "Yes," and inside the speed of light, Patty and Lizzy were knocking on the door.

When Nicole let them in, they said, "Hi," as they breezed past her surrounding me on the sofa.

Unaware of what was in store, I sat still with hands in my lap. "You girls look very chipper." I used that word to see if they knew what it meant.

They looked at each other, and as usual deciding who would reply.

Lizzy got it that time. As she tilted her cute head, she asked, "What's that? Did you call us a name or something?"

I was having fun. "Nope. Chipper means bright, happy, looking good."

They both gave me light hand slaps on my arms, each with an "Oh, you."

When they do that, it makes me wonder who taught them to. Or is it internal? No, not internal, 'cause lots of women don't do hand slaps, even to their main guy.

"Okay, okay. What did you come up here for, except to slap me around?"

Patty pulled two pictures from her pants pocket. As she handed them to me, she informed me, "Nathan and Andre gave us these. The pictures you wanted."

They had no idea how much I wanted to see that mantle picture. But they had two.

"You should know that your visit tonight is very special. Feel free to knock on my door anytime." That got more grins, but a question announced itself. "Did the boys know where these were taken?"

Lizzy said, "Some place in Germany. Sounds kinda like Maine."

Patty bounced a little. "Main with a Z added. Maze or something. Doubt I said it right, Uncle John. It's a really weird name."

"You're close, Patty. It's Mainz, like saying mines with a z. It's a tricky word, and adding the German pronunciation really throws it off the norm."

Patty tilted her head and asked, "How'd you know that, Uncle John? Have you been there?"

I briefly returned the tilt as I examined the pictures. "Nope, but my brother, Jake, has. And, Jane and Paul, my pilots, are there now."

Nicole was sitting on the bed being ignored. I motioned for her to join us. She did, but she sat on the floor between my legs, looking up at me. I gave her one of the pictures to look at.

She glanced at the picture then added, "John, everybody takes at least two and usually more. I know I do, to be sure I got a good one. There are mountains in the background. The only difference is the buildings. One has more of the building, and the other has less."

Lizzy chimed in, "Yeah. Buildings, yuck. But the mountains are cool. Must be some kind of resort or something for everyone to go there." Her hands waved a little showing her uncertainty.

They both got my interest. I decided a little query was needed. "Both of you may have a clue. Both are photos of the family at the same location, just at different angles, like Nicole said. But the most interesting thing is the pictures were taken by someone else. Did the boys say who took them?"

Patty did a quick head shake at Lizzy, who returned one. Then Patty started really shaking her head and tightening her face in frustration, "No, but we didn't ask them. Oh! We're so dumb sometimes. I didn't even think of that. I mean, I'd like to know, too. I'm so sorry, Uncle John."

"Me too," added Lizzy with a matching expression.

I threw my arms around them both and gave them a snug hug. "All right, you two. I will not have my most special nieces feeling bad. You got me the pictures, and I'll ask the boys or their mother about 'em." I gave the girls a little shake. "Now, I want to see two smiles."

That got me a pair of hugs. Nicole gave me a wink from each eye. Guess she thought it was doubly cute.

I released the girls and laid the pictures on the table beside the sofa. My hands returned to my lap. "Hey. Tomorrow's Thursday. Whatcha got planned?"

It took at least a second for both girls to perk up 110 percent. Their faces were filled with smiles. Nicole shifted to the bed. The floor may have gotten hard and her view was always up.

Both girls started talking. I called time, flipped a coin, and gave Lizzy the okay, which she took and ran with.

"The boys, as you call them, our boyfriends will pick us up and take us to their house for breakfast. Their mother cooks some real fun food. It's so nice."

When Lizzy stopped, there must have been some internal female hint to Patty.

Patty took the signal. "We may go back to the Louvre again. We thought about trying to walk all the way around the river. There's so much to see."

I added, "And, I suspect, so many places to be with, hmm, now, what is the word I'm looking for? Oh yes, with your boyfriends."

I gave them a crooked grin. Two hands tapped my cheeks. It was a cool feeling.

Nicole's hands were resting on the bed. Up to that point she'd been watching, when her posture straightened. I recall she'd made a decision and decided we all should know.

"Okay, girls. It's getting late, and Uncle John and I have plans of our own to talk about."

That got ohs and nos followed reluctantly with okays from both sides of me.

It was time to see if they needed any funds. I managed to get a hand into my hip pocket and pulled out my wallet. The girls saw it.

Patty's words rushed out as she shook her head. "No, no, Uncle John. We don't need any money. You've given us plenty."

Lizzy loaded her voice and sent me a nod. "It's okay. Really. We have some money left."

I pulled my wallet and asked, "Just how much money do you have?" Something didn't sound right. I did quick looks at both girls and with a grizzly growl I added a firm, "I wanna see your wallets."

They glanced at each other, then at me, then at the sofa.

That caused a question to arise, "And just what will you do without money?"

Nicole picked up the pace. "John, you know very well they don't have any money. They're ashamed to be asking you again, right, girls?"

That got two slow nods still eyeing the sofa.

I let go of my wallet and lifted their heads up. "You are two of the sweetest and prettiest girls I know. I may be a distant uncle, but I'm your uncle and I like it, and you will take some money. NOW! Ya got that?"

I pulled out two hundred euros, splitting it between the two. That got me extended hugs and kisses and thank-yous.

As Lizzy leaned back, I saw a puzzled look. She asked, "How can you have so much money over here?"

That was an easy one. "I was planning to be in England in a few weeks and had Susan get me some traveler's checks. I've just been cashing them in as needed. You're in need, so stop saying no. I like yes best."

The two excited girls headed for the door as Nicole joined me on the sofa. I told them to hold on a bit and pointed to the bed. They both jumped on it, sitting up on their crossed legs.

Wasn't sure how to get started so I just dove in. "Lizzy, been meaning to ask. What's your mother's name? All I know is Rebecca. And what's your full name?"

"My name's Lizzy Hanna Patrick. Mother's is Rebecca Renea Patrick. I always thought it was a pretty name."

Nicole gave me a finger punch in my side. She didn't know what I was doing, and I would pay the price. I gave her a smile. She didn't return it.

With a little knowing, I uttered, "Renea. Lizzy, did you know that's a French name?"

From my brief times in France I had learned some things, mostly about women, it appeared.

Lizzy's eyes went wide open, "It is? No, I didn't know. Oh, my. That's so amazing. No one ever told me."

"And, I'm thinking that Hanna is also French, a very old French name."

Her hands grabbed each other. "Really? I'm in France and I have a French name. That's the most wondrous thing. I never knew."

"Hang loose. I got more."

Lizzy gave me one of those uh-oh looks. Patty was speechless, but her eyes were narrowed accompanied with a slight head tilt. She was suspicious.

"Lizzy, I want to bring your mother over. With your permission, of course, I can have her here tomorrow afternoon, if she will come."

Patty and Lizzy grabbed hands.

Lizzy's eyes got even wider. The rest of her, while temporarily frozen to the bed, eventually thawed and she spoke. "Uncle John, I miss her so very much. I've never been away from her this long. I'd love to have her here. You do mean that, don't you? Please."

I hadn't even answered, and their faces grew happier.

"Yes, I mean it. Between us we'll talk her into it." I turned my head to Nicole and mouthed, "Am I okay?"

I got her approval with a cheeky kiss.

Lizzy gave me a long-lasting, teary-eyed hug and shifted to my other side.

"Lizzy, we have a choice. We can call her now at well after one in the morning her time, or wait till the morning."

"Oh, please. Please let's do it now. It might scare her, but if we start now, you can get her here for sure tomorrow, right?"

"With her cooperation, yep."

Lizzy started clicking buttons. I won't bore you with the details, but between Lizzy, Nicole, Patty, and I, we convinced her mother to make the trip. She would stay in the same room as all the women, with the one exclusion to my room.

Rebecca was worried about her house while away. I took care of that and called Susan.

After about thirty minutes of informing me where my body parts would be found, she agreed to getting someone to watch over both Patty's and Lizzy's houses. And to be sure Rebecca got on the plane. Susan still liked me.

I just needed someone to watch over me when I got back to the office.

With all that taken care of, I stood up and put my arms out in a hugging position. The girls entered my huggable arms. With bye-bye hugs, they were gone. I called the lobby and told them Rebecca Patrick would be arriving and the room she'd be using.

Nicole had sat down on the bed watching the girls head out. I joined her. She took my hands. "John, you never cease to amaze me. That was the kindest thing. Lizzy will love you forever. Me too."

"Hey, they were practically French and needed to be here, together. Let's forget about that, okay?"

"I won't forget it, but I'll let it lie still, for a while. So, what're we doing?"

It was picture time. I retrieved them. There was one picture of particular interest. "Did you take a close look at the building in this picture?"

I handed her the one that had a little more of the top edge of the building visible.

"No. Not really. Dumb thing to have in a great picture of the mountains. A building. You can't even read the letters on the building."

"Would be a great time to have a magnifying glass."

I held a finger up to be patient. I found a piece of paper, a book to write on, and a pen. I wrote the top parts of the three letters visible on the building.

"Okay, bright eyes, what do you see?"

She looked and shook her head.

I didn't give up. "Make that Nicole with the sweet eyes." I paused. "I see the tops of three letters. SSC. And what I think is the dot of an i and the top of a t and an l. Look at the order I just wrote the letters. Tell me what you see."

"I'm sorry, John. I just don't." She stopped dead in her tracks. "What's the full name of Signature?"

That was easy. "Signature Security Consultants." I gave her a hint. "You see the top of an s two times, don't you?"

"Yes. Oh, God. The S and i and t, then another capital S, then . . ." She paused again. "Signature Security Consultants." Her smile lit up the room.

"Yes" was all I could say.

Her excitement began to diminish. "But that only means they have an office there."

"Have an office, or had an office," I added.

Her eyes lit up again. "His boys in the picture are young. It was taken back then." Her head began to shake, again. "But John, he just had a picture taken back then. He worked for them. People take pictures of their offices. I have a couple of the newspaper office."

What she said was totally true and possible. But there was still one question I needed the answer to.

"That's true. It doesn't tell us much. But I wonder if your father took the picture. You could be holding a picture where he was holding the camera."

She quietly put the photo flat against her breast as tears started flowing.

I pulled her close. Through her tears, she asked, "We don't really know, do we?"

"We'll find out. Noémi will know. So will the boys."

"But why wouldn't they have told me?"

She had a good question. "Your father was a close friend. He could have taken many pictures of them. This could be just one of many. If so, he, too, had been to Mainz."

With tears subsiding, "Maybe they took some of him."

"I'm thinking the same thing." I put my hand under her chin and raised it to see into her wet eyes. "We'll find out tomorrow. Now, let's get ready for bed. Tomorrow will be busy, I do believe."

"What day is tomorrow?" she asked. I wondered why.

"Thursday, my sweet. And I believe it will be a bright one."

CHAPTER 23

MAINZ, NO; CRÉTEIL, YES . . . OOPS

My eyes opened. I knew it was Thursday, and an early morning thereof. I had set the alarm for 6:00 a.m., but it never had a chance.

Nicole was up sometime before six. I didn't know exactly when because she had turned off the alarm and put on clothes.

I either woke up or she caused it when she hit the bed. All I knew was, when I opened my eyes, hers were latched on to me while sitting on her knees.

"You can get up, Mr. Lazy Eyes. The world awaits us." Her arms went up. She did not attempt to keep it low key.

Her arms dropped. I mumbled, "What time is it?"

"Six thirty."

I went up on my elbow. "You're dressed."

"Yep. Just gotta put some shoes on and I'm ready to go."

My head flopped back down on my pillow. "Okay."

"You, sleepyhead, gotta get up, too."

I needed to be up, again, so my elbow slipped back under my chin—again. "Go? Going? Where're we going?"

Out came, "Mainz," on a bright, smiling face.

Then I realized what her morning was all about. "You do know it's a six hour drive just to get there, then six back."

"No, sleepyhead. We'll use your plane." Her smile was still there, and her hands were spread, palms up.

"Ah. I thought you knew. The plane's here, but my pilots are in Mainz."

"Oh." Her hands fell to the sheets.

It was time to be close. I sat up and snuggled close, picking up her hands. She needed encouragement, and I wanted her back to happy.

I gave her my plan. "What I thought we'd do is visit Noémi this morning and ask her about the picture."

Before I said another word, Nicole added her thought in almost a question, "And, she'd know who took the pictures and we'd know where to go."

"Sorta." When I said that, her head did a quick short twist, so I kept talking. "*And* that will tell us if we need to go to Mainz or not."

That got another "Oh," with her encouragement moving up the scale.

I still had her hands. I shook 'em a little. "Now, don't lose the excitement. I'm excited. If your father took the pictures, they may have more. You'd like that, wouldn't you?"

Her face bubbled back with a smile as she pulled our hands to her chest. "That would be the most wonderful thing ever."

The sweet expression I saw was enjoyable. I only hoped it would remain with whatever the day gave her.

I pulled her hands in and gave them a kiss. "Yes, it would. I suspect it will. Okay, I gotta get dressed. You call Patty and ask if we can see Noémi today, this morning."

She gave our hands a little swing. "John, my dear, you may not have noticed, but it's just barely six thirty."

"If you recall, they're going for breakfast. Maybe a true French breakfast. And we need to pick up Rebecca at the airport this evening."

She figured it out and gave my earlobe a little wobble. The day was in gear.

We got to Noémi's home a little past eight o'clock. We'd called the girls, who called the boys. The boys got the okay with their mom for us to show up and eat breakfast. Then I remembered the boys were picking up the girls. Guess Andre got permission to use his mom's car.

As for me, I was hoping the pictures would prevent a day long trip to Mainz. The other side of me asked why I kept tripping over Mainz.

I parked on the sidewalk, again. I wasn't alone in that endeavor. At the nearby houses, there were no cars in the obviously empty and roomy garages.

Lizzy and Andre, holding hands, met us at the door. Andre shook my hand. Lizzy gave me another hug. On the way to the kitchen, Lizzy mentioned she'd told Andre and everyone there about her mother coming. Another indicator that many things were being shared, which was good.

The kitchen had two tables joined together, fortunately big enough for seven eaters. Both boys took seats there.

The real unexpected thing was seeing the girls helping Noémi prepare and serve breakfast. Nicole saw it, did a little nod, and gave me a *Do you see what I see?* stare. I thought she was going to trip over a dust particle. Didn't stop her. Nicole joined the girls with their chores.

Me, still standing hadda ask, "I didn't know you girls could cook."

Patty tossed me a smile. "You didn't ask." Then the two of them glanced at each other.

Lizzy confessed, "Mother Noémi has been giving us lessons. This will be the French version of breakfast."

"Don't worry, Uncle John," added Patty, "eggs are common. We'll scramble yours. And, we got ham and some delicious little pastries."

I took my seat at the table and threw out a tease, "What? You mean I don't get Pop-Tarts?"

Both girls looked at me with *huhs* on their faces.

"Just kidding. Eggs are great. I do get croissants, don't I?"

The boys were enjoying all of this. Nicole was, too. Noémi kept a tiny grin as she pulled the croissants from the oven. Lizzy and Patty gave up on my shenanigans, make that ignored, and finished scrambling the eggs.

The boys did coffee. The girls, Nicole, and Noémi had hot tea. The girls had prepared me the French version of my favorite: hot tea with ice and sugar added.

There was lots talked about as we ate. I found that Nathan, being eighteen, had a learner's license. Andre was nineteen and had a full ready to drive license, but for some reason, his mother didn't let him drive much. At least he'd started picking up the girls, on occasion.

I tried to believe it was the cost of driving, because gas was not cheap. It's sold by the liter for about 1.40 euro, but that's one quarter gallon. So, times four, it's $5.60 a gallon. Her car was small but would hold four young ones, all of whom must be slender. She could be cutting costs, except for this morning.

Or had they picked 'em up? Maybe they took a taxi? I started to make a note, but my note pile was too high to reach the pad.

With breakfast finished and the girls washing the dishes, Noémi joined us at the table. I was anxious for this time and pulled out the pictures she'd given me.

Before I could ask the who question, Nicole did. "John and I were wondering who took the pictures."

Noémi said, "Forgive. Pensée, non, non. May you know." She looked at Nathan, who said, "She thought you knew, Nicole. Your father did." That caused turmoil at the kitchen sink. Both girls dropped their plates, carefully, and wash rags and stormed the table.

Patty gave Nathan a hard love slap on his arm. "You didn't tell me that. Why didn't you tell me?" Fear was etched on his face. He started to speak but she gave him a, "Shut up. I don't want to hear it." She had the situation well in hand.

Nearly at the same time, Lizzy planted the hard love pat to Andre. "You too." Andre threw up his arms attempting to protect himself. He got a, "I don't want to hear it." It wasn't Lizzy's father, but the girls did stick together.

I was happy they left the plates in the sink. The boys needed some help.

"Girls, I'm certain the boys weren't trying to keep this a secret. Ya gotta remember, Patty, your father spent a lot of time with these guys and their family. I suspect he was a member of the family, right, Noémi?"

"Oui. Ami and family."

Andre translated, "Friend and family. Very much."

"Now, girls," I added, "you need to apologize to your boyfriends. I suspect your father was as close as an uncle."

Andre spoke to his mother, "Oncle." I guessed it was a translation and found it startling how the two are pronounced so much alike.

The girls didn't move immediately, so I gave them an order. "Okay, you two," pointing at them. "The boys deserve a hug and a kiss."

My command was accepted. I got one of my own from Nicole.

With my success so far, I took a chance and asked, directing my words to Noémi and her boys. "So, when are you going to show us the rest of the pictures? And the other things your father left you?"

Couldn't hurt, and I wanted to see what they had.

Next thing I knew we were in the living room, Noémi was in her chair and the rest of us on the floor with a box of stuff between us. There was no top to the box and virtually no dust. Must have been in a closet, most likely with other stuff piled on top.

You know how it is. If you don't look at it often, things get piled on top of it. And if you don't look at those things on top for years, stuff gets piled on top of the stuff.

I asked Noémi about the Signature building in the photo. She said it was closed several years ago and torn down. I knew Signature had been kicked out of some countries. Guess Germany was one of them.

Nothing in the box gave me anything new to chase. It was mostly photos and a tall, thick stack of newspapers. Those I did ask to take with me. Noémi gave her okay.

"Noémi, thank you for loaning me these newspapers. The dates look old and could be worth looking at. I promise to return them."

She replied, "I non them years," then said something to Nathan, who told us, "Father read much. Purchased many newspapers. He kept them, and we did, also." He said something to his mother. She said something. Then Nathan said, "Mother kept them because Father liked them. A memory for her."

With that, I knew I must take good care of them, and I told her so. Still, I wanted to do a serious go-through. They were history. It had dawned on me they would all be in French, which would be a challenge. I kept them anyway, even after Nicole sent me one of those *You gotta be kidding* looks.

Nicole and I gave our thanks for breakfast and left with our goodies. Nicole was given several pictures, mostly of her father.

We headed back to the hotel. After that, I wasn't sure where we were headed. We had just about run out of leads. Truth was, we had.

"John, did you notice there was no mention of the kidnapping?"

"No. No, I hadn't. I had other things on my mind, but I see what you mean. That was a life threatening event and no one mentioned it."

"If it hadn't been for you, those kids could easily be dead. You too! She could have at least thanked you." She uttered a *hmph*. and added, "Well, I'll be sure they remember it next time we visit. I won't let them forget."

"Oh, you don't have to do that."

"Maybe I don't, but I will. She should be down on her knees thanking you, John. Oh, when we leave the hotel, I want to go see Pappy." She did a fast switcheroo.

With no reason to wait, I gave it a go. "Let's just go see him now."

"No. I need something from the hotel." I raised my eyes and looked at her asking silently. She answered my soundless question. "I need to change out a pad. Are you happy?"

That was a question no man wants to answer. I attempted to sneak around it.

"Yes. I'm happy 'cause I'm here with you, and you'll get your pad and I'll buy you dinner anywhere you like."

Oh shit came to mind. If I hadn't been driving, I'd have slapped my head.

Nicole's hand attached itself to my shoulder. "Sweetie, you made that offer once before, and look where it took you. Not to worry. Pappy's place will be perfect for lunch, and even dinner. I'll go wherever you want. You seem to have a knack for taking care of a woman."

"If you don't mind, I don't think I should say much on that subject. But, we could do lunch at Pappy's, if you'd like to?"

Her hand slithered down to my arm heading for my hand. I grabbed hers as it grabbed mine.

"Pappy's will be perfect. Maybe he's got something new to tell you. Oh, and this afternoon, why don't you look through those newspapers? I might could help."

I snatched a glimpse at her, then back at the road. "Sometimes you are the scariest and yet most provocative women I've ever met. I was thinking of the newspapers."

"I read your thoughts. I knew that's what you wanted to do. It's okay."

That fired up my curiosity. My eyes darted between her and the road more times than I could count. "Am I that obvious?"

"Sometimes you are. Most times, I got no idea what you're thinking." She gave my hand a squeeze. "This time I could see the newsprint in your eyes."

I gave her a wink and kept quiet with eyes on the road. Fortunately, the hotel was in sight.

She did her pad thing and we headed for Pappy's place. I kept the newspapers in the car. Pappy might also want to delve through them.

CHAPTER 24

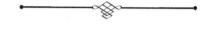

A NEW KID IN TOWN

Seems every time we entered Pappy's restaurant, there was always something different or ready for us to head for some danger. This time the real surprise was Antoine, Pappy's son, behind the bar talking to and watching Sasha pour drinks.

Antoine was thirtyish when Pappy asked me to help him. That would make him thirty-three or so, now, looking like twenty-five. Some guys got it.

What I really remembered was all the girls crawling over him. Okay, maybe there was a bit of envy, but he, from what I'd been told, never wanted to settle for one woman.

"Who's that you're looking at? Do you know her? And who's the guy?"

"Huh? No, not at her. Him. That's pappy's son, Antoine."

"Antoine. Ooh, I like that name. Good looking. Introduce me."

I gave her the kind of look she'd given me more times than I could count. Men can't do the look. It's indescribable and best left undescribed, but when a guy sees it, he knows he's in trouble.

She gave me a, "What? Why are you looking at me like that?"

"That's the look I get from you when I see or say something you don't like."

She did it. I got the look along with, "I don't do that." She ignored me. "You going to introduce me, or do I have to?" She wasn't even looking at me when she said that.

As always, I had no choice. I grabbed her hand and headed for the bar. I almost dragged her, but made no difference. She helped.

Before I could say a word, Antoine saw us. He beat me to it. "John, it's been a long time. How's it going?" He was stepping from behind the bar as he spoke.

"Couldn't be better. Thought you were in Switzerland?"

Talking as he approached us, "I still live there, but Pappy called me. Said he had something he wanted me to do and would fill me in when I got here."

Keep in mind, when he reached us he was facing me, but his eyes kept drifting to Nicole. Granted, that was understandable. I would've done the same thing.

Still, bet you have the same thoughts I did. I was there. Suddenly he was there with a Pappy invite.

I asked the obvious. "Did he mention me being here?"

Nicole was standing beside me. Her hand was out of sight tugging at my shirt.

He started talking, but he wasn't really speaking to me. "No, he didn't. Who's this beautiful woman standing beside you?"

Obviously, an intro was needed. "Antoine, I'll keep the charade going. This is Nicole Powell, and I'm here to find out what happened to her father." I figured he only heard two words. Her name.

"Hi, Nicole. I'm Antoine Armand. Pappy's my father." He ignored me. Don't think he heard a word I said.

Nicole's eyes looked like they met his halfway. She took a half step, which put me that half step behind her. "I thought that's who you were. Did Pappy force you to come here? Maybe to give John a little help." She was on the same track and attacking.

I gave her a hidden punch in the back. She jumped a little. I smiled at Antoine.

He looked at Nicole, then at me, with his eyes shifting between us. "No. I don't? I mean I didn't. This is strange. I promise you, Father called yesterday and asked that I come and help him do something. At least that's what I thought it was." His eyes stopped on Nicole. "If there's something I can help with, I'd be happy to."

She sent him a smile, but I wondered what may be behind it.

Antoine put his hand on my shoulder as he looked at Nicole. "Had it not been for John, I'd be destitute."

From my experience with Antoine, he's a good and, best I know, honest man. One that women will fight over. And, the timing was going to be just what I needed. He could speak and read at least three languages, and that would be to my advantage.

Maybe he didn't know, but I fully thought Pappy brought him here to get involved in the case. If so, I had no choice and he could be useful.

"We're about to have some lunch. Why don't you join us?" I wanted to see where the encounter would lead.

As we picked our own table and sat down, Celeste brought menus. But she wasn't through.

When she turned to leave, she laid her fisted hand against Antoine's back. Firmly, I might add. It travelled about three inches before it landed. It wasn't a friendly tap.

With her hand resting on his shoulder, she apologized, but it wasn't just the I'm sorry words.

Bending just a tiny bit, enough for him to see her, she said, "Oh, I so sorry, Antoine. Thought saw a bug." She didn't wait for a response. Guess it was one of those sister-brother disagreements. Antoine was probably glad she wasn't carrying a cake.

We politely ordered, and he and I began talking over old times. That was enjoyable.

When we started eating and I'd taken maybe two bites, Nicole lay down her fork and asked, "Are you here to help find my father? 'Cause if you are, it's time you told us. At this point, there's only one man I trust to help me and that's John. Pappy, too, but sometimes I wonder what his real goal is."

Within a second of her last word, she slid her plate forward just enough to cross her arms and rest them on the table. At that moment,

I was gladly not on her list. If there was a staring contest between Antoine and Nicole, she was winning.

Antoine had just taken a bite and was chewing, but that changed. He almost choked as he swallowed whatever it was. He grabbed his drink and took several gulps.

To give him time to recuperate his throat, I added, "Antoine, she has the same suspicion I do, that you're here to help us. Which is okay. We'd just like an answer, either a yes or no? We're waiting."

He had two pairs of eyes drilling into him.

When the napkin had cleared his lips, he said, "John, Father told me there was something he wanted me to do. He did not get specific. He didn't tell me you were here or, Nicole, anything about your father. I promise you he didn't. He said he would give me the details when I got here."

I took a bite of food and signaled the others to eat. Antoine took me up on it, which gave me a chance to ask, "So, how long have you been here?"

"I had walked into the restaurant and Celeste told me Father would be out soon, so I started talking to Sasha. That's when you came in. Please believe me."

That sounded like Pappy. "I believe you. Pappy can be vague and mysterious at times. And, I suspect he probably had some reason to not see you, knowing we were coming."

Nicole ate a bite and shook her head, and calmly said, "Pappy didn't know we were coming."

My comeback she was not going to like but I gave it a shot. "I think he knows every move we make." Nicole looked shocked. I added, "Outside the hotel."

She tracked what I said and meant. Her eyes were wide, but she remained calm. "I don't like that, John. Tell him to stop," then paused for half-a-second and switched to pissed. "NO. *I* will."

We had to get over that hurdle to make any progress. "Nicole, if he's having us followed, it's to our benefit. It keeps us safe. You safe. If he had been watching the girls, they would never have been kidnapped."

Antoine was watching Nicole and I battle it out, but that got his attention. "Who was kidnapped?"

He didn't know, and it sounded legit. "Nicole's sister, her friend, and the two girls' boyfriends. You didn't know, huh?"

"No. Look, I've been living in Switzerland. Working there. Father doesn't tell me everything, and he sure didn't say anything about a kidnapping."

"Okay. I've heard enough. We'll finish eating and deposit ourselves in Pappy's office whether he's there or not." I added, "I bet Nicole's mother will be there."

That gave Antoine another surprise. We shared what we knew and finished our food along with a bottle of wine. It was free. Antoine had some timely influence.

I knocked on Pappy's door, opened it, and we three walked in. Pappy and Mother Betty were sitting on his sofa, fairly close and holding hands. Feelings were revealed to many. He wasn't expecting us, at least not announced.

If you wonder why I didn't knock, well, I wanted to know just what was going on between those two. I and others knew something was, but in public there was no evidence. We then had that evidence. When a girl lets a guy hold her hand, they're connected. They got a relationship. Unfortunately, someone was not happy.

"John, what the enfer are you doing? You knock when you enter my office."

I suspected the English version of that word started with an H. I gave him a calm but direct reply. "And when you bring a new guy in to help me, you should let him know what he's getting into, and you should let me know. Antoine, you or Nicole have any thoughts on my entry?"

Nicole took the stage and Pappy was in her line of fire. "I do. Pappy, I know you like Mama, and that's a good thing. I like it, and it's time to stop keeping it a secret. But I don't like you sending Antoine down here without telling him why, and we see him and have to figure it out ourselves." She started to tear up but kept going as she took my hand. "And, if you don't want us here, John will take me home. Mama can stay. I don't care. My father is dead, and I don't care."

I pulled her close. She rested her tear-filled face on my shoulder. I whispered, "Good words, girl. I'm proud of you."

Mother Betty hadn't said a word, but her face was trying to tell me something. Possibly it was to get the heck outta Dodge. If you don't know, that's an old Western phrase the sheriff tells the bad guy. Means get out of my town, or else.

Antoine was stunned.

It was my time. "She's crying because she does care. She wants her mother to be happy. She wants to hold her father. Maybe I should've knocked, but maybe not. Seems the air has been cleared a bit. Pappy, why don't you tell us why your son is here?"

His eyes flipped between all three of us till he settled on mine. "John, I only asked him here to help you. He speaks fluent English, and I knew he would like to."

Before I had a chance, Antoine joined in. He was somewhat disturbed. "Then why didn't you tell me why I was coming? I'd have jumped at the chance." He turned to me. "John, I'm jumping at the chance now, if you'll let me. You lead, I follow."

Mother Betty stood up. "All of you, be quiet!" She paused a moment then added, "Please." She placed her hand on Pappy's shoulder. "Pappy is protecting me. I asked him to have his son come here."

She glanced down at Pappy.

Shock was on all our faces.

Nicole shot out one word, "Mama!" leaving her mouth open, briefly, till she looked at me.

Think I was supposed to say something, but that was NOT going to happen. I was awaiting in the next second, deciding to duck or run.

Mother Betty's eyes converged on me. "John, I'm so thankful for what you've done for me. You saved my young daughter from being killed while risking your own life. You've given Nicole hope for her father. John, I only thought Antoine could help because he was born here. And you should know, I'm so sorry for how I treated you when we met. You're a very special man."

Mother Betty sat down as tears started. Nicole elbowed my side. I whispered out of the corner of my mouth, "Hey. I know what to do."

Pappy gave his girl a tissue.

I went and squatted beside her. "Thank you for the kind words. Antoine will be of good use. And, I will not stop till I know what really happened to Nicole's father."

That was not the time to say husband.

Then something happened that was not expected. She hugged me. Unexpected, but welcomed. She was holding my head sideways, directing my eyes at Nicole, who still had tears flowing down her cheeks.

Mother Betty loosened her hug. I gave her a little cheek kiss and stood up. The room was yelling for sound.

Attempting to slide to a new subject, I said, "Nicole, there was something I was going to ask Pappy. Do you remember what it was?" That got her attention. My wink at her helped.

Nicole brushed the tears away. "I remember. Those newspapers. You thought Pappy might want to see them."

I gave Mother Betty's hand a kiss, and on my way to join Nicole, I added, "Noémi gave me a lot of old newspapers. Some about ten years old, and many seven and eight years ago. All in French, of course."

As I sat beside Nicole, "Pappy, I was thinking you might want to see them, but with Antoine available, he can help me look over them."

Antoine gave me a nod. He was in the game.

Pappy did the same. "John, those papers could be very valuable. Once again, you've pulled a kitten out of a hat."

Mother Betty did one of those leans to Pappy, then straightened up. "Pappy, it's not a cat. It's a rabbit. Magicians pull rabbits from hats, not cats." I saw some invisible connection as she lightly slapped his arm. "Oh, you stinker. You know that."

I read that as an "I like you" tap. Maybe a *very* "I like you" tap.

Pappy returned a brief shoulder-to-shoulder lean but said nothing to her. He focused on me. "Handle those with care. Just let me know of any interesting finds."

"We will, Pappy. If you two will excuse us, we have some reading to do."

With Antoine along, we headed for the hotel and my room.

I didn't expect to find any funnies.

CHAPTER 25

NEWSPAPER NEWS

I broke out the stacks of newspapers. They were in date order with the older ones on the bottom. Antoine counted them. There were fifty-six editions.

Nicole took our pictures with the newspapers in the background. She took a couple extra of Antoine. Her story was he'd be working the newspapers—we hoped.

Sitting on the sofa, Nicole and I took a try at the papers. To be truthful, we looked at the pictures.

Antoine had been watching and decided we needed help.

He took possession and added them on the desk and just stood there. He crossed his arms and sorta looked at them. Nicole and I just watched. Without warning, he flipped the stack over. He was going to begin with the oldest. He sat and started paper digging.

Before long, paper dust was covering the desk. Every now and then we'd ask how he was doing. A wordless hand would go up. That was going to be his signal, a signal to leave him alone.

Nicole appeared with a bottle of wine. I'd not even thought about the room fridge. Within a few minutes, we all had a glass in hand. I was still on the sofa. Nicole was walking, no, plodding around the room, comforting the wineglass with both hands.

She would sit a spell, walk a spell. After a few walks, the sitting lasted longer.

My new fear was the possible replacement of thinning carpet.

Antoine called me over and told me of a find. In a 2010 paper, he found a small mention of Gustav Gagnon and William Powell, American, being laid off from their government jobs. The article wasn't harsh. Why that would appear in a paper was odd.

After looking at the article, I thought out loud, while eyeing the female in the room, "Wish I had the US paper of that date."

The walking Nicole saw me giving her the eye. Her hands flew out and gave me a moderately loud, "What!"

The hands dropped as she took a couple steps closer to me.

I took that as opening a talking door. "Any idea if you or your mother has a paper with an article about your dad being laid off?"

Nicole took a couple of steps closer. "Nah. We read 'em and trash 'em." That sentence ended with a quick question two steps closer, "Why would you want to know?" She joined me sitting.

I was hoping some bells might ring. "The article Antoine found is in 2010. What month was your dad laid off?"

Nicole thought for a second. Her head was lightly shaking, as if trying to remember something. Suddenly, she grabbed my arm then blurted, "April! April 2010. I remember because it was on Tax Day. April 15."

Antoine looked at us, adding his nickel. "This paper is dated April 18. I'd say that was a match," he said with only a modest sign of excitement.

I tossed in my two cents. "Too close for a coincidental match. Had to be on purpose. I wonder if it was coordinated between countries."

Nicole's hands were shaking wildly. "John, they were great guys. Not movie stars or high-ranking government people. Unless us regular people rob a bank, shoot someone, or save a dog, we don't get names in a paper."

"She has a point, John," added Antoine.

He got my attention. "As to some history, both men were laid off from similar government jobs, investigative type, then rather quickly both got jobs with Signature Consulting."

I began walking around the room, with two pair of eyes tailing me.

Nicole stood beside Antoine and leaned on his shoulder. "He's thinking again. He does that. You got any idea what he's thinking?"

"No idea. But, he has a point of the two being laid off and getting on with same company. The weird thing is different countries."

She answered, "Yeah. I agree. But they knew each other."

"They did?"

"Oh, yes. You didn't know? Yeah, they—"

I tuned back in. "All right, you two, quit horsing around."

Nicole grinned.

Antoine glanced at me, then up at Nicole. "Horsing around?"

"It's an old saying, Antoine. Just means having fun." She tapped his shoulder as she continued grinning.

While ignoring their words and taking control of the pair, mostly the female one, I did the ol' finger waving in the air. "Now, if I wanted a person to get a job at a certain type of company, an announcement officially stating he'd been laid off from a similar company could be a door easily opened."

Antoine latched on to that one. "They wouldn't have to know each other because someone else was getting them the job."

"Good point, Antoine, but in this case both Powell and Gagnon had been working together in France for some length of time. That had to be why they were picked."

Nicole objected. "John, you can't know that. Daddy could've been working with anyone."

"Possibly. We need to check that out, but it seems the length of time your father spent with Noémi's boys teaching them English," I paused a few seconds, "had to be more than a year."

Yes, that was a guess, which I preferred to label as an educated one.

Her voice began to show emotion. Her hands were moving randomly. "But Daddy was at home a lot even while he was traveling so much. I told you that. He was gone for short times then longer times, but he was at home between them."

I eased close and put my arms around her. "I didn't mean to cause this. I only meant to say your father had to be a smart man, an intelligent man, and I think both governments knew that. He was a man to be proud of."

Nicole hugged me, calmed some, and stepped back. "Thank you. Please don't let anything change that."

Antoine was quietly listening.

I added, "From what I've seen and heard, nothing can bring him down."

She returned a quiet "Thank you."

The paper explorer started his own subject coated with frustration. Or was it annoyance? "Okay, you two. I need guidance here. I'm jumping to the two August issues. Please," the word please took at least four seconds to exit his mouth, "tell me what I'm looking for?"

He had a good question. That paper was the last one Mr. Gagnon saved, meaning he was still alive. Then my brain caught up. Unless Noémi had saved it. We had to look for their deaths. That watchman's death. Then I heard a female voice.

"Antoine, he's doing it again. John. John! Stop thinking and start talking."

"Nicole, I'm not sure what I'd do without you. Okay, Antoine. Take notes." I pulled out mine. "I'm looking for deaths. William Powell. Gustav Gagnon—make that Gustav Louis Gagnon. Noémi's husband. And anything related to Karthos. It was a manufacturing company. Ah, and Marcel Moe Clair. Moe Clair is his last name. He was and sorta is foreman there. These are wild, but look for Ludovic Rousseau and Jules Pelletier, and . . ."

I lost it. My brain was colliding with my mouth. I sat down.

Nicole was grinning as she threw a pointed finger at Antoine. "Hey. Add Gabrielle to the list."

Antoine looked at me for a reply. Poor guy was stunned.

"It's okay, Antoine. She's a serveur Nicole and I met last night at dinner."

His mood changed and he came back smiling. "I'm quite familiar with Gabrielle. No need for this list. She's already on *my* list."

I laughed out loud. Nicole did not. I added, "Hell, add George Kaplan to the list. That's all I got."

They stared at each other, wondering, I suspected, then at me. They said nothing.

"Kaplan. George Kaplan. That name was used in an Alfred Hitchcock movie and at least two TV shows. I've seen it in e-mails. Kaplan, the character, never existed, but he was made to be real by the plot of the story. You guys really need to . . . never mind."

It got quiet for second as they shot questioning looks at me. The kind you get when they think you've gone bananas.

Through it all, another dawn dawned on me. "Nicole, I knew there was something wrong when we met with Larry."

Antoine asked, "Who's Larry?"

I lit his light for the nickname. "Ludovic Rousseau. Larry was easier to remember. Listen. We were questioning Larry about what Nicole's father and Gagnon were doing. Rousseau told us what his part was. And, he was lying."

Nicole's hands must have been frustrated. They went into the air. "So what's new? We figured he'd lie. I think everybody we've been talking to are liars." We both gave her a *Who me?* stare, which she saw and answered. "Not you guys! I mean all these people who are supposed to know something. John, how can you know for sure?"

"You do have a point, ma'am. I saw it when he said he was not privy to secretive projects. A person's eyes look to the right when remembering. To the left when being creative. He was being creative. He was lying. He knows more or all of what happened to those two. I just don't know the specifics."

Poor Antoine was stuck in the middle. He kept trying to decide who to watch.

Nicole wasn't satisfied, "Now, how do you know that? Did you just make that up as an excuse?" Her demeanor made that sound like an accusation.

A suit of armor would've been useful. My confident hands went into the air with palms up. "I'll have you know, I read it in a book." Then I wasn't sure and my hands dropped. "Or maybe a website, but it works."

Antoine had quit listening. I saw him go back to the papers. I would've liked to join him.

I motioned for Nicole to sit. She did, and close to me.

Antoine was going through the papers at a decent pace. He was scanning every page top to bottom. Pictures and column headings. I heard him once say to himself, "Why so many people dying?" Obviously he was reading the obits.

Nicole got quiet. She was dozing on my shoulder. My eyes were attempting to close, but I prevented that for about a second.

After some period of time, my shoulder shook. As I opened an eye, it was Antoine. He whispered, "I found something." He sat back at the desk, waiting.

I nudged Nicole. She wiggled, and her eyes slowly opened. I did the whisper to her. We joined Antoine.

He glanced at me, then at the article. "This man, Lucas Berart, worked at Karthos and died. Heart attack, the obit says. He was a night watchman. What'd you think?"

I couldn't read it, but it was a promising start. I pointed at the paper. "That's a very good find. We have a starting point."

Nicole got interested. "Maybe we can go see Marcel? He would know."

She was on track. I called Marcel and asked if we could see him. He said we could, but not at the plant and not his home. He got off at five and he hadn't eaten at Pappy's, so I invited him to meet us there at five thirty. He accepted.

Curiosity set in, and I asked him who came in when he was off duty.

He said, "They have special sensors I turn on when I leave each day during the week. I don't work weekends, so I turn off the sensors when I get back on Mondays at six in the morning."

I thanked him for the info.

It was close to four, so we had time to kill. We kept reading old newspapers looking for new clues.

What was so unimportant they had sensors half the day and weekends? Yet someone worried that someone would be rambling around the place and needed a guard during the day. Was there an unknown entity guarding the place in the off hours?

Hell, I walked in and the guard put me on the floor. Nicole then put the guard on the floor. Was he only for show? She was the show—showing me to never get her beyond pissed off.

CHAPTER 26

DEAD FRIENDS IN QUESTION

We got to Pappy's early. The day was getting long. It was approaching five o'clock. I called Lizzy and told her I might not make it to pick up her mother. I confirmed the hotel knew of her pending arrival and that she'd be staying in their room.

Nicole didn't like it but understood.

Lizzy was pleased and liked picking up her mother with no adults around. Bet it felt good. I also told her if I couldn't, I'd have a rental delivered there, to check with the front desk about it.

With the flight time and the time difference, arrival at the airport would be close to eleven o'clock. They'd be lucky to be in bed by midnight.

The way my day looked, I might not make it by midnight.

With that covered, there were some pre-meal things I needed to do. If Marcel would not meet at his home, there must be something he feared. If someone were watching him, Pappy's restaurant would be a good place to spot any prying eyes.

To offer a bit of scrutiny, I asked Pappy to have one of his guys be in the restaurant watching for anyone paying us too much attention. Pappy provided two, Franco and Jacques. I kept that little endeavor between myself and Pappy.

We'd gotten everything in place. It was dead on 5:30 when Marcel came in. He was dressed casual. Celeste escorted him to our table.

I had picked a table for four. I wanted to keep this informal fact gathering limited to Antoine, Nicole, Marcel, and myself. Pappy probably already knew—speaking of prying eyes.

Everyone stood and I introduced Marcel to Antoine. I mentioned Antoine was Pappy's son.

After introductions, I made sure Marcel sat near Nicole. My hope was Nicole might offer him some memories and even assist with our questions.

A second before I sat, I casually eyed Franco and Jacques. I got the okay sign and sat down.

The plan was if they saw someone about to do something suspicious, they would intervene. If that someone was observing unnaturally, and as we were leaving, Franco and Jacques would, shall we say, prevent that person's or persons' departure until a purpose was known.

We hadn't been eating long when Marcel must've gotten worried, impatient, or just interested. "John, you said you had questions about someone dying at the plant. I'll do what I can. What did you want to know?"

"Marcel, anything you can give will be appreciated. I mentioned we have some old newspapers and we found that a night watchman died about seven years ago. Does that ring any bells?"

He finished chewing and answered, "Yes. But no acid death," nodding as his eyebrows went up.

His voice sounded as if he was apologizing for disappointing me.

He had more. "Oh, I should explain the unusual shifts we had. There were two watchmen on duty Friday night through Sunday night, two shifts, twenty-four hours per. The third shift was six hours. They rotated that one. One did two shifts one week. The other guy did two the next week. When you had to do the second and third, you were there thirty hours straight."

Nicole grimaced when she heard the hours, "I can't believe anyone would do shifts that long. Besides getting food, when would you sleep?"

He tilted his head to her with a little smile. "Yes, Nicole, that's a long shift, but it paid very well and the watchman just had to make a round every ten hours. And a round only took an hour or so."

That got her interested. She laid her fork down. "So, they could sleep, I guess? But what about food? They wouldn't let them leave, right?"

He patted her hand. "Good observation, my dear. They got sleep between rounds, but they brought food with them or family would bring them food. We had a refrigerator back then. Oh, and there was a télévision. Or a TV as, Camille would say."

The two got combined smiles with those words.

We needed to get to the real subject. "Marcel, you said there was a death?" I motioned for Nicole to take a bite. She ignored me.

The old man paused, as if thinking. "Yes, one of the watchmen back then did die. It was Lucas. Lucas Berart."

My fork was filled with food, but his words cornered my interest. I rested the fork. "How do you know this? You said you were on day shift."

His eyes grew wide open, and he nodded in almost a circle. "Oh, I knew. He was a close friend." His head steadied. "Lucas ate supper with Camille and I at least once a week. Sometimes three times. I always took him food on at least one of his weekend shifts. He loved Camille's cooking. Lucas was an older man, fifty-seven, if I recall. Wife was dead. Parents had passed away. He was pretty much all that was left of his family."

I liked what I was hearing. "Then how'd he die?"

"Well, he didn't die from acid. He had a heart attack. The Monday morning watchman came in about eleven fifty that Sunday night. When Lucas wasn't at the desk, the watchman started hunting for him. He found him in the restroom, sitting there on a toilet with his clothes on."

I hadda ask. "Was the toilet flushed?"

Marcel grinned. "I know what you're thinking. I spoke to the watchman who found him. Yes, flushed. Lucas almost had his belt buckled when it happened. Lucas was just sitting there slumped over. We think he was standing when it started and just sat down."

"Any idea what the doctor said?"

"Lucas was my friend, and I was going to make sure I knew what happened. The doctor came to the plant and found he'd had a heart attack. The medical examiner came to the same conclusion. I know you're looking for acid, but not that time."

Nicole leaned toward Marcel. "He was your friend. I'm glad that didn't happen to him. I mean, I'm sorry he died, but it had to be less painful, as, as with that stuff." Her nose crinkled up and her mouth wrinkled as if she had taken a whiff of Limburger cheese.

He must have understood, for he politely ignored her expression. "Those are kind words. Camille had the same kind feeling. She was comforted he died so naturally. If he had any pain, no one knew." Marcel extended his hands palms up.

Everyone had finished eating, or was close to it. Most of us, me included, were sipping our wine.

Maybe it was the wine, but more questions came to mind.

Addressing Marcel, I said, "I don't know how it works here. Was he buried or cremated?"

"The service was at the maison funéraire home. Excuse me, Maison Funeral Home. He was buried in their cemetery. There weren't many people there. Most were people he worked with and a couple of neighbors."

Nicole said, "Oh, I'm so glad you and Camille attended his funeral. I can easily believe you two were as close a family as he could have."

She grabbed his arm and gave it a little hug. When she let go, he laid his hands on the table.

Those were good words. I wanted to ask him something, but I also wanted him to know he was with friends.

"Marcel, I have a question you may not want to answer. If you don't, I'll understand."

His hands remained on the table but flipped open palms up along with an agreeable nod.

I asked, "Could you tell me why you didn't want us to meet at your home? Has someone threatened you?"

Nicole leaned toward Marcel. "He does that. One question turns into two and often more. Truth is, he's a nice guy. Honest, too."

"John, you have a very convincing woman who's impossible to disobey. I know I've said it, but she so much reminds me of Camille. Beautiful and strong willed and so compassionate." He paused a moment, placing his hand on hers. "If I had a daughter, this one would have been my choice."

That did it. Her arms went around his neck with her chin resting on his shoulder. No tears, but glistening eyes.

"I do know what you mean, sir."

After a few moments passed, he answered, "For long time the French agents, like your FBI and CIA, come around looking at the place and asking if I'd seen or talked to anyone. Except for your visit, my answer is always no."

"That's seven years. You mean all those years?"

"No. My mistake. My memory sometimes fails me. When they closed the plant, the owners asked three of us to watch over it. Just three years ago, they decided only one was needed and they chose me. Not until about six months ago did the ISD first show up and they started asking if I'd seen anyone. Their visits are au hasard, I mean, random."

"Have they ever given you a reason for that kind of question?"

"No. I've asked why, but was never given a reason. I do know they didn't like my asking. So I quit asking and just answered."

I saw the look on Nicole's face—fear. "What did you tell them about our visit?"

Marcel had good news. "They haven't been around since you were there."

A real worry lit the question tree. Could they have been watching when we were there?

I had to know. "Marcel, when and if they do, I want you to tell them I was there asking about a man who died there. Do you remember the name I gave you?"

"Sure. My friend, Lucas Berart."

"Good. Then you can be honest because I asked about Lucas. That I found his name in an old newspaper. And that's true. We did. I didn't tell you why, but I said I'd be digging more."

Nicole's opinion would put holes in the sun. "John, I don't like that. You'll put yourself in more danger. This isn't worth it. Maybe we should quit looking."

Marcel was no longer smiling, and I needed a referee. I looked at Jacques and mouthed, "Pappy." He nodded his head. I made some arguments to buy me some time. Within two minutes, Pappy was at our table. I introduced Pappy to Marcel and explained how I knew him.

Marcel told Pappy all he told me, and I added what I was looking for at the factory. Pappy remembered.

Then I asked, "Pappy, what should I do? Continue my investigation or leave town?"

Nicole didn't let that question remain unanswered. "Pappy, John's in danger. Please tell him to stop?"

"Nicole, I don't believe that's needed. If John was on the ISD list, I'd know. I have my own internal snitches, as I believe is the American term. John should continue his own investigation. He has already revealed more than I have."

I appreciated his favorable words, but there was still much unknown. I wished the revealed would reveal itself to me.

Unsure who knew, so I asked, "Pappy, what's the ISD?" I knew who they were, but wanted no one to ever know why.

He looked at me a bit puzzled. I nodded and winked, and he explained, "The French version is Répertoire de Sécurité Interne. But you would recognize it as the Internal Security Directory, ISD. It's like a combo of your CIA and Homeland Security."

I wasn't particularly excited about being on their radar, again. I saw Nicole's demeanor.

She didn't like it, but I wanted to ease her concern. "Pappy, is the ISD a legitimate group? What I mean is, if they wanted to talk to you, would they just pay you a visit and talk, or maybe take you to their headquarters, peacefully?"

Pappy did a nod and smiled "I understand what you're asking, and they would not kidnap and torture you. Depending on what they had, they might ask you to go to their headquarters."

It was late. We needed a break, and I had something to do. "Lady and gentlemen, it's approaching eight o'clock and I'm ready to call it a day. Anybody in the same boat?"

Everybody's hand went up except Pappy's, but he had to hang around and manage the restaurant and hold hands with Mother Betty.

Marcel added, "I should get home. There's no one there, but I could use the rest." After a short pause, he added, "Pappy, the food was perfect. I have really enjoyed meeting all of you."

He stood. Nicole shot up right beside him and without hesitation asked, "Can we take you home? I really wouldn't mind doing that. And, I know John would be okay with it."

His face brightened up. He offered his hands, and she took them. "That's nice of you to offer, Nicole, but I have my car outside. I can get home okay."

I had a different perspective. Him getting home okay didn't sit well after all we talked about. I had an alternative in mind. "I'd be glad to drive you home, but I understand."

Nicole wasn't happy with that.

Marcel hugged Nicole and gave us his goodbyes.

Just as Marcel left the restaurant, I pulled Pappy aside. "Could you have your guys follow him home and maybe hang around his place very out of sight for a few hours? I want to be sure he's okay."

Pappy agreed and immediately made some signal with his hand and fingers to his guys. They took off.

After watching them obey his silent command, I had to at least recognize I was aware of it. "I take it they're off to follow him?"

Pappy crossed his arms while offering a half smile. "Well, you did ask."

Just as Pappy said that, Nicole was close to instantly standing beside us. "What are you two doing? I saw you two."

She backhanded me in the chest. I took it she wasn't pleased.

"Nicole, my dear, I asked and Pappy has his guys following Marcel home to be sure he gets there safe. Do we have your approval?"

I immediately knew I'd pay the price.

She stepped in front of me. Only steamy air was between us, along with a finger planted on my chest. "You do. Next time you want to do that, you will include me, understood?"

Pappy was behind her with a very big, silent, tooth filled smile.

Grabbing her finger, I leaned a little closer. With only a breath away, I said firmly, "I believe I need to kiss you."

She answered in a dramatic tone, "Well, you should do what you say, Mr. Stone."

I embraced her face with my hands and kissed her then immediately let go and said sternly, "I'm headed for the hotel. You coming with me?"

Her expression acquired a mischievous if not naughty appeal. She stepped back and gave me a tight-eyed stare. With no hesitation, she grabbed my hand and started dragging me out. It wasn't the first drag and I doubted it would be the last.

I did a walking sideways thing and waved goodbye to Pappy. If you can burst out laughing in silence, he did.

Antoine was watching us with raised eyebrows, a fixed expression, and an open mouth. Yeah. Clueless. Again.

Once outside, Nicole stopped at the passenger door. I took the silent order and opened it for her as she sat down.

No sooner than I was sitting on my side about to turn the key, when my phone rang. It was Mac. I whispered it to Nicole, then answered. "Hi, Mac. When you call, it often means I should head for cover." I heard him laugh. He was enjoying this.

"John, this time it may be appreciated. I have an update for you, but first, I want to talk to Nicole."

"And, why would you think she was with me?"

"My friend, I've known you too long, and I suspect your magnet for attracting girls hasn't ended. Besides, it's nighttime. And it's even later where I am. Now, may I speak with her?"

I innocently passed the phone to her, simply saying, "It's for you." She took the phone with an expectant smile. "Hi, Mac. You must be as sweet as John, from what he tells me," and with a guileless expression she added, "with all those women hanging on to you." He said something. She grinned and said, "Yeah, that's what he keeps saying." She shook her head and said, "I still like him." He said something. She added, "Me too. Here he is. Oh, we're going to meet soon, aren't we?"

With a wicked grin, she allowed me to use my phone.

"Okay, Mr. Mac, I figure you just got me in a heap of trouble," with Nicole listening to every word, "so give me the scoop and I'll take my punishment."

Her hand swung around and gently slapped my arm. That action told me I'd learn more later. To gain some control of the call, I clicked the speaker and held the phone between us.

"Not to worry, my good man. It will be a pleasant learning. As to the call, my source informed me that Alivia Béringer got married maybe five or so years ago. Don't have the exact year. Her married name is Marceau, but she still intros herself as Béringer. That's all I know now, but it got my interest up and am checking other sources."

I was unsure where that would lead, but it was welcome information. "Marceau is a new addition to my ever-growing list, but that fits, as her roommate still speaks of her as Béringer."

"Maybe we'll know more. Don't recall if I told you, but her parents live in Mainz, Germany. You probably remember Jake had an assignment there a few years ago."

"When I first heard Mainz, I remembered Jake being there. All I know is some Frenchman was killed. Do you think there's a connection?"

"Don't believe so. And your memory's close. Jake was there working on a government official kidnapping case. Jake saved the official, but ended up killing the kidnapper."

That brought back more memories. "Yeah. With the kidnapper dead, they never figured out who ordered it."

"Good memory, young man. Guess I best go. Got some guests waiting. Take care of yourself and that young beauty I spoke with, and I hope to meet soon."

"Will do, Mac. Keep in touch."

No sooner than I'd clicked the button, Nicole spilled her thoughts. "She got married. So what? Women do that. Why would he have called you with something like that?"

"It's information. Maybe worthless, but we can't know that. I find something, tell him, and he gets me details. Sometimes someone he asked will keep digging and get him more info."

My words got me to thinking, why now? Why not tomorrow? I couldn't make myself believe his call was a coincidence.

Don't know why I thought that, but I acted on it. I cranked the car and told her we were going to see Alivia.

Her pretty head whipped in my direction. "It's eight o'clock. And, if you hadn't noticed, that's followed by the letters p.m. It's getting dark. Too late to go ringing a doorbell this time of night. How do you know she's there? You can't know she's there."

"It's good to see we're on the same side." That got a twisted lip with an eye boring stare. "We know she lives there and comes and goes. I figure if we slip in this late, we may surprise her."

She gave me her thoughts, covered with potential retaliation. "You're obviously getting search crazy. Okay, I'll let you have this one, but if she's not there, I'll be sure to remind you many times."

That came with a waving finger pointed in my direction. Had it been a laser, my head would've had slices.

With that logged into my future, I headed for Montrouge. The discussion had yet to stop, including the fact I wasn't able to convince her of a need for the visit.

My thinking was I hadn't yet talked to Alivia. And, her two possible cohorts were not even close to helpful. Larry was a liar, and his buddy Jules was best put as inhospitable. Alivia had become a mystery that needed at least some research.

It was almost nine o'clock when I parked at her hotel. I should mention I liked the hour, because it was late and she might possibly be home waiting for the surprise I mentioned.

The lift deposited us on the fourth floor as before, and there we were standing at her door, D1.

Nicole was holding my hand tightly. "You sure you want to do this? Now? Either of the women could open the door with a gun in her hand."

I gave Nicole a raised eyebrow stare as I knocked on the door. In maybe a minute, I heard a female voice behind the closed door say something in French.

Responding in English was my only choice. "Hi, Nicolette. This is John Stone and Nicole Powell. We were here a couple of days ago."

The female voice sounded agitated. "Why are you back?"

"I have a couple of additional questions I'd like to ask. May we come in, please?"

The door opened a small crack and I saw her look at us. I tossed a hi with my hand. She accepted and opened the door, but did not offer us entrance.

Her eyes narrowed. "Is late. Why you back?"

Nicole gave it a chance. "When we were here, you were so kind trying to help me find my father. We just wanted to talk a few minutes more."

Nicolette stepped back, letting us in. She shut and locked the door. She did not offer us seating.

I gave it a go. "Is there any way I can talk to Alivia? She may know nothing about Nicole's father, William Powell. If I could at least ask, it would remove one more person and we can work other possibilities. If she's here, or even by phone. Anything would help."

Nicolette said nothing. Her expression appeared curious. After a few moments, she said, "I call her. You not talk more than few minutes."

I took that as a command. "Yes. Just a couple of minutes. I promise."

Nicolette picked up her phone from a table and pressed screen buttons. Within seconds she was speaking to someone. I heard the name Alivia. Nicolette handed me the phone, which I passed to Nicole.

Nicole started, "My name is Nicole Powell. My father, William Powell, was in an automobile accident seven years ago and was killed. All I know is he was working for a private company." Alivia, I assume, said something. Nicole continued. "It was a security company. He was burned to death. Oh, and his friend, Gustav Gagnon, died falling into a vat of acid at a manufacturing plant north of Paris."

Something else was said, but Nicole told Alivia to wait and handed me the phone.

"Alivia, my name is John. Please share with me what you told Nicole."

"I told her much not. I didn't know of her father. I read papers well and did read about man killed with acid. That was many years past. I didn't know of them."

She may have been honest with us, but I wasn't convinced. It was her speech. Her words were mixed with what I've heard where the person knows just a little English, but she used contractions. Contractions are not heard unless the person knows and uses the language well.

"Alivia, a close friend reads the papers as well. He told me you were married a few years back. It may be late, but congratulations."

Her reply was delayed. I couldn't see her face, but I could hear her heavy breathing. She finally responded, "Yes. I was married almost six years ago."

A perfectly worded reply. Six years. That was close enough to what Mac told me.

But, we were getting nowhere. I took it to the next level. "Do you recall passing by Nicole and me as you exited the hotel lift a few days ago?"

"No, I do not. And, how would you know it was me?"

"Your perfume. I got a good whiff of it as you walked between Nicole and me. Later, I smelled the same perfume when we visited Nicolette here. It was the same. No question about that. And as I described you, Nicolette showed me a picture. It was definitely you."

Her reply was delayed, but I knew what it would be. I held the phone away for a moment, looking at Nicolette then back at the phone. The first three numbers were a Frankfurt exchange from my calls to Jake. I read the other eight into my brain as many times as I could. With luck, that might etch them on a memory muscle.

Alivia's reply was quick and angry. "I've spoken enough to you. Give the phone back to Nicolette."

Her English was getting better. Someone was a good teacher.

"Will do. And, I find it astonishing how perfectly you speak English. Bis bald."

Adding the German words for bye seemed appropriate. That's pretty much the only words I remember from my calls to Jake.

I handed the phone to Nicolette and pulled out my own, keying in Alivia's number as best I could remember. "I better call him before I forget," which meant nothing, but an excuse to be clicking numbers.

Nicole returned a silent "WHAT?" to which I mouthed, "Nothing!" along with a tiny shake of my head. I turned to face Nicolette and receive my departure request.

She and Alivia were talking as Nicole and I were doing our silent thing, so I heard nothing they said. Of course, it was in French, as expected.

Nicolette gave the order. "You should leave. No. You *will* leave. You're no longer welcome here. Do not return, or I'll call the police."

Odd. The more these two women got pissed at me, the more their English equally improved.

I put my arm out for Nicole to latch on to and we departed. I left the door open for Nicolette to shut, which she did with gusto. I think the building shook.

We stopped at the lift. Nicole stared at the door but didn't press the button. "Don't think we'll be welcome there anymore."

I raised her hand and gave it a kiss, then added, "Not until we give them a good reason to invite us."

With a doubtful gaze, she included a question along with the answer, "We're not going with them to pick up Rebecca, are we?"

"Nah. I doubt your mother will be with them. It will be a thrill for Lizzy to do that herself."

"You do know she doesn't have a car or a driver's license?"

"Not to worry. Andre does. Remember, I ordered a rental to be delivered to the hotel, and they'll call Lizzy when it arrives. Now, if Andre wants to drive his car, I think Lizzy will be very agreeable."

"You do seem to have all things worked out."

"I try. It's been a long day. You sleepy?"

Still giving me the eye, she replied, "You do remember I got the pad thing happening?"

I turned and pressed the lift button. "Snuggling is fun."

She agreed.

CHAPTER 27

RADIATING QUESTIONS

My alarm woke me only because I had set it for 7:00 a.m. It also woke the woman lying next to me. Both of our heads were lying on pillows. Eye to eye.

The woman said, "Maybe we couldn't do everything I'd like you to do, but you snuggle very well. I think you've had practice." She emphasized her words with an alluring wink.

With a very exaggerated no teeth visible grin, I said, "I'm a quick learner."

A fist gently hit my chest with the purpose made clear with words, "You better be sure I'm the only teacher you have or need. Got that?"

I put my free arm across her and answered with the only words a man dares say, "Yes, dear."

The fist made contact again.

My arm retracted as she asked, "Did we learn anything from that fiasco last night?"

She was going in a new direction, so I had to tweak it a little to add some fun. "Do you know you just spoke a French word?"

Her face lifted a bit off the pillow. "What *are* you talking about?"

"Fiasco is French. Means failure, or close to it."

Her hand flew up against her cheek as she rested on her elbow. "All right. Quit stalling. Cut the crap and answer my question, Mr. Fiasco."

The problem was, if I knew anything, I didn't know what it was. But I had to give her something.

I joined her by resting on my elbow hand. "First, Alivia spoke very good English, but only after she got pissed. So did Nicolette. Alivia was making up the words she spoke. She tried to make it appear she didn't know her words well. That was a lie. She speaks English better than I do. That goes for both of 'em."

"I don't understand. I mean, so what? She knows English. Maybe Alivia took a course."

"Or maybe she's been around a bunch of Americans."

"Tell me again why we even wanted to talk to her? It was a waste of time. Ours and hers." She was as perplexed as me.

"All I know is Pappy gave me Alivia's name because he had some vague reason. He didn't even know. Some flag must've gone up and got his interest."

"A flag? You mean a French flag? That's dumb. They're all . . ." She stopped. She saw me smiling. "Oh, a flag of interest." She got a little upset with me. The hand supporting her head crashed down on her pillow, leaving her elbow supporting her body and her face cushioned only by air. "Why didn't you stop me?"

I kept it short. "I liked you walking down that road. You looked cute. Just like you do now."

She leaned forward. Our lips were no more than an inch apart. In a whisper, "You think I'm going to kiss you, don't you?"

Her whispered breath caressed my face. "That's the hope of every man on earth." That was going to get me some points.

"What're our plans for today?"

"Huh?" Yeah. I was as surprised as you are.

She brushed my nose with her finger. Keep in mind, her finger nearly brushed both our noses. "I'm sorry, John. I shouldn't have done that. I was trying to be playful, and you're being sweet." Her hand went under my chin and she planted a lingering kiss. When our lips parted, still an inch away, she asked, "Am I forgiven?"

Only one word came to mind, "Forever." I didn't leave it there. I hitchhiked on her earlier words with a variation, "As to plans, we're stopping by your mom's room to give Rebecca a hi."

"That's also my plan. Glad you'll be there with me. I'm so happy she's here. And, after that?"

"After that, we'll be paying a visit to Karthos this morning."

Her eyes widened. "Ooh. I like that. I'll see Marcel again. He's a sweet man."

He was not in the plan. I had my reason and I dreaded telling her. "Well, not quite. Not this time. We're going to—"

She heard all she wanted. Our lips were suddenly a foot apart, along with our emotions. "And why the hell not? We'll be there. It's Friday and he'll be there, and we're going to visit him."

I sat up on my knees. "If you remember, the ISD stops there and they always want to know if anyone visited. The more we visit, the more trouble we cause him. This is a special trip."

Nicole shot up on her knees with angry piercing eyes. Her fists were balled on her hips. "You should've told me. You made me think we were seeing him." Her hands flew out, fingers spread. "And, why would we go there just to see the building?" Her hands dropped to her side.

I took her hands into mine. "I do apologize. I didn't mean to— Look. I'll arrange times for us to see him. Meet him somewhere. I like him, too."

"Okay. That's good, but what are you really doing?"

"Here's my thinking for today. Why would the ISD even care about that old, dusty, dying building? It's been seven years. Today, I just want to walk around the outside."

She waved our hands. "The outside! What's that going to tell you? You think they got a parking ticket?"

That got a needed laugh outa me. I returned the gesture. My hand went up, still holding hers, and I pointed a finger at her. "Now, that's an interesting thought. But, doubt the police will let me know that. Truth is, I'm not sure what I'm looking for. Marcel sees the inside daily. I want to know why ISD even cares, and the outside is a start."

Still holding hands, she swung them a little, adding a smile. "That's a good idea. And you thought of it. Nobody else has. Oh, maybe we'll find an old shed out back filled with gold. No, diamonds."

She literally bounced a couple of times when she said that.

I liked her excitement. "Ya never know. Somebody cares about the place where a man died in acid, and it all just doesn't fit. And, I want to know why. Might recover some diamonds."

Nicole pulled our hands to her breast. "Me too. I mean, the who and why." She kept holding my hands and put a finger on my chest. "Not the diamonds. Let's get some breakfast and raid the place."

We took our showers, she got a fresh pad, and we got dressed. She picked up her purse. It was a small, flat one that hung down to her waist. Very feminine, in my opinion. She was wearing a loose pink blouse, white shorts, and the sandals I liked. They laced up close to her cute knees.

She took my hand and led me into the lift and pretty much down to the tenth floor.

I knocked on her mom's door, but before anyone could open it, Nicole did. She held up her key card, sorta flipping it around, for my benefit, enhanced with a smile.

We were about one step in the room when an attractive woman rushed to Nicole and gave her a hug. I heard undecipherable shared words.

The two parted and Nicole, holding my arm, with a hand pointing at me, "Rebecca, this is John Stone, the fellow who got you over here."

Smiling, Rebecca hugged me, then granted me release while capturing my hands. "John, thank you so much. It's so wonderful to be here."

I was about to say something when she hugged me again. I put my arms around her gently.

Nicole came to my defense. "Rebecca, go easy on him. He's got some work to do."

Rebecca let go and took a step back. "Nicole, I'm so sorry, but no one has done anything near this. John, thank you again. Lizzy is so happy."

With fear diminishing, I added my words, "Thank you, Mrs. Patrick. It just didn't seem right with all of us over here and you at home. Oh, and I should add, that daughter of yours is a sweet and lovely young woman."

"John, everybody calls me Rebecca, and so will you." I accepted the order.

I managed a nod as Patty and Lizzy came to my rescue and pasted themselves on my sides.

Nicole politely stepped back when she saw them coming.

A pleased Lizzy informed her mom, "Mother, we told you how Uncle John helped us. Well, this is Uncle John."

Mother Betty had a positive expression, which I appreciated.

My trouble was I wasn't sure what they'd told her mother. There was that little kidnapping thing that my meddling had caused.

Patty saw my distress and must have signaled Lizzy.

Lizzy gave my arm a little hug and added, "It's okay, Uncle John. Mother knows of the kidnapping and how you saved us."

That girl laid it right out there with no hesitation, after reading my mind. My head was nodding, and my eyes were getting dizzy trying to know who was next.

Guess Patty didn't want to be left out in the cold. With a gentle tug, she added, "That's why we love him and why he's our Uncle John."

From behind I heard a sigh of relief. Nicole added, "Girls, he's surrounded by women. I think you're making him nervous."

The girls gave me a grinning kiss and let go. Rebecca was just watching.

Nicole grabbed me and led me to a sofa. I whispered, "Thank you."

To the girls, I said, "So, what do you gals have planned for the day?"

The girls sat down on the floor in front of me with the ladies in chairs.

Patty answered, "We're going to Noémi's home to spend the day. And, Mama's coming."

Lizzy jumped in. "My mother's coming, too. We've told her all about Nathan and Andre. I'm so glad Mother will meet them."

They had the day in gear. "Yeah. That'll be fun. Do I need to drive you there?"

Patty answered, "No, Uncle John. Andre and Nathan are picking us up." She pointed at me. "And, you're not giving us any spending money. And you won't need to give them cab fare."

Fanning my face, I made a *whew* sound. That got a smile from the girls and an elbow in my side via Nicole.

I wanted to be sure the new mother was aware. "Rebecca, you'll soon learn that these two girls have a serious crush on those boys. And the boys, likewise. Right, Mrs. Powell?"

Mother Betty was surprised at my question, for I had innocently directed it to her.

"John, you and Nicole have been around them more than me, but I'd agree with you from what I've seen."

With that covered, I needed the girls' attention. "Girls, Nicole and I need to git going. Would it be okay for us to stop by Noémi's when we get our stuff done?"

"Of course, Uncle John," said Lizzy with added excitement.

I stood up and Nicole joined me. The girls gave me a hug. Mother Betty did the same. She hadn't done that often, so I felt a treat.

Rebecca joined the huggers. "John, I can tell my girl thinks a lot of you and pays attention to you." She added, "And I like it. Feel free to send her to her room without supper." She let out a wild laugh.

"Mother!" broadcast Lizzy. I think the lobby heard it.

With a finger pointed at Rebecca, I added, "That'll still be your job. I like hugs better."

Having caused a mother-daughter dilemma, it was time to head for the hills. Actually, I saw smiles, so felt all was okay.

I was surprised to find Mother Betty was going with the girls to Noémi's home. I was equally astonished that the boys were picking them up. Course, it saved me cab fare.

Saint-Denis and Karthos were our targets. I just had to remember where Dépôt Raspail was. I did, after a couple of wrong turns.

My main concern was watchers. For all I knew, the Repertory ISD guys were parked and watching, unknown to all. To ease my mind a bit, I drove around several streets looking for men or women in suits sitting in a car, watching.

After circling a couple of streets, Nicole asked, "What *are* you doing? Why are you going in circles?"

"Sorry. My concentration was focused. We know ISD asked Marcel if anyone was there asking questions. That may mean they're also watching. So, I'm looking for cars that appear to be watchers."

Her head was shaking like a tree in a tornado, with hands blowing in the wind. "John, get real. I know you mean well, but you can't know that."

"I know that, but I had to check the area. I haven't seen anything suspicious."

She came back with a toe-curling yet calm expression. "Thank you."

I added, "Just so you know, I'm going to park on the opposite side from where Marcel is. We'll get out and look around." She started to say something, but I caught her. "Not now. Let me finish." Her arms folded. "We may never see inside. We're going to look in any side buildings. Anywhere something may be hidden."

I stopped on purpose, waiting for the rebuttal.

It took close to forever for her reply. Her arms unfolded. That time she was doing the thinking. "Dear God. I know what you're thinking." She began looking around as I was pulling into a parking space. "This place was closed soon after those two men died. People die. Closing it must've had a separate reason. And, now, that DSI or ISD or ISS or ABC or whatever group is watching the place. But why?"

"That's the ultimate question. Come on, Sherlock, we got digging to do."

We stayed together as we looked around. There were no cars, no trucks anywhere. There were four separate buildings behind the main one, two large ones and two smaller ones. There were no locks on the two larger ones, and we found nothing but dusty, rusty, crumbling, unidentifiable things. There weren't offices. Must have stored something there. Acid, maybe.

One of the smaller buildings was similar but more of a designing place. It had a large drafting table, broke and totally unusable. The other smaller building was different.

As we went inside, I flipped the light switch just to see if it worked. It did. The lights in the other buildings hadn't.

As I saw the place, I asked Nicole, "What's your impression of what you see?"

She had already been eyeing the place. "No dust. Someone cleaned it enough to live here. I've seen apartments dirtier than this place. Still can't live here. One chair. And that table looks more like what I've seen in a hospital. What's that pile of stuff?"

"That, my dear, is a protective blanket for when you work around radioactive material, and some gloves." Without any serious thinking, I lifted it. I saw the hazmat suit.

"We're gettin' outta here!"

With both hands on Nicole's waist, I pushed her out the door, flipping off the light. I didn't see any radioactive containers, but the gear meant there was some there or might be some coming.

Once outside she asked, "Are we gonna die?"

"No. Don't think so. That's what you need to work around things like uranium. Uranium is kept in containers, and I didn't see any. We're leaving."

I left the door as we found it, locked, and the knob area wiped clean of prints. The entry slab was concrete, and I didn't see any identifiable shoe prints we may have left.

Heading for the car, I looked up, down, whirling around, looking, but saw nothing moving and no one watching.

Nicole headed for her side. I to mine. When I put my hand on the door handle, I froze. I turned to face the building. An uneasy thought had revealed itself to my brain. Did I leave the stuff on the table as I had found it?

Once we were in the car, Nicole sat but continued to fidget, watching all around. I cranked the car and put my hand on her shoulder. "We're okay. I'm heading for Pappy's place. I got questions."

She gave me a pair of tense words. "Go. Please."

I parked and walked briskly, keeping Nicole in the lead into the restaurant. As soon as I saw Celeste, I told her I needed to see Pappy like right then. She told me he was alone in his office, which was enough for me.

This time I knocked and got an okay to enter. We pretty much collapsed on the sofa. Once we had calmed a little, I told him what we found. Nicole excitedly told him the same thing in her own words, only creepier.

Pappy was listening while leaning back in his chair. Once he heard our story, he leaned forward resting on his desk. "John, you may have found something the ISD has been attempting to find for months. Uranium is always being smuggled everywhere, but that's by major groups. There is a small group that's on the ISD list, but they haven't been able to successfully track them."

"Are you saying I've got myself and Nicole tangled up with that group?" I almost said, *Again*.

"It's possible."

A bad thought drifted into my brain. "You said you'd know if I was on their list, and that I wasn't." I waved a finger in the air. "Suppose those guys talking to Marcel are imposters and they're just trying to be informed if anyone notices what they're doing at the plant. Like me."

My words caused unintended concerns. I knew it when I saw Nicole, who was on the brink of screaming.

Her head shook as her hands turned into fists. "Oh, no, no. Not again."

Pappy put his hands out, palms up. "Don't worry, Nicole. As soon as I tell my contacts at ISD, they will have that place under surveillance within the hour."

Pappy made the call. I have no idea who he spoke to at the ISD nor what he said, but the call seemed positive. He did mention my name twice, and after the call, he gave me a contact there. Henri Dumas. I already had his number, in my phone, from when I helped Pappy and Antoine. Dumas wasn't happy with what I did.

We hung out at Pappy's place for just over an hour and left for Noémi's. Nicole had calmed. Pappy was happy, and after two years, I'd have to face Dumas again.

I paused to consider how long being pissed lasts.

CHAPTER 28

OLD CONTACTS EMERGE

I'd barely left the parking lot when Nicole's face lit up. She turned to me. "It's going to be relaxing being with Mama, Rebecca, the girls, and Noémi."

"After this morning, it will be amazing and relaxing." That was my hope. It was needed.

She was watching the road and me. "We did get a lot done, didn't we? I mean, we found that place they were using and got it reported. It was frightening, but you kept us from getting hurt." She rested her hand on my arm.

We'd been talking for ten minutes or so and I started watching a car I suspected was following us. I'd made four turns since leaving the station. It had made the same turns. I kept talking but decided I needed some test turns, watching what they did.

Nicole caught on to my screwy driving. "Why are you talking to the rearview mirror?"

I jumped.

"Geez. Will you stop doing that," still eyeing the review view mirror.

After two more turns, I was certain.

Nicole noticed. "I don't know *what* you're doing, but you're frightening me. What *are* you doing?"

I managed to gain a little control of myself. "I thought we were being followed. Did some test turns, and yep, we are. I bet it's the ISD imposter uranium guys."

She started to look back. I told her not to. To keep looking ahead.

Her hands were strangling each other then she wrapped them tight around her chest. "I thought this was over. What can we do?" Her hands gripped the armrests.

"Don't worry. There's a police station not too far up this road. I remember it from before. I'm heading there now. If they try to corner us, I'll run every light I can find and let the police arrest me."

"I gotta look. I'm going crazy." She immediately focused out the rear window. Within a second, her eyes were focused on me. "How do you know there's a police station up ahead?"

Ignoring her question, I managed to get an okay out.

She said, "The gray car. Two men, right?"

"Yes." That's when I saw them pull around another car to gain ground. I floored the pedal and ran a stoplight. They did, too. I'd normally prefer not to have a police car following me, but at that time, I wanted one real bad.

"John, they're getting closer."

"I know."

Pointing she said, "There's a police car behind them. Do they know who they're following?"

"Yes. Us. The cops are following the bad guys, and the bad guys are following us. If we were in the States, I'd call 911."

"John, it's no time to try being cute. Can we shoot 'em or something?" She never took her eyes off them.

"They haven't fired any shots and probably won't with a cop behind them." Then I saw it. "There it is. Boulevard Vagard, or some such. The station is couple of minutes away."

Nicole saw where we were. "Looks like we'll get to the station before the police car does."

And we did. I pulled in and slammed on brakes, taking two parking spaces. The bad guys decided to take another route, but not before I got the car model. The police car followed them. Guess they figured the station boys would handle me.

I grabbed my wallet, passport, and phone as I was flying out of the car. Told Nicole to do the same. Pulled out my driver's license. As all that was happening, I was clicking Pappy's number. I had one hand by my ear and the other in the air, waiting.

Policemen started rushing out of the building. I was the target.

Nicole rushed around the car and jumped between me and the police. Whether or not she knew it at the time, that gave me needed seconds to get Pappy to answer and give him two sentences.

The officer said something. Nicole threw her arms out with a *got no idea what you're saying* gesture. He grabbed her arms and moved her several feet off to my side.

The only words I got out were "No speak French. Please talk to my ISD guy here." I pointed to the phone. Pappy heard me say that.

Nicole stepped back close to me, grabbed the phone, and started talking to Pappy.

She was giving Pappy everything when the cop tried to get the phone. She told Pappy to wait. To the cop, she let him have it, in words, "Hey, you. I'm using this phone. Pappy, don't hang up."

Nicole was not to be stopped. She undid a blouse button and stuck the phone inside. With that brave action, she crossed her arms. Believe me, that guaranteed considerable protection.

The officer stood there snookered. Two more officers joined the fun. They decided to leave the phone in its cozy snug venue.

Between the officer's commands to me and to Nicole, I told him, again, to talk to the guy on the phone. "We were being followed. Please. The man on the phone knows Henri Dumas, with ISD. They can tell you what has happened. Please."

Nicole followed suit, saying, "Please." With her fingers pointed to her blouse.

Then the proverbial stuff hit the fan. The next officer approaching I knew very well—unfortunately.

Standing there with arms in the air, I greeted him, smiling. "Lieutenant Grenier. It's good to see you again."

I left it at that. He didn't return the greeting.

Nicole stepped beside me. With a hand slap on my arm. "What're you doing? You trying to make friends with these guys? They want you behind bars. Maybe a padded cell."

Lieutenant Grenier stepped into the crowd of officers, waving them aside.

He was standing a few feet away, with arms crossed. "Mr. Stone. I have you in my custody, again. For what occurrence do I have the privilege of your presence?"

At least he still spoke good English. I, unfortunately, already knew that.

Nicole's eyes, along with her head and emotions, were flipping between us. I knew explanations were in my near future. One to the lieutenant and one to the woman. My brain was in favor of the LT.

I turned to Nicole. "Is Pappy still on the phone?"

She gave me a nod. She withdrew the phone from its cozy domain and extended her hand holding the warm phone. She said nothing. The phone probably would have complained of sweating.

"Lieutenant. Two things I need to tell you. I ran the red light because a car with two guys was following us. It was a dark blue four door Peugeot. Late model, I think. And, first letters of the tag were PD29."

Nicole decided I needed help with, "PD29JFH," grinning.

"Nice. Thank you, Nicole. Lieutenant, I had to do something stupid hoping one of your guys would see me and arrest me. And, second, Pappy Armand is on that phone." I pointed to Nicole's hand. "I managed to tangle with some uranium smugglers, and—"

"Stop." The lieutenant gave me very definite order. Then turned to Nicole and without hesitation he ordered her with his hand stretched out, "Give me the phone."

With no hesitation and no fear, she officially approached him. With very a steady hand, she placed the phone in his hand with an audible slap.

In spite of his surprised demeanor, obvious by his open mouth, he looked ready to give her more orders. He never got the chance.

Ignoring him, Nicole turned facing me with her back to him. She stepped beside me and turned back facing the lieutenant. Then came the pièce de résistance, and I ain't talking about fish. She simply stood erect with her hands clasped behind her back, smiling and displaying splendid points of interest.

The pink blouse, white shorts, and sandals added feminine power to the view.

Her small purse hung freely on her side brushing just below her waist.

The officers around him were enjoying the spectacle. I swear they were ready to clap hands.

It was time to bring him and his guys down to earth. "Lieutenant, I highly suggest you listen to what Pappy Armand has to say. Possibly, my associate here may need to give you phone instructions?"

Hey, I was up to my knees in trouble, and the LT would prefer to have it up to my—well, we'll leave it at that.

The LT stared at the phone. I knew when he heard the name Armand, his own concerns jumped at him. Courage, or possibly fear, forced him to put the phone by his ear. I heard "Bonjour" and some other words, and he said his name and a lot of French. The LT was angry at first, but he calmed down. Possibly because he was told to.

They didn't talk long. I heard a quick "Au revoir" from the LT.

He extended the phone to me. "He wishes to speak with you."

I took the steps, accepting the phone, and returned beside Nicole. It was time I knew my fate. "What's happening, Pappy?"

"There will be no charges against you. The episode will not appear on any books."

"Thanks, Pappy. So, what's our next step?"

"I only gave the lieutenant the high-level information. You need to give him as much detail as you know. Because we don't know what the smugglers will do regarding you. You need cover. I asked the lieutenant to put cuffs on you as if being arrested, in case they are watching. Once inside, he will give you a car to use temporarily. They will have someone drive your car to the hotel later."

"Sounds good. Will they be watching the plant?"

"Yes. And, you stay away from it, at least for now. If the smugglers show up there tonight or whenever, they'll grab them. The lieutenant knows you are the one who figured this out. And, I will make sure he doesn't forget."

All that was overwhelming. "I'll cooperate as needed. Pappy, I owe you one."

"John, you helped my son. I owe you more than can ever be paid."

We said our goodbyes. I put the phone in my pocket and gave a nod to the LT. I turned my back to him, waiting for the cuffs.

Nicole reacted and was about to take a swing at the LT when I said, "No."

I told her to come close and gave her the short version but told her to continue to complain in case someone was watching. She returned a twisted lip smile. I knew both me and the LT would regret the walk to the building.

And yes, the LT's walk to the building was not pleasant. Nicole played her part well. The other officers didn't know the script and tried to slow her down, without success.

Once inside, she grabbed the officer who put the cuffs on me and dragged him behind me. In unpleasant English, she told him to remove the cuffs. The LT nodded an okay.

Rubbing my wrists, I asked the LT if we could talk in private. He agreed and led us to his office.

Nicole and I were in separate chairs.

He was letting me off, but I needed clarification. "Lieutenant. I know you're in charge, so is there anything I can do to help with the smuggling ring?"

"At this point, I think not. But, if you recall anything more, please let me know."

I gave him a recap of what we knew and saw at the plant. And that Marcel Moe Clair was a big help and to be sure he wasn't hurt. Nicole added some details, some of which he did not know.

He thanked us. To my surprise, he added, "I fully understand why you drove as you did. You had no idea what they might do, and you had this charming woman to keep safe. Your actions are understood."

By what he said and how he said it, I felt he knew my concerns. But I wondered of his concerns.

The LT then asked, "So that I'm aware of where you will be, may I ask what your plans are for the day?"

I eyed Nicole as to who should talk. I got the nod.

"We're going to visit Noémi Gagnon. Her husband was a close friend of Nicole's father. She lives in Créteil on Buisson. That's all of the address I recall."

Nicole sweetly queried the LT, "I know we can't use our car, John's car. Are we going to get a car? Hope it's not a clunker."

The LT did the head tilt, which I read as he had no idea what she meant. I nodded to Nicole.

With a captivating smile and briefly touching her fingers to her lips, she added, "Oh, I'm sorry. A clunker is a car that is either old and falling apart, or a new one that's noisy and falling apart. A car you would never let your girl drive or ride in." He smiled. She leaned forward a little and added, "You would never have me ride in a car like that, would you?"

He was hooked, and she was ready to drag him in. I was a little jealous.

"Miss Powell, I will make sure you have a very fine car." He emphasized *very*.

He picked up the phone, pressed some buttons, and spoke with someone, in French, of course. The only word I recognized was clunker. Suspect there's no French version.

Nicole asked, "Did you order me a car?"

Order *her* a car? I'd become second banana in the script.

"Yes. The Mercedes will be here in fifteen minutes."

If his smile had been any brighter, we would've needed sunglasses. I felt like I'd vanished.

She added, "Lieutenant, you may call me Nicole, if you like."

"Yes, please. Your name matches your face. And, you must call me Jonathan, please."

I threw up my finger to speak, but no one saw it.

Ignoring me, Nicole kept her play going. "I would never have thought that was a French name." Maybe she wasn't acting.

"The background is Hebrew. My mother's great-grandparents moved here from Israel, and she picked the name. But I'm pure French and love it."

Their eyes were glued on each other—and she had the glue.

My only way to be known to exist was lighting a pack of firecrackers or maybe stripping down naked and dancing around the room.

I decided to stand. "Ah, feels better standing up." Speaking to the LT. "Could the car possibly be waiting for us?"

Without looking at me, he gave the answer to Nicole. "I'll get a call. Nicole, where do you live in America?"

I sat back down, with clothing intact.

"It's a small town in Georgia. Marietta. It's a sweet old town. Has a great square. But we don't have an Eiffel Tower. Oh, and we do have the Statue of Liberty. Thank you for that."

"You're very welcome. Have you ever visited it?"

"No. Never been to New York."

The phone rang. I welcomed the interruption.

The LT picked up the phone, spoke a few words, hung up and informed Nicole, "The car's here. Let's go see if it meets your approval."

He wasn't looking at me when he spoke those words.

We three went out the back entrance. The red Mercedes was there. No one else was around. Guess it was the LT's show. There were no visible public streets, so at that point we were hidden.

Nicole walked around it twice with hands caressing it. "Jonathan, it's magnificent. Perfect. Thank you."

She stopped at the passenger's side. I started toward it but was overtaken by Jonathan, with his hand already on the handle. I continued around to the driver's side, opened the door and stood there.

The keys were in the car. Leaning on the roof, "Nicole, get in," was my simple command. "Lieutenant, I'll get this back to you tomorrow."

He gave an okay sign.

Nicole hadn't obeyed. Again, I asked, with a bit more emphasis, "*Nicole.* Get in or stay here."

She gave me an unpleasant frown but got in.

I joined her and cranked the car. Just as Nicole was letting her window down, I drove off. I considered burning rubber, but my freedom may still have been in question.

From the second I left the police station and turned on the main road, Nicole was quiet. If the windshield could complain of staring eyes, it would have.

I asked, "Is there a problem?" I was pretty certain I knew the answer, but I wanted to talk about it.

Her face showed no anger. She was looking down. Her fingers were flipping around like they were playing with each other, but I knew she wasn't watching them. I'd hurt her feelings.

She looked at me. "Why did you yell at me back there? I was trying to say goodbye to Jonathan. I was going to thank him for being kind, understanding, and generous. But you drove off."

I wasn't happy with what I'd done. "I do apologize. I'm so sorry. The way you were talking to him and looking at him, I think I was jealous. You should never forgive me."

She put her hand on my arm. "I never meant to make you feel that way. To be honest, I did enjoy talking to him. I understand now. All I did was talk to him. I ignored you. That wasn't nice to you. It's me who's asking to be forgiven." She gave my arm a little squeeze.

It was time to offer a compliment, "You did get us a great car to use." I threw a quick glance at her.

"You do know why I was so nice to him about the car we'd get?"

"Ya got me there, girl." I didn't know, but she heightened my interest.

"Out front while he was arresting you, I saw a bunch of old cars on the side of the building. They were inside a tall fence. And, from the cop shows I've seen, that's where they keep cars related to cases. The ones I could see were old and yucky. Soooo, I got nice."

"You snookered him!" She was considerably good at that. I could only do it on a snooker table.

"Yes," with a brilliant seductive smile tossed in my direction.

"There's nothing more dangerous to men than a sneaky, pretty woman. And, I ain't kidding." I knew I'd pay for that observation.

"It's good you know that, Mr. Stone. Now, look. I didn't want to be sneaky, but I didn't like the way Jonathan looked at you in the parking lot. He acted and talked like he knew you. I didn't like it and started playing the game right there."

"I must admit, you had us both fooled. I had no clue what you were doing. Oh, and you saw the cars. I didn't. Truth be known, if you hadn't been there, I'd be in a cell right now."

Her head swished like a rocket in my direction and stuck there. "He did know you!" She paused a split second, possibly considering if she should devour me. "Okay. Spill it. Now!"

"We're getting close to Noémi's place. We can talk about that later." And, yes. I was pleading for an innocent ruling.

She managed to do a half side turn while buckled in, crossed her arms, and gave me the verdict. "You'll tell me now, or you'll wish you were in a cell. I'm waiting."

"Okay! I give. Back when I was helping Antoine, I determined who the embezzlers were. I set up a couple of bank accounts and made it appear I had financial problems to get their attention. They approached me with false solutions, and I turned them in to the police."

"That sounds dangerous, but you got the bad guys in jail. Seems a good thing to me." She was right on both counts.

"Depends on which end of the stick you're holding."

"Stop throwing out the puns. Fill in the gaps!"

"The ISD, which you now know is the French version of our FBI, had been after those guys for almost a year. The lieutenant and his guys were assisting the ISD."

"Ah, I see. You butted in and solved the case. No wonder Jonathan knew you."

"I didn't mean to. I was just helping a friend."

She was still sitting sideways, but her head dipped a little then back to me. "And now you're helping me, and look what I've caused. I bet you wish you'd never met me on the square. I've caused you nothing but trouble and more trouble."

A direction change was needed. I could let her keep feeling bad about all this, or I could give her a piece of my arm to chew on. "That was a given. Women are always trouble." I was ready to duck.

She smiled. She leaned over and brushed her hand on my face. "Sometimes we are trouble, but I know what you really meant. You wanted me to get angry at you and forget my feelings. No way. You're too sweet to get away with that. And, I do feel better."

"I'll have to remember that cure."

"Best not. It only works once."

Warnings are always welcome.

I was about to reply when my phone rang. I gave it to Nicole. It was Pappy wondering what happened. She gave him the update. She held the phone close to my ear and I told him about the Peugeot. Nicole gave him the tag number. He told me to keep the incident between us till we knew more. I agreed. Nicole heard and agreed as well.

He had nothing else for us, so we said our byes and headed for Noémi's place.

We hung around Noémi's home for couple of hours. The ladies made two batches of cookies, a French batch and a US batch. That was good. Between that coffee, my French iced tea, and lots of talking, the afternoon went well.

The good news was Rebecca was fitting in. I did mention her and Lizzy's middle names were French. That got a lot of discussion going. I caught Nicole watching me in that venture, but I didn't know why.

I also learned Noémi has a sister whom she visited once a week. She usually stayed overnight, sometimes two nights. Her sister was older and had medical problems. The boys stayed at home to watch over the place. With us being around, she hadn't visited her sister. I offered my apologies. Noémi said it was okay.

Next stop was Pappy's. Mother Betty decided to return with us. I needed updates to make plans, though I wasn't sure I wanted updates. Rebecca stayed, which I saw and hoped was a good thing.

What I really wanted was to sit in Nanna Bolton's lap and let her tell me about life. I had no knowledge back then, but grown up I realized what life was like for her. But, you wouldn't know it. I'd be sad and sit in her lap, and in a minute, she'd have me smiling and laughing.

When I grew up and she was gone, I always hoped when she was young she had a lap to sit on and smile.

CHAPTER 29

LIARS AND LIES

We got to Pappy's about four thirty. It was Friday afternoon and approaching the hour I first saw Nicole on the sidewalk. That dinner invite had turned into Paris, kidnappings, being tailed, and—wasn't sure I wanted to know the next *and*.

I opened the car door and Mother Betty stepped out. Nicole took my hand as I opened the door for her, and she held it all the way into Pappy's office. The sofa felt good. Mother Betty took her chair beside Pappy.

There was a bundle of stuff she was about to learn.

As I sat, I spoke. "This has been quite a day, and believe me, I feel lucky to be here. That luck was made possible by you and this woman sitting beside me." I got a soft hand squeeze.

Pappy gave me friendly nods. "Glad you're here. I have some interesting news. But first, the police tracked down that car that was following you. Those two are in custody at Lieutenant Grenier's precinct."

I was surprised. "That was quick."

"When the lieutenant has an urge, he makes it happen." A pointing finger went up. "There's more. From those two and their phones and papers, they were in league with the Signature guy, Bastien Vadinoye, and his guys. All are part of the uranium smugglers."

Then it clicked. "Damn. I see. When we first visited the plant, his men saw us, they got Vadinoye going and the kidnapping. I would have never made that connection."

"Neither would I. Yes, and they decided you needed to be disposed of. If you had turned the kids over to that guy, the girls, the boys, Nicole, and you would be dead. That was the plan."

"And when Nicole and I paid a second visit to the plant, they must have seen where we went."

Mother Betty had heard all she wanted. She was more than pissed. Her hands went wide, each with a finger pointed at me and Pappy. "I can't believe what I'm hearing. You two nearly got my daughter killed, again. That's twice. How many more times do you have to try?"

Nicole had let go of my hand. If it's possible to listen intensely she was, and the daughter decided to take a stand.

"Mama, you should remember all this is my fault. All John wanted was to take me to dinner. I convinced him to find out why Daddy was killed." She grabbed my hand again. "Instead, he's almost been killed and nearly put in jail. Don't you dare accuse him or Pappy of anything but trying to help me. Me!"

Nicole wasn't crying, but she had my arm entwined with hers. Her defense meant a lot.

I tugged on our entwined arms looking at her. "You're on target, beautiful."

To everyone I added, "And, we're not going to quit. My muddled brain says we're close. I've met truth tellers and liars. I've been told some truths and, I think, many lies. This I know. If a lie is needed, there must be—no, there *is*—a reason."

Nicole was watching all this a foot away from my vocal cords. "And you're going to find that reason. I'll do anything you want to help. I'm pissed, too."

Mother Betty was stone silent. Stunned probably fit. Pappy was quiet. Pleasantly quiet. But then, he always appeared to have the edge we needed, and then delivers even when we don't know it.

Somebody had to say something. The silence was making me nervous.

"Okay, everyone, here's the plan. Nicole and I are going to dinner somewhere."

She immediately intervened. "And I know where. Sweetie, we're going to that quaint café where your girlfriend works."

Surprised was not even close to what I heard. My reply was simple. "Gabrielle?"

"Yes."

"Villa le 42?"

"Yes."

With that yes, her hands positioned my lips in line with hers, where she planted a kiss. "That's to remind you who your current girlfriend is."

Pappy smiled. Her mother was unsure what to do. I decided to leave that challenge to Nicole.

After recovering, I added, "After dinner, Nicole and I are going to do some serious soul searching."

Nicole couldn't let that stay unrecognized. "And, Mama, you will do your own soul searching with Pappy. You will *not* hold anything that's happened against him. He's been a perfect gentleman and protector." Looking at him, she added, "I suspect he's helped more than we know."

At that point, I thought the daughter needed some recognition. "Mrs. Powell, your daughter was brave and stood her ground at that police station. She didn't back down. You should be proud of her. I know I am."

Nicole placed my hand in hers again.

Her mother finally let her feelings out. "John, until you stepped into my house a week ago, my life was calm and uneventful. You changed all that, yet some things," she turned to Pappy, "are better different, and you're to thank. My husband's dead, and I'm at peace with that."

"I'm glad you are, Mama."

Mother Betty looked directly at me. "John, I want you to keep doing what Nicole wants. She still needs closure, and I know you're the only one to give her that."

Wow came to mind. "I much appreciate that, and it's my goal. Are you coming with us to the hotel, or is Pappy going to make that happen?"

Pappy finally spoke. "I'll see that she gets there. John, as always, keep me informed of anything you find or need, and I'll see that you get it."

With that said, Nicole and I headed for Villa le 42 in the Mercedes.

The moment we stepped into the café, there was Gabrielle. Nicole and I were holding hands, but that didn't slow Gabrielle down. She rushed and gave me a hug. Both her legs were off the ground, knees bent. I held her tight to keep her from falling, of course.

That forced me to return the hug, with one hand. Nicole was gripping the other.

Gabrielle released me and returned both feet to the ground. "John now for moi?"

I turned to Nicole. "Think she said I was here for her."

"Oui. Oui." Gabrielle understood that. So did Nicole.

I knew it was Nicole's idea to go there, only to give me trouble. Well, two could play at that game. Extricating my hand from Nicole's, I grabbed Gabrielle with both arms and swung her around, carefully missing Nicole, of course.

Having committed an act of war, I let her loose and did my best to tell her to find us a table. She held up three fingers. I shook my head saying, "No," and held up two fingers, pointing to Nicole and myself.

Gabrielle's face went sad, dropping her head just a little with eyes staring up at me all with sexy, pouting lips. That extra exhibition was fully on purpose.

There were two guys with their dates standing off to the side. The men's eyes were glued to Gabrielle until their women punched them in the side.

From the reaction of the guys, those were not love taps.

My woman didn't slug me. But I knew I was in serious trouble.

When we got to our booth, I assisted Nicole being seated. Gabrielle left the menus and did an over-her-shoulder bye-bye wave as she turned and left.

We were alone and I had to find out my future. I leaned on the table to be closer to my her. With hands flat on the table, "Okay. What's my status?"

Nicole didn't laugh, but she had that grin women have when they know they have full control. She leaned forward and put her hands on mine. "John, you made that little sweetie very happy. I'm proud of you."

Then I knew what happened. "You did all that on purpose? We came here so you could see her grab me."

That time I had the finger pointing at her.

She recaptured my hand and calmly said, "Yes, I did," then with a moment's pause, "but I like the food and I really like the cozy, romantic atmosphere, especially with you. I mean that."

I liked her reply. "Then we'll eat and enjoy each other's company. It's a good way to celebrate our anniversary."

"I was thinking the same thing, along with a little cozying at the hotel."

The food and atmosphere were good causing us to be there almost two hours. Gabrielle didn't visit us while we were there. Luck was with me.

We were about to leave when I realized I hadn't checked on the girls. I called Patty's phone. They were in their hotel room and so were their mothers. Pappy had delivered Nicole's mother and the boys had delivered Rebecca and the girls.

I was surprised they were in their room. It wasn't that late. Still, I knew where they were and that they were safe.

The day had been long. We were sitting together on the sofa in my room admiring the quiet.

At least I was till Nicole added sound. Her legs were curled under her, knees resting on my legs. She was leaning against the sofa.

"It feels so nice to be here relaxing with you. I can forget about all the bad things of the day and just think of us." She grabbed my arm and threw it over her shoulder as she rested her knees and legs more over mine. "John, this is so nice."

I gave her a gentle hug. "I agree. You're soft and cuddly."

From her cuddled position, she was looking at my chin. After a couple of minutes, she asked, "Are we ever going to find why my father was killed?"

That I didn't expect, yet I'd had the same question. If she never knew, it would haunt her for the rest of her life. I didn't want that to happen, yet I wanted to encourage her without lying. "I wish I could say absolutely. I can't, but this I do know. We've run into a bunch of liars. Liars lie for a reason. It's usually to hide something."

"You make it sound so easy." She was shaking her head as she spoke those words.

"I wish it were easy. The liars add difficulty. So, we zero in on the why they have something to hide."

She smiled. "Sweetie, you just said that."

"When we were talking to Noémi, she didn't appear sad, but I would say she was truthful."

Nicole gave her feelings. "Me too. I think she was truthful. I remember her saying her husband was a good man."

Her words clicked a button. "Do you remember exactly what Noémi said when we were there about her husband?"

"I just told you. You've really got to listen better."

"No. No, listen. Noémi said her husband was a good man then, meaning back then. In the next sentence, she said he *is* a good man. Was a man. Is a man. How can he be a was then an is?"

"John, that's just the way people talk. We think about the past and want it to be now. And remember, she knows little English. Her boys had to interpret what she said from what she thought she said."

"Yeah, you're right. I sometimes gnaw at the wrong end of the bone."

"Yes, but John, sometimes you gnaw and the truth is exposed."

"I remember something Nanna Bolton said. She told me once, 'You don't never want nobody to shoo you the wrong way. If they do, they got sumptin bad waiting for ya.' I've always wondered how she would know that. I hoped maybe it wasn't her who personally found out."

"That is so sweet how you used her words. She was lovely. Do you think someone lied to her and caused her something really bad?"

"I don't know. She never went to school. Maybe when she was young, even before my father knew her. Best I know, her life had always been bad. I never saw her oldest son. Maybe he was working. Money had to come from somewhere. I doubt whatever my dad was paying her was enough."

"I wish you could go back in time and make her life better. Make her happy. You could do that."

"I'd love to try. Let's get off that subject. We need to think about tomorrow."

"Let's do that thinking tomorrow. I'm going to take a bath, then you, then we snuggle. You good for that?"

"Always."

I hoped reminiscing about Nanna Bolton might cause a fresh lead to avail itself. With a little luck, sleep might clear the cobwebs from my brain.

CHAPTER 30

CELL MYSTERY

The alarm went off as usual. Don't know why I even set it. I wasn't interested in getting up early. I had no specific plans. My Saturday was empty.

I turned to snuggle against the woman who had gone to bed with me, but she wasn't there. I sat up to find her sitting on the sofa, her legs under her. She was focused on her phone as if it was lonely.

The words of an old song came to mind, which I attempted to sing. "Hey, good looking. Whatcha got cooking?"

She simply replied, "Nothing, I guess."

Her words told me she wasn't listening to my attempt to add some cheer to her secluded state. "Guess you never heard the song."

She looked up, "What song?"

"I don't know the name of it. The few words I know are, 'Hey, good looking. Whatcha got cooking?' The song then asks if she's got something cooking with the guy doing the singing. In this case that's you." My attempt was less than poor.

That brought a tiny smile, but she didn't change much. Solemn might describe how she looked. "That's cute and sweet of you to try to cheer me up. You've sung to me twice."

That didn't go too well, so I joined her on the sofa. I was in my pajamas and she her nightie. We were a good match, so long as no one walked in.

"So, whatcha doing?"

"Looking at some pictures of Daddy. I'd almost forgotten they were there."

She held the phone where I could see and flipped through several. "He's a handsome man. How old are the pictures?"

"I took this one," giving me a close look at it, "which was taken the last time Daddy was at home. That July."

"You've kept them that long." As I said that, a thought occurred. "How long have you had your cell phone?"

"Oh, I know it's old."

"But it's not the same phone you had when you took those pictures, right?"

"No. I got a new one about three years ago. They told me all the contacts and photos would be there. And they are. I'm so glad I have them to look at."

"I noticed you had a landline at home. Did your father call you on this phone?"

"Oh, he called me lots of times, and I called him."

"He called you?" Her reply got me excited. It shouldn't have been news. Too obvious, but it was promising.

"Yes. Many times. All the time. So what?"

We needed a break, and her phone was added to the list. At that moment, it was all there was.

"Always from his cell phone?"

"Sure, I guess. I mean, it was his phone. He bought us the same kind as his. All I did was go back to the store and get a newer one. It's what everybody does."

"May I see your phone?" I held out my hand, hoping.

"Sure. But it's just a regular cell phone. Daddy liked it, so I bought the same kind."

Now, the chances of his number still being in the phone were better than slim, and if she never had her phone professionally wiped or it had reset itself, and that does happen, such will hang around forever, even when you buy a new one. All contacts, photos, and text messages are normally transferred to the new one.

I checked her recent calls. She had five favorites set up. I counted over two hundred numbers in the recent list, many duplicates on different days, which is common.

"Do you ever edit or delete numbers?"

She tilted her head and tossed her hands out. "No, not much. A little, maybe. Why you ask?" I got her interest up along with mine.

At the bottom, I found ten or so from William Powell. There were others from area codes I didn't recognize, except for one, but my memory of it was unclear. I showed them to Nicole.

"Yes, those are from him. See, that's his number. I mean, was his number."

"Hmm, wonder if the number's still good?"

I saw her face change when I said those stupid words. I was thinking out loud.

Her reaction was what I regretted. "Oh, dear God. I can call him! I never thought."

She snatched the phone from my hand and started to dial. I grabbed her wrist and took the phone, stopping the call. She started crying and hitting my shoulders. I put the phone down and gently held her wrists.

With a meager struggle, she pleaded, "Please let me go. I want to call him. Please." She continued to cry, but less. I let go of her wrists. She stopped hitting me and put her arms around me.

Whispering, "I want you to talk to him, but it might alert him at a bad time. If he's alive and trying to stay off the grid, your voice may cause him to act. He has no knowledge of my existence. Let me call, okay?"

She pulled away just a little. Her glistening eyes focused on mine. I held her phone in my open hand, trying to show how much I cared for and trusted her.

"Yes. You should call."

"I know that wasn't an easy decision. We're going to the lobby, and we'll use a phone there."

She wiped some tears from her cheeks. "Why? It's more private here."

"If someone else answers, I'm not ready for them to have my name and number."

"I see. I guess."

I wasn't sure she did, but at that moment I had her trust and was not going to let it get away.

We both dressed quickly. Nicole tied up her hair; I just used a comb. She had recovered some from her crying and looked cute even without makeup.

She took my hand and we headed downstairs. I could have used the phone in my room, but that could also publicize a clue to my whereabouts. The hotel would do the same, but not as direct. I was unsure what the hotel system might send to the other end.

I found an available phone by the concierge desk. The concierge wasn't up yet. Nicole was kneeling beside the chair I was sitting in, ready to make the call. Didn't like that, so I confiscated a nearby chair and placed it right beside me.

I clicked the buttons. It was a 678 number, which fit for Georgia. I held the phone so Nicole could hear.

The phone rang several times, then a woman answered speaking French.

I chose English, "I'm trying to reach William Powell." I wanted to know if she spoke English.

"Who you?" She responded in decent English.

"My name is John. Can I speak to William?"

There was a brief pause. "I not know him. I not know you."

"You have his phone."

"No. This my phone. I buy." She hung up with no other words spoken.

With the phone still in my hand and eyes staring at Nicole, I said, "She's gone."

Nicole had been focused on the phone. She looked at me but didn't cry. "I heard what she said, but I don't understand. It's his phone number."

"True, but we now have another mystery. Why does she have his phone, with the same number, for so many years?"

"Daddy had a very good, expensive phone. It would certainly last."

"Expensive or cheap, if not dropped too often, it will last a long time. Updates need to be made, but don't think that would cause the phone to stop working. That's his phone. It's a US phone number, and she couldn't have the phone unless he gave it to her."

"Oh, God, maybe she stole it from him. Maybe she—"

"Now, don't think that. Still, if it were truly hers, she would've had to go to America, buy a phone, in Georgia, with that exact number. Not gonna happen."

"But she has his phone. How can that be?"

"Look. Someone must be paying the bill, because the number is still active. Ah, betcha it's a company phone. Maybe his company is still paying the bill. I mean, Signature Consulting. But why would they? It's been seven years. Hmm. Unless they're trying to cover up something. That's doubtful. Maybe."

I couldn't be sure of all that. Did seem probable, but I didn't want to raise Nicole's hopes too high. That French woman was using it to make calls, or she was keeping it for Nicole's father, or he just didn't want to answer the calls. And, it might seem to be in use to whoever gave it to Powell. Or the woman was paying the bill.

Regardless, the bigger question was, how did she get the phone? And the much bigger question—who was she?

"John, why are you so quiet?"

"Sorry, been thinking. Let's go back to my room."

Seated back on my sofa, Nicole was sitting with her legs curled under her, holding my arm, giving me a thoughtful gaze.

As for me, I was staring blindly at the wall trying to gather my thought particles.

"Nicole, the woman who answered his phone spoke French. She was expecting to speak French to a caller. When she spoke English, I could tell it was a second language. Meaning, if she did buy the phone on some black market—Oh, no, that's crazy. The phone has the same number. She stole it, or your father gave it to her."

That got Nicole's attention. "Either way, she met Daddy. She knew him."

"Agreed." I pulled out my phone.

"What're you doing? You're going to call her, aren't you?"

"Yep. We'll settle some of this for sure. Whoever she is, she will have my calling card."

"Huh?"

"My name and phone number."

Nicole held her phone up so I could key in her dad's number. I held my phone so Nicole could hear.

"Bonjour," said the woman.

"I'm calling with an offer to give you five thousand euros if you answer my question."

"Want none you money. I no need. Who are you?"

"Forgive me, Miss. My name is John Stone, and I really need to get in touch with William Powell."

"You called. Told you. I not know him. Stop call me." She hung up.

Nicole was shaking her head, sighing. "We still didn't learn anything, did we?"

She rested her head back on my shoulder.

"No. We didn't. But if I hear her voice again, I think I'll recognize it. Ain't much, but she has your father's phone and number. She knows or knew him."

"I don't know who she is, but I want her to know him."

"Me too. Let's keep this between us for now. I need to put more thought into the phone thing. I'm not ready to mess with questions."

She sat up and nodded. "I agree. This may be good news. Maybe not. I don't know what to think. But I do know I'm hungry."

That was my next thought. "You do your shower first. I can do a shower and be dressed quick."

Her attention jumped several notches. "And, just what do you mean by that? Are you saying I'm a slow dresser?"

Must I always open my mouth and immediately put my foot in it?

"No, no. Not at all. It's just that you girls have more to do than us guys. I just shower and put clothes on. Ten minutes, tops."

With hands balled up on hips, "Well, Mr. Stone, you should be appreciative that we girls want to look nice. Half the time you guys look like you stepped out of a pigpen. Just so you know, I'm going to take that shower, and I may make it a long one just to make you WAIT!"

The only answer I could think of was "Okay," as she gathered her bath stuff and slammed the door.

Her shower gave me time to send Mac an e-mail asking if he could trace a couple of phone numbers. Yeah. One was her father's number. There had to be a reason it was still active, but I wanted to know before I told Nicole. I didn't want the answer to cause her more grief than she already had.

He said he'd try, but sometimes it takes a spell.

CHAPTER 31

GERMANY ON THE HORIZON

I did my shower, we dressed, and we headed for breakfast. As we were leaving the room, I had to ask, "White shoes and long pants. What happened to the sandals and shorts?"

She held my hand. "I wondered if they were distracting to you. Taking your mind off the search." Why she was smiling caused me to wonder, too.

"The shorts were certainly distracting to anyone we were talking to. Helped me know what to ask."

Doing a little lean against me, "Well, I was hoping you'd be distracted."

"Why do you think I asked so many dumb questions?" I was hoping for points.

We stopped at the lift. I pressed the button with my spare hand.

She gave me a warning. "You never ask dumb questions. Why do you think I'm keeping you around?"

The door opened, so I kept quiet. There were others traveling the same path.

On the ground floor, we departed company with the other lift dwellers. Heading for the breakfast table, I added, "Just remember. I'm driving a Mercedes."

"Suspect you're back to the rental, Mr. Stone. I still like having you around."

"Better than the lieutenant?"

That didn't slow her down. "For a while."

She spoke those words while grinning and facing the restaurant. As for me, I wondered how long a *while* was.

The morning continued with surprises. At the restaurant door, I saw both mothers and the girls. The boys were just sitting down, next to their girls, naturally.

Approaching the table, I whispered, "Did you arrange this?"

"Yes."

"When?"

Nicole took my hand. "While you were taking a shower. I did more than dress during your shower, Speedy." She was enjoying every second of this.

Fortunately, we were at the table, 'cause I didn't have a comeback.

An oddity occurred. I was seconds away from pulling the chair out for Nicole, when the boys stood for her. They hadn't been doing that. At their age, I can guarantee you they didn't figure that out on their own. That courtesy isn't done as often as it once was. I don't do it every time. Hmm, maybe things are different in France. If so, why now?

Everyone ordered and started eating, accompanied with lots of small talk. I discovered that Rebecca was a talker.

At an opportune time, I decided to give the boys some recognition. "Nathan, Andre, I want to compliment you on the special gesture you made when Nicole was about to sit. You stood up. That's not done often enough, and I thought it was a super thing to do."

Smiles came to their faces. Nathan spoke first. "Thank you, Uncle John. Mother told us we should do that."

Andre wasn't going to be outgunned. "It wasn't something we normally did, but I like it."

Within a split second, Lizzy kissed him on the cheek. Within the other half of that split second, Nathan got his from Patty. Hands were also being held.

"Boys, that's a good thing—" I was interrupted by a kiss from Nicole. There were lots of smiles occurring as I attempted to regain my composure. "Okay, so we all got rewards. Boys, I highly suggest you keep that in mind."

We guys are also to stand when the woman stands to leave. I was just going to watch.

Then Nicole joined the game. "Mama, does Pappy do your chair when you sit?"

"Sometimes he does, and that's fine. He's a sweet, gentle man. I don't expect him to do that every time."

Opportunity knocked. The boys were in my sight. "Don't know why all this made me think of this. Has your mother been to see her sister yet?"

The boys did their decision glance. Andre got elected. "No, not yet. With all of you here, she doesn't want to interrupt the visit. Mother has really enjoyed all the visits."

Nathan decided to add his thought, "Yes. This week has been one of her most enjoyed times. It has been special for Mother, and for me and Andre."

I saw Nicole's reaction to their words and tossed in mine. "I must say, you boys and your mother have made our time here very memorable. I'm sorry it has delayed your mother's time with her sister. Would you mind giving me her sister's name? I just like to know the names of the people I meet. Adds memories."

Nathan was pleased to let me know. "I can understand. It's Elsia Gauthier. No, is Elsia Myriam Gauthier."

He finished that with a smile and a nod. He definitely enjoyed saying her name.

Andre perked up with his own name giving, "Mother's full name is Noémi Hanna Gagnon. Her father's name was Jocquez Leron Lavoisier."

Both boys' faces lit up. It was obvious they were proud to give me, all of us, the names. I was pleased, but at the time wasn't sure why I asked. I was pencil-less.

"Would you guys e-mail or text me that info? I love those names, but no way I'll get the spelling right."

Nathan replied, "Yes, sir, Uncle John. We'll get those to you when we finish eating."

I nodded with a wink, trying to decide if those names would be of any value. I knew more about the families, and did I care.

Looking at the boys, "Guys, Mrs. Gauthier would be older. How's her health? She okay? I'm thinking your mother said something about that."

Nathan responded, "Bad health is all we know."

"Sorry to hear that. Where does she live?"

My vague curiosity caused me to ask that. I didn't expect to gain much from asking, but names can sometimes connect when least expected.

Andre had the answer. "She lives in Saint-Avold. It a small town up close to German border. About three hour drive. Maybe little more. I text it to you."

Food and fun had finished. Nicole and I excused ourselves to my room. Without a reason being mentioned, the girls displayed a pair of sheepish grins. As we turned to walk, I did a partial body twist and returned their expression with waggling eyebrows. I saw that in a movie once.

Nicole's back hand hit my chest, and she wasn't even watching.

CHAPTER 32

A DERRIÈRE EXPOSED

The sofa must have gotten lonely, because it sensed the door open and drew us to it.

Nicole took her usual position beside me, with legs drawn up under her, feet bare. Personally, I liked that position. Sorta showed she wasn't going to run away first chance.

She caught me. "Why are you looking at my feet?"

"I was just thinking." Her feet were still in my focus.

My chin was captured by a small hand and twisted for a better view. Her eyes. "There're other parts of me I'd rather you be thinking about."

"I know. I started further up and worked my way down." I had, but chances of that working were slim. Hey, a guy has to give it a go.

That got me three soft cheek slaps. "I'm still doing the pad thing. What did you have in mind?"

I had my own thought, so I gave it a go. "We need to go over the info we have and see what our next step is. Your input will help make it so."

"Thank you for not giving up." She watched for my response. "With just about anyone, you can see their faults and lies and still get what you want. So, what's the next step?"

We had to start somewhere. "First, let's just say what we know."

Nicole started, "I'll take a shot. We found uranium smugglers."

I jumped in. "The boys stood while you were being seated. That was suddenly different, and I wonder why."

"Noémi has an older sister somewhere. And I agree, John. We should know where, just to rule her out. Finding her might rule her in. No wait. We do. It's Saint-Avold. The boys are to send you that."

"Good deduction. That's three. Noémi said her husband *was* a good man, then he *is* a good man." That one puzzled me most.

"I agree that sounds odd. Let's see. Ah, both men died in unusual ways. Acid. Fire. Oh, and a French woman has my father's phone. That's unbelievable."

"Yes, and that's one we need to clear up. Oh, forgot to mention it. I asked Mac to trace your father's phone number. I'm not sure that's something he can do, but I want to know who that woman is."

She wrinkled her nose. "When were you going to tell me that?"

"Please. It was a spur-of-the-moment thing. Okay? I was sitting there listening to your shower. More like picturing you in the shower, and that did it. Guess I lost some points, huh?"

"You can never lose points."

"Then keep thinking. We must be missing something. Make that *I* gotta be missing something."

Having exhausted what we knew, my phone had a timely ring. It was my pilot Jane.

"Jane, what's happening? Haven't heard from you. You must be having a ball."

"John, we are. Being here with my friend and seeing her so happy is wonderful. This is so different than Australia. I was worried she'd hate it."

"I'm glad. With all that fun, why call me? I should be calling you."

Nicole heard what I said. I know because she punched me. I uttered a quiet grunt and held my phone so she could hear.

"A blessing, John. I finally got my phone fixed. The pictures should be in your inbox by now. Just family stuff. Hope you enjoy them. Any questions, call me."

"Looking forward to seeing them. Hope you're in some."

"Paul and I are in a couple. Guess I better go. Oh, when we need to come back to Paris, give us some warning. It's a six-hour drive."

"I'll give you plenty of time. Glad you're having so much fun."

We said our byes and hung up.

"John, that's so nice of you to do for them."

"I didn't do anything. They just drove there and are having a great time. I tried to cover their expenses, but they didn't want it. Enough of that, let's check out the pictures."

My laptop would be better viewing. I retrieved it from the desk and put it in my lap, pressing the power button. Nicole adjusted its position for a better view.

I started pulling up the pics. The first two were Jane and her friend. Then I got a total surprise. Shock would be a better word.

When I pulled up the third pic, there she was. Alivia in the picture flesh. The brunette with blond stripes holding a little girl, also brunette.

My fingers froze.

When I didn't click the next one, Nicole asked, "She's pretty. Do you know her? Who is she?"

All I could think to say was "Alivia."

Nicole leaned closer, pointing. "Her? The one with the ass?"

"Yep. She's the sister of Jane's friend's husband, in Mainz, Germany."

"No way. It can't be her. She lives in Paris."

"Mac said she was married. That must be her kid. It's her. Remember we were with Nicolette when she called Alivia. I said the area code looked familiar."

"Yes, I remember. Something about your brother."

"Right. Jake was in Mainz. That was the same code number."

"But do we care? Big deal. She's married and doesn't know my father. We don't even know why Pappy gave you her name."

"I know, but Mainz keeps jumping out at us. Get dressed for a long, fast drive."

"Now? You don't even know where they live in Germany."

"But I do. Mac got me her married address, in Mainz."

The question was who to tell. I wasn't ready to tell anyone. Nicole and I did some serious discussing, and she agreed. She was a bit undecided. I reiterated everything I knew and convinced her that Mainz was firing red flares.

We told everyone we needed a break and were taking a two-day vacation to clear our minds. We were asked where we were going. We just said we weren't sure, only that it was far away from Paris. I was undecided on sharing all the details with Pappy, and for once, I truly hoped he knew why and where we were going.

It was after eleven and it was a six-hour drive. We'd be lucky to get there by six.

We quickly packed a few essentials and loaded the two small bags in the back seat.

I was ready to start the car when I rechecked with Nicole. "Are you sure you want to do this?"

Her face showed her agreement. "Yes. I want to. Maybe more than you. Finding the truth will ease my mind, and this is a possibility."

Uttering, "Cool," I cranked the car. I stuck a CD in the player. "I hope you like the Eagles?"

She didn't like the first song and clicked till she found one that made her grin—"Witchy Woman."

I mentioned, "You know she had raven hair. You have blond hair."

"That isn't the half of it. I suggest when dealing with me, you remember that sparks flew from her fingertips."

Her fingers wiggled, most likely as an omen. She restarted the song more than once and sang along with the Eagles, hands moving in unison.

The rest of the trip consisted of childhood stories and experiences. I supplied some stories, and Nicole filled all empty spaces with her mom and dad. The more I heard, the more I knew I had to find the right answer. The right conclusion.

Once I was walking with Nanna Bolton out back of her shack. She was picking berries. I was about ten and was scared I'd forget my mother. So, I asked her. She told me, "Ya can't member it all, but da good stuff ya not gonna fegit. You jist think 'bout where she took ya. An all 'hem time she say she love ya. Some part ever day, ya just think a her. She be lisen, and she help ya."

Everything Nanna knew was from living. Books were useless. She wasn't allowed to read. She just knew people, by how they treated her and her loving personality. From the things she told me, I knew her life wasn't all pleasant. But her will overcame it all.

I didn't realize it at the time, but she, as a loving default, had become my mother.

CHAPTER 33

A SURPRISE HOMECOMING

The trip was long, but arriving safe was a good thing. I had constantly watched for anyone following us. No one should know where we were. Why anyone would know eluded me, but the feeling remained.

The speed limit was an obstacle I ignored on this trip. Not my normal driving pattern, but I needed speed.

It was close to five thirty when we approached Alivia's home. I hadn't announced our coming. Hope was all we had for finding Alivia there.

There was a driveway, but I didn't want to use it. I parked across the street. A good size lake was to my left, offering a great view from her home.

Nicole questioned my parking decision. "What're you doing? You do see her driveway?"

"I'm taking no chances. We're showing up unannounced, and I'm—"

She cut me off. "You thinking she'll open the door with a nine-millimeter?"

"She might," then I let her know the rest. "I don't want you standing there."

"I doubt it, buster. And, I will be standing right beside you!"

"No, you won't. I got this feeling, and it worries me."

"You're just now deciding to tell me? We've been on the road for six hours."

"No! It was when I saw the house, I saw questions."

"And what do questions look like?"

"Please. Please, stay in the car till I know she's at least at the door. Please?"

"Okay, I'll stay here. I'm sorry I said all that. You care. I like that. But, soon as you know it's safe, tell me." Her immovable attitude had a concrete base.

I said, "I will," and took off.

Alivia's house was an older one with six steps leading to a porch stretching the front of the house, with a swing. Wood had been replaced with plastic. It looked well kept. The front door was wood and protected by a glass door. There was a pair of windows across the front of the house, one on each side. Room windows, I guessed.

I pressed the doorbell, wondering how I'd be greeted. "Welcome" was not expected. My main concern was it may be the entrance to Pandora's box.

The curtains covering the narrow windows beside the door moved. A woman's face was visible. It was Alivia. I knew her, but would she know me?

The wooden door opened. She left the glass door shut and most certainly locked.

I donated my info. "Hi. I'm John Stone. We spoke on the phone yesterday."

Her expression told me my presence was not welcome. Her words proved it. "What are you doing here?" Her question was not asked in friendly terms.

"It is my belief you know something about the death of William Powell. Please know that I come in peace. Along with his daughter," pointing to the car, "I ask you with a heartfelt please to let us come in."

While facing me, her head did a brief glimpse down a hall. As she began to unlatch the glass door, I signaled Nicole. That was all it took. She was halfway across the street before the car door shut.

Nicole and I were led through a small, open foyer into the living room. It was large, with fireplace, long couch, a small sofa, two armchairs, and what appeared to be a kitchen/dining room off to the right.

The moment we were there, with no offer to sit, Alivia had her say. "I do not understand why you keep bothering me about your father. You are wasting my time."

Standing close beside me, Nicole replied with tender words, "I'm sorry for all this, but I miss him, and his death was questionable. And, and, if there is even the tiniest chance he's alive, just to know would mean so very much."

Alivia said, "But I can't help."

I heard more than a glimmer of sadness as Alivia spoke.

So did Nicole. She posed a companionable question to Alivia. "Your father. Is he alive?"

Alivia's expression did a serious change. It went from sad to sorrow. "My father died a long time ago. I was fifteen." Her eyes began to glisten.

"I know how you feel. You remember those few years with him, and they mean so much. I'm doubly sorry for even asking."

Nicole didn't stop there. She moved toward Alivia, with her arms rising. Alivia's arms rose to meet her. The two did a fully combined hug.

To my left I saw the shadow of an image moving. My right hand slowly eased into my back pocket, where I was packing a two cylinder derringer. Small, but deadly at close range.

A man wearing jeans and a T-shirt stepped from the shadows.

Smiling, he initially said nothing, but he was visible to Alivia. I didn't know if she already knew, but she knew at that moment.

Alivia pulled back from Nicole. With arms helping she simply said, "Turn around."

Nicole turned. Her hands flew to her lips and she cried one word. "Daddy!"

She ran into his arms.

I wondered how I would react and felt if that had been my mother standing there. But it wasn't time for that.

Moving beside Alivia, I whispered, "Thank you."

There were tears on her cheeks. Maybe they were from wishing it was her father who had walked into the room.

Still in his embrace, Nicole pulled back and said, "I love you, Daddy."

William returned the words and pulled her back into the hug. It didn't last forever, but the moments made up for the years.

But, he can't still be using William. Alivia married a Marceau. I held off for a spell.

Alivia's arms went around me with her head against my neck.

We had a new serious decision to make. Nicole's father was alive with a new name, identity, and wife with child. That meant his life had been in serious danger seven years ago and he had to be legally dead. At that moment, knew he was putting more than *his* life at risk.

At one of those appropriate moments, I uttered, "We should sit down. We have lots to talk about."

Nicole and her father sat on the couch, with Nicole holding her father's arm. She was making up for lost time. I sat on the sofa, and to my surprise, Alivia joined me.

Seated, I gave it half a second and got things going, "Mr. Marceau, I believe there're things you can't tell us, but anything would help. Can we have your new name?"

He gladly gave it. "James Frank Marceau."

Nicole still holding on to him, "I like it, Daddy."

That was good to hear, but I had a little more to add. "I should also mention that I believe Gustav Gagnon is alive and is also using a new name."

"Mr. Stone, you've done your homework, and I thank you. I never expected to hold my daughter again."

He leaned his head toward Nicole. She returned the gesture with a brilliant smile.

"You're welcome, sir, but Nicole gave me the desire to do the hunt. You should know she's not only lovely, but has a beautiful heart and a will that's tricky to overcome. I have bruises to prove it." I supplied a crooked grin.

That brought Nicole back to the now. "I'm trying to decide if I should throw something at you."

To her father, I confirmed, "See what I mean? A very determined woman."

She blew me a kiss, accompanied with a smile. I caught it.

But there was more I wanted. "Mr. Marceau, back to my original question. What can you tell us?" Then a sudden thought popped into my mind. "Is there anyone watching over you?"

"Yes, there's someone watching over me and my family." Within a breath, he knew how that sounded. He turned to Nicole. "By family I mean Alivia and my little girl. Please understand."

Nicole's heart blossomed. "Oh, yes. A little girl. Daddy, can I see her?"

Alivia said, "She's in her room taking a nap. It's about time to wake her anyway."

In maybe two minutes, Alivia brought the little girl and gave her to her father.

He introduced her as she settled into his lap. "Babette, this is your sister Nicole. We haven't seen her in a long, long time."

I saw Nicole's eyes begin to glisten. She held the tears back, saying, "Hi, Babette. It's so good to finally see you. How old are you?"

Babette looked at her father, who gave her a go-ahead nod. She said, "Five." Then, excited, she said, "I got a birthday in August."

Both she and her mother spoke English very well. With my eyes, I wrote on the wall to ask about French. If you recall, the notepad was full.

That's all it took. Nicole dropped to the floor, motioning for Babette to join her. She did. If heartwarming can be used multiple times, that's what happened. Those two sat there talking. Nicole showed her the picture Jane had sent. Babette jumped up, ran to her room, and came back with a picture of her with her mom and dad.

That went for several minutes till Nicole suggested they get back on the couch.

Alivia took Babette to the kitchen to get her something to eat. I believe she did that so we could talk more about adult things.

Nicole picked it up. "Daddy, why was it necessary for you to go dark or vanish or whatever you call it?"

Still gazing at Nicole, with glances back and forth between me and Nicole, he began. "Gustav and I became aware of a major syndicate that was planning to kill foreign leaders. We were discovered by them and had to vanish, as Nicole put it. What we knew would put our families in danger. Other than saying their plans were foiled, I can't tell you more."

"Mr. Marceau, you need not tell us more. I understand and believe Nicole does, too. Right, Nicole?"

"Yes, John. I understand, and as much as I'm so happy to be sitting here, I know we must leave. And," she looked at her father, "I know I'll never see you again."

He put his arm around her. She snuggled close and didn't cry.

Alivia, from the kitchen, asked, "I understand how you found me, but why did you ever look for me?"

"I was looking for related information in any way touching William Powell, and your name was among them. And, I can now drop you as the subject." I added a smile.

Alivia wasn't smiling when she asked, "You know of my past, don't you?"

"We don't need to discuss that." And I didn't want to.

Alivia was sitting at the table, talking while playing with Babette.

"John, my past is just that. I was going down a bad road. When I met James, things changed. When I fell in love with him, I told him what I'd done. He helped me correct it. Repay those I hurt."

Nicole added her feelings, "He didn't abandon you. He loved you more, didn't he?"

"Yes, he did. He and Babette are my life now."

Nicole went to the kitchen and met Alivia standing. They shared a long, heartfelt hug. That was good and needed. It helped me to know even though they may never see each other again, they had an understanding relationship.

Alivia brought Babette back to the couch. Nicole joined her father.

Once they settled down, I had another question directed to Nicole's father. "Yesterday, in our searching for you, I called your number that's still in Nicole's phone. A French woman answered. Has that caused you any problems?"

With a wink to Nicole, he said, "Sweetie, this man is quite thorough."

"He's very thorough, Daddy. He digs in the right places, and sometimes doesn't know what he's digging for."

I jumped in. "A likely story."

She ignored me. "One of his closest friends told me this week that he knows things he doesn't know he knows. But he always finds what he's looking for."

Her dad turned to me, then back to Nicole. "Now, that's confusing."

She kept at it. "To us, yes, but not to him. I would say that unknown knowledge gets tucked away in some corner of his brain, then pinches his mind to do something. The only reason we came here was because he couldn't find Alivia, and Mainz kept biting his butt."

Everyone got a laugh out of that except me. "Let's not forget the picture taken by my pilot Jane," I turned to Alivia, "with you and Babette."

Alivia smiled. "I remember the picture, but how could you know it was me? Do you know my brother?"

Nicole knew the answer. "It was your perfume."

Alivia tilted her head a bit and asked, "My perfume?"

Nicole decided to do the follow-up. "John and I were at Nicolette's hotel waiting for the lift. It opened, and you blew by us never looking. I paid no attention. But John saw you and caught a breath of your perfume. He smelled it again in the apartment. What's the name, John?"

I wasn't expecting that. Slipping on my thinking cap, I replied, "Hmm. It's. It's a French Victoria's Secret brand. Don't recall the name. No. Wait. Think I remember. Amour Affaire." And, don't ask. It would not be wise to spill those beans.

Alivia's eyes opened wide along with a positive "Yes."

Nicole replied, "See?"

Babette quietly said, "I like Mommy's perfume. I use it sometimes when Mommy lets me. Don't I, Mommy?"

Alivia said, "You sure do. I like it on you, too."

Babette smiled and bounced a little, then ran over and jumped in Nicole's lap.

They started talking and laughing. Nicole told Babette who I was and to give me a hug. She did and rushed back to Nicole. I didn't mind. The hug was worth it.

Nicole's father asked her, "I take it you're fond of this man?" He looked at me then at Nicole, with an approving little smile.

"More than fond, Daddy. But for now, we need to decide what to do." Then her focus switched to me. "John, anything else you need to know?"

Her question came with a suspicious twist, as if she *told* me I had one.

How she knew, I do not know. But I did. "Yes. There are two men we spoke with who had some fuzzy input. Have you ever heard the names Jules Pelletier and Ludovic Rousseau? They somehow knew you."

His eyes went wide. My impression was I'd caught him unaware. "How you know they exist is beyond me." He shook his head. "Difficult to believe, but you do." With a brief pause, "All I can say is they helped me and Gustav vanish. Vanish was their term."

"Yes, they and others used it often. They're connected to Signature Consulting. Does Signature know you're alive or dead?"

"They helped. To Signature I'm dead, but don't spread that around." His words had a serious tint.

I gave him a serious reply. "No worries. It's our secret."

My concern was that Pappy may want to know. May ask. Course, he may already know, and if I tell him lies, he could hate me forever. The future wasn't going to be easy to manage.

Nicole was talking softly to Babette about something. If I didn't know better, I'd say one ear was listening to Babette and the other to whatever. Why? Because she heard me.

"I know he won't." Turning to me, "John, I really don't want to ask, but what do we do now?"

Looking at her father, I asked, "One more question. Where did the bodies come from?"

Nicole leaped on that one, with a vigorous opinion. "John, that's gross. Do we have to know that?"

Her father slipped in with an answer, "Not much I can tell you, except the bodies were of dead individuals not claimed by anyone."

Speaking to all, I added, "Now, to answer your question, Nicole. I'm relatively certain no one followed us. I had many opportunities to check. All those I know in France don't know where we are. All that to say, we need to head for Paris. We have less than three hours of daylight left for travel."

Nicole put Babette down. The little one got interested in something else.

We all stood and began doing last and most likely final hugs.

I asked for and got Alivia's number. The purpose was to have an emergency number I could call. Many people knew she and I had talked, more than once. So, there was a connection.

Alivia okayed that idea. "John, thank you for caring. I just wish things could be different."

I gave her my number while Nicole and her dad were saying their goodbyes. When their hug ended, her father told her to wait.

Babette saw him and ran after him.

He went in a back room and returned with a gift, with Babette tailing him. "Nicole, I want you to have this." It was a bracelet. "This belonged to my great-grandmother. Your mother may remember it, so be aware." He put it on her wrist. "I was planning on giving it to you when you were older. This is the time."

He put it on her wrist. That was an emotional sight.

Nicole held her wrist and the bracelet, with tears again on her cheeks. "It's so very beautiful. Thank you, Daddy. This is a memory

I'll never forget. With it, I'll always have you with me." With those words, her arms wrapped around her father's neck.

Nicole squatted to let Babette see it. Babette gave it a tender touch as Nicole said, "I like it, Daddy."

He smiled at them both. "I had a ring I was going to give Patty, but they needed it for—you know."

She stood. "I understand, Daddy. I only needed a hug. That's all Patty will need. Daddy, there's something I need to tell you."

"I'll listen to anything you say. I love hearing your voice."

"Daddy, do you remember when I was young and you didn't want me to wear a bikini?"

"Yes, I do. You didn't like my doing that."

She looked down, then back to her father. "Well, when I was sixteen, I saved some allowance, and Mama gave me some money, and I bought a bikini. I only wore it with friends when you weren't with me. I'm so sorry, Daddy. I should have told you."

"Sweetie, I knew of the bikinis. I gave your mother the money to buy them."

"But—but—you didn't want me to wear them."

"I know, but you were showing your independence and strength at that age, and I knew bikinis were the rage. I said nothing and told your mother to go along with anything you wanted."

The tears began to flow as she hugged him again.

Nicole stepped back and wiped her tears. "Thank you. I love you, Daddy."

Babette just stood there and stared at what happened. I guess her young mind didn't understand. Her arms went up for her father to pick her up. The little one had good timing. With the confession in the open, everyone hugged everyone one more time as we said our goodbyes again. I made sure those goodbyes were inside the house. I didn't want her father visible outside with her, just in case.

As Nicole walked through the front door, she turned to see her father holding Babette. She took a picture—one that would not be in the story she would send to her paper.

It was almost seven o'clock and we were on our way.

We'd been driving for about ten minutes when Nicole broke the silence. "John, what you did for me today, I'll never forget. I saw my father and my new sister. It was wonderful. I know you aren't destined for me, but I'll say a prayer for you every night."

I told her thanks, but a prayer wasn't necessary.

She returned with an absolute, "I will anyway."

"I've seen confessions, but yours was nothing like anything I've seen. Your father was a super father letting you have what you wanted and never saying no. Does it make you wonder how many other things he knew but would never say no?"

"John, today you gave me a father who knew me more than I ever dreamed."

I didn't know what to say next, so I changed the subject, hoping.

With a glance at her and back to the road. "Yeah. It was pretty special. When I think about it, all we did was discover a deceitful search."

She gave me a questioning stare. "That sounds crazy."

"Yes, it does. Look. We have two men's deaths leading everyone to believe were accidental with a twist of maybe."

Her face brightened. "John, I see. Two bodies found, dead, unidentifiable, and we talked to people who might know and got lies."

"And we must continue with the deceit part to protect your father and his family, and Noémi's husband and her children."

"I'll do whatever is needed to keep them safe."

My concerns were when we got back to Paris with everyone waiting and wondering what we did, what would we tell 'em? Nicole knew no one else could know and she'd accepted that.

I wondered if Pappy already knew. I did know Mother Betty could never know, as I had the premonition she would be staying in France—with a new husband.

What I really didn't like was Patty not knowing. At her age, one might say she had less to remember and grieve over. That *one* would not be me. The young age when she knew him was a special time to love. We'd just seen proof of that. A young Babette with her father, collecting memories.

I didn't like any of it because we'd be lying to them all. Nicole kept talking. I talked some and kept driving—and thinking.

During that thinking, it dawned on me he never told us what happened to his phone.

CHAPTER 34

BUDDHA CONFLICT

It was after one in the morning when we got back. Without much said of the visit, we decided to shower and go to bed. However, the first stage was when Nicole crawled into bed. Remaining vertical, sitting on her knees. I received a silent command with fingers waving me up.

I joined her. "You'd be beautiful even if you were upside down standing on one arm."

That was an attempt to be humorous because I had a burning sensation of what we'd be discussing.

She put her hands out for me to hold, which of course I did. "You gave me the most wonderful day of my life." She must have seen my expression. "And you are the second most."

"I like being number two, but remember, I had your help in all this. You gotta give yourself some credit."

"John, I don't want any credit. All I want is you and my father forever, and I know I can't have either. You, I've come to terms with. You'll leave and be gone from my life, and that's okay. Believe me, I truly understand. But I know where my father is, and I can't hug him."

"There are times I've thought it best we would find he'd died. And there are times like now, I'm glad we found him alive and I could see you hugging him. That was a forever moment for me."

Her hand went to my face, touched it then dropped back to my hand. A soft question came out. "What do we do now?"

I was waiting for that. I pointed a finger up. "First, I believe your mother will want to move to France and marry Pappy. What do you think?"

"I've only been alone with her a few times since she reconnected to Pappy. She does love him. If he asks her to marry him, she'll say yes."

"And, we know he'll ask. But, I'll check privately. If that happens, what about Patty? Will she stay or go home?"

"When I was alone with her in Noémi's kitchen, she told me she loves Nathan. It may take a year for her to fully fall for him, but it'll happen. And if Mama stays, she'll stay. That's a given."

"What about Lizzy?" I was most worried about her, while hoping Andre might be her French anchor.

"I can't be absolute, but I don't believe there's anyone back home she's interested in. Her mother lives like a hermit. Sure, we see her, but she doesn't have a love life."

"Hmm. So, if Lizzy wants to stay, her mother will stay, too?"

"Yes. And if Mama stays, that will give Rebecca more of a reason to stay."

"I like that thought. Guess you know you still have a job in Marietta?"

"Of course I do, you ninny." I got a soft cheek slap. "I made some notes and took some pictures. Some you know nothing about. I'll do the article and include the death of my father and the happy times here with you, and a couple of possible boyfriends."

Now, that was a surprise. "Boyfriends? Who's my competition?"

She swiped my nose with her finger. "That, you may never know. I'm sleepy." She dropped flat and slipped under the covers. "I'm ready for some snuggling."

She lifted the inviting blanket.

The morning came early. My eyes opened at 6:00 a.m. and closed immediately. At 8:30 a.m., someone pinched my nose.

I opened one eye. "Oh. It's you." As I closed it, someone began tickling me all over. I opened both eyes and grabbed her hands. "Okay. I give. Why aren't you asleep?"

"I'm hungry. We're getting up." Those words filled the air with a pleasant but demanding tone. Not sure how to describe that, but yes was the only sensible answer.

Knowing I had no say in the matter, I needed something to say. "Now? I've barely had six hours sleep."

"You have a choice. Get dressed, or you'll be sleeping on the sofa."

I decided clothing was the solution.

Within twenty minutes, she had gotten dressed, including long white pants, her pink blouse, and sandals. She called her mother, who was already eating breakfast with all the other girls. We joined them.

That wasn't what I'd planned for the first part of the day. Yet there we were, sitting at the table providing a requested update. That update, for the moment, was that we finally believed her father was dead. With Mother Betty present, it was the only version we could give and may ever give.

I was surprised no one cried. Sadness did appear on all faces. I suspected the absence of heavy emotions was due to the years that had passed, where they had already accepted William Powell's demise.

But there was Nicole. She knew the truth, and her own sorrow was visible. I told myself I must find a way to mend that grief.

When I found that the boys were picking up the girls and heading for Créteil, Noémi's home, I told Nicole we were going to tag along, in my car.

The opportunity was good for something I had in mind.

Once we got moving, I asked Nicole, "If the girls knew of your father, knowing the situation, would they tell their mothers?"

As seemed always, my view was darting between Nicole and the road.

"They might. But, if they understood it could ruin Mama's life, and put their mothers and Daddy in danger, I don't think they would.

With the kidnapping, they already know life has dangers even when you've done nothing wrong."

She had given me the needed reply. "That's good thinking. When we get there and pick a good time, I want you to get Noémi alone. Tell her we found your father and we know her husband is also alive. See what she says."

Nicole's sweet eyes lit up as her hands flew open. "Ah, I see. Once she knows, maybe I can find out if the boys know." She ended that with a delightful smile.

"Girl, you're on the right track. Now, I also need you to get with the girls. We need to know how they really feel about the boys and if they'd like to stay in France. Maybe they've got marriage on their minds."

That request took a moment to soak in, but she had an answer along with an excited nod. "I can do that, but they'll have to keep that to themselves for now."

"Yes. They'd have to know for sure."

"John, you, me, we're doing a lot here. I'm worried all this might go bad and Daddy will be hurt."

I could see the worry on her face, but it didn't obscure the hope.

"It's chancy, I know, but I don't believe the secret will remain so long as the girls and boys continue their relationship. Time and closeness will expose everything."

"You're right. If the boys know, it will spill out somehow, and the girls will know both deaths were faked. And, any relationship they have with the boys would suffer. Oh, dear God, you'll be gone."

Her hands went to her face but no tears. She kept her strength.

I offered my hand. She took it. "Now, you listen. Don't worry. I got a plan, but we have to do what we just talked about. We have to know who knows about Gustav."

Still holding my hand, she shook it a little. "You're not going to tell me your plan, are you?"

"Oh, but I did. At least I think I did, but I don't know the whole plan yet. We gotta know who knows what to see what we can do for whom."

With a sweet grin, "You realize you repeated what and who and know so many times I have no idea what you said. Except, I know you know. See, I did it, too." She giggled. "I know I love you and that you won't let me or my family down."

Just as she finished, I parked on the sidewalk in front of Noémi's house, as I'd done before, in less tense times. This visit would be a telling.

It was close to eleven o'clock as Patty and Nathan greeted us at the door and welcomed us in. We followed them into the kitchen, joining everyone else. The boys were sitting at the table. I joined them, watching.

Noémi started doing some indescribable cooking thing as we were informed that lunch would be a little delayed and there was a chocolate layer cake in the works. Seeing it was a good time, Nicole asked Noémi if she could see the bedrooms.

Step one was in motion.

The girls joined me and their boyfriends at the table. I mentioned how good something smelled. When the girls looked at each other, I knew they had something to say.

Patty got chosen. "Uncle John, when will you be leaving us?"

Talk about blindsided. No, I really wasn't, for I knew that question would raise its ugly notion.

"Well, I haven't thought of a specific time. In a few days, I guess." I responded such that it implied I would be leaving alone.

Lizzy added her kind thoughts, "We don't like it, but we knew it would happen. We'll miss you more than you can know. What about us? Do you think we can stay here in France?"

With a tiny grin, I supplied one solution. "I know what you're really asking. Lizzy, Patty, you know that's a decision your mothers will have to make."

Both were not wearing happy faces.

Patty added, "We know, but we hoped maybe you could help them say yes. Mama must be in love with Pappy. If she stays, maybe I get to stay, and I want Lizzy to stay, too. We just don't know what to do. Please help us?"

Subbing for Nicole, I put step two in play. "Girls, I need to talk to you, alone. We're having a private meeting in my car. Come on," implied with a wave of my hand.

That short tête-à-tête was going to delay lunch, but hopefully the encounter would leave them with full hearts.

I took off. They followed, leaving the boys stranded watching us walk away.

In the car, we three were in the back seat. I was facing them. It was a bit crowded, but I wanted it to be personal.

I took off with questions. "I need to know your relationships with Nathan and Andre. How close are you? What personal things have you discussed? I hope you can share that with me."

Patty was ready. "Uncle John, we like sharing with you. Nathan is wonderful. Every minute I spend with him is so special. He does what I ask but will question things, too. He's sweet, and I know he cares about me. He wants me to be happy."

Lizzy would not be outplayed. "Andre treats me the same. He's kind, sweet, and gentle. I actually feel lonesome when I'm anywhere without him."

That I expected, but they only spoke of now. "I understand, but what about the future? Do you want to just be friends with them if you stay?" I did a little look-see from the corner of my eye. "Or do you want more?" I added a saucy grin with waggling eyebrows to emphasize the question.

Lizzy reached around Patty and slapped my leg. "Uncle John, sometimes you're such a cutie. And we love it. Okay, Andre is nineteen. He'll be twenty in four months. I'll be nineteen in three months. We don't have the money to do college and neither does Andre, but he has a job lined up starting next month. He told me he wanted to save money for us. When he said 'us,' I was so happy."

Patty was sitting almost at attention waiting her turn. "Uncle John, we'll both be nineteen next year, and if we stay, we can finish school here. Nathan is starting a part-time job next month. He's asked me to marry him. We know we'll need to wait a year or so, but we want to be together."

What I heard was what I'd suspected. The boys starting jobs was kinda sudden, though I assumed it was due to the girls and their future together.

"Helping you stay is one thing. Your future with the boys is different. Do your mothers know how you truly feel about the them?"

I thought I knew the answer, but wanted to hear it from them.

Patty got the signal. "No. They know we like the boys, but we haven't said much more."

Glancing at both of them, "Girls, I assume Noémi knows all this?"

Patty put her hand on mine. "Yes, she does, and she's told us she'd love to have us in her family."

There was still more I needed. "This also will be strange, but I need to know. Do the boys talk of their father, and how do they talk of him?"

Lizzy in some unseen way got the okay to answer. "When you were here a few days ago and Mama Noémi was talking about Mr. Gagnon, Patty and I saw you take notice. When she used present tense, you saw it. Yes, he's alive. She goes to see him at her sister's house."

I needed clarification. "That's Elsia Gauthier, who lives in Saint-Avold?"

Lizzy smiled. "I knew you'd remember. You know everything, Uncle John."

Patty added, "When we found out, I so very much wanted Daddy to be alive."

Lizzy said, "Me too. I miss him. If me and Patty wanted to go somewhere, if Daddy couldn't take us, Mr. Powell would. We both got Christmas presents from them. They were so kind and thoughtful, it was like we had two fathers."

My eyes glided back and forth between them. "You two have given me so much information, some that I knew and some that I wanted to know. Let's go inside and see what Nicole and Noémi have been sharing. This could be a very pleasing chapter in your lives."

The car had been a perfect place for our talk, but it was time for more to be revealed in a homier setting.

As we entered the living room, there were the boys and the two women. There wasn't much room. Nicole and I had chairs and Noémi had her usual seat. The girls sat on the floor beside each other. With hands in the air aimed at their sweethearts, the appropriate boy joined them.

The room was full and the next few minutes would confirm that telling.

Nicole was first to speak. "John, your knowledge of Noémi was right on track." Her wink told me just what I needed.

"Noémi, I want to thank you for sharing with Nicole." Turning to the girls. "And thank you for sharing with me. You should know all this was for a purpose. Knowing that Mr. Gagnon is alive and well means a lot."

It was time for the kicker.

"Girls, please don't be angry with Nicole and I, but we had to know your situation. What we have to tell you will have present and future consequences."

Almost on top of my last word, Lizzy's face lit up as her hands grabbed themselves landing on her chest. With firm excited words, "Mr. Powell's alive, isn't he?"

Nathan repeated her words in French.

Patty's hands went to her face in silence.

Lizzy's hands didn't move.

I nodded at Nicole. She took my cue, "Yes. We found him." She started crying the moment she said the words. Her hands went to her lips.

Andre did the French repeat. Noémi's hands went together as if in prayer.

The girls shot to their feet, dragging the boys with them. I got up. Figured I'd be drug up anyway. Nicole joined me, with everyone hugging and sharing teary eyes. Noémi remained seated but still got her hugs.

Awaiting an appropriate time, I kindly asked all to get seated.

Directing my words first to everyone, but knowing the girls would be in the direct path.

"Patty's father being alive must be kept a secret. You should know he's living under a new name. A complete new identity, just like Noémi's husband. He's married and has a little girl."

I stopped there. I didn't know how having a new family would be taken.

Nicole added the needed words focusing on the girls, "Please understand. Daddy had no choice. Both he and Mr. Gagnon had to have new identities, or they would be killed. Patty, if Daddy remained with us, he would've put us in danger. Both men had no choice."

Patty gave a sad slow reply, "I understand. Knowing that makes me love him even more. And, I'm glad he found someone to share his new life with." She had one of those little sweet grins that you know told the truth. You would also know Patty would hold him tight in her heart.

Lizzy was ready. "Me too. What he did makes him a wonderful man." She turned to Patty. "We want his new life to be happy, don't we?"

They hugged each other as Patty said, "Yes."

That told me they had the kind of love every man dreams of. And, just the words I wanted to hear. The girls were young, but had the knowledge to accept his faith. But there was still a lie at stake.

I sat down in front of the girls. "Patty, we're pretty certain your mother will stay and marry Pappy. That means she can't know of your father's new life. She must believe he's dead. Do you agree?" Nicole joined me on the floor.

Patty gave me a tear filled, "Yes."

I sent a nod to Lizzy. "The same goes for you. You can't tell your mother."

Lizzy came back with her heart speaking, "I don't like it, but I know we can't tell them. I would never want anything to happen to him. Never. Or his new life."

"I know that wasn't easy for either of you. It shows your heart's in the right place."

The girls sent sweet, tender smiles that told me they were sincere. Andre translated for his mother at appropriate times. She listened and saw our reactions. Her silent and pleasant expression told me she was on board.

It was time for me to share some details related to our trip to Mainz.

"Now, just so you know, I'm certain no one knows where we went yesterday. I started off in a crazy direction, making sure I took some twists and turns to confuse any possible followers."

Nicole added, "I wondered what you were doing. I kept quiet. But, after meeting Daddy, I forgot."

"Hey, it worked. I saw no odd cars on the road that appeared to be following or watching. Ditto when we parked at his house."

Nicole's reply was a body bump. Sitting on the floor didn't hamper her meaning.

As I finished, I saw Patty watching with her head tilted a bit. "Patty. You have a question?"

Her head stiffened and her eyes grew wide. I'd startled her, but she recovered quickly, and asked, "Is there any way I can see him sometime?" She put her hand on Lizzy's. "Me and Lizzy?"

I knew that was coming. Nicole had had the same wish so I gave them an intro to my direction. "It's possible with careful planning. Nicole may not like this, but I was thinking—"

Nicole ended my sentence and asked, "Might not like what?"

That got needed laughs from the girls.

"Well, I was going to tell you, if you'll let me. Now, keep quiet." I paused as she gave a *humph* and went silent. "You could wear a brunette wig, odd clothes, and drive up in a rental. Maybe meet him halfway."

Luck was with me. She caressed my arm. "John, I'm sorry. You were already thinking of that, weren't you? No fibbing. You were? Weren't you?"

"Yep. Got to thinking about it on the way back."

"Yesterday? Yesterday! And you're just now letting me know."

The room was filled with more laughter. Nathan translated the situation to his mother. At least, I think he did. It was, of course, in French.

I firmly grabbed her shoulders and turned them so we were eye to eye. "Now, you listen closely, beautiful. I had to consider a disguise. Where to meet him. Whether his family could be with him. I didn't want to disappoint you. Is that clear?"

Her expression went from pleasant as she said, "Yes," to a kiss.

The kiss might've went longer except for the women clapping their hands.

I made sure everyone heard the risks. "Remember, this can't go beyond this room. You can't tell anyone. This group, right here, must keep the secret. If you tell even a friend, it won't stop there. Do I make myself clear?"

Andre told his mother.

There was more. "Noémi, when you meet your husband at your sister's home, is he alone?"

Andre did the translation, again, then answered, "Yes, he comes alone. There have been no problems since he started over six years ago. We see him, too. You know that, but wanted to say again."

"That's good to know. Also, as I said, I don't think Pappy should know. Course, he may already know of all this." I then thought aloud, "Even if he does or learns later, he would never tell your mother. He cares for her too much. Besides, there're things he doesn't and isn't going to tell me. I do trust he'd tell me if there could be harm."

Nicole had the obvious question, "When can we start?"

"Hold a sec. A wild thought just shot by me. A better plan. Here's the deal. My pilots are in Mainz visiting a friend. Jane is staying with her friend, whose husband is Alivia's brother."

Nicole added, "Think I know where you're headed. Are you sure that would work? We'd all be showing up there to see him."

"To everyone else, you're going with me to visit with my pilot and her friend. Ah, I'll call Jake and he might could join us. That would add some extra reason for going. For those who don't know, Jake's my brother. He spent lots of time in Mainz a few years back."

Nicole added her wish, "Please call him. I know I'd like to meet Jake, and I bet the girls would, too."

That got lots of yeses and claps, to which I added, "So does every female on earth."

Only the girls smiled.

Action was back in my court. "I'll call Jane and ask if we can go there for a visit. That I wanted you to see a little bit of Germany and have the boys meet her and Paul. Now, guys, your mother shouldn't go. I'd like to keep this visit parentless. Okay?"

As I hoped, Nathan translated to Noémi and got a positive response.

"I'd like you boys to go with the girls. I want him to meet you. To know you." I pointed to Nicole, Patty, and Lizzy getting their attention. "You girls would like that, wouldn't you?"

Nicole gave me her okay first. "Yes, John, that would be perfect. We want them with us as often as possible."

I got nods and happy smiles on the girls' faces. Nicole, too. For Nicole, this meeting could have more effect. She was older and had known him longer, with more memories collected.

It was closing in on two o'clock, and there was much to be done. Nicole and I said our goodbyes and headed for the hotel.

There was only one real worry.

This excursion was in dire conflict with Buddha's wisdom: "Three things cannot be long hidden: the sun, the moon, and the truth."

CHAPTER 35

THE MIRAGE

No sooner than we entered the room, Nicole hit the sofa and ordered me to join her. She offed the sandals and pulled her legs under her, resting an arm on the back of the sofa.

I liked it, except it gave her a better spot for staring and scaring.

She wasted no time. "Do you have any idea of all the things you have to do?" My mouth opened to speak, but she beat me to it. "Just to get things started, you have to contact Jane to set up the visit. There's Jake to invite. We have to make up a valid story to tell Mama, Rebecca, and Pappy. And you gotta rent a minivan that will seat six."

"Nice. I was going to make a list and you just did."

She put her hand on my shoulder. "*Sure* you were." With the emphasis on that first word.

"Hey, I was going to." When I heard myself say that, it sounded like a little boy trying to convince his mother. "Wait a minute. Let me rephrase that, Mother." Nicole threw her head back, laughing. "Now that I've got your attention, I'll make a list when I'm ready, because everything you said probably won't happen as we think."

"Okay, I get it. I shouldn't have said that. But, John, you never make a list."

"If I make a list and forget something, you'll tell me it was on the list. If I don't have a list and forget something, you won't know what I forgot."

Her hands went up, I suspected, filled with frustration. "Will you just do something?"

Those hands fell hard enough to bruise the sofa. I knew because I heard a groan. It was me. One came down on my shoulder.

Recovering, I said, "Thought you'd never ask," giving her a big, toothy visible grin.

As I was pulling out my phone, she let me have it. "So, what *are* you going to do?"

"Quiet. I gotta make a call."

Her hands went up again, returning softly to the sofa. Much appreciated by me.

My first call was to Jane, and I told her I'd like to bring the girls and their boyfriends there to meet her and her friends and see parts of Germany. She liked the idea, and I got her blessing. Told her we'd be there about five or six o'clock tomorrow. Mentioned we'd stay overnight and would need a hotel. Jane said she'd take care of that.

When Nicole saw me hang up, she made her presence known, again. "I guess she liked the idea, right? I mean, you didn't let me hear what she said."

"You noticed. Now, for my next call."

Nicole started to speak, but she knew I wasn't listening. She scrunched up her nose and pouted. It was a cute look that I had to ignore.

My next one was to Jake. I told him we were having a party in Mainz and wanted him to join us. I mentioned girls, and he said he would be there about five o'clock tomorrow. That was perfect. I briefly told him of the Nicole-father relationship. He had the kind of contacts I believed would help keep all of it safe and under control. Jake understood and told me he would be prepared.

"You didn't mention my meeting Daddy. Why didn't you?"

"Thought it best to tell him in private and in person." No sooner than the words flew out of my mouth, I knew a question was about to be asked. "Yes, you'll be there with me."

She gave me a mild, "Thank you."

No sooner than I'd got that done, Jake called me with an update. He would be bringing a close friend, the ISD man who watched over James Marceau and his new family. Jake knowing the man meant he had confidence in him, which was a serious plus. It just might make all this easier and keep Alivia and James protected.

Having him meet Nicole and the boys and girls would be good. At least I thought so. He would then know who would be visiting often. Knowing the watcher was attending, I told Jake how I found and met James Marceau, Nicole's father. I asked if his friend knew of our visit there. Jake didn't know but would find out.

I briefed Nicole and told her that needed to be our little secret. She like the idea.

Almost forgot one important call. Alivia. I told her Nicole and I were coming to see Paul, Jane, and her friends. I gave her the plan, asking for her to meet us alone when we got there.

I was giving Nicole a pleasant stare when my phone rang. I jumped. It was Susan.

Holding the phone where Nicole could see and hear, I answered, "Hi, Susan."

"John. I hope things are going well there. How's Nicole?"

Nicole replied, "Hi, Susan. I'm here, and all is well. Ah, you're calling John because he forgot something, right?"

"Nicole, you know him better than I thought. He has this knack for finding answers, yet his memory sometimes has holes in it, letting important things leak out."

"Do you two always have to gang up on a guy? Me! By the way, Madam Executive Secretary, why'd you call?"

"Glad you asked, Boss. Louisiana Governor Haggerty called. That's Jacob Barton Haggerty to refresh your memory. Wants you to come see him in a couple of months. He said no hurry. Had to get some funds allocated through the state legislature. Good bunch, he said, just slow."

"Did he give any details of what he wanted?"

"No, but when he mentioned seven mil, I got interested."

"That's a lot of money for a state to invest in just IT. They already have their own full IT department. There's gotta be more to it."

"I agree. I pressed him a bit, and he gave me one word. France. Never got any deeper."

"That do sound interesting. Hmm. And you're calling me today, because?"

"Because he called me today. Five minutes ago. Thought you'd like to know."

"Just teasing you a bit. Glad you called."

I was thinking of saying something when she switched gears. "Nicole, you there?"

"Yes. I can't let this guy out of my sight. Girls are always trying to grab him."

"Don't worry. He only lets the ones he likes grab him."

That got laughs from a cute mouth and an expensive phone. Almost everyone was enjoying themselves.

They needed words from the almost, "You're picking on me, again. Just thought I'd mention it."

Ignoring me, Nicole asked, "Did he ever tell you about Gabrielle?" Nicole was becoming a tattletale.

"Oh, a sexy name. No, he didn't."

"Her whole body's sexy. I forgave him. She's an old flame that's been put out."

They did the laughing thing again.

"Okay, you two. I give. You win. Can I accept defeat and hang up?"

"Susan, maybe we better. Not to worry, I'll help him feel better."

"She's a prize, John. You take good care of her. I'll send you an e-mail with the governor's contact details. Bye-bye, you two."

We said our goodbyes as I pressed the stop button.

Nicole, now with knees on my legs and arms crossed over my shoulder, said, "You do know the reason we pick on you is because we love you."

"There must be some mysterious secret training manual women have that's passed down from generation to generation on how to conquer men."

"It's our woman's intuition." The usual intimidating smile came with those words.

What I wanted was to get away from it all. Clear the mind. "Being outnumbered, maybe we should do some sightseeing. I've done all I can for tomorrow."

"Are you saying you don't like sitting here with me?"

She ended that question with her head lying on her hands, which were still on my shoulder. This was not going to be easy.

I gently lifted her head and gazed into her eyes. "I love sitting here with you, especially right now. Maybe I'm nervous about tomorrow. If our plan puts your father in the limelight—" I couldn't say the words. My hands dropped.

Her hands took over. One held mine while the other caressed my face. "Pappy may have given you names to find, but that was for his longing for Mama. Nothing was done for my mother or father for seven years. You knew me for a few days and magically put me in my father's arms."

"It wasn't magic. It was a lot of walking and talking."

"Looking back on it, it was fun. Now is better. John, you're about to make it possible for me to be a part of his life again. That knack of yours will make it happen." She gave me a wink. "I should mention today is my last pad day. Tomorrow, I'm pad free. Let's do that. Go somewhere."

"Yeah. I was actually thinking about taking a ride in the French countryside and finding a place for a midafternoon snack. Somewhere away from all this we're doing."

"I'd like that, too. Then what?"

"We should have dinner at Pappy's place. Unsure of the boys and girls, but most likely your mother and Rebecca will be there. We can let them know of the trip to Mainz."

Nicole asked, "Have you thought they might want to go with us?"

"Sure, but they have to know you want to go there to meet some new people, make new friends, and see a little of Germany."

"I know I need to talk to Mama about her staying in France with Pappy."

"Yes. That's a big move for her, and you and Patty. This is real life." I thought for a moment. "Let's head southwest of Paris. We might find a small town and a place for dessert or some such."

With that decision made, we were on the road. I attempted to avoid tomorrow's adventure, and that's exactly what it would be. The ending was the uncertainty.

After an hour or so we found Dreux, a small, picturesque town. Next step was finding a place to eat. We found one called Le Petit Café. I was pretty sure it meant small café, because it was a small cafe.

We had hot tea and shared a chocolate dessert called The Mirage, which translates to Le Mirage. Yes, it's a French word. It had dark, milk, and white chocolate, with a thin, flat cracker hidden inside. Delicious was the only word that fit. That word itself must have been at least half French, because the owner understood when I gave him a thumbs-up and said, "Delicious."

The dessert and the afternoon in that small French café brought out more reminiscing of our childhoods.

Talking didn't end there, as our plans for tomorrow and after just wouldn't depart. We must have explored every nook and cranny of our plans, if there could've been such.

After driving round the town, scenic as it was, we headed for Paris and more pondering. Nicole called her mother and told them we were coming for supper, and maybe she and Rebecca could join us.

They said yes.

Phase one—bringing the team together and planning—was done.

Phase two—informing the bystanders—was the next challenge.

The game was on, and it wasn't a mirage.

CHAPTER 36

THE SMELLY ANNOUNCEMENT

It was close to six o'clock when we parked at Pappy's restaurant. I looked at Nicole, tilting my head. "You ready?"

She grabbed my hand. "I'm ready, coach."

I promise you I didn't mention the game thing.

But, as it was in play, I replied, "You're the best cheerleader I've seen in a long time. And the prettiest."

With a wink, I got out of the car, heading for her side, but by the time I got there she was standing there waiting.

I got about one foot from her when she grabbed my hand. "I bet you say that to all the girls don'tcha, coach? Come on." No answer was needed.

She led me into the place—make that dragged me in—and told Celeste we needed a table for seven. The funny part was Celeste headed for one table, and Nicole, still doing the dragging, headed for what could only be known as our family table. Celeste joined us, laying menus and silverware on the table with a festive flair.

Nicole called the mothers and they joined us rather quickly. I was unsure if they were hungry or Nicole's mention of a trip got their attention.

I saw them approaching, but Nicole stood and welcomed them.

Unsure how I was going to help them be seated, so I stood to give it a try but was waved off by both women. They sat where they wanted. Truth be known, I was surrounded.

Mother Betty kicked things off. "I'm excited. What's this trip you're taking?"

Her daughter wasn't ready. "Mama, let's at least order first, okay?"

Nicole got okays from her mama and Rebecca, who didn't seem nearly as excited as Mother Betty. The word "worry" came to mind.

We ordered, and as the serveur took the menus and departed, both women were staring at me.

Nicole came to my rescue. She placed her hands on the table, eyes on the mamas. "I asked John if I could see some places in Germany. Mama, you know his pilots are there now with friends. Well, John called, and they said we could join them for a day or two. Isn't that wonderful?"

Her eyes darted between the two mothers.

I added my nickel. "We're planning to take Patty and Lizzy and their boyfriends with us. I've confirmed all that with Jane, my pilot. She got the okay with the family they're visiting. We best keep it with that crowd."

The eyes of those two women focused on me. My hands being in my lap grabbed the edge of my seat. The feeling I acquired was that of the Thanksgiving turkey watching the water boil.

Under the table, unknown to all, Nicole snatched one hand and yanked it free.

"Mama, wouldn't that be a good thing? The girls are so happy about going, and they really don't want any mothers watching. Please understand?"

A pleasant smile appeared on Rebecca's face. "Nicole, I agree with you. That's a time for the young ones to enjoy. They don't need us old fogies hanging around."

I liked what she said, and the mild understanding that accompanied it. "Rebecca, are you sure?"

"Yes, John. I think the young ones need the adventure. It's a new country. Let them enjoy it with the young." With a pleasing smile, she added, "That includes you and Nicole."

Mother Betty had been quiet, but with encouragement from Rebecca, she gave in. "Rebecca's right. I'm happy right here." The smile remained.

Rebecca continued, "Me too, but I'm looking for a man. A French one wouldn't be a bad idea." She had the most mischievous grin I'd seen.

Next thing I saw was a similar grin on Nicole's face. "Rebecca, I know just the guy. Very French. About fifty-five. Handsome, sweet as can be, and single. Does that offer you any interest?"

The two continued to share that grin that would unnerve every man on earth. "When can I meet him?"

"It may be too late today. But don't worry, I'll arrange it."

"You've seriously got my interest. Maybe you can arrange it now!"

"Not now, but I promise. I'll contact him today. I just want to prepare him."

Rebecca replied, "Okaaaaay," waving her hand back at Nicole. Her single-word reply sounded pleased, but a bit unsure.

The food arrived at a timely time.

The only other interesting topic was when Nicole told her mother, "I know you love Pappy, but we haven't talked about that much. Has he asked you to marry him?"

Mother Betty's answer was short. "Yes, I do love him. And yes, he's asked me to marry him."

Nicole's response was even shorter. "And?"

The answer came. "He asked me this morning. I gave him a yes and a hug."

Leaping out of the chair heading at lightning speed to her mother, Nicole gave her a hug. Her face shone with tears and a barn-burning smile. Rebecca and I clapped. I decided to join the pair. Many in the restaurant clapped, not even knowing why. Must have been the fact two women were hugging.

Kneeling on the floor, I just watched. When Nicole dropped to her knees, I gave Mother Betty my own hug and added, "Pappy will do everything in his power to make and keep you happy. I have no doubt whatsoever."

Nicole gave me a super smile. Mother Betty gave me words, "I have no doubts either."

There was a question, however, that needed an answer. "You remember the thing that happened to the girls where you got really angry at Pappy? Does this mean you forgave him?"

My hand was on the arm of her chair. She put her hand over mine. "Pappy explained everything. I have full trust in him, and you, John."

I patted her hand and stood up. Nicole stood, and we retook our chairs.

Nicole put her hand on mine. "John, I'm tired. Let's go to our room."

I felt she'd let me know when she was ready, but that was sudden. We said our ta-tas and headed to my room.

We hit the sofa again. Nicole pulled her knees under her and laid her head on the back of the sofa, holding my hands. She was getting good at that position.

It was time to know what was going on. "Were you really tired, or just wanted to be alone with me?"

"Both, John. I'm physical and mentally tired. The dinner was great, but all we didn't say tired my brain."

"I can imagine it was. I let them know what was best for them and your father. You did the same because you love them. So did I."

She lifted her head from the sofa. and quietly asked, "What time is it?" She really was tired—too tired to look at her phone.

"Almost eight thirty."

"I'm so tired I don't want to take a bath. Do I smell bad?"

"If you were sweaty, you'd smell great. If you did, I'd still curl up next to you."

"That's so sweet. Maybe I should take a shower."

"Let's both shower in the morning."

She gave me an "Okay," stood up, and took all her clothes off except the bikini undies, and slipped under the covers.

The woman was truly worn out. The day, filled with so many family things happening, had taken its toll. It was now up to me to ensure nothing disturbed her. Tomorrow would be both tiring and, hopefully, rewarding.

With dinner consumed, we'd finished step two. Or had we? Unanswered questions flooded my also tired brain.

With Nicole sleeping, I needed the bathroom. I closed the door and started making calls. The morning needed precise timing. I called the girls to confirm they knew we'd be hitting the road about nine in the morning and we'd meet them and the boys in the hotel lobby for breakfast at eight.

That would be step three.

I invited the mothers and got their confirmation. Those two women gave in awful easy. Rebecca I could understand. She just wanted her own man. Mother Betty was too easy. I wanted to consider that thought further, tomorrow. And no, I didn't add it to any pile. You really must get your mind off that.

The woman in my bed was already asleep.

I donned my PJs and hit the sofa.

CHAPTER 37

MAINZ ON THE HORIZON

I was woken up about six in the morning by a woman wiggling around in my bed. I was in my bed due to that same woman waking me up at two with orders to git off the sofa.

At that moment, she was facing me. I nudged her a little. Her hands brushed over me as she turned to face the wall.

I snuggled up close and put my arm around her. "You ready to get up?"

That got a simple, almost silent, "No."

Whispering why was my next try. "We have two hours to get some packing done and eat breakfast with our traveling companions. You need to get up."

That time I got a soft almost blurred, "You first."

Drastic measures were needed. Still low, but above a whisper, I said, "If you don't get up, I'll pick you up, put you in the shower, and turn on the water. Get up now, or else," with emphasis on else.

She must not have been happy with the wall. She chose me instead, with eyes open. "What's the 'or else'?"

Getting nowhere was in sight. I needed a diversion. "I'm counting to three. On three, I pick you up, put you in the shower, and turn on the cold water. Now make up your mind."

With a tiny pause I said, "One."

"You really mean that, don't you?" Her eyes were very wide open.

"Two."

"Wouldn't you rather stay here with me?" The eyes did rapid blinks.

"Two and a half."

She pushed away from me. As she started rolling over, she gave me a piece of her displeasure. "Okay, okay. I'll get up, spoilsport." She only rolled halfway and stopped. In an instant, she whirled back around. "I'll remember this."

Success. She got up. We did bathroom things and packed bags. Nicole called the girls before we left to be sure they were getting ready. They were and would see us in few minutes. It was about seven fifty as we headed downstairs.

We parted company on the ground floor, for about three seconds, till Nicole decided to follow me. Together we verified the three-seat minivan was present.

I'd acquired a table for eight assuming all invited would join us. Talk about timely, or due to my phone calls, but by 8:00 a.m. on the hour all seats were taken.

About two seconds after sitting, there were five women discussing many topics with we three men attempting to join the conversations. At some point, we ordered food, after which experiences were shared. Humorous things the boys did, gossip, and a little dishing of the dirt.

Lizzy asked me a question. It must have had a pause button, for all talking ceased. "Uncle John, I forgot. How far is it to Mainz?"

"Five hundred forty kilometers."

She wiggled a finger aimed direct at me. "I know just what you're doing," adding a tilted, tight eye stare for emphasis. "They use kilometers here, and you did that on purpose." Her arms crossed. "I want it in miles, Monsieur Sneaky."

"Nice touch, Mademoiselle."

Her hands went flat on the table with one of those expressions that entices the man to obey. "Okay, Uncle John, you're cute. Now stop being cute and answer my question, please?"

She was young, but life had already given her lessons.

"Okay, I give. It's about three hundred forty-five miles. The real number to know is drive time—about six hours."

That got their attention. Patty and Lizzy shared stares at each other.

It was my time for a rescue. "Our transportation will be an SUV, which is waiting right outside as we speak. I checked"—Nicole's foot hit mine—"make that me and the big sister checked its presence earlier. It's a triple seater with good back-end storage. It has a CD player, and I have CDs. Anyone else have any CDs they like?"

Everyone was looking at everyone.

Nicole gave me a direction, this time without the use of her foot. "John, tell them what singers and groups you have, and let's go from there."

"Good thought. I have the Eagles, Credence, Chicago, Beatles, and some other singers. Does that interest anyone?"

Out of the blue and quiet, Nicole's mother said, "I like Chicago and Janis Joplin."

I clapped my hands. "Me too."

Patty's hands went up. "Beatles!"

Lizzy's hands did the same. "Chicago, Eagles, Beatles, Beatles, Beatles."

I couldn't pass that up. "Lizzy, you said Beatles three times."

Her hands were hugging each other under her chin. "I really like them. Daddy did, too. Didn't he, Mama?" The cute smile signaled she meant it.

Rebecca softly answered, "Yes, he did, sweetie. He loved listening to them with you cuddled in his lap. Oh, my. It's been a long time since I thought about that. Thank you for remembering."

The sharing was a good thing, along with speeding up the eating. With eating passé, Nicole intervened with something more interesting. "Rebecca, remember that nice man I mentioned yesterday? Can I share him with you?"

"If he's good looking and sexy, I won't share him, but I'd like to meet him."

That got giggles and smiles.

I knew who this man was. If Nicole wanted to pair them up, she must have known Rebecca well enough to give it a try.

Nicole started the intro. "I can't speak for sexy, but he's a super nice, honest, sweet man. His name's Marcel Moe Clair. I told you he's about fifty-five, give or take. He was married to an American woman, Camille. She died a few years back. Five, I think. Would you like his number?"

Her eyes went wide open. "Sure!"

Nicole took Rebecca's phone and added Marcel's number.

"I'll call Marcel and tell him you're going to call him. That'll get him prepared. He works days at a local manufacturing plant. I don't recall his exact hours. but he has nights free."

Rebecca was interested. Her hands began to wave her desires. "Well, whatcha waiting for? Call him!"

"Think I'd like to do it in private." Nicole stood and told Rebecca to sit tight. Nicole took a picture. "Rebecca, he's going to like this picture." She took off for the private call.

As soon as she was out of hearing range, Rebecca asked, "Does anyone know this man?"

Mother Betty's finger focused on me. "I bet he does."

I threw my hands up as if being arrested. "Okay. I do. I can't speak from a female's perspective, but he's smart, intelligent, and speaks English better than me."

Rebecca asked, "What does he look like?"

"Let's see. He has a good head of hair." That brought unexpected smiles. "Maybe five ten or five eleven. Slender. Does security now, but was a foreman in the factory. He furnished me with good information searching for Mr. Powell."

"John, you got me very interested." Rebecca was rubbing her hands together. Maybe cooking up a plan.

The timing was on target. Nicole walked up just as Rebecca was doing some serious thinking.

Nicole's hands encircled her slender waist, resting on her cute derrière. "And, just what have you, all of you, been talking about?" For some reason her eyes focused on me.

I saw no escape. "Rebecca asked about Marcel and I gave her a little info. She's interested, right, Rebecca?"

Her only reply was a sexy, "Very."

More giggles occurred.

Nicole picked up on the feeling. "I'm glad, Rebecca. So is Marcel. He really liked your picture. He's going to call you after work today, at six."

Rebecca did a tiny hand clap, "This is exciting. I'm about to date a Frenchman. At least I hope I do."

Nicole expressed her relief. "You will. He's going to invite you to dinner. I gave him the name and address of a perfect place for a first date. John knows the place well."

I got a stare, but she left it at that.

Rebecca rescued me from the stare, "I wanna know the name. Please tell me the name?"

"It's a small, very romantic café called Villa le 42. Wait, I have a picture." Nicole did some clicks on her phone and showed Rebecca.

Rebecca did some serious staring. I was afraid the phone would start melting. "I love it. Oh, my. A French man and a French café."

Nicole added, "If lucky, Gabrielle will be the hostess." She turned to me, calmly asking, "John, do you have Gabrielle's phone number?"

"Think I lost it." Not sure why, but the table started laughing. So did everyone sitting at the table, except me. I confessed, "Yes, I have it. But I'm not sharing it without permission." I wanted to add "for fear of my life" but decided against it.

Patty got interested and looked straight at Nicole. "Is Gabrielle competition?"

Before Nicole could pin me to the wall, the one with the imagined target, I spoke. "No, Gabrielle isn't competition. I dated her a few times years ago. Okay?"

The real question was why was I defending myself.

After the laughter died down, Nicole came to my rescue. "Everyone understand, I was just teasing with John. Gabrielle is a beautiful young woman." She paused and directed her gaze at me. "He's not planning to date her again. Are you, John?"

I attempted to answer through all the giggles. "If you recall, she was the one coming after me." The older parties at the table got quiet. The girls were enjoying it. "Just kidding. I'm not going to date her again, unless someone keeps challenging me." I gently took Nicole's chin in my hand, giving it a slight turn aligning it with mine. "You're not going to bring this subject up again, are you?"

Her apologetic no came out with a pout. Her next words were softer. "And I won't tease you about her again." Her lips showed a silent maybe.

"And I promise not to call her."

She took my chin holding hand and lowered it, "Now, I might want to eat there again."

"Any time," was my reply.

"Okay," was hers.

Patty brought us back to reality. "Will you two cut that out? Save it for your hotel room. We need to leave."

Having been brought back to reality, I agreed, "Patty, you have a point." Standing, I informed the travelers, "Get your stuff and have it at that door," I pointed, "in ten minutes."

With quick byes to Mother Betty and Rebecca, we all headed for our rooms and met at the aforementioned door close to the ten-minute mark.

With Mother Betty and Rebecca waving us off, the day had finally begun.

CHAPTER 38

SECRETS OUTED

The six-hour drive started with fun talk and music, filled mostly with Beatles songs.

We'd been gone maybe ten minutes when it occurred to me I hadn't even mentioned this trip to Pappy. "I forget to tell Pappy." Why I said it out loud, I didn't know.

Nicole said, "Mama will tell him."

"Yeah, but I always tell him what I'm doing. He might have details that could be useful."

That was a stupid thing to say, but something was clawing at my brain.

"John, you're going to call him. So do it. Why are you even worried about it? We've been there already."

I turned off to the side of the road and pulled out my phone. Nicole may have been right. I was looking at my phone trying to decide if I needed to call Pappy or wait.

Then the ton of bricks fell on me, with an answer. The last four digits of Pappy's number was also on Nicolette's phone. It was one of the two sets of four I saw. The number was in red, which told me Pappy had called her. Maybe only four digits wasn't enough, but that would be one heck of a coincidence.

Decision made. "Calling him ain't enough. We're going to see Pappy. He has some e'plaining to do."

I did a slick fast U-ey heading for the restaurant.

Me and the car had made it about ten feet when three females asked, "What?"

One of them got very unhappy. I was in Nicole's line of fire. "Have you gone mad? Telling him will make no difference. Mama will tell him all he needs to know."

My head was switching back and forth between Nicole and the road. "The number I saw on Nicolette's phone was Pappy's. Remember I saw the numbers? It was his. He called her. He knows her. I want to know why and how."

"What are you gonna do? Storm in there and start yelling at him?"

"I'll yell politely."

Nicole turned to the occupants in the back seats. "Sorry for all the crazy talking and yelling. Are you all okay?"

Patty fired her feelings at us. "You're scaring me. Both of you. Why are we heading back?"

Lizzy was calmer, but she didn't hold back. "Yeah. What're you doing?"

"We're headed for Pappy's restaurant. John discovered something he thinks Pappy knows and hasn't told us. John will confront him."

Patty threw in an alternate destiny, "What if Pappy goes after him?"

Nicole turned to me. "We'll order dessert."

As I stepped in the restaurant door I asked Celeste if Pappy was available. With a brilliant smile, she said, "Yes, Monsieur Stone. He is in his office." That was different. Why did she get so formal in French? Why not Mister? Why the smile?

My attempt to see Pappy alone didn't work. Me and all the car inhabitants were standing at his door.

If my theory for being there wasn't correct, I'd be toast. Burnt toast. I was hoping, at least, for a tasty filling and a favorable understanding from everyone.

My knock got a "Come on in, John." It was Pappy's voice. Many times, I've wondered if someone pinged him when anyone was headed his way.

I took three steps into his office. The girls and boys decided to hang back, just inside the door, in case shots were fired.

"Does Celeste always tell you when someone is about to knock on your door?"

"That she does, young man."

"Hmm, you must trust her a great deal."

"I should. She's my daughter."

"I know that." I wasn't building my case well.

Nicole smiled. "How sweet."

But that was not what I had come to find out. "That's one semi-secret revealed. Let's dig into a better subject. Why does Nicolette have your phone number? Why did you call her?"

By the time I finished my question, Nicole and I were standing in front of his desk. Nicole's attention shot at me. "Hey! Why did you wait to tell me today?" Those words told me someone had a finger on the toaster.

"It hadn't clicked till I was about to call him in the car. When I was looking at my phone back in the car—"

"You had many opportunities to tell me. I should mention we've been in a car alone more than once. We've been in a hotel room *very* alone."

One of her fingers was again attempting to drill a hole in my chest.

A possible answer glided out. "No. No Listen. I told you the numbers looked familiar in Nicolette's apartment. But it wasn't clear till I did the U-ey. I didn't remember till then."

"You don't forget anything. You may not know you know something, but when you do know, you know."

I was running out of answers, so I just grinned. "You said 'know' four times."

My answer wasn't good enough because the back of her hand plowed into my chest. I was lucky. The toaster was unplugged.

Pappy saw I needed some help. "Be nice, Nicole. This man knows more than he knows he knows. But sometimes it takes a place, an action or a woman to bring the answer to the surface. And I believe the woman was you."

Nicole's expression showed sadness. Her hands dropped then wrapped around me. "John, I'm so sorry. I was angry and not listening. You told me when you knew."

As we separated, her hand gently slid off my chest. I gave her an okay wink and she stepped beside me holding my hand.

Pappy gave her a nod then began his reply. "To answer your question, my friend, a little background is needed. I've known Mac far longer than you have. I didn't know of you till you came to my restaurant the first time."

That was true. "And your restaurant was among the three Mac gave me. And, that was on purpose?"

"True. If you recall, I gave you names to interview for your potential France office, remember?"

"Of course I do. But—" The sky was full of dark clouds as he interrupted me.

"You also know Alivia's name was among the three I gave you to visit."

The truth was about to emerge. I had just found the corner pieces of the puzzle. "Pappy, you knew of Alivia and Mr. Powell, I mean James Marceau." This time I was pointing the finger. "You knew they're married." It wasn't a question.

"I didn't know all that when I gave you the names. After the kidnapping, I did my own checking and found that Alivia was married. I called Henri and he gave me a little more detail. You were the key informant. The more you found gave me more, and I called Henri again." Then he waved his hand, "Betty, you can come out now."

The sky cleared. My mouth opened, and I managed to get one word out. "Yes."

Mother Betty came in and stood near Nicole.

It didn't matter what my word was because Nicole blew it to smithereens. "Mama, did you know all this? And I don't mean *his* daughter."

Mother Betty took her daughter's hands. "Yes. Pappy told me. He got a call from someone after you found your father."

Pappy said, "Henri."

"This morning, Mama, all our talk about going, you knew what we were really going to do?"

"Yes. I knew you were going to see him and I just couldn't spoil it. I could see the happiness in your face, all of you."

They did a mother-daughter hug. It was something you never forget.

Nicole's mother turned to me. "John, please understand. Pappy loves me and wanted no secrets. Neither did I, because I love him." She patted Nicole's cheek, whispering, "I love you," and sat down by Pappy. They were holding hands.

Nicole asked a poignant question. "Does Rebecca know?"

I winked at Nicole. Wish I'd asked that one.

"Yes, my dear, she knows. I've told her. Once she knew how I felt, she felt the same."

Nicole gripped my hand tight and gave her our plan, "John and I and the girls have been so worried about that. We were afraid it would ruin your life with Pappy. John planned so much and did so much to keep you from being hurt." She turned to me. "John never gave up. I found my daddy because of him."

Tears started, and Nicole's arms encircled me. Patty and Lizzy did the same.

The room was quiet. The truth was exposed.

After a moment or two, still bound with arms, I quietly uttered, "We need to get back on the road. Okay?"

Nicole gave her answer, "Yes, we do," ending the words with a cheek kiss.

Mother Betty added, "Nicole, all of you, I should have told you, but I was afraid what it might cause. Because I didn't, John did two unforgettable things. He found your father and found Rebecca a man who may just be who she needs."

"Yes, he did, Mama. It's okay. Love causes a lot of things." She gave me confirmation. "Let's go, John."

With goodbyes, we took off for Mainz.

CHAPTER 39

MAINZ... ING AGAIN

The six-hour drive started, again, but this time talking filled the air. I thought all would be angry at Mother Betty, but after many words, they weren't. Everything we didn't know had built new families. New relationships.

After a time, for some relaxation, I taught 'em the old I Spy game. Taught is the right word. They had no idea what it was, but grew to love it, for about half an hour. That is, till I told them to look for signs or anything related to family, fathers, or screwy guys. They found a lot of large rocks and named them after me.

Those names will not be made known.

Beatles music snatched a chunk of time, with everyone trying to sing along.

I stopped every couple of hours to keep the legs relaxed and stomachs supplied with snacks. About halfway I stopped in a small town, Metz. The restaurant name I can't pronounce, much less spell, but we did try some unique French dishes.

Jake called to let me know he wouldn't be there till Wednesday. He didn't say why, and I didn't ask. His work involves things I best never know.

There was a lot of discussion about what we'd do when we got there. For me, it was simple. The only two who knew nothing about the father things were Jane and Paul. They had no reason to know.

The plan was to keep them in the dark. I trusted them, but the more who knew, the wider the exposure.

First stop would be Jane and the Béringers' place. Jane would have us a hotel lined up, so no worries there. I wanted all of us to meet and hopefully give our hosts a good impression.

I'd called Jane and asked her to watch for us.

After turning off the main street through a wall of tall, green shrubs, I was in the driveway.

First thing I saw was a small castle. Okay, not a castle, but there were three stories and a four-car garage. If I didn't know better, and I wasn't sure I did, the brick looked special made. It wasn't the usual red rectangle. Off to the side was a second two-story house, or so it appeared, with steps up the side to the second floor. I'd only seen those in movies.

No sooner had I put the vehicle in park, Jane, with Paul close behind, came running out the castle door. If it hadn't been for the six steps, each at least four feet long, she would've opened the car door for me.

Two steps out of the car, Jane gave me a bear hug. Make that grabbed me. "John, it's so good to see you and seeing you here makes it even better."

Paul and I shook hands.

Inside we met Erwan Béringer and his wife, Jane's friend, Jessica. Our good fortune was Alivia and James weren't there. Had they been, it would've gotten sticky.

My plan already had too many humans involved.

Having said our hellos, I found that the hotel accommodations were outside, in the two-story house I saw on the way in. The guesthouse, they called it.

Everyone was ushered into a large room filled with bookshelves loaded with books. There were two long couches and three expensive looking wingbacks. Two were facing the fireplace. One looked like a recliner. The other was a very old, make that ancient, design with the frame visible. Maybe a hand-me-down. Couldn't recall the name, and didn't want to recall the price.

Jessica and Erwan led us to a window. A very large window. She opened the curtain, exposing the guesthouse.

With an open hand, she formally introduced it. "There's one master bedroom upstairs and two downstairs. All have bathrooms with showers and tubs. That's where you'll be sleeping. A hotel just wasn't what Jane and I wanted."

The girls, holding their guys' hands, stood amazed by the view. I know because the girl's mouths were wide open.

Jane gave her thoughts on usage. "From what I see, you'll need two of them."

Nicole took my hand and added, "We'll need all three."

The girls giggled at her words. Me and the boys had our own thoughts of the rooms and probable usage.

Jane confessed, "Jessica, looks like they'll need all three rooms you prepared." She added one of those wicked grins as she looked at me.

Nicole said, "Thank you. I love the guesthouse. It looks so much like ones I've seen in the movies I watched with Daddy."

Patty added, "I didn't see it in any movies, but I like it too." She pulled the hand holding Nathan's to her breast, pressing it with her other hand. "It's beautiful."

Nathan was pleased, but he wasn't looking at the window.

Lizzy's eyes were also fixed on the guesthouse. One hand was holding Andre's and the other limp by her side. She was so enamored with what she saw, her thoughts emerged. "Maybe we could stay forever."

Patty agreed with her own, "Yeah."

At that point, the girls realized they were in a dream world and decided to be embarrassed. The place filled with understanding, agreeable laughter. Then it happened. If I didn't know better, I'd believe it was planned.

Jessica had been standing behind the girls watching their reactions, especially when Nicole spoke. I couldn't help but watch them all myself. When I looked sideways at Jessica and no one else was watching her, she looked pleased. I hoped I was reading her feelings correctly.

Leaning a tiny bit, I looked to my side past Nicole at Jessica. Jessica saw me, but so did Nicole. I gave Jessica a pair of wide open eyes with, "What's going on?"

Nicole caught me. "What're you doing?"

I kept quiet.

Jessica shared her secret with us all. "Staying here a while would be a good idea. Nicole, Patty, your daddy will be here soon. Lizzy, from what I hear, you'll be happy to see him, too."

More humans knew. So much for calling Alivia. The secret was out.

There was total silence for every bit of half a second when the room started vibrating caused by all the bouncing and laughter. There were tears. Girls hugged boys. Girls hugged girls. Us guys just shook hands; there wasn't much time for that. The women kept doing re-hugs.

When I hugged Jane, I quietly asked, "So, you know who Daddy is?"

She whispered back, "We know the whole story."

I stopped worrying about humans.

When the hugging and tears had ebbed, Jessica asked all to be seated. My man-cave inclination headed for the recliner, but Nicole led me to a couch. Paul and Jane picked the opposing couch. The girls ushered their boys to the other end of the couches. Erwan picked the old wingback.

Jessica stood by the fireplace. No fire, obviously, but it was enhanced to be appealing. Granted, it did offer ambience, or *ambiance*, if you want to kick in a little French. Or maybe she just wanted to be facing everyone.

With calmness taken over our group, she began her story. "Back in Australia when I was with Jane, I never believed I'd meet such a kind, sweet man as Erwan. His family has welcomed me in so kindly I now have a mother and father, here."

She stopped her story, paused for a breath of air and said, "Jane, I'm pregnant."

That last word filled the other female faces with desirous grins attempting coverage with fingers.

Jane jumped up and they hugged again. Acting as if embarrassed, she quickly slipped back on the couch. She wasn't. She's a strong woman.

Jessica wasn't through. "I love that woman. Now, where was I? It was about six years ago when Alivia met James. She brought him to see us and visit us often. Super guy from day one. When he knew they were in love, he told Alivia about his past. They kept it between themselves until you, Nicole, showed up at his home."

Nicole took hold of my arm and quietly added, "John brought me. He didn't exactly know why, but he believed we needed to talk to Alivia. He caused it to happen."

The fingers of Jessica's hands laced together just under her chin. "Nicole, when you spoke with Alivia and asked about her father, she tried but couldn't hold it back. She knew how you felt. Alivia and James talked and decided we, his family, needed to know, and that you needed to be with your father as much as possible."

Nicole raised her arm, showing the bracelet. "This is the bracelet Daddy gave me that day. It was his great-grandmother's. I've worn it every day since." Looking at me, "John, did you know I was wearing it?"

My arm was already around her. I gave her a gentle snug, "Yes. You forgot to take it off last night."

"I did forget. And you noticed." Her head leaned against mine.

But my concerns were still there. "Some precautions must have been put in place to protect James and Alivia, and even everyone who knew."

Erwan got up and stood by Jessica, grasping her hands. "Knowing all this was sudden, but we all were glad to know it. Still, it caused worry. I first called Henri and told him what happened. I also have contacts in both the German and French governments who have departments that watch over people like James. If anything is spotted, they contact Henri. That gave me, all of us, much relief."

Patty had been sitting restless. "I—I want to see Daddy as much as I can. Can I do that and not hurt him?"

"Me too," said Lizzy and Nicole. Their words were close together and lovingly said.

"And you will," said Jessica. "They'll be here in about an hour. You'll meet him and eat with him and visit him at his home. And spend the night there, if you wish."

"Really?" asked Patty.

Jessica gave her a gentle nod and a, "Yes."

I needed clarification. "I called Alivia last night telling her to meet us first because I thought no one else knew. Jessica, she didn't tell me you knew. She didn't tell me *anyone* knew."

"She wanted it to be a surprise. John, finding her changed her life, for the better, forever."

Nicole patted my cheek. "He's like that."

"So, how did Pappy Armand get involved?"

Jessica continued. "You, I think. Mr. Armand had lost contact with James's first wife and family until you called. He contacted Henri. They talked and shared some information. Not everything, so I was told. Now, why Henri would share anything with Mr. Armand, or anyone for that matter, I don't know."

Nicole was beaming a smile. "Do any of you know how all this got started? Patty does. Anyone else know?"

Jessica jumped at that. "I don't! Ya gotta tell us."

That was Nicole's cue. "I was walking on a sidewalk in Georgia and a man sang to me."

Laughter burst out all over the room.

Jessica almost yelled, "AND?"

"It was late afternoon, and Patty and I were walking back to our car when this man, right here," she poked me, "was watching us. We saw him but ignored him. He had to jump off the sidewalk. We just walked on by him. Didn't even look at him."

More laughter.

Talk about new news. "You never told me that. I thought you just didn't see me."

"John, dear, you don't have to know everything."

The laughter grew louder.

Nicole continued her story. "We kept walking. Then he yelled that someone had written a song about me. John, what was the name of the song?"

She was doing her best, successfully, to embarrass me. "'Long Cool Woman in a Black Dress,' by The Hollies. Okay?"

"I walked back to him, stopped maybe a foot away, and told him to sing it. He did, well, about two lines. I had him shaking in his shoes. But he did it so sweet."

The women clapped.

Erwan asked the obvious. "But you came to France. How'd that happen?"

Nicole was enjoying herself. "John asked me to dinner. He told me I could go anywhere. Being difficult, on purpose, I told him I wanted to go to the Le Beaujolais restaurant. When he said yes, I almost choked. He knew Pappy, and here we are."

She got much louder applause.

Lizzy gave her thought. "If he hadn't done that, I'd never have met Andre."

Patty joined her. "And I'd never have met Nathan."

Their boys got kisses after those words.

Jessica, still standing with Erwan, pulled him close. "That's about as romantic as anything I've ever heard. Someone ought to write a book about that."

Nicole wasn't finished. "I know I've said it, and I'll say it for the rest of my life." She squeezed my arm. "This man found my father. It wasn't easy. People lied to us. He got knocked out, got into a gunfight, and was chased by smugglers. With all that, he didn't give up. After seven years, he put Daddy in my arms."

That got aahs. From the women, of course.

Lizzy put her arms around Andre. "He has a knack for doing that."

Patty agreed, "A sweet knack."

Lizzy added, "That's why we call him Uncle John."

It was getting awful mussy. I politely asked, "Could we talk about something else? Maybe order a pizza or something?"

The room stood and laughed. Everyone must have taken that as a command to go unpack. With smiles all over the place, we got our belongings and headed for our respective guest rooms. On their way out, when they passed me, some patted or slapped my back.

There are times I wish I had a zipper on my mouth. This was not the first.

While Nicole and I did what little unpacking we had, I found a sofa—yeah, another one. It was a light blue.

"It's getting close to seven. Your father should be here soon. You ready?"

She shut a dresser drawer and dropped beside me. "I'm more excited for Patty. I want her meeting him to go so well. I'm a little scared."

"Not to worry. She's a smart, strong girl."

Nicole curled her legs under her. "I know, but it's been so long."

"It'll be just like when you saw him. Lots of hugging and hanging on."

"Yeah. That's how I hope it'll be for her."

"Actually, both the girls will be doing the hanging, from what I know."

"You're going to be leaving soon, aren't you?"

Her asking wasn't a surprise, and not something I really wanted to talk about. Ever. But it was needed.

I picked up a hand and held it. "Yeah. Tomorrow or Wednesday, probably. Sooner, if you want me to get out of your way."

Her head was laying on the back of the sofa, looking up at me. "You can never be in my way. Wait till Wednesday at least, okay?"

"No sooner. I promise."

Her hand went around my neck and met me halfway. We kissed, not so passionate, but a long, endearing one.

When we parted, still inches apart, she asked, "Wonder what the girls are doing now. Maybe same as us?"

I knew that answer, "If the boys are smart, they've got their girl in a separate room."

"Oh, I'm sure they are. If I know Patty and Lizzy, they made sure that happened. The boys will sleep in separate rooms, but that'll be the only separation."

"Women. Always in control, right?"

"Always." After that one word, our lips connected again. As our lips parted, she let me know her wish. "I'm especially looking forward to tonight."

I knew she would. "Meeting your dad again will be a special time."

She gave me a soft cheek tap, "No, silly. Here. With you. The pad's gone, and I miss you."

"Are you sure you want to do that? You should be mad at me for leaving."

"I'll miss you, but I'm not upset. I know it has to be. I just want to be close to you till the last minute." She moved back a couple inches, with eyes wide open. "You do too, don't you?"

"Yes, I do. I must admit, you have a piece of my heart I'll miss. That doesn't happen often."

"Megan had a piece of your heart, didn't she?"

"Yeah. She has a piece. I'm sorry, I shouldn't have said it that way."

"It's okay. I understand. Here's what I think. One day, Megan will tell you to give her piece to another woman. Now, don't get upset. We women are like that. She hasn't told you to give it to me. But, one day, she'll tell you the lucky woman, and you'll have no choice."

"You're not making my departure easy."

"That's another thing we women are good at. On that flight back to the States, you'll have me on your mind every second. It's time. Let's get up and join the others. I'm hungry."

With that, we got ourselves ready and headed for the main house. On the way I mentioned, "You have a strange way of switching horses."

She only smiled.

We drifted into the castle and into the big room. The girls and their boys were there, chatting away with Paul, Jane, Erwan, and Jessica.

When Jessica asked where we'd been, Nicole beat me to it. "Let's just say we were doing some serous kissing." We hadn't even sat down yet.

As expected, that got oohs and aahs, emphasized by faces fanned—as if cooling down.

With a wink at Nicole, I asked, "Has anyone asked why in the rooms below us there were a girl and boy, alone, in each?" I ended that with no particular expression.

Patty stared all around. "Uncle John, you don't know that. How did you know that?"

My expression changed to a wide, toothy grin. Never said a word.

Patty and Lizzy did that stare again.

Lizzy's eyes closed tight accompanied by scrunched-up face. If I read her silent lips right, she said, "Oh, crap." Her hands flew out. "Patty, he didn't know till you told him."

"Oh, I did. I told him. You—you—Uncle John! You're not my uncle anymore." She crossed her arms for emphasis.

"All right, you two. So, you got caught. Big deal. I've done the same thing when I was your age. Now listen. I don't know exactly what you did, and I don't care. You wanted to be alone with the man you love. *That* is very normal. Everybody who agrees with me, raise your hand."

Nicole's shot up fast. Jessica's and Jane's hands went up along with Paul's and Erwan's, after the women nudged their hubbies. I think the boys were frozen in their seats.

Patty uncrossed her arms. "Thank you, Uncle John."

"You're welcome. You too, Lizzy."

Lizzy added her feelings, "Uncle John, we didn't do anything bad. We kissed and talked about our future and everything. That's all."

"I know, Lizzy. Just remember, you're my nieces, and I protect." She liked that. "Jessica, any word from Alivia or James?"

She picked up on my question. "Alivia called me. They'll be here in a few minutes."

That information brought eager expectation to all. When that topic slowed a bit, I asked and Erwan told me his firm assisted the German government with mishandling of security documents. That got my interest. Meaning he had government contacts—a good thing.

After several minutes, there was a knock on the door. We heard it open. Jessica jumped up, heading for the foyer telling us it was Alivia and that she had a key.

Nicole, Patty, and Lizzy stood up. Anxious for who they would see in seconds. I stood behind them. I heard the footsteps heading our way.

Alivia and James, with Babette between them, were holding hands. Alivia put her hand on James's back. It was a signal. He looked down at her and accepted her request.

James managed two more steps before three women nearly dove on him. With arms spread and within seconds his were wrapped around two women, both crying.

Nicole held back. She picked up Babette and wiggled her finger at Alivia to join her.

I stood there watching and trying to describe the scene. Simple. The room was filling with water. I could have sworn the walls were crying.

We three along with Babette were entwined in arms. I had some tears myself. Erwan wiped a tear as Jessica joined him.

Babette was trying to understand what she saw. Her inquisitive face only added to her cuteness.

Can you imagine an eighteen-year-old girl seeing her father for the first time since she was eleven? Were the tears from the years missed or memories recalled?

And Lizzy. She was hugging who might be appointed her adoptive father, possibly remembering all the times she had with both. One she could never hold again, one she could.

I was too young to have many memories of my mother. My father told me things that added to my own memories. And I have Nanna Bolton memories.

Why are some memories etched in stone and easy to remember, while others are like sand on a beach? You know they were there, yet you have to brush the sand to remember. Over time, the brushing does no good.

Alivia took Babette as Nicole kissed my cheek and walked to her father. He then had three tear-makers gripping him. He looked up at me. I gave him a little salute. He returned it with a smile and a nod.

I heard James tell the girls to meet their little sister.

That's all it took. The two gently walked to Babette and Nicole introduced the girls to her. I don't recall all that was said, as emotions clouded the words. I was excited to see the young Babette talking to my nieces. I took a quick picture.

At some point, all this would have to slow down and verbal reacquainting would have to start. It wasn't going to be me. But someone had the bravery to move things along.

Jessica softly took the challenge. "This has been the most emotional time of my life. Let's sit down. We need to share many things."

Her wish worked.

The girls sat on the couch beside their father, holding Babette. Lizzy took a piece of Patty's fatherhood. Nicole sat on the floor in front of him. I was headed for the recliner when I saw Nicole's finger wiggling for me to join her. It was best I did as instructed.

When the sharing was well underway, Jessica and Alivia headed for the kitchen. About five minutes later, Nicole excused herself—and me. That left James listening to the three young girls get acquainted. With what, I had no idea. I think they were all talking at the same time. Babette was fitting in well.

Nicole and I joined the ladies in the kitchen. I asked if anything I could do to help. They told me to sit at the table and watch.

After a couple of years, make that an hour, food was ready. Babette sat in a chair next to her father, with legs curled under her. Me and the boys sat where the women told us. Together the women finished the food and delivered it to the table, where we helped our plates.

The variety was intriguing. There were items from Australia, Germany, France, and Southern Georgia.

I found it interesting that with the size of the house, there wasn't any paid help. Perhaps they had been dismissed for the homecoming. Secrecy was needed.

Along with good food, the talking was all over the place. There were six men and seven women. Yeah, I included Babette, as she kept up with the talking. Even without her, we men would be outnumbered.

Something I noticed. At first, Andre and Nathan were having trouble joining in. Their girls saw it and would switch to a subject one of their beaus could relate to. I wondered if the boys knew just what their girls were doing. I guess love does conquer all.

The day and evening were filled with lots of joy. But it had to eventually end. That happened about eleven thirty, when most got tired and decided it was bedtime.

Nicole and I retired to our guesthouse room. She never stopped talking and I never stopped listening, even as we joined each other under the covers.

I decided to query my mate. Keep in mind, she was inches away.

"If you could put it all together in a few sentences, what did the day mean for you?"

Her hand touched my face. "A new life. Pappy will love and care for Mama, and I'll have him as a father. I'll have my real father and a new sister nearby to visit or call or eat with or anything. I'll have to find work here in France."

Our hands were touching under our adjoining pillows.

"You're an amazing woman. You put that together fast. Suspect you been thinking on it."

She gave my hand a tiny squeeze. "I have. When I saw how Mama was feeling for Pappy. When I spent time with you showing me Paris and how I can love someone. Any reason I needed to go home was fading. You'll soon be gone. And now, with Daddy back in my life, Paris, I guess, is my new home."

"I just wish there was more I could do."

She put her finger to my lips. "All the best friends, girls, women I've ever known, no one did anything near what you've done for me. After all the names I called you, trouble I caused you, fussing about anything and everything, you didn't give up. I don't know how physically strong you are, but your personal strength never lets you give up."

I felt myself smiling. "You *were* a challenge. A scintillating challenge."

She pinched my nose. Guess it was handy.

Then she said, "Daddy once told me there are intelligent people, and then people with street smarts. He said an intelligent man will know the temperature of the moon, but a street-smart man will tell you the best time to avoid getting caught."

"About negative three hundred degrees Fahrenheit and two in the afternoon."

She uttered a low, "Huh?"

"Don't ask me to repeat that. Not sure I even said it." I wasn't kidding.

"How did you? Never mind. I'll talk to Daddy about it. I think you threw his words out the window." Without stopping, she added, "Enough talk about this street-smart guy. I think you should find a subject you can enjoy without words."

For once, I *wasn't* clueless.

CHAPTER 40

PARIS AND MAINZ COLLIDE

It was Tuesday morning. I was preparing to sleep longer. I knew that because I'd set the alarm for 7:00 a.m. However, the alarm didn't go off. It would've, had the earth reached that hour. I suspected the cause was the someone sitting up in bed on her slender knees.

The one with the knees asked, "You awake?"

"No."

"Good. We're going to Daddy's house for breakfast."

"Your knees are cute. Did we just decide that?"

"Glad you noticed. Yes."

"I got no choice, do I?"

"Nope. Move it, Mr. Stone!"

The knees and all other body parts left the bed. With that encouragement, I got up.

We did our teeth and clothes things and headed for the castle. I later learned Miss Nicole had called Alivia and they had got all this going. Nicole had also called Patty. The ground-floor members were following her orders as well.

Jessica had been informed, and along with Jane, they waved as we drove off.

I knew the way. Ain't easy to forget a route when all you did was watch for suspicious cars with suspicious inhabitants. You sorta notice everything. Of the people who knew of Powell and Gagnon's new lives, they struck me as being legit and on their side.

That morning the car was full of happy people talking, laughing, and singing. Still, my suspicious nature wouldn't rest. I watched for cars paying too much attention to mine.

This trip I did only short, quick stops, mostly for drink buying and restroom visits.

The trip was nearing its end when I saw Alivia's street up ahead, which got me to thinking.

In the middle of the night I'd sent Mac an e-mail with the name of every person I'd come in contact with since I met Nicole. And, yes, that even included Nicole. If all they did was give me a hi or hello, they were on the list. I asked Mac to look for any reason anyone would want to take out Powell or Gagnon after seven years.

My nature just had to know.

Out of the corner of my eye, I saw Nicole waving at someone and pointing at me.

She was waving at the gang in the back seat. "See him? He's thinking again."

That started everyone either smiling or laughing.

"John, can you join us now?"

"Now, cut that out. I gotta think sometime. When I'm around you, I can't. You absorb my brain."

I shouldn't have said that. The car was shaking from all the noise.

"Okay, everyone, let's calm it down. My man's driving."

That dropped the laughter volume about half a decibel.

"Sweetie, what were you thinking about?"

I glanced over at her and back to the road. "I was thinking about last night. And I'm not going to elaborate on the thinking."

That was not fully the truth. It was not the time to say more.

The car started shaking again.

Nicole waved everyone down a bit as she patted my cheek. "Understood," was her only word until she saw where we were. "We're here, everyone."

She saw the driveway. I saw an extra car from last time. It had a French Paris area tag. I drove past to the next house and pulled to the curb.

"Everyone. Listen. Stay in the car. I'm going in first."

Nicole went after me. "What're you doing? You missed the driveway."

"Nothing may be wrong, but I have this feeling. Please. Stay in the car. I'm going to the house first. None of you are going till I know it's safe. Understood?"

"You are *not* going alone. I'm going with you."

"No, you're not." I grabbed and shook her arm for the first time. "You're staying here. Is that understood?"

The girls were on the verge of tears. Nicole was scared enough to stay put. She nodded. I let go of her arm. It was time.

All I had was my derringer and surprise.

I left the car shutting the door slowly and quietly, heading for the French one. Touched the hood. Hot. Very hot. I slowly eased up the steps. Kept low. The front door windows still had curtains. Could be my lookout or my enemy.

One of the curtains had a little open gap to the door side. A quick peek told me the story. Nicolette was holding a gun on Powell, I mean James. He had Alivia corralled behind him. I didn't see Babette. Nicolette was yelling and waving the gun at James. A thirty-eight special.

I turned with my back against the wall to think. There was Nicole sneaking up the steps. She stopped right in front. I told her what was happening. She handed me a thirty-eight. I kissed her.

She whispered, "I'll tell you about the gun later. What do we do?"

Whispering I said, "I'm going in and draw her attention to me. Once inside, you keep watch through this window. When I give you the signal, put a bullet through it right there." I pointed to the upper frame. "I want a sudden, loud noise. Got it?"

I gave her the thirty-eight. She was not happy.

Through her fear she gave me her desire, "Yes. If you get killed, I'll hate you forever. You got that?" Her hand flat on my chest gave her meaning extra attention.

I tapped her nose and moved her to the side so she wouldn't be seen when the door opened. I stuck my derringer behind my belt as low as it would go.

After taking three deep breaths, I started knocking hard on the door yelling, "Alivia, James, have I got one for you! Let me in! This is exciting."

My knocking and yelling was quickly answered.

The door opened with just a crack, to see Alivia, "John, please go. This is not a good time."

Ignoring her, I pushed the door open, shifting her to the side. As out of the way as I could get her. I waved at James and Nicolette. While ignoring them and I turned back to Alivia talking a mile a minute. Between words, I mouthed to her, "I know what's happening."

I continued to go in circles till I was near Nicolette. Her gun was still pointed at James. I took a chance. I spun one more time, winked at Nicole, and fell backward right at Nicolette's feet, looking like I'd tripped.

A shot came through the door window. Nicolette's eyes focused on me then the shot. With one hand, James grabbed her gun hand. With the other, he put his fist into her nose.

She went flat to the floor landing beside me.

James had her gun in his hand. Alivia attached herself to James.

In an instant, so it seemed, Nicole was kneeling beside me. Actually, she was hitting me in the chest. "You, you idiot! That was a crazy thing to do! You could've been killed."

I took hold of her hand. "I didn't dare get killed. You'd hate me forever."

She sat up and gave a tight-eyed stare. She called me some name, hit me one more time, then fell on top, kissing me. When finished, she rolled off beside me.

Everyone was smiles till another figure emerged through the front door—with a gun. It was Duane Naude. He wasn't happy. He raised his gun in James's direction. A horn blew. Naude got distracted.

I pulled my derringer, yelled, and within a second, fired both rounds.

James got off three bullets between my two.

Naude was caressing the floor—dead.

Babette came running into the living room, crying. Alivia picked her up. Nicolette was recovering and started to sit up, but Nicole slugged her. Nicolette was back on the floor. Nicole was rubbing her hand.

I took her hand in mine. "Remind me to never get you pissed at me."

The girls and their guys came running into the house, talking and screaming unknown stuff.

Patty almost yelled, "Is everyone okay? Uncle John?"

I took the cue. "All is well. Who blew the horn?"

With arms snuggled around Nathan, Patty said, "Nathan did. He saw the gun."

Nathan corrected, "Andre saw the gun. I blew the horn."

Nicole asked, "How'd you know to do that?"

Lizzy wasn't going to be left out. "That guy," she pointed to the body. "He came up from somewhere, unlocked the car out there, and took something. Patty said if he had a key, he's one of the bad people. So, we needed to do something."

Nicole was sitting up by then. "You all could have gotten hurt doing that."

Lizzy had her answer, "No way. We didn't do anything till we saw that guy." She pointed at Naude again. "We stayed in the car till Nathen blew the horn and we heard the shots."

Patty added, "Yeah. We waited."

Lizzy backed her up. "True. We did just what Uncle John told us. Don't fuss at us! You didn't. But what you did was needed. We all helped."

Nicole looked at Lizzy. "You sure did. All of you!" She then stood beside Alivia and Babette.

I was sitting up by then. "Every one of you, Nicole included, did just what needed to be done. That horn blew at just the right second. Perfect interaction." I paused a moment. "Anybody know how to call the police?"

James raised his phone and dialed something. When he hung up, he said, "They'll be here in fifteen or so minutes. Most likely so."

With that, we all moved to chairs and couches, careful not to disturb anything. We did tie up Nicolette, keeping her lying just where she was.

Nicole asked, "Why did they do this?"

That was my time. "Let's not discuss anything more till they take Nicolette away."

Nicolette heard that and yelled, "You not going to know anything! I get loose and kill all of you."

Nicole walked over to Nicolette, grabbed her blouse, pulled her head up and said, "Shut up, you bitch," and slugged her, again.

An opportunity arose. "Thank you, Nicole." Addressing Alivia and James. "What would cause that woman to come after you with a gun? Whichever you it is."

Alivia chose to answer. "Me. Nicolette and I were partners in our schemes. I told you just a little. It's so embarrassing. We lied to elderly couples promising them ways to make money for their later years. We took their money and gave nothing back. When I quit all that, she was angry. When James helped me repay my victims, she got really upset. At first, I went to visit her almost every month trying to help her get her life right. Together we found legal ways to help her earn money."

Nicole moved near Alivia and held her hands out. Babette accepted those hands.

I asked, "I take it that didn't work?"

"At first, yes. John, I kept seeing her, helping her. At least, I thought I was helping. The more we saw of each other, her anger got less and less. At least I thought it did."

"Did she ever come here?"

"No. She knew I lived here in Mainz, but she never had my address. I never gave it to her."

"What about him?" I pointed at Duane Naude. I was asking anyone.

James stated his angle. "I never knew him with my new identity." All I heard meant something or someone must've told him recently. James needed to know how I knew. Might ring a bell.

"Nicole and I never knew your new identify until Mac, a close friend, told me your married name was Marceau. And, Alivia, he told me you still introduced yourself as Béringer."

"That's right. In Paris, everyone knew me only as Béringer."

Alivia sounded very certain, and I believed her. Knowing her husband had a new name could easily have sealed her secrecy. Besides, it had to be reasonably easy being Béringer in France and Marceau in Germany.

Something kept digging at my memory. "Here's a thought. Duane Naude. He worked for a security firm. That would allow him to have a reason to inquire about a name."

Babette was holding on to Nicole's neck, who added, "John, remember, he knew that Phillips woman at the embassy or consulate, or whatever you call it."

"Beautiful, you're on track. Phillips knew Naude. Between those two, anything would be possible. I'm not saying Phillips had any evil intent, but she could easily have provided assistance to a security guy, Naude, thinking it was needed. James, is that possible?"

James topped off the mystery. "Yes. Signature Consulting was a hot item and still is. Believing it would be kept confidential, they would give Signature any info they asked for."

Two police cars with sirens blazing pulled up outside. The forensic van joined them.

To everyone, I said, "I believe we can share most of whatever is needed with the police." To James I added, "But your watcher needs to be present. Don't you think?"

"I'm calling him now."

The police came. When Alivia saw them coming, she took Babette back to her room.

The forensic team did their thing. Bodies were examined and carried off. Nicolette was led off yelling and screaming.

Everyone went to the police station. Henri Dumas, James's watcher, met us there. Henri knew me from times past, but he ignored that era and made sure James's past was not revealed. Nicolette started running her mouth. Dumas made a phone call, and she pretty much became an odorless vapor. After more than three hours, we were released and headed back to James and Alivia's home. I made sure Henri knew I appreciated all he did.

Hunger was on our minds. The women, all four of them, fixed us lunch, which was great. We spent the rest of the day talking and sharing past and future. Well, at least the girls, their boys, and Nicole did. They had lots of future thoughts. Babette was happy. Her crying had stopped, and I guess with her child's mind, she had forgotten the morning. I hoped so.

I made a couple of discreet phone calls regarding that future.

After lunch and talking time, we said our goodbyes and headed for the castle and our two-story abode. We also made a stop at the big house and gave them an update.

By the time we finished with the shootings, the police, and the castle update, it was after six o'clock, and the women told us we were dining out. The Béringers took us to a club with a band and dance floor. They played fast and slow songs. Apart from the fact they were in German, the music was okay. I was going to pay, but Erwan picked up the tab and we headed for the castle.

CHAPTER 41

ENDS WRAPPING UP

It was well after eight o'clock when Nicole and I flopped down on the sofa in our room. No sooner had we done that than there was a knock on our door. It was the first-floor inhabitants, all four of them. The girls dropped to the floor in front of me and Nicole, snuggling close to their respective mate.

Patty gave us the purpose of their visit. "Uncle John, you're leaving tomorrow, aren't you? We heard a couple of words when Jane said something to Jessica."

This was personal. I joined them on the floor. Nicole joined me.

"I've done all I can. I believe you're safe, and you have a father to spend time with, and a new sister. I've got some business things I need to do and some personal things to finalize."

Lizzy shared her feelings, "I wish you could stay forever." Tears were forming in her eyes.

With a gentle shake of her head, Patty asked, "Will we ever see you again?"

"Absolutely. And, I mean that. It will take me a couple of years to get the French IT branch fully underway, but I'll be back at least a couple of times a year. Probably more." Waving a finger, I added, "I'll be back for graduations, birthdays, and possible weddings." I ended that with a simple smile.

"Do you really mean that, Uncle John?" asked Patty.

"Yes, I do. I promise you I will see you many times. But I want you to think about your father. He's a real father. I'm just a make-believe uncle."

Lizzy's sad, pretty face was something I didn't ever want to see. But it was there.

She said, "You're my uncle for the rest of my life." Her tears began to flow as her arms circled me.

Patty did the same. I hugged them both. Nicole's hand was rubbing my back.

I let that last for about half a minute. I was enjoying it, too. "Okay, let's unhug. You're cutting off my circulation."

They let go slowly.

It was still my show. "You need to know I made some phone calls today."

Nicole didn't know. "Again?"

"When I was out of your sight." I grinned. She didn't. She was about to speak when I put my fingers firmly against her lips. "Not now. Later." I took her hand and held it close. Focusing my attention on them all, "I called Dumas, your father's watcher, and had all of you added to his watch list. Boys, you're already on it. Nicole and you girls got added."

Nicole spoke without hesitation as did a firm squeeze of my hand. "I *do not* want anyone following me around."

My hands went palms up and fingers spread. "Now, no one's gonna be following you around. They'll just watch for actions of others who may want information about you. That's not new. It's done all the time."

We were not holding hands at that moment.

I got support from an unexpected admirer, Lizzy. "I like it. It's an invisible protective shield."

"I see. Yes, I do, too," said Patty.

Nicole reclenched my hand. "John, I'm sorry. You're doing what you've been doing. Keeping us safe."

"I should've let you know sooner. It just took some time."

She put her head on my shoulder. "I understand. You've got more, don't you? What's next?"

"Here's the deal, and this is for you." I lifted Nicole's hand. "I'll ride back with Paul and Jane. The SUV will be here for your use. I've informed the rental agency, and it's in your name, Nicole. Just return it within two weeks. It'll be paid for."

"You don't have to do that. We can find a car."

"I know you can, but this is just in case. The hotel rooms are also covered. Just return the car and check out within two weeks."

"Don't worry, I will." She tilted her head on my shoulder again.

"Now, this I know. Pappy will take care of anything you need. Frankly, I suspect you girls will move in with him. He has his own castle."

That got a positive nod from Nicole.

Patty lit up. "We could move in here." She paused a split second with an indecisive eye. "No. Forget that. I love everyone here, but I want to be in France with Nathan."

Because they might have more ideas of things I need to do, I asked "So, what'd I miss?"

There was silence till Nicole spoke as she held my hand, "I like everything you've done and planned for us. I only wish there was something you could do to stop us from missing you."

"I'm going to miss you all of you, too. And, remember, you will see me many times."

Nicole was still holding my hand. "If no one has any more questions, I want to be alone with this man."

Her request was answered. After two hugs and two handshakes, the room shrunk to two.

Still standing and holding hands, I asked, "Shall we watch some TV?"

"No," said the lady as she took off her clothes. "I'm taking a bath. Then you take one. I'll be waiting in bed."

Somewhere in the neighborhood of seven o'clock, my clock alarmed. That was different. I had expected a female to wake me.

I turned over to face her. "You ready to get up?"

"No."

"Why?"

"If I get up, you'll leave."

"I could get ready, pack, and give you a goodbye kiss right here in bed. That would be something to remember."

"Wish I had amnesia. I'd remember everything except you. You'd leave, and I'd give you a bye-bye wave and never remember you."

She didn't come down with amnesia. Instead, we dressed and joined the others doing their getting ready to leave or watch those leaving.

We ate breakfast, went outside, and said our goodbyes.

I pulled Nicole aside. I told her I'd miss her more than any woman I'd ever been close to. That was the truth, and I told her as much.

I've done a lot of leaving in the past, but this one wasn't as easy. Nicole was different. She had never let me get away with anything. Must have been reading my mind. Maybe it was what she said about Megan giving me to the right woman.

Whether it would be helpful or not, I had to do something. I called Lieutenant Grenier and told him where Nicole would be and gave him her number. He already had it, but he was glad I called. Antoine was my next call, and I made sure he had Nicole's number.

I'd done that before, directing suitors to the woman hoping she'd be happy. I've asked myself why, but didn't know the answer or maybe just afraid to know it.

Paul was driving, and Jane was in the front seat. On that trip, I wanted to be in the back so I could watch Nicole, the girls, and the boys for as long as I could.

They followed us to the street. I saw their tears as hands waved. I felt my own tears as they grew smaller.

I sat there watching the scenery fly by. Watching and wondering why I'd made the calls. Nicole was a strong, lovely, caring person. She would find her man. Still, maybe I had helped. Maybe I did love her and was afraid to say it. I'd only said it once before.

In Paris, I dropped in on Pappy at his restaurant. I gave him a rundown on how things were. He promised to take care of Nicole and the girls for whatever they needed. Mother Betty and Rebecca were at his house making themselves at home.

Pappy mentioned that Rebecca and Marcel had hit it off well and she may not be hanging around his house much longer. I tried to determine who was the fast worker between those two. Most likely she and Marcel decided he'd go along with her plan.

I'd done nothing for my French IT division, but the future would make its own plans. I left with memories and the role of an uncle to keep alive. That was going to be fun.

I left the Eagles and Beatles CDs in the car.

CHAPTER 42

MEMORABLE DEPARTURE

The plane was in the air. Paris was behind me. Memories were flooding my mind as I watched the French landscape fade.

Leaving as I did brought to mind a movie I saw with my dad when I was a teenager. A movie called *Gator*. You can look up the actors. In the end, the man and woman who loved each other went their separate ways. Their combined love let it happen. They knew it had to be.

Had to be, or maybe not. That was my destiny, at least this time.

Nanna Bolton was as close to a mother a little boy can have. But she never let me forget my mother. She knew I was always wishing I could've been with Mama longer. I believe we all think that.

One time in particular, Nanna told me, "You keep remembering her. Ever time you think of yo mama, she be right beside ya. And not worry. One day you be right thar with her gittin a hug."

That woman was smarter than most people I know. Her spoken words might have been Deep South, but her wisdom came right from her heart.

About the Author

Winnfred got his writing interest in Mississippi, where he met many authors as newsletter editor for the Mississippi Writers Association (MWA). He was born in Griffin, Georgia, where in the tenth grade he took a typing class. He was one of two boys among twenty girl students. Ponder that influence.

The first story he wrote was a short story. While in Mississippi, Winnfred woke up one morning at two o'clock and wrote a short about his grandmother. It's titled "Angel in the House" and appears in his first short-story book, *Southern Shorts*. Except for a little grammar, there were no other changes to that early-morning family story.

Winnfred has been called a romantic, which you will experience in his stories as he blends mystery and romance.

CPSIA information can be obtained
at www.ICGtesting.com
Printed in the USA
BVHW030842060221
599131BV00006B/100